U0039573

最激勵人心的
英文演講

Words of *Wisdom*

宣揚理念 ╳ 畢業致詞 ╳ 勝選演說 22 篇

政治、企業、影藝、學術、人權　各界名人智慧精華

Word Power Made Easy

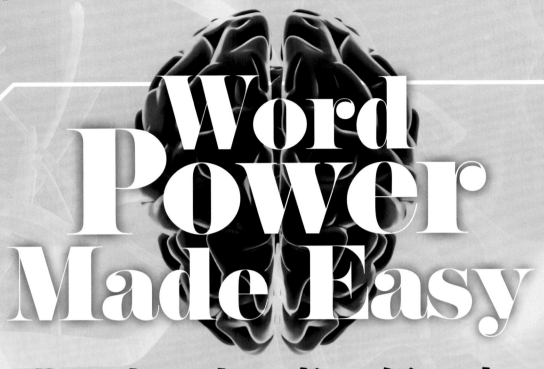

英文字彙解密

字源及衍生字完全記憶法

英文字彙書史上最強銷售紀錄

★ 出版至今全球長銷熱賣超過兩百萬冊！

★ 全美公認 No.1 英文字彙學習書，美國學生準備 SAT、GRE、GMAT 必備參考書

★ 2013 年獲選為美國英語教師協會推薦書籍

30 倍字彙量！

擴充字源知識，啟動字根、字首、字尾記憶鏈

每天 30 分鐘！ 30 天內字彙程度大躍進

成人再次突破字彙量的祕訣！ GRE、TOEFL、SAT 必備參考書

諾曼‧路易斯教授將使你相信：

「讀完這本書，你將不再是原來的你。絕不可能！」

暢銷熱賣超過六十年的英文字彙經典鉅作
《Word Power Made Easy》全新中文化，重裝上市！！

成功人士皆具備優越的字彙量；
而本書的對象，就是立志活出成功人生的讀者。

透過作者的學習安排，你將能在兩、三個月內迅速且有系統的習得大量字彙。更重要的是，
這些字彙將永遠改變你的思考模式，並幫助你在學業、商場及其他專業領域獲得成就。

由主題概念（IDEAS）引導學習
本書各章節分別探討十個用來表達某個主題概念的基本字彙，然後把這些字彙當成跳板，
探索其他在字義或語源上相關的單字。所以一個篇章就會探討、教授和測驗近一百個單字。

用字源 學單字，啟動腦內字彙記憶鏈
你將會學到為單字賦予獨特意義的希臘或拉丁字源，以及其他含有相同或相關字源的單字。如此一來，
你便能不斷學習相關領域的單字，且不會因為要學的單字太多而搞糊塗了。

豐富的單元小考，掌握學習成效
每課皆有單元小考以及章節總複習。題型包括發音練習、字義配對、是非題、填充題等。
從發音開始反覆練習，強化對字彙意涵的了解。

LEWIS 教授英文專欄，精進文法概念
缺乏正確的文法概念、流利的口語能力，再多的字彙也無用武之地。
本書的英文專欄將幫助你認識正確的文法，並學習自然的英文口語表達方式。

英文字彙解密
人格、職業、科學與行為
字源及衍生字完全記憶法
定價：380 元

英文字彙解密
語言、事件、個人特質
字源及衍生字完全記憶法
定價：380 元 (暫定)

CONTENTS

6 12 18 24 30 36

© Helga Esteb / Shutterstock.com

© Paolo Bona / Shutterstock.com

© Jaguar PS / Shutterstock.com

© JStone / Shutterstock.com

© Everett Collection / Shutterstock.com

© NASA/MSFC

42 **54** **60** **102** **114** **120**

J.K. 羅琳哈佛大學畢業演講
J.K. Rowling's Harvard Commencement Speech
The Benefits of Failure

© Everett Collection /Shutterstock.com

為了今天的演說，我絞盡腦汁，費盡心思。我自問，現在的我希望大學畢業時，自己該知道些什麼，以及我畢業後到現在為止這二十一年來，我學到了哪些重要的教訓。我得出了兩個答案。在這美好的日子裡，我們齊聚一堂，慶祝你們學業有成，但我想跟各位分享關於失敗的好處。還有，當你們站在所謂「現實生活」的入口，我想宣揚一下想像力有多至關重要。

Important Lessons
重要的教訓

I have racked my mind and heart for what I ought to say to you today. I have asked myself what I wish I had known at my own graduation, and what important lessons I have learned in the 21 years that have [1]**expired** between that day and this. I have come up with two answers. On this wonderful day when we are gathered together to celebrate your academic success, I have decided to talk to you about the benefits of failure. And as you stand on the [2]**threshold** of what is sometimes called "real life," I want to [3]**extol** the [4]**crucial** importance of imagination.

Looking back at the 21-year-old that I was at graduation, is a slightly uncomfortable experience for the 42-year-old that she has become. I was convinced that the only thing I wanted to do, ever, was to write novels. **GM** However, my parents, both of whom came from [5]**impoverished** backgrounds and neither of whom had been to college, took the view that my overactive imagination was an amusing personal [6]**quirk** that would never pay a [7]**mortgage**, or [8]**secure** a [9]**pension**. I cannot remember telling my parents that I was studying Classics; they might well have found out for the first time on graduation day.

回顧二十一歲大學畢業時期的我，對於現在四十二歲的我來說是有點尷尬的體驗。我當時堅信自己唯一想做的事、也一直想做的事就是寫小說。不過，我的父母皆出身貧困，都沒上過大學，他們認為我那過於豐富的想像力只是令人莞爾的個人怪癖，對於繳房貸或取得退休金

VOCABULARY

1) **expire** [ɪkˋspaɪr] (v.) 到期，滿期，終止
When does your passport expire?

2) **threshold** [ˋθrɛʃhold] (n.) 門檻，開端，起點
At the age of 30, Steve Jobs was on the threshold of success.

3) **extol** [ɪkˋstol] (v.) 頌揚
The book extols the benefits of exercise and a healthy diet.

4) **crucial** [ˋkruʃəl] (a.) 關鍵的，決定性的
This election is crucial to the country's future.

5) **impoverished** [ɪmˋpɑvərɪʃt] (a.) 窮困的
Haiti became even more impoverished after the earthquake.

6) **quirk** [kwɝk] (n.) 怪癖
Mark finally found a woman who could accept his quirks.

7) **mortgage** [ˋmɔrgɪdʒ] (n.) 房屋抵押貸款
How many years are left on your mortgage?

8) **secure** [sɪˋkjʊr] (v.) 獲得，取得
Richard managed to secure a loan from the bank.

9) **pension** [ˋpɛnʃən] (n.) 退休金，養老金
Does your company have a pension plan?

是無濟於事的。我不記得是否告訴過父母我主修的是古典文學，他們甚至可能在我畢業典禮那天才發現。

The Benefits of Failure
失敗的好處

I cannot criticize my parents for hoping that I would never experience poverty. They had been poor themselves, and I have since been poor, and I quite agree with them that it is not an [10]**ennobling** experience. Climbing out of poverty by your own efforts, that is indeed something on which to pride yourself, but poverty itself is [11]**romanticized** only by fools. What I feared most for myself at your age was not poverty, but failure.

關於父母希望我永遠都不要經歷窮苦的生活這點，我無可厚非。他們體驗過貧困的日子，我自己後來也經歷過，所以我同意他們，這不是什麼使人昇華的經歷。靠自己努力擺脫貧困，確實足以令人感到自豪，但只有傻瓜才將貧困視為浪漫的事。在你們這個年紀的時候，我最害怕的不是貧困，而是失敗。

[12]**Ultimately**, we all have to decide for ourselves what constitutes failure, but the world is quite eager to give you a set of [13]**criteria** if you let it. So I think it is fair to say that by any conventional measure, a mere seven years after my graduation day, I had failed on an [14]**epic** scale. An [15]**exceptionally** [16]**short-lived** marriage had [17]**imploded**, and I was jobless, a lone parent, and as poor as it is possible to be in modern Britain, without being homeless.

我們最終都要自己摸索出失敗的定義是什麼，但只要你願意，這個世界總是迫不及待給你一套標準。所以，我可以這麼說，以任何傳統的標準來看，我在畢業後七年就經歷了慘敗。格外短命的婚姻已宣告破裂，而且我當時沒有工作，成了單親媽媽，可以說達到了現代英國最貧窮的標準，只差沒有流離失所。

> 66 We do not need magic to change the world, we carry all the power we need inside ourselves already: we have the power to imagine better.
>
> 改變世界不需要魔法，我們內心已具備所需的能力：想像更美好世界的能力。
>
> *J.K. 羅琳談想像力*

© Ken Schwarz

J.K. Rowling
J.K. 羅琳

一九六五年七月三十一日生，是一位英國知名奇幻小說家，代表作為《哈利波特》系列作品。《哈利波特》暢銷全球，熱賣超過四億本，成為史上最暢銷的書籍之一；其同名改編電影也成為電影史上票房收入最高的電影之一。

J.K. 羅琳的人生宛如《灰姑娘》故事，在短短五年內從接受政府濟助的貧窮單親媽媽，成為富可敵國的暢銷作家。《時代雜誌》也以她「對哈利波特迷在社會、道德與政治方面的影響」評為二〇〇七年時代年度風雲人物第二位。

10) **ennobling** [ɪˋnoblɪŋ] (a.) 使人昇華、尊貴的
Some believe that suffering is ennobling.

11) **romanticize** [roˋmæntə͵saɪz] (v.) 使浪漫化、理想化
It's common for women to romanticize marriage.

12) **ultimately** [ˋʌltəmɪtlɪ] (adv.) 最後，總而言之
Stress can ultimately lead to heart disease.

13) **criteria** [kraɪˋtɪrɪə] (n.)（判斷的）標準、準則、尺度，即 criterion 的複數
Every applicant who meets our criteria will be considered for the position.

14) **epic** [ˋɛpɪk] (a.) 史詩般的，宏偉的
The people's epic struggle for freedom is finally over.

15) **exceptionally** [ɪkˋsɛpʃənəlɪ] (adv.) 異常地，優異地，特殊地
Yo-Yo Ma is an exceptionally talented cello player.

16) **short-lived** [ˋʃɔrtˋlɪvd] (a.) 短暫的，短命的
Most of Michael's relationships have been short-lived.

17) **implode** [ɪmˋplod] (v.) 崩潰，瓦解
Some economists believe the economy is in danger of imploding.

So why do I talk about the benefits of failure? Simply because failure meant a stripping away of the [1)]**inessential**. I stopped pretending to myself that I was anything other than what I was, and began to direct all my energy into finishing the only work that mattered to me. I was set free, because my greatest fear had been realized, and I was still alive, and I still had a daughter whom I [2)]**adored**, and I had an old typewriter and a big idea. And so [3)]**rock bottom** became the solid foundation on which I rebuilt my life.

那我為什麼要談失敗的好處？只不過因為失敗可以幫你擺脫不必要的東西。我不再需要偽裝自己，並開始將我的所有精力都放在完成唯一對我重要的事。既然我最恐懼的事已成為現實，我就自由了，更何況我還活著，還有我最寶貝的女兒，又有一台老舊的打字機和滿腦子創意。於是谷底成了我重建人生的堅厚基石。

The knowledge that you have emerged wiser and stronger from [4)]**setbacks** means that you are, ever after, secure in your ability to survive. You will never truly know yourself, or the strength of your relationships, until both have been tested by [5)]**adversity**. Such knowledge is a true gift, for all that it is painfully won, and it has been worth more than any [6)]**qualification** I ever earned.

挫敗會讓你變得更有智慧、更茁壯，代表從此以後你的生存能力便是安全可靠的。在歷經逆境的考驗之前，你永遠不會認識到真正的自己，也不會知道自己人際關係的力量。這樣的知識才是真正的禮物，雖然得來的過程是痛苦的，但比起我曾獲得的其他資歷都還要值得。

The Importance of Imagination
想像力的重要性

Now you might think that I chose my second theme, the importance of imagination, because of the part it played in rebuilding my life, but that is not [7)]**wholly** so. Though I personally will defend the value of bedtime stories to my last [8)]**gasp**, I have learned to value imagination in a much broader sense. Imagination is not only the uniquely human capacity to [9)]**envision** that which is not, it is the power that enables us to [10)]**empathize** with humans whose experiences we have never shared.

你們也許會認為，我之所以選擇想像力的重要性做為演講的第二個主題，是因為它在我的人生重建過程中扮演了重要角色，但事實並非完全如此。雖然我個人就算剩最後一口氣，都會捍衛床邊故事的價值，但我已學會用更廣泛的意義來評價想像力。想像力不但是人類獨特的預想能力，也是一種同理心的力量，讓我們能夠體會他人經歷，即使和自己的經歷全然不同。

One of the greatest [11)]**formative** experiences of my life [12)]**preceded** Harry Potter, though it informed much of what I [13)]**subsequently** wrote in those books. This [14)]**revelation** came in the form of one of my earliest day jobs. Though I was [LG] sloping off to write stories during my lunch hours, I paid the rent in my early 20s by working

> ❝ There is an expiry date on blaming your parents for steering you in the wrong direction; the moment you are old enough to take the wheel, responsibility lies with you.
>
> 抱怨父母害你走錯路的行為是有期限的；當你大到可以自己做主時，責任就在你自己了。
>
> *J.K. 羅琳談責任*

VOCABULARY 🎧04

1) **inessential** [ˌɪnɪˈsɛnʃəl] (a.) 不重要的，非必要的
We try to avoid spending money on inessential items.

2) **adore** [əˈdor] (v.) 熱愛，愛慕
Gilbert adores his wife and children.

3) **rock bottom** [ˈrɑk ˈbɑtəm] (n.) 最低點，谷底
Stock prices have reached rock bottom.

4) **setback** [ˈsɛtˌbæk] (n.) 挫折，失敗，阻礙
The project was delayed due to setbacks.

5) **adversity** [ædˈvɜsəti] (n.) 逆境，厄運
We all must learn to deal with adversity.

6) **qualification** [ˌkwɑləfɪˈkeʃən] (n.) 資格，能力
What qualifications does the applicant have?

7) **wholly** [ˈholi] (adv.) 完全地
The government isn't wholly responsible for the crisis.

8) **gasp** [gæsp] (n.) 喘氣，喘息。last gasp 即「奄奄一息，最後一搏」
At his last gasp, the man confessed his crime.

9) **envision** [ɪnˈvɪʒən] (v.) 想像，展望
It's hard to envision a world without war.

at the African research department at  Amnesty International's headquarters in London. Every day, I saw evidence about the evils humankind will [15]**inflict** on their fellow humans, to gain or maintain power. I began to have nightmares, [16]**literal** nightmares, about some of the things I saw, heard, and read. And yet I also learned more about human goodness at Amnesty International than I had ever known before.

在寫哈利波特之前，我有過許多重大的成長經驗，其中一件最重要的人生啟示，是出現在我早年其中一份工作，而且這個經驗對我後來的作品也有不小的影響。二十歲出頭時，為了付房租，我在國際特赦組織倫敦總部的非洲研究部門上班，不過我會利用午餐時間偷偷去寫小說。我每天上班所看的資料，都是人類為了爭奪或掌控權力而殘害同胞的證據。我開始作惡夢，是真的睡覺作惡夢，夢到我白天所看到、聽到和讀到的事情。不過，我在國際特赦組織也學到了許多人性的善良之處，是我以前從不知道的事。

> 66 Wherever I am, if I've got a book with me, I have a place I can go and be happy.
>
> 不論身在何方，假如我有一本書，我就能遁入其中怡然自得。

J.K. 羅琳談閱讀

© Tracy Lee Carroll

美國奧蘭多環球影城的霍格華滋特快車（The Hogwarts Express）© Yobab / Shutterstock.com

日本大阪環球影城的霍格華滋城堡（Hogwarts Castle）© Veerachart / Shutterstock.com

美國奧蘭多環球影城的哈利波特魔幻世界（The Wizarding World Of Harry Potter）© Daniel Horande Photography

10) **empathize** [ˋɛmpə͵θaɪz] (v.) 表示同情，empathy 即名詞「同感，同理心」
It's easy to empathize with the characters in the novel.

11) **formative** [ˋfɔrmətɪv] (a.) 影響（某人）成長、發展的
Kevin spent his formative years in rural England.

12) **precede** [prɪˋsid] (v.) 處在⋯之前
In English, verbs are preceded by the subject.

13) **subsequently** [ˋsʌbsɪkwəntlɪ] (adv.) 隨後的，後續的
The man was arrested and subsequently charged with murder.

14) **revelation** [͵rɛvəˋleʃən] (n.) 揭露，顯示
The book is filled with revelations about the star's private life.

15) **inflict** [ɪnˋflɪkt] (v.) 使遭受（損傷等），加以（處罰或判刑）
Even small dogs can inflict fatal injuries.

16) **literal** [ˋlɪtərəl] (a.) 照字面的，確實的，不誇張的
Some Christians believe in the literal truth of the Bible.

Amnesty [1]**mobilizes** thousands of people who have never been [2]**tortured** or [3]**imprisoned** for their beliefs to act on behalf of those who have. The power of human empathy, leading to [4]**collective** action, saves lives, and frees prisoners. Ordinary people, whose personal [5]**well-being** and security are assured, join together in huge numbers to save people they do not know, and will never meet. My small participation in that process was one of the most humbling and inspiring experiences of my life.

國際特赦組織動員成千上萬人來為那些因為自己的信念而遭受酷刑或受到監禁的受害人發聲，他們本身沒有同樣的受害經歷，但人類同理心的力量能帶動眾人一起拯救生命、釋放俘虜。他們只是普通人，原本過著幸福平安的生活，卻願意大量聯合起來，共同拯救他們從不認識、未來也見不到的人。在這個過程中，我只是參與了一小部分，卻是我人生中最感到謙卑、也最受啟發的經歷。

The Wisdom of the Classics
古典文學的智慧

One of the many things I learned at the end of that Classics [6]**corridor** down which I [7]**ventured** at the age of 18, in search of something I could not then define, was this, written by the Greek author Plutarch: What we achieve [8]**inwardly** will change outer reality. That is an [9]**astonishing** statement and yet proven a thousand times every day

of our lives. It expresses, in part, our inescapable connection with the outside world, the fact that we touch other people's lives simply by existing.

十八歲那年，我在古典文學的走廊裡探索，尋找著一些我當時說不出來的事，在走廊的盡頭，我學到了許多東西，其中一個是希臘作家普魯塔克所寫的：「我們內在所成就的將改變外在的現實。」真是令人驚訝的一句話，但在我們生命中每一天都能驗證上千次。這句話的部分意思是說，我們與外在世界的連結是無可避免的，我們單就存在這世上，就與其他人的生命有關連。

And tomorrow, I hope that even if you remember not a single word of mine, you remember those of Seneca, another of those old Romans I met when I fled down the Classics corridor, in retreat from career ladders, in search of ancient wisdom: As is a tale, so is life: not how long it is, but how good it is, is what matters.

而明天，就算你完全不記得我說過的話，我也希望你記住哲學家塞內卡——他也是我躲到古典文學走廊逃避職涯階梯、尋找古老智慧時遇到的古羅馬人之一——記住他說的其中一句話：就跟故事一樣，人生的重點不在於長短，而是在於它有多美好。

I wish you all very good lives.

祝大家有美好的人生。

VOCABULARY 🎧06

1) **mobilize** [ˋmobə͵laɪz] (v.) 動員，調動
The government mobilized troops to defend the border.

2) **torture** [ˋtɔrtʃə] (v./n.) 刑求，折磨
Many captured soldiers were tortured by the enemy.

3) **imprison** [ɪmˋprɪzn] (v.) 監禁，使入獄
The terror suspects were imprisoned without trial.

4) **collective** [kəˋlɛktɪv] (a.) 集體的，共同的
The event has become part of our country's collective memory.

5) **well-being** [͵wɛlˋbiɪŋ] (n.) 康樂，安康
Practicing yoga has increased my sense of well-being.

6) **corridor** [ˋkɔrɪdə] (n.) 走廊，迴廊
My office is at the end of the corridor.

7) **venture** [ˋvɛntʃə] (v.) 冒險，大膽行事
Our cats never venture far from home.

8) **inwardly** [ˋɪnwədlɪ] (adv.) 在內心裡
Ellen looked calm, but she was inwardly nervous.

9) **astonishing** [əˋstɑnɪʃɪŋ] (a.) 令人驚嘆的
The magician performed astonishing tricks.

© paintings / Shutterstock.com

rack one's mind/brain
絞盡腦汁

rack 當動詞有「過度使用」的意思，過度使用腦子，就是「絞盡腦汁」的意思囉。

A: Did you remember where you put your keys?
你記得你把鑰匙放在哪裡嗎？
B: No. I racked my brains, but I still can't find them.
不記得。我已經想破頭了，但還是找不到。

Classics 西洋古典學

也稱為 Classical Studies，是一門古希臘羅馬歷史、哲學、文學、律法、藝術、建築……的文化研究，是西洋人文學科的根源，尤其著重於古典古代（Classical Antiquity，西元前 600 至西元 600 年間的）的文學作品。

slope off / slip off 偷溜，開小差

英式英文的 slope off 即美語當中的 slip off。slip off 可以表示「（把衣物）隨手一脫」，但若用在與地方、位置相關的說法，則表示「偷偷跑到某處」。

A: Do you know where Robert is?
你知道羅伯特在哪嗎？
B: I think he slipped off to smoke a cigarette.
我猜他溜去抽根菸吧。

Amnesty International
國際特赦組織

成立於一九六一年的非政府組織 Amnesty International 致力於國際人權監察，呼籲全人類均享有《世界人權宣言》揭櫫的所有權利，以支持言論自由、保護婦女及同志權利、營救各國良心犯（prisoner of conscience 又稱 POC，即因思想信仰、種族、性取向……被拘禁者）、追究侵犯人權者的責任為主要任務。Amnesty International 是國際人權組織的始祖與楷模，一九七七年獲頒諾貝爾和平獎。

on behalf of 代替某人

意思是「代替某人去做某件事」、「做某人的代表」。也可以說 in behalf of sb.、on / in sb.'s behalf、in sb.'s name。

· The producer accepted the award on behalf of the director.
= The producer accepted the award on the director's behalf.
那位製作人代替導演領獎。

A: Rob just called. He's sick and can't attend the meeting today.
羅伯剛剛打電話來。他生病了，今天無法參加會議。
B: Oh. Can you go on his behalf and report back to me?
喔。你能代他去開會，再向我回報會議結果嗎？

另一種意思是「為了某人的緣故」。
A: Are you sure it's safe to take a bus home this late?
你確定這麼晚搭公車回家安全嗎？
B: Yes. Don't worry on my behalf. It's perfectly safe.
確定，別為我擔心，絕對安全。

Plutarch 普魯塔克——西方傳記文學鼻祖

Plutarch（約西元 46-125 年）是以希臘文寫作的羅馬傳記作家，以二十三組古希臘、古羅馬傳奇人物對比傳記（如亞歷山大對比凱撒），加上四個單篇帝王本紀所組成的《名人傳》傳世。

在《名人傳》當中，Plutarch 融匯歷史、文學及人生哲學，將人物刻畫得栩栩如生，並保留許多已經散失的傳說及文獻，他樸實的筆調及生動的敘述風格對歐美散文、傳記影響深遠，莎士比亞許多劇作都取材於他的作品。

Seneca 塞內卡——古羅馬著名悲劇作家及哲學家

Seneca（約西元前 4 年至西元 65 年）是西班牙人，隨父親定居羅馬，後來從政，並在皇帝尼祿十一歲時成為他的老師。西元 59 年，尼祿二十一歲時陸續謀殺母親及兄弟，Seneca 為避禍遠離羅馬，他著名的哲學著作「致門徒盧基利烏斯的 124 封信」即在這個時期完成，這些信的倫理及神學觀念，對後來的基督教思想頗具影響。西元 65 年，尼祿以謀反的罪名下令 Seneca 自殺。

J.K. 羅琳示範演講、文章好用的「however」

副詞 however 在句義上屬轉折語，常用在敘述長句中，熟悉掌握各個轉折語的意思，有助於寫作時讓句子更通順。however 的常見含義有三個：

● 然而，但是，相對地
解 此用法可將 however 置於句中或句首來連接前後兩個子句，後面務必加上逗點。

例 **However, not every invention is necessary.**

解 放在句中時，若前面為完整子句，however 前面需要再加上分號，若是直接插入句中，則前後都是逗號。

例 **The first test was quite easy; the second, however, was much more difficult.**

● 不管，無論如何（方式）
例 **At our company, we're allowed to dress however we like.**

● 不管，無論如何（程度）
例 **However much we disagree with other people's views, we should still respect them.**

二○○八年六月五日，J.K. 羅琳接受哈佛大學頒發榮譽文學博士學位（Honorary Doctor of Letters degree），並於當天畢業典禮上發表此篇演說。

面對全球首府哈佛畢業生，這群世界上學業最成功的人，J.K. 羅琳要送給他們的禮物就是「失敗」，因為「你們對成功的渴望，應該跟你們對失敗的恐懼一樣大……你們失敗的經驗，可能跟平常人成功的經驗一樣少。」

Be True to Yourself

Ellen DeGeneres' Tulane Commencement Speech

艾倫狄珍妮杜蘭大學畢業典禮演講

© TULANE UNIVERSITY

Common Cement
一般的水泥

Thank you, President Cowan, Mrs. President Cowen, [1]**distinguished** guests, undistinguished guests—you know who you are, honored [2]**faculty** and [3]**creepy** Spanish teacher. And thank you to all the graduating class of 2009, I realize most of you are 🔲 hung over and have [4]**splitting** headaches and haven't slept since 🔲 Fat Tuesday, but you can't graduate till I finish, so listen up.

謝謝考恩校長和校長夫人，各位貴賓，平凡的賓客——你們知道自己是誰，備受尊崇的教師和怪怪的西班牙語老師。還有，謝謝所有二〇〇九年畢業班的學生。我知道從狂歡節到現在，你們大部分人都還在宿醉，頭痛欲裂，甚至都沒睡；但在我說完之前，你們還不能畢業，所以仔細聽好了。

When I was asked to make the [5]**commencement** speech, I [6]**immediately** said yes. Then I went to look up what commencement meant which would have been easy if I had a dictionary, but most of the books in our house are Portia's, and they're all written in Australian. So I had to break the word down myself, to find out the meaning.

貴校請我在畢業典禮上致辭時，我立刻答應了。然後我就去查 commencement（畢業典禮）這個單字有什麼含意，假如我有字典的話，應該會簡單得多，但我家的書大部分都是波蒂亞（艾倫的伴侶）的，所以都是澳洲文。因此我就自己來拆解這個字，找出它的含意。

Commencement: common, and [7]**cement**, common cement. You commonly see cement on sidewalks. Sidewalks have cracks, and if you step on a crack, you break your mother's back. So there's that. But I'm honored that you've asked me here to speak at your common cement.

把 commencement 這個單字拆開，就是 common 和 cement，一般的水泥（common cement）。你一般會在人行道上看到水泥。人行道上有縫隙，俗話說：踩到縫隙，你媽媽的背就會摔斷。差不多就是這個意思。不過，我很榮幸你們邀請我來這裡，在你們的「一般的水泥」上致辭。

I Didn't Go to College
我沒上過大學

I thought that you had to be a famous **LG** alumnus, alumini, aluminum, alumis—you had to graduate from this school. And I didn't go to college here, and I don't know if President Cowan knows, I didn't go to any college at all, any college. And I'm not saying you wasted your time, or money, but look at me, I'm a huge [8)celebrity.

我以為能在貴校畢業典禮上致辭的只有著名的校友之類的，我的意思是說，要從貴校畢業。我沒念過這所大學，而且我不知道考恩校長是否知道，我沒念過任何大學，任何一所都沒有。我的意思不是說你們在浪費時間或金錢，但看看我，我是個大名人。

I'm here because I love New Orleans. I was born and raised here, I spent my formative years here, and like you, while I was living here I only did laundry six times. When I finished school, I was completely lost. My point is that, by the time I was your age, I really thought I knew who I was, but I had no idea. Like for example, when I was your age, I was dating men. So what I'm saying is, when you're older, most of you will be gay.

我今天來這裡，是因為我愛紐奧良。我在這裡出生長大，我的成長階段是在這裡度過的，就跟你們一樣，我住在這裡時，只洗過六次衣服。我高中畢業時，生活完全沒有方向。我想說的是，在你們這個年紀時，我真的以為我知道自己是誰，但其實一點底都沒有。比如說，我在你們這個年紀時，我是跟男孩子約會。所以，我的意思是說，等你年紀漸長，你們大部分人會發現自己是同性戀。

66 I ask people why they have deer heads on their walls. They always say because it's such a beautiful animal. There you go. I think my mother is attractive, but I have photographs of her.

我問一些人為何要把鹿頭掛在自家牆上。他們總是說因為鹿是一種很美的動物。我覺得我媽也很漂亮，但我掛的是她的相片。

艾倫談保護動物

Ellen DeGeneres 艾倫狄珍妮

© Jaguar PS / Shutterstock.com

一九五八年生，美國喜劇演員，主持電視脫口秀《艾倫狄珍妮秀》（*The Ellen DeGeneres Show*）獲多次艾美獎肯定，並曾主持兩屆奧斯卡金像獎頒獎典禮。

艾倫於一九九七年在《歐普拉秀》當中出櫃，她主演的影集角色也同時向歐普拉飾演的諮商師表明自己的同志身份，造成轟動，從此感情生活成為娛樂新聞追逐焦點。她與女星 Portia de Rossi 於二〇〇八年結婚。除了為同志人權發聲，艾倫也是著名的愛護動物人士。

7) **cement** [sɪˋmɛnt] (n.) 水泥
   Be careful not to step in the wet cement.

8) **celebrity** [sɪˋlɛbrətɪ] (n.) 名人
   Have you heard the latest gossip about that celebrity?

© Natalia Bratslavsky / Shutterstock.com

© Pieter Morlion

Fat Tuesday 是美國歷史最悠久，也最多采多姿的慶典之一，遊行隊伍會向觀眾投擲珠串、小紀念品、塑膠硬幣。

There Must Be a Purpose
一定有其意義存在

Anyway, I had no idea what I wanted to do with my life, and the way I ended up on this path was from a very tragic event. I was maybe nineteen, and my girlfriend at the time was killed in a car accident. And I was living in a basement apartment; I had no money; I had no heat, no air; I had a [1]**mattress** on the floor and the apartment was [2]**infested** with fleas. And I was [3]**soul-searching**—I was like, why is she suddenly gone, and there are fleas here? I don't understand, there must be a purpose, and wouldn't it be so convenient if we could pick up the phone and call God and ask these questions?

反正當時的我並不知道自己想做什麼，我會走上現在這條路，是因為發生了一件非常悲慘的事。那時我大概十九歲，我當時的女友在一場車禍中喪生。我那時候住在一棟公寓的地下室，我沒錢，沒有暖氣，也沒有冷氣，我只有地板上的一張床墊，飽受跳蚤侵擾。我當時在自我反省——我在想，為什麼她突然消失了，跳蚤卻一直都在？我不懂，這一切一定有它的意義存在，假如我們能打個電話給上帝，問祂這些問題，那豈不方便多了？

> 66 I had everything I'd hoped for, but I wasn't being myself. So I decided to be honest about who I was. It was strange: The people who loved me for being funny suddenly didn't like me for being... me.
>
> 曾經，我希望擁有的東西都有了，但我不是在做我自己。所以，我決定要忠於自己。奇怪的是：那些因為我很搞笑而喜愛我的人，忽然討厭做自己的……我。

艾倫談出櫃

And I started writing, and what poured out of me was an imaginary conversation with God, which was [4]**one-sided**. And I finished writing it and I looked at it and I said to myself, "I'm going do this on the 〔LG〕 *Tonight Show* with Johnny Carson, and I'm going be the first woman in the history of the show to be called over to sit down."

於是我開始寫東西，將我腦海中想像與上帝的對話都寫出來，不過都是我一個人的獨角戲。寫完後，我看著這些對話，告訴自己：「我要在強尼卡森的《今夜秀》表演這段脫口秀，而且我要成為節目有史以來第一位獲邀坐下來受訪的女性。」

And several years later, I was the first woman in the history of the show, and the only woman in the history of the show to sit down, because of that phone conversation with God that I wrote. And I started this path of [5]**stand-up**, and it was successful and it was great, but it was hard because I was trying to please everybody and I had this secret that I was keeping, that I was gay.

幾年後，我成為《今夜秀》節目有史以來第一位、也是唯一獲邀坐下來的女性，這都是因為我寫的那些與上帝通電話的對話。於是我開啟了單口相聲之路，而且非常成功、非常棒，不過很辛苦，因為我試著討好所有人，而且要守住自己是同性戀的秘密。

I Decided to Come Out
我決定出櫃

〔GM〕 Then my career turned into, I got my own [6]**sitcom**, and that was very successful, another level of success. And I thought, "What if they find out I'm gay? Then they'll never watch." And this was a long time ago—this was when we just had white presidents. But anyway, I finally decided that I was living with so much shame, and so much fear, that I just couldn't live that way anymore, and I decided

to  come out and make it creative. And my character would come out at the same time.

然後我轉型了，拍了自己的情境喜劇，而且非常成功，那是我的另一個事業顛峰。於是我想：「假如他們發現我是同性戀會怎樣？他們就不會看我的節目了。」這是很久以前的事了，當時我們的總統只有白人。不論如何，我終於決定，我受夠了恥辱，受夠了恐懼，我不想再過那樣的生活，於是我決定出櫃，而且要用充滿創意的方式。我飾演的角色也會同時出櫃。

And I thought, "What's the worst that could happen? I can lose my career." I did. I lost my career. The show was cancelled after six years without even telling me; I read it in the paper. The phone didn't ring for three years. I had no offers. Yet, I was getting letters from kids that almost [7]**committed** [8]**suicide**, but didn't because of what I did. And I realized that I had a purpose. But I felt like I was being punished, and it was a bad time. I was angry, I was sad—and then I was offered a talk show.

我還想過：「最糟糕的結果會是什麼？我可能失去我的演藝生涯。」我確實是失去了我的演藝生涯。那個做了六年的節目突然喊停，而且還沒有事先通知我，我是看報紙才知道的。接下來三年，沒人打電話給我，也接不到工作。不過，我收到差點自殺的年輕人來信，他們因為看到我出櫃，打消了自殺的念頭。於是我意識到，我做的事是有其意義存在的。但我當時覺得自己像是受到了懲罰，那段日子很難受，我變得易怒、感到悲傷。然後，我接到了一個脫口秀的節目。

> 66 Why don't they give us things we can actually use? I don't need a thinner phone. You know what I need? I need a tortilla chip that can support the weight of guacamole.

為什麼他們不給我們真正有用的東西？我不需要更薄的手機。你知道我需要什麼嗎？我需要能支撐酪梨醬重量的玉米脆片。

艾倫談需要

© TULANE UNIVERSITY

7) **commit** [kə`mɪt] (v.) 犯（罪、過失等）
The woman was sent to prison for a crime she didn't commit.

8) **suicide** [`suə‚saɪd] (n./v.) 自殺
The man committed suicide by jumping off a bridge.

The Tonight Show《今夜秀》

這個一九五四年開播的深夜廣播／電視節目，是史上最長壽的脫口秀。拜電視普及所賜，目前大眾最熟悉的主持人應為傑雷諾（Jay Leno，主持期間為 1992-2009 及 2010-2014），但演講稿中所提 Johnny Carson 的主持期間最長（1962-1992），他的節目形式及主持風格對美國電視界影響深遠，也造就許多明星，喜劇演員無不以在節目中博 Johnny Carson 一笑、坐上該節目客座主持椅為至高榮譽，大衛賴特曼（David Letterman）、傑雷諾、傑利賽菲爾德（Jerry Seinfeld）、艾倫狄珍妮均名列其中。

Stay True to Yourself
忠於自己

Really, when I look back on it, I wouldn't change a thing. I mean, it was so important for me to lose everything, because I found out what the most important thing is, is to **LG** be true to yourself. So in conclusion, when I was younger I thought success was something different. I thought when I grow up, I want to be famous. I want to be a star. I want to be in the movies. When I grow up I want to see the world, drive nice cars; I want to have
1)**groupies**.

But my idea of success is different today. And as you grow, you'll realize the definition of success changes. For many of you, today, success is being able to **LG** hold down 20 shots of
2)**tequila**. For me, the most important thing in your life is to live your life with 3)**integrity** and not to give in to peer pressure and try to be something that you're not, to live your life as an honest and
4)**compassionate** person, to contribute in some way. So to conclude my conclusion, follow your passion, stay true to yourself.

說真的，回顧過去，就算人生再走一遍，我也會做同樣的事。我是說，失去一切對我來說很重要，因為我發現最重要的事，是忠於自己。總結來說，我年輕時，我所認為的成功跟現在是有點不一樣的。當時我想，等我長大後，我要出名，我要成為明星，我要演電影；等我長大後，我想要看看這個世界，開名車，我想要有粉絲。

但我現在對於成功的想法不一樣了。當你年紀漸長，你會發現對成功的定義會改變。現在對你們許多人而言，成功是可以乾掉二十杯龍舌蘭。對我來說，人生中最重要的事，是活出真誠，不要因為同儕的壓力而屈服，也不要試著變成別人；帶著悲憫情懷活出坦率的人生，在某些方面做出貢獻。所以，總結一下我的結論，就是追隨自己的熱情，忠於自己。

© Helga Esteb / Shutterstock.com

VOCABULARY 12

1) **groupie** [ˋɡrupi] (n.) 追隨樂團、想跟團員在一起的粉絲，通常是少女
The band invited a bunch of groupies onto their tour bus.

2) **tequila** [təˋkilə] (n.) 龍舌蘭酒
Most tequila is made in Mexico.

3) **integrity** [ɪnˋtɛɡrəti] (n.) 正直，誠實
The principal was a man of great integrity.

4) **compassionate** [kəmˋpæʃənɪt] (a.) 有同情心的，慈悲的
The nurse gave the patient a compassionate smile.

The Ellen DeGeneres Show
《艾倫秀》

經常被暱稱為 Ellen 的《艾倫秀》二○○三年開播至今，這個節目除了有一般脫口秀的搞笑橋段、名人訪談，還會與現場觀眾互動，對一般市井小民的生活及夢想也多所著墨，極為收到大眾歡迎。Ellen 不只叫座，也很受到好評，至今已獲得三十八項日間節目艾美獎的榮譽，已確定與電視台簽約至二○一七年。

be hung over 宿醉

hangover 是「宿醉」的名詞，當我們説 have a hangover，就是指酒喝太多，造成隔天頭痛、噁心的後遺症。動詞形式則為 be hung over。

A: Did you have a hangover after that party last night?
昨晚的派對有給你帶來宿醉嗎？

B: Yeah. I was really hung over this morning.
有啊。我今天早上宿醉超厲害的。

Fat Tuesday / Mardi Gras 狂歡節

Mardi Gras（法文，Fat Tuesday「油膩星期二」的意思）是美國歷史最悠久，也最多采多姿的慶典之一。每年二月或三月，在美國南方路易西安那州的紐奧良（New Orleans, Louisiana）、阿拉巴馬州的莫比爾（Mobile, Alabama）、密西西比州拜洛希（Biloxi, Mississippi）等有法國傳統的城市，都會舉辦慶祝活動。

要認識 Mardi Gras，必須先了解 Lent（四旬齋）這個基督教／天主教活動，也就是從復活節起往前算四十天（週日不算）的齋戒，第四十天會落在星期三（被稱作 Ash Wednesday，聖灰星期三、塗灰日）。在這段期間，教徒藉由禁食、懺悔來贖罪，讓自己的身心靈潔淨，以迎接耶穌光榮復活的日子。而聖灰星期三之前的那一天，是四旬齋之前最後能夠吃喝狂歡的機會，傳統上會舉辦嘉年華（Carnival，源自拉丁文 carne vale「告別肉食」之意，以巴西最負盛名）。

而紐奧良狂歡節獨具特色，不同於巴西嘉年華的原因，在於一八二九年一群年輕人從巴黎回到美國，模仿巴黎人舉辦慶典時身穿豔麗服裝沿街跳舞；一八五七年，一群自稱 Mistick Krewe of Comus（科莫斯神秘克魯隊）的當地商人加入，開啟遊行隊伍向觀眾投擲珠串、小紀念品、塑膠硬幣（統稱為 throws）的傳統。

Grammar Master

Then my career turned into...
艾倫狄珍妮娓娓道出人生的轉折
——插入語法

當説話者想在一句話中同時表達多樣、細微的敘述時，即可使用插入語——將一個獨立單字、片語、子句或句子插入原本那句話，用來修飾、説明、強調或連接句子。再説得直接一點，文章中常見用括號、破折號及逗點補充説明的地方，就是插入語。附帶一提，若一個插入語與主詞屬於同等關係時，即為我們常説的「同位語」。

例 **There's no reason, though, to dismiss him.**（獨立單字當插入語）

例 **What—in your opinion—is the cause of global warming?**（片語當插入語）

例 **The idea that pandas only eat bamboo (though not exactly correct) isn't too far from the truth.**（省略語當插入語）

例 **Yo-Yo Ma, a world-famous cellist, was born in Paris.**（與主詞同等關係片語當作插入語，即「同位語」）

回到演講稿中這一句：
Then my career turned into, ~~I got my own sitcom, and that was very successful~~, another level of success.

→ Then my career turned into another level of success.

艾倫在此使用的插入句，用前後兩逗點夾插一句題外話 I got my own sitcom, and that was very successful，將此句刪除，剩下的句子 Then my career turned into another level of success 才是真正主要重點。

alumnus, alumini, aluminum, alumis 畢業生

alumni 這個複數名詞源自拉丁文，一般被當作「畢業校友」的統稱，但原本的用法如下：

	複數	單數
女性畢業校友	alumnae	alumna
男性畢業校友	alumni	alumnus

所以嚴格來説，「全體男女畢業校友」應該是 alumni and alumnae，不然也可以用比較口語的 alums 或 graduates 來避免性別差異。而艾倫在演講稿中的 alumnus, alumini, aluminum, alumis，除了第一個字 alumnus（單數男性畢業校友），其餘都是胡謅，引人發噱，除了諷刺拉丁文／學術界的酸腐，也暗合接下來要講的內容「她沒上過大學」，以及她無視男女界限的同志身份。

come out 出櫃

come out 是 come out of the closet 的簡稱，用衣櫃（closet）來比喻同志們暗藏自己性向的狀況，而走出衣櫃的動作就是形容向大眾公開自己的性傾向。

A: Don't say anything about Gary being gay—he hasn't come out of the closet yet.
不要和別人説蓋瑞是同志的事，他還沒出櫃。

B: OK. His secret's safe with me.
沒問題，我會保守他的祕密的。

be/stay true to oneself 忠於自我

true 除了表示「真實的」，也有「忠實的」意思。當我們説 be / stay true to oneself 時，就表示不欺騙自己，面對真實的自我。

A: I want to major in art, but my parents want me to major in engineering.
我想要主修藝術，但我父母希望我主修工程。

B: You need to stop listening to your parents and be true to yourself.
你必須停止聽命於父母，要忠於自己的想法。

hold down 能夠消化，不吐出來

在這裡是指能把食物吞嚥下去而不吐出來，也表示有辦法喝很多酒又不會吐，「酒量好」的意思，在這個定義時也可以説 hold one's liquor。

A: Has Dan eaten anything since the operation?
丹在手術之後有吃任何東西嗎？

B: The nurse gave him some broth, but he couldn't hold it down.
護士有給他一點高湯，但他還是吐出來了。

A: Is that Eric over there throwing up in the toilet?
那個抱著馬桶吐的人是艾瑞克嗎？

B: Yeah. He can't hold his liquor.
對啊。他酒量不好。

本文是 Ellen DeGeneres 於二〇〇九年在杜蘭大學（Tulane University）畢業典禮上的演講。杜蘭大學位於紐奧良市，成立於一八三四年，是一所私立的研究型大學，常被譽為「南方常春藤」、「南方哈佛」。邀請與紐奧良地緣深厚的 Ellen 演講，顯得別具意義。

Stay Hungry, Stay Foolish

Steve Jobs' 2005 Stanford Commencement Address

史蒂夫賈伯斯 2005 年史丹福大學畢業典禮演講

© Charis Tsevis

I am honored to be with you today at your commencement from one of the finest universities in the world. I never graduated from college. Truth be told, this is the closest I've ever gotten to a college graduation. Today I want to tell you three stories from my life.

我今天很榮幸能參加全世界頂尖大學的畢業典禮。我大學沒畢業,坦白說,這是我距離大學畢業典禮最近的時候。今天我想告訴各位我人生中的三個故事。

 Connecting the Dots
串連生命中的點點滴滴

I [1]**dropped out** of Reed College after the first 6 months, but then stayed around as a [2]**drop-in** for another 18 months or so before I really quit. Reed College at that time offered perhaps the best [3]**calligraphy** instruction in the country. Because I had dropped out and didn't have to take the normal classes, I decided to take a calligraphy class to learn how to do this. I learned about [LG] serif and

---

VOCABULARY 🎧 14

1) **drop out** [drɑp aʊt] (phr.) 輟學
   My parents would kill me if I dropped out of school.

2) **drop-in** [`drɑpˌɪn] (n.) 沒有預約、順便拜訪的人,旁聽生
   (v.) **drop in**
   We do accept drop-ins, but it's better to make an appointment.

3) **calligraphy** [kə`lɪɡrəfi] (n.) 書法,書寫
   The poem was written in beautiful calligraphy.

4) **typeface** [`taɪpˌfes] (n.) 字體
   What typeface will the book be printed in?

5) **typography** [taɪ`pɑɡrəfi] (n.) 活版印刷術,字體設計、排版
   Graphic designers should have a good understanding of typography.

6) **subtle** [`sʌtəl] (a.) 含蓄的,微妙的
   The coconut milk gave the curry a rich, subtle flavor.

sans serif [4)]**typefaces**, about varying the amount of space between different letter combinations, about what makes great [5)]**typography** great. It was beautiful, historical, artistically [6)]**subtle** in a way that science can't capture, and I found it [7)]**fascinating**.

剛進里德學院半年後我就輟學了，但我又另外旁聽了十八個月後才真正離開學校。在當時，里德學院提供的書寫課程也許是全美國最好的。由於我輟學後，就不必修正規的課程，所以我決定旁聽書寫課，學習如何寫一手好字。我學到關於襯線和無襯線字體，如何調整不同字母組合之間的空間，以及漂亮的字體設計漂亮在哪裡。字型設計不但美妙、具有歷史感，更帶有含蓄的美感，是科學所無法體現的，我覺得那很迷人。

None of this had even a hope of any practical application in my life. But 10 years later, when we were designing the first Macintosh computer, it all came back to me. And we designed it all into the Mac. It was the first computer with beautiful typography. If I had never dropped in on that single course in college, the Mac would have never had multiple typefaces or [8)]**proportionally** spaced [9)]**fonts**. And since Windows just copied the Mac, it's likely that no personal computer would have them.

這些看似對我的人生一點用處都沒有。但十年後，我們在設計第一台麥金塔電腦時，這些全派上了用場。我們將這些設計都用在麥金塔電腦，於是麥金塔成為第一台使用漂亮字體的電腦。假如我在大學時沒有旁聽那堂課，麥金塔電腦就不會有各種不同的字體和等間距的字型。由於微軟視窗電腦是抄襲麥金塔的，因此可以說是沒有個人電腦會使用多種不同字型的。

If I had never dropped out, I would have never dropped in on this calligraphy class, and personal computers might not have the wonderful typography that they do. Of course it was impossible to  connect the dots looking forward when I was in college. But it was very, very clear looking backward 10 years later.

假如我沒有輟學，就不會去旁聽書寫課程，而個人電腦可能也不會有這些美妙的字型。當然我在大學時，是不可能事先想到學書寫課跟之後的麥金塔有所連結。但在十年後，再回顧過去，兩者的關連是極為明顯的。

> " I think if you do something and it turns out pretty good, then you should go do something else wonderful, not dwell on it for too long. Just figure out what's next.
>
> 我覺得如果你做了一件事，結果相當不錯，接下來你該去做其他了不起的事，不要耽擱太久。快想想下一步是什麼。
>
> 賈伯斯談卓越

Steve Jobs
史蒂夫賈伯斯

© Denys Prykhodov / Shutterstock.com

生於一九五五年，蘋果公司、Pixar（皮克斯）動畫工作室、NeXT 軟體公司創辦人，麥金塔系列電腦、iPod、iPhone、iPad 及 Pixar 以電腦軟體製作的新型態動畫，都是賈伯斯主導催生的結果，對電腦、影音娛樂業的影響極為深遠，曾七次登上《時代雜誌》封面。

賈伯斯並非電子工程師，他在電腦業的成就，來自於他極強的商業眼光，與對極簡美學與直覺式設計的堅持而來。二〇一一年十月五日，賈伯斯因胰臟癌相關併發症去世。

Steven Jobs

7) **fascinating** [ˈfæsəˌnetɪŋ] (a.) 迷人的，極好的
The movie had a fascinating plot.

8) **proportionally** [prəˈporʃənəli] (adv.) （成）比例地，均衡地
Crime is proportionally higher in urban areas.

9) **font** [fɑnt] (n.) 字型，字體
If you use a larger font, the page will be easier to read.

最早的麥金塔電腦
Macintosh Classic
© Marcin Wichary

 **Love and Loss**
愛與失落

I was lucky—I found what I loved to do early in life. 🔵 Woz and I started Apple in my parents' garage when I was 20. We worked hard, and in 10 years Apple had grown from just the two of us in a garage into a $2 billion company with over 4,000 employees. We had just released our finest creation—the Macintosh—a year earlier, and I had just turned 30. And then I got fired.

我很幸運，我在早年時就找到自己熱愛的事。我二十歲時，就和沃茲在我父母家的車庫創辦了蘋果公司。我們努力工作，十年間蘋果就從只有我們兩個人在車庫裡，成長為營業額達二十億美元的公司，並擁有超過四千名員工。在這前一年，我們剛發表最棒的作品——麥金塔——而我正剛滿三十歲，然後我就被解雇了。

What had been the focus of my entire adult life was gone, and it was [1]**devastating**. I was a very public failure, and I even thought about running away from the Valley. But something slowly began to [2]**dawn on** me—I still loved what I did. The turn of events at Apple had not changed that one bit. I had been rejected, but I was still in love. And so I decided to start over.

我整個成年後的事業重心全部付諸流水，令我痛不欲生。我成了公眾眼中失敗的示範，甚至想過要逃離矽谷。但我漸漸開始明白一件事——我還是熱愛我所做的事。在蘋果公司遭遇到的轉折並沒有改變這一點。雖然我被否定了，但我還是熱愛我的工作，所以我決定重新開始。

During the next five years, I started a company named 🔵 NeXT, another company named Pixar, and fell in love with an amazing woman who would become my wife. Pixar went on to create the world's first computer [3]**animated** [4]**feature** film, *Toy Story*, and is now the most successful animation studio in the world. In a remarkable turn of events, Apple bought NeXT, I returned to Apple, and the technology we developed at NeXT is at the heart of Apple's current [5]**renaissance**

接下來的五年，我創辦了 NeXT 軟體公司和皮克斯動畫工作室，還愛上一位了不起的女人，她後來成為我的妻子。然後皮克斯製作了世界第一部電腦動畫電影，《玩具總動員》，現在也成為全世界最成功的動畫工作室。又一次神奇的轉折，蘋果公司收購了 NeXT 軟體公司，我又回到蘋果公司，而我們在 NeXT 軟體公司研發的技術，成為蘋果公司目前復興的重心。

I'm pretty sure none of this would have happened if I hadn't been fired from Apple. It was awful-tasting medicine, but I guess the patient needed it. Sometimes life hits you in the head with

66 My model for business is The Beatles. They were four guys who kept each other's kind of negative tendencies in check. They balanced each other and the total was greater than the sum of the parts. That's how I see business: great things in business are never done by one person, they're done by a team of people.

披頭四是我經營事業的楷模。這四個人能好好抑制彼此的怪癖。他們相互平衡，成果大於個別加總。我對事業的看法就是如此：偉大的事業絕不會靠單打獨鬥，而是一群人做出來的。

賈伯斯談合作

1) **devastating** [ˈdɛvəˌstetɪŋ] (a.) 使人痛不欲生的，使人感到震驚的
The news of their son's death was devastating.

2) **dawn on** [dɔn ɑn] (phr.) （為人所）頓悟、開始明白
It finally dawned on Richard that his wife wasn't coming back.

3) **animated** [ˈænəˌmetɪd] (a.) 動畫（片）的 (n.) **animation** [ˌænəˈmeʃən]
What's your favorite animated movie?

4) **feature** [ˈfitʃə] (n.) （電影）長片、正片、本片
The movie won the award for best feature film.

5) **renaissance** [ˈrɛnəˌsɑns] (n.) （固定大寫）文藝復興，類似的藝文復興運動
The city is experiencing a cultural renaissance.

6) **external** [ɪkˈstɜnəl] (a.) 外部的，外面的
You shouldn't judge people by their external appearance.

a brick. Don't lose faith. I'm convinced that the only thing that kept me going was that I loved what I did. You've got to find what you love. And that is as true for your work as it is for your lovers.

我相當確定，假如我沒有被蘋果公司開除，這一切都不會發生。良藥總是苦口的，但我想我這個病人就是需要這種良藥。有時人生會給你來一記當頭棒喝。不要失去信心。我相信唯一能讓我繼續走下去的，就是我熱愛自己所做的事。你一定要找到你所熱愛的事，不論那是事業或是所愛的人。

Death
死亡

When I was 17, I read a quote that went something like: "If you live each day as if it was your last, someday you'll most certainly be right." It made an impression on me, and since then, for the past 33 years, I've looked in the mirror every morning and asked myself: "If today were the last day of my life, would I want to do what I am about to do today?" And whenever the answer has been "No" for too many days in a row, I know I need to change something.

我十七歲時讀到一句名言，那句話差不多是這樣的：「把每一天都當作人生最後一天來過，總有一天你會證明自己是對的。」這句話令我印象深刻，自那時候起，也就是過去這三十三年來，我每天早上照鏡子時，都會問自己：「假如今天是我人生中最後一天，我會去做我今天要去做的事嗎？」假如連續好幾天的答案都是「不」的話，我就知道我必須做些改變。

Remembering that I'll be dead soon is the most important tool I've ever encountered to help me make the big choices in life. Because almost everything—all [6]**external** expectations, all pride, all fear of embarrassment or failure—these things just fall away in the face of death, leaving only what is truly important. Remembering that you're going to die is the best way I know to avoid the trap of thinking you have something to lose. You're already naked. There's no reason not to follow your heart.

提醒自己生命將走到盡頭，是我體驗過最重要的方法，可以幫助我做出人生重大抉擇。因為幾乎每一件事 —— 所有外界的期望、所有名譽、所有對困窘或失敗的恐懼 —— 這些事情在面對死亡時都會退散，只有真正重要的事才會留下。提醒自己生命將走到盡頭，是我所知道最好的方法，避免讓自己掉入害怕失去的陷阱。既然你已經毫無牽掛，就沒有理由不去追隨自己的心。

© catwalker / Shutterstock.com

你的時間是有限的，所以不要把時間浪費於活在別人的陰影裡。不要被困在教條中，也就是不要活在別人的思維窠臼中。不要讓別人嘈雜的意見淹沒自己內心的聲音。而且最重要的是，鼓起勇氣，追隨自己的心和直覺。你的心和直覺冥冥中早已知道你真正想成為什麼。其他一切都是次要的。

 Stay Hungry, Stay Foolish
保持渴望，保持傻勁

When I was young, there was an amazing publication called 🔲 *The Whole Earth Catalog*, which was one of the bibles of my generation. It was sort of like Google in [4]**paperback** form, 35 years before Google came along—it was [5]**idealistic**, and [6]**overflowing** with [7]**neat** tools and great [8]**notions**. On the back cover of their final issue was a photograph of an early morning country road, the kind you might find yourself [9]**hitchhiking** on if you were so [10]**adventurous**. Beneath it were the words: "Stay Hungry, Stay Foolish." And I have always wished that for myself. And now, as you graduate to begin [11]**anew**, I wish that for you. Stay hungry, stay foolish.

我年輕時，有一本很棒的雜誌叫《環球概覽》，是我們這一代人的必讀經典之一。在三十五年前還沒有 Google 時，那本雜誌對我們來說就是平裝書形式的 Google——內容充滿理想主義，以及好用的工具和偉大的想法。在最後一期的封底是一張清晨的鄉間小路照片，假如你喜歡四處遊歷的話，就像那種你在搭便車時會看到的景象。照片底下是一句話：「保持渴望，保持傻勁。」我總是以這句話自我期許。現在，你們畢業了，即將展開另一段旅程，我也以這句話期許你們。保持渴望，保持傻勁。

Your time is limited, so don't waste it living someone else's life. Don't be trapped by [1]**dogma**—which is living with the results of other people's thinking. Don't let the noise of others' opinions [2]**drown out** your own inner voice. And most important, have the courage to follow your heart and [3]**intuition**. They somehow already know what you truly want to become. Everything else is secondary.

VOCABULARY 🎧 18

1) **dogma** [ˈdɔgmə] (n.) 教條，既定的信念
Don't let yourself be blinded by political dogma.

2) **drown out** [draʊn aʊt] (phr.)（聲音）壓過、淹沒（其他聲音）
The loud music drowned out our conversation.

3) **intuition** [ˌɪntuˈɪʃən] (n.) 直覺
Sometimes it's best to trust your intuition.

4) **paperback** [ˈpepɚˌbæk] (n.) 平裝書，hardback 是「精裝書」
Holly bought a paperback to read at the beach.

5) **idealistic** [aɪˌdiəˈlɪstɪk] (a.) 滿懷理想的，理想主義的
Most people are more idealistic when they're younger.

6) **overflow (with)** [ˌovɚˈflo] (v.) 充滿，洋溢
The girl's heart was overflowing with joy.

7) **neat** [nit] (a.)（口）美妙的，很棒的
Tom's toy robot is really neat.

8) **notion** [ˈnoʃən] (n.) 概念，觀念，想法
I only have a vague notion of what Ryan does for a living.

9) **hitchhike** [ˈhɪtʃˌhaɪk] (v.) 搭便車
Evan hitchhiked around the country after graduating from college.

10) **adventurous** [ədˈvɛntʃərəs] (a.) 大膽的，愛冒險的
If you're feeling adventurous, you should try the stinky tofu.

11) **anew** [əˈnu] (adv.) 重新，再一次
Dennis wants to move away and start his life anew.

© Apple

serif and sans serif 襯線與無襯線

serif 是討論字型時常見到的字，serif 類的字型，字母筆畫的起點及終點有小小的裝飾凸起。sans serif 的 sans 是「沒有」的意思，顧名思義這類字型一筆一畫乾乾淨淨，不會有任何裝飾。

connect the dots 拼湊線索

小朋友都玩過「連連看」的美術遊戲，只要照著數字順序把圖上的小黑點連起來，就會得到完整的線條圖，看出在畫的是什麼。這個說法引申為拼起看似無關聯的線索，找出其中的關聯後，得出結論。

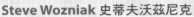

A: The police finally charged the woman's husband with her murder.
警方終於起訴那名被殺婦人的丈夫謀殺罪名。

B: I guess it took them a while to connect the dots.
看來他們花了點時間拼湊線索。

Steve Wozniak 史蒂夫沃茲尼克

沃茲尼克是一名電腦工程師，與賈伯斯同為蘋果電腦的共同創辦人。他創造了第一代（Apple I）及第二代蘋果電腦（Apple II），Apple II 風靡美國七、八〇年代個人電腦市場，沃茲尼克可謂將電腦成功推入家庭的大功臣，因此有 Wonderful Wizard of Woz（神奇巫師沃茲，與《綠野仙蹤》The Wonderful Wizard of Oz 諧音）的稱號，賈伯斯在演講中即稱他為 Woz。

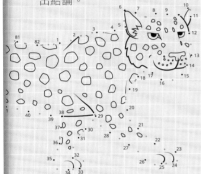

© Viappy / Shutterstock.com

NeXT 軟體公司

賈伯斯被逐出蘋果公司後，於一九八五年成立 NeXT Software, Inc.，初期專門開發製造高等教育及商業用途的電腦工作站 NeXT Computer，一九八六年跨足電腦軟硬體，開發 NeXTSTEP 系統，並釋出其應用設計介面（API，Application Programming Interface）OPENSTEP。

由於硬體銷售不彰，NeXT 在一九九三年結束硬體業務，專注於 OPENSTEP 等軟體開發。一九九六年，蘋果公司收購了 NeXT 的 OPENSTEP 及開發人員，賈伯斯最後也回歸蘋果公司，重掌領導權。整體來說，NeXT 不論軟硬體產品都未能在市場上獲得成功，但蘋果公司的 Mac OS X 作業系統就是建立在 OPENSTEP 的基礎之上，對電腦產業影響深遠。

The Whole Earth Catalog 《環球概覽》

簡稱 WEC，是作家史都華布蘭德（Stewart Brand）創刊於一九六八年的嬉皮文化雜誌，內容涵蓋各種 DIY 產品、天人合一觀念、自給自足生活、另類教育等，WEC 的標語 access to tools（找到好工具）揭示其為一本工具型錄的特性，從書籍、工作服、園藝工具，到個人電腦無所不包。但這本理想主義色彩濃厚的雜誌並不搭配廠商宣傳新品，也不販售任何產品，而是在產品圖片旁邊附上試用報告。一九七二年後改為不定期出刊，賈伯斯演講中提到的是一九七四年十月號。這本雜誌的全部圖文都已上網 www.wholeearth.com。

賈伯斯演講中提到的《環球概覽》封底
© Marcio Okabe

keep 的用法

動詞 keep 的意義與用途很廣，常見的有：

● keep (sb./sth.) + adj./adv. 表示保持某種狀態

解 此用法中 keep 意思跟 stay 意思相同。

例 **You should keep calm during an earthquake.**
地震來襲時應該保持冷靜。

例 **The boy's parents told him to keep quiet.**
那個男孩的父母叫他保持安靜。

● keep + Ving 表示持續（做某事）

例 **Mike kept interrupting the professor during class.**
麥克在課堂上一直打斷教授。

賈伯斯於二〇〇三年罹癌之後，健康問題一直受到媒體猜測，二〇〇五年這次演講時，他的癌症已經移轉。在演講中，他娓娓道來自己大學輟學、創業、事業跌入谷底、遇見真愛、重回蘋果，最後進入「死亡」這個話題。藉著這個機會，賈伯斯第一次公開得到癌症的消息，也以 *The Whole Earth Catalog* 最後一期的臨別贈言 Stay Hungry, Stay Foolish. 作結，為現場即將畢業，大好人生正要展開的聽眾帶來極大的震撼與啟發。

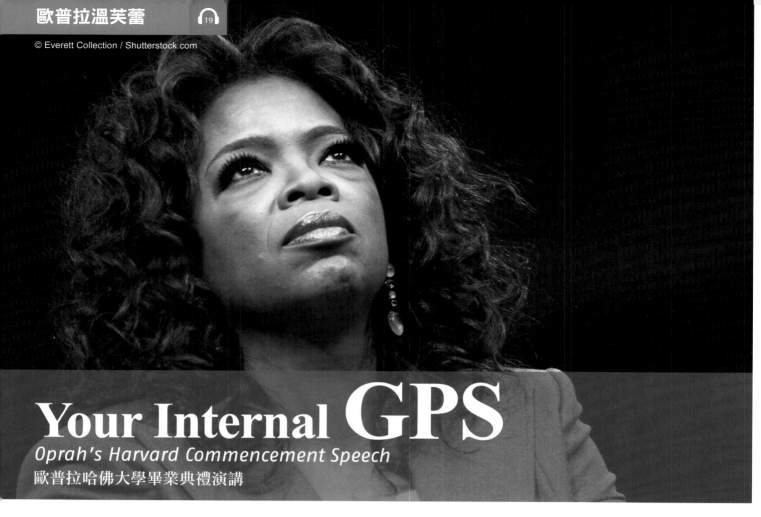

Your Internal GPS
Oprah's Harvard Commencement Speech
歐普拉哈佛大學畢業典禮演講

 An Honorary Doctorate
榮譽博士學位

I'm at Harvard! Wow! I thank you for allowing me to be a part of the conclusion of this chapter of your lives and the commencement of your next chapter. To say that I'm honored doesn't even begin to [1]**quantify** the depth of gratitude that really accompanies an [2]**honorary** [3]**doctorate** from Harvard. Not too many little girls from rural Mississippi have made it all the way here to Cambridge. My one hope today is that I can be a source of some inspiration.

我來哈佛了！哇！感謝你們讓我參與你們這段人生篇章的總結，還有你們下一段人生篇章的開端。表示深感榮幸仍不足以表達我對獲得哈佛榮譽博士學位的感激之情。沒有多少來自密西西比州的鄉下女孩能一路走到劍橋市的哈佛。希望今天的我能激勵到某些人。

I'll be honest with you. I felt a lot of pressure over the past few weeks to come up with something that I could share with you that you hadn't heard before, because after all you all went to Harvard, I did not. But then I realized that you don't have to necessarily go to Harvard to have a [4]**driven**, [5]**obsessive** LG Type A personality. But it helps. And while I may not have graduated from here, I admit that my personality is about as Harvard as they come.

VOCABULARY　20

1) **quantify** [ˈkwɑntəˌfaɪ] (v.)（使）量化，以數量表示
The benefits of the arts are difficult to quantify.

2) **honorary** [ˈɑnəˌrɛri] (a.) 名譽的（學位、職位，稱號等）
The actor was awarded an honorary degree.

3) **doctorate** [ˈdɑktərɪt] (n.) 博士學位
How long did it take to complete your doctorate?

4) **driven** [ˈdrɪvən] (a.) 奮發圖強的，積極進取的
You have to be driven to succeed in business.

5) **obsessive** [əbˈsɛsɪv] (a.) 過分關心的，執念的
Sandra is a little obsessive about her weight.

6) **journalist** [ˈdʒɜnəlɪst] (n.) 新聞工作者，新聞記者
The journalist has won many awards for his reporting.

坦白告訴你們，這幾個星期以來我感受到很大的壓力，我在想還有什麼你們沒聽過的事能分享，而且是，因為你們畢竟都是哈佛的畢業生，而我不是。不過我也發現到，不一定要念哈佛才會擁有積極進取和偏執性的 A 型人格，但還是有幫助的。雖然我不是自哈佛畢業，但我承認我的個性就跟哈佛人差不多。

我十九歲時上了電視。一九八六年，我推出自己的電視節目，而且下定決心一定要成功。和他人競爭讓我感到緊張，但後來我成了自己的競爭對手，每年都把標準提高，不斷給自己壓力，把自己逼得越來越緊。各位聽起來是不是相當熟悉？

 ## An Unexpected Career
出乎意料的生涯

You know my television career began unexpectedly. As you heard this morning, I was in the Miss Fire Prevention contest. That was when I was 16 years old in Nashville, Tennessee, and you had the requirement of having red hair in order to win up until the year I entered. So during the question and answer period the question came, "Why, young lady, what would you like to be when you grow up?" I had seen Barbara Walters on the *Today Show* that morning, so I answered, "I would like to be a [6)]**journalist**. I would like to tell other people's stories in a way that makes a difference in their lives and the world."

各位知道，我是無意間踏入電視圈的。正如各位今早聽說的，我參加過消防小姐選拔賽。當時我十六歲，住在田納西州的納席維爾，而且以往最後都是紅頭髮的選手贏得比賽，直到我參選那年才打破這個慣例。那麼，在問答階段時有這麼一個問題：「小姑娘，你長大後想當什麼？」那天早上我看了芭芭拉華特斯主持的《今日秀》，於是我回答：「我想當記者，我想報導其他人的故事，為他們的人生和這個世界帶來某種程度的改變。」

Well I was on television by the time I was 19 years old. And in 1986 I launched my own television show 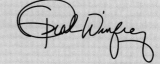 with a relentless determination to succeed. I was nervous about the **competition**, and then I became my own competition, 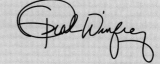 raising the bar every year, pushing, pushing, pushing myself as hard as I knew. Sound familiar to anybody here?

> **66** If you concentrate on what you have, you will always end up having more. If you focus on what you don't have, you will never, ever have enough.
>
> 如果專注於自己擁有的東西，你總是會越得越多。如果老是想著沒有的東西，你永遠不會覺得足夠。
>
> *歐普拉談知足*

© Helga Esteb / Shutterstock.com

Oprah Winfrey
歐普拉溫芙蕾

一九五四年一月二十九日生，美國脫口秀主持人，其《歐普拉秀》（*The Oprah Winfrey Show*，1986-2011 年全美聯播）是史上收視率最高的訪談秀節目，對美國大眾文化影響至深。

歐普拉被譽為 Queen of All Media（媒體女王），除事業跨足各傳播領域，累積巨大財富，更獲美國總統歐巴馬頒贈總統自由獎章（Presidential Medal of Freedom）、受哈佛大學及杜克大學頒發榮譽博士學位。

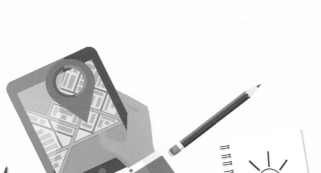

Time to Break New Ground
創造新突破的時候到了

The Oprah Winfrey Show was number one in our time [1)]**slot** for 21 years, and I have to tell you I became pretty comfortable 🄶🄼 with that level of success. But a few years ago I decided, as you will at some point, that it was time to recalculate, find new territory, 🄻🄶 break new ground. So I ended the show and launched OWN, the Oprah Winfrey Network. So one year later after launching OWN, nearly every media [2)]**outlet** had [3)]**proclaimed** that my new [4)]**venture** was a [5)]**flop**. It really was this time last year the worst period in my professional life.

> I've talked to nearly 30,000 people on this show, and all 30,000 had one thing in common: they all wanted validation. I would tell you that every single person you will ever meet shares that common desire.

我在這個節目上跟將近三萬人對話,這三萬人有一個共同點:他們都想得到認同……我可以告訴你,這是你所遇到的每一個人的共同渴望。

歐普拉談認同

二十一年來《歐普拉秀》的收視率一直是同時段的第一名,我必須告訴各位,對於這樣程度的成功,我是挺心滿意足的。不過,幾年前我決定,該是重整腳步的時候了。你們也會在某個時間點這麼做的,尋找新的領域,開創新天地。於是我結束了那個節目,推出「OWN 歐普拉電視網」。推出 OWN 一年後,幾乎所有媒體都聲稱我的新事業是個失敗。去年此時確實是我生涯中最悲慘的一段時間。

It was right around that time that President Faust called and asked me to speak here, and I thought, "What could I possibly say to Harvard graduates, some of the most successful graduates in the world in the very moment when I had stopped succeeding?" So I got off the phone with President Faust and I went to the shower. And I thought as I got out of the shower, "I'm going to 🄻🄶 turn this thing around. And when I do, I'm going to go to Harvard and I'm going to speak the truth of it!" So I'm here today to tell you I have turned that network around!

VOCABULARY 🎧22

1) **slot** [slɑt] (n.) (電視節目)時段
My favorite show was moved to a late-night slot.

2) **outlet** [ˋaʊtˏlɛt] (n.) (媒體)公司,出版社,商店
The company sells its products through retail outlets.

3) **proclaim** [prəˋklem] (v./n.) 聲稱,聲明,公佈
The suspect continued to proclaim his innocence.

4) **venture** [ˋvɛntʃɚ] (n.) 新創事業,投資事業
The business venture ended in bankruptcy.

5) **flop** [flɑp] (n.) (作品,演出等)失敗
The director's last movie was a box office flop.

6) **mourn** [mɔrn] (v.) 哀悼,哀痛
The woman is still mourning the death of her husband.

恰好在這個時候，佛士德校長打電話給我，邀請我在畢業典禮上演講，於是我心想：「我能跟哈佛畢業生說什麼？在世上最頂尖的畢業生面前，就在此時，在我停滯不前的時候？」我跟佛士德講完電話後，就先去洗澡。洗完澡時，我心想：「我要扭轉局面。而且等我扭轉成功時，我要去哈佛，把這件事實說出來！」所以我今天來到這裡，就是要告訴你們，我已經讓電視網起死回生了。

This is what I want to share. It doesn't matter how far you might rise. If you're constantly pushing yourself higher, higher, the law of averages—not to mention the Myth of Icarus—predicts that you will at some point fall. And when you do, I want you to know this, remember this: there is no such thing as failure. Failure is just life trying to move us in another direction.

這就是我想和各位分享的。你能爬多高並不重要。假如你不斷給自己施壓，把自己推向更高的位置，根據平均法則的預測——更別提伊卡魯斯神話了——你在某個時間點就會跌落。當你跌落谷底時，我希望你們能知道一點，並且記住：沒有失敗這件事。失敗只是人生想要讓我們轉個彎而已。

Your Internal GPS
你內在的導航系統

Give yourself time to [6]**mourn** what you think you may have lost, but then here's the key: learn from every mistake, because every experience, encounter, and particularly your mistakes are there to teach you and force you into being more who you are. And then figure out what is the next right move. And the key to life is to develop an internal moral, emotional GPS that can tell you which way to go.

給自己一點時間，哀悼你覺得可能失去的東西，但關鍵是：從每個失誤中學習，因為每一個經驗、遭遇，尤其是失誤，都是在教導並強迫你打造真正的自己。

然後要思考正確的下一步。人生的關鍵，是打造出一套內在道德和情感的導航系統，這個導航系統會告訴你該往哪裡去。

The challenge of life, I have found, is to build a [7]**résumé** that doesn't simply tell a story about what you want to be, but a story about who you want to be. It's a résumé that doesn't just tell a story about what you want to accomplish but why. A story that's not just a collection of titles and positions but a story that's really about your purpose.

我發現，人生的挑戰是建立一份履歷，這份履歷不僅僅是在講你想成為什麼的故事這樣簡單，而是在講一個你想成為誰的故事。這份履歷不只是在講你想要什麼樣的成就，而是為什麼你想要那樣的成就。你所要講的故事，不只是一連串的頭銜和職位，而是關於你的目標。

> **"** Whatever you fear most has no power—it is your fear that has the power.
>
> 你最害怕的東西其實都沒有力量——有力量的是你的恐懼。
>
> 歐普拉談恐懼

7) **résumé** [ˈrɛzjʊ͵me] (n.) 履歷
An internship will look good on your résumé.

歐普拉造訪卡崔娜颶風災民的臨時避難所，並為救災募得超過一千一百萬美元，她個人捐款就佔了一千萬。　© FEMA photo/Andrea Booher

📍 The Angle Network
天使網絡

For me, that discovery came in 1994 when I interviewed a little girl who had decided to collect pocket change in order to help other people in need. So I asked for our [1)]**viewers** to take up their own change collection and in one month, just from pennies and [2)]**nickels** and dimes, we raised more than three million dollars that we used to send one student from every state in the United States to college. That was the beginning of the Angel Network. And together we built 55 schools in 12 different countries and restored nearly 300 homes that were [3)]**devastated** by hurricanes 🔠 Rita and Katrina. I have been on the air for a long time, but it was the Angel Network that actually focused my internal GPS.

一九九四年我訪問了一名小女孩，她決定將口袋中的零錢收集起來，幫助其他需要幫助的人，對我來說，這件事讓我有了新的啟發。於是我請觀眾也將零錢收集起來，一個月後，僅僅從這些一分錢、五分錢到十分錢的硬幣，我們募得了超過三百萬美元，然後我們從每一個州選出一位學生，用這筆錢資助他們上大學。這就是「天使網絡」的緣起。我們在十二個不同的國家建了五十五所學校，並為麗塔和卡崔娜颶風近三百戶災民重建被摧毀的家園。我在電視圈待了很長的時間，但真正讓我啟動內在導航系統的，是天使網絡。

From time to time you may [4)]**stumble**, fall—you will for sure, 🔠 count on this, no doubt—you will have questions and you will have doubts about your path. But I know this: if you're willing to listen to, be guided by, that still, small voice that is the GPS within yourself, to find out what makes you come alive, you will be more than OK. You will be happy, you will be successful, and you will make a difference in the world. Congratulations, Class of 2013!

你這一路上偶爾可能會失足跌倒——你一定會的，相信我，不用懷疑。你會對自己走的路有質疑、有疑惑。但我知道一點：假如你願意傾聽來自你內心 GPS 的一個小小聲音，願意接受它的指引，找出讓自己活起來的目標，情況就會好轉。你將會帶著愉悅的心情邁向成功，為世界帶來改變。二〇一三年畢業班，恭喜你們畢業了！

VOCABULARY 🎧 24

1) **viewer** [ˋvjuɚ] (n.) 電視觀眾，觀看者
Millions of viewers watch the Super Bowl each year.

2) **nickel** [ˋnɪkəl] (n.) （美國、加拿大）五分幣，鎳
A nickel contains 25% nickel.

3) **devastate** [ˋdɛvəˏstet] (v.) 摧毀，重創
Parts of the town were devastated by the tornado.

4) **stumble** [ˋstʌmbəl] (v.) 蹣跚而行，絆倒
The drunken man stumbled down the street.

Type A personality A 型人格

A 型人格、B 型人格與血型無關，而是一種個性區分法，在一九五〇年代由心臟病醫師的研究首先提出，他們發現 A 型人格的人罹患冠心病的風險，是 B 型人格者的兩倍。

	A 型人格	B 型人格
個性	具野心、掌控慾強、在意身份地位、缺乏耐性	懂得紓壓、容易有成就感、面對競爭或失敗不會鑽牛角尖
工作	常為工作狂、傾向接受高壓及時間緊迫的工作、要求精確	工作較穩定、傾向從事需要創意及協調能力的工作

raise the bar 提高門檻

這裡的 bar 可以想像成跳高比賽的橫桿，每當有選手跳過一個高度，桿子就會被往上調，桿子越高就越難跳過。因此當我們說某個事物 raise the bar，就是那個事物讓一件事變得更加困難。

A: What do you think of the new iPhone?
　你對新 iPhone 看法如何？
B: It's excellent. Apple has really raised the bar for smartphones.
　非常棒。蘋果公司確實提升了智慧手機的水準。

break new ground 有所突破

當有人獲得前所未有的突破，或是在某個領域有新發現，就可以說他 break new ground，他的成就也就可以用形容詞 groundbreaking 來形容。

A: Did you see that show about new cancer treatments?
　你有看到那個介紹癌症新療法的節目嗎？
B: Yeah. Those researchers are really breaking new ground.
　有啊。那些研究人員真的大有突破。

表示「附帶狀態」的介系詞 with

歐普拉這段演講中，以自身為主題，與畢業生分享自己經歷的各種「狀態」。她利用「with + 受詞 + 補語」的句型就可以簡短解釋那樣的狀態。受詞補語可以是現在分詞、過去分詞、形容詞或介系詞片語。

例 **You should never fill the tank with the engine running.**（補語為分詞 running）

例 **I became pretty comfortable with that level of success.**（補語為介系詞 of success）

with 另一個常見表達為「伴隨的情況或原因」，作「因為」或「隨著」解釋。with 可放在句首或句中。句型為：S + V 子句 + with + 名詞片語

例 **We need to make a lot of changes in our lives with the arrival of our baby daughter.**

= **With the arrival of our baby daughter, we need to make a lot of changes in our lives.**

turn sth. around 扭轉局勢

turn around 就是「轉 180 度」，當某事物有了 180 度的翻轉，就表示情況已經跟以前完全不一樣。一般用於形容扭轉頹勢，讓情況好轉。

A: Is Chile still in a recession?
　智利還處於經濟衰退嗎？
B: No. The new government is turning the economy around.
　不了。新的政府已經扭轉經濟局勢。

Myth of Icarus 伊卡魯斯傳說

希臘神話當中有一則故事，說到 Icarus 的父親 Daedalus 是偉大的建築師及工藝家，國王命他建造無法逃脫的監獄監禁半人半牛怪，於是他建了一座迷宮，任何人進去之後都無法逃脫。國王後來宣布，雅典人民每九年必須將七對男女送進迷宮獻給牛怪，Icarus 因此進入迷宮。

為了救兒子，Daedalus 用蠟和羽毛製作了兩對翅膀，要帶他飛離迷宮。儘管 Daedalus 提醒 Icarus 乖乖跟著他飛，不要飛得太低，以免打濕羽毛，也不要飛得太高，免得太陽把蠟曬溶，但 Icarus 一飛沖天之後得意忘形，越飛越高，等到發現時，翅膀的羽毛已經落盡，他只能墜入海中。

Rita and Katrina 麗塔颶風及卡崔娜颶風

© AP Photo/U.S. Coast Guard,
Petty Officer 2nd Class Kyle Niemi

二〇〇五年下半年，北美洲大西洋沿岸極不平靜，活躍的氣象打破許多紀錄，其中一項紀錄是有多達七個三級以上颶風（相當於強烈颱風等級），其中八月的 Hurricane Katrina 引發潰堤，紐奧良市區 80% 都浸在水中；九月 Hurricane Rita 來襲，紐奧良再度淹水，讓城市的重建雪上加霜。

count on 指望，預期

count 當動詞有「預期」的意思，當你 count on 某人事物時，表示你必須依賴它，或是相信它一定會發生。

A: Do you think we'll get a year-end bonus this year?
　你覺得我們今年會有年終獎金嗎？
B: I wouldn't count on it.
　我不敢期待。

本篇演講發表於二〇一三年五月三十日，當天歐普拉獲頒哈佛大學榮譽法學博士（Honorary Doctor of Laws），並發表演說，與哈佛師生分享她那幾年由盛極而衰，再反敗為勝的心路歷程與致勝法則。

歐普拉出身極為貧困，早年際遇悲慘（九歲被強暴、十四歲懷孕生子，兒子夭折），但她在念高中時得到第一個廣播工作機會之後，就一路積極向上，腳步從未停歇——「自我激勵」之道，歐普拉絕對知道。

© Charis Tsevis

We Are What We Choose

Jeff Bezos' Princeton Commencement Speech
傑夫貝佐斯普林斯頓大學畢業典禮演講

Summer Road Trips
夏天開車旅行

As a kid, I spent my summers with my grandparents on their [1]**ranch** in Texas. I helped fix windmills, [2]**vaccinate** cattle, and do other chores. My grandparents belonged to a [3]**Caravan** Club, a group of 🄻🄶 Airstream trailer owners who travel together around the U.S. and Canada. And every few summers, we'd join the caravan. I loved and [4]**worshipped** my grandparents, and I really 🄻🄶 looked forward to these trips. On one particular trip, I was about 10 years old. I was rolling around in the big bench seat in the back of the car; my grandfather was driving; and my grandmother had the passenger seat. She smoked throughout these trips, and I hated the smell.

孩提時代，我都在德州爺爺奶奶家的農場過暑假。我幫忙修風車、替牛打疫苗，還會做其他家務。我爺爺奶奶是露營拖車俱樂部的會員，那是一群擁有清風露營拖車的車主組成的俱樂部，他們會相約一起在美國和加拿大各地開車旅行。每隔幾個暑假，我們就會加入他們。我喜歡我的爺爺奶奶，也很崇拜他們，而且真心期待參加開車旅行。有一次旅行時，我大約十歲。我爺爺在開車，我奶奶坐在乘客座，而我就在車子後面的長座椅上滾來滾去。我奶奶一路上都會抽菸，但我討厭菸味。

VOCABULARY 🎧26

1) **ranch** [ræntʃ] (n.) 大牧場
My uncle owns a cattle ranch in Texas.

2) **vaccinate** [ˈvæksə͵net] (v.) 注射、接種疫苗
Did you get your dog vaccinated for rabies?

3) **caravan** [ˈkærə͵væn] (n.) 車隊，露營車，拖車
The gypsies parked their caravans by the river.

4) **worship** [ˈwɜʃɪp] (v.) 崇拜，敬仰
Tommy worships his big brother.

5) **mileage** [ˈmaɪlɪdʒ] (n.) 油耗，省油性
Does your car get good mileage?

6) **statistic** [stəˈtɪstɪk] (n.) 統計資料（常用複數）
Have you seen the latest sales statistics?

7) **puff** [pʌf] (n.) （抽）一口菸
The boy took a puff of the cigarette and started coughing.

At that age, I'd take any excuse to make estimates and do minor arithmetic. I'd calculate our gas [5]**mileage**, figure out useless [6]**statistics** on things like grocery spending. I'd been hearing an ad campaign about smoking. I can't remember the details, but basically the ad said, every [7]**puff** of a cigarette takes some number of minutes off of your life. **LG** At any rate, I decided to do the math for my grandmother. When I was satisfied that I'd come up with a reasonable number, I [8]**poked** my head into the front of the car, tapped my grandmother on the shoulder, and proudly proclaimed, "At two minutes per puff, you've taken nine years off your life!"

在那個年紀，我會找任何機會做估算和一些簡單的算術，比如計算我們的平均油耗、在飲食開銷之類的事情上做一些沒有用的統計。我當時聽到關於抽菸的宣傳廣告。我不記得細節了，但那個廣告基本上是在說，每抽一口菸，就會奪走你幾分鐘的生命。反正我當時決定要幫奶奶計算一下。等我覺得自己已經算出一個合理的數字時，我把頭探進前座，拍了拍奶奶的肩膀，驕傲地宣布我的計算結果：「一口菸兩分鐘，妳會少活九年！」

It's Harder to Be Kind
體貼別人要難多了

I expected to be [9]**applauded** for my cleverness and arithmetic skills. Instead, my grandmother **LG** burst into tears. **GM** My grandfather, who had been driving in silence, pulled over onto the shoulder of the highway. He got out of the car and came around and opened my door and waited for me to follow. Was I in trouble? My grandfather was a highly intelligent, quiet man. He had never said a harsh word to me, and maybe this was to be the first time? My grandfather looked at me, and after a bit of silence, he gently and calmly said, "Jeff, one day you'll understand that it's harder to be kind than clever."

8) **poke** [pok] (v.) 伸出，探出
The mole poked its head out of the hole and sniffed the air.

9) **applaud** [əˋplɔd] (v.) 鼓掌，喝采
The audience applauded at the end of the play.

Airstream 的 RV 休旅車
© ken ratcliff

我期待聽到他們誇讚我有多聰明，算術能力有多強，不料，奶奶突然哭起來。一直默默開車的爺爺，將車子停在高速公路的路肩上。他下車，繞到車子的另一邊，打開我座位旁的車門，等我隨他下車。我惹麻煩了嗎？我爺爺是個很有智慧、沉默寡言的人。他從來沒有對我說過重話，也許這會是第一次？爺爺看著我，沉默了一會兒後，他溫和平靜地說：「傑夫，有一天你會明白，比起表現得聰明伶俐，對人體貼要難多了。」

> " Your margin is my opportunity.
> 你的利潤就是我的機會。
>
> 貝佐斯談商業競爭

Jeff Bezos
傑夫貝佐斯

© Doc Searls

生於一九六四年，於一九九四年六月創立亞馬遜網路書店，並迅速擴展商品線，成為全球最大網路百貨零售商。貝佐斯年幼時父母就已離異，母親在他四歲時再嫁給古巴移民 Miguel Bezos，跟母親及繼父同住的貝佐斯，暑假都會去德州南部的外祖父家幫忙。

貝佐斯除了是 Amazon 的董事長及執行長，還跨足許多營利及非營利事業，更於二〇一三年斥資兩億五千萬美元現金，以個人名義買下《華盛頓郵報》 *Washington Post*。

Airstream trailer 清風拖車

Airstream 是一個高級休閒旅行拖車的品牌，以閃亮的鋁製渾圓車體造型聞名。這個將近一百年歷史（1920 年代末創立）的牌子歷久彌新，許多人以翻新改造老車款為樂，它的忠實愛用車主甚至有個專門的字代表：Airstreamer。

Airstream 古董拖車，這是屬於車體較短的版本 © dwstucke

這個品牌的車主俱樂部於一九五一年成立，以創辦人 Wally Byam 為名，現在每年夏天，The Wally Byam Caravan Club International（WBCCI）在美國國慶日前後都會有盛大的聚會，全美各地還有十幾處該牌車隊專屬的露營度假村。

Choices Can Be Hard
選擇有時並不容易

What I want to talk to you about today is the difference between gifts and choices. Cleverness is a gift, kindness is a choice. Gifts are easy—they're given, after all. Choices can be hard. You can [1)]**seduce** yourself with your gifts if you're not careful, and if you do, it'll probably be to the [2)]**detriment** of your choices.

我今天想告訴你們的是，天賦和選擇的不同之處。聰明伶俐是天賦，對人體貼是選擇。天賦很簡單，畢竟那是天生就有的。選擇有時是很難做的。假如你不注意的話，就會隨著天賦的引誘而誤入歧途，若是如此，可能會危害到你的選擇。

This is a group with many gifts. I'm sure one of your gifts is the gift of a smart and capable brain. Your smarts will **LG** come in handy because you will travel in a land of marvels. We humans will [3)]**astonish** ourselves. We'll invent ways to [4)]**generate** clean energy and a lot of it. Atom by atom, we'll

> 66 There are two kinds of companies: those that work to try to charge more and those that work to charge less. We will be the second.
>
> 公司有兩種：一種試著提高價錢，另一種努力降低價錢。我們屬於第二種。

貝佐斯談亞馬遜網路書店

assemble tiny machines that will enter cell walls and make repairs. I believe you'll even see us understand the human brain. As a civilization, we will have so many gifts, just as you as individuals have so many individual gifts as you sit before me. How will you use these gifts? And will you take pride in your gifts or pride in your choices?

你們是一群富有許多天賦的人。我相信擁有精明能幹的頭腦一定是你們的天賦之一。你們的聰明才智一定會派上用場，因為你們會遊走在一個充滿奇蹟的世界，連我們人類自己都將為之震驚。我們會發明大量生產乾淨能源的方法，用一個個原子組成微型機器，穿過細胞壁進行修復。我相信你們甚至可以看到我們解開人類大腦的密碼。在文明世界中，我們將擁有如此多的優勢，就如同在座的你們各自擁有許多天賦。你們要如何運用這些天賦？你們會為自己的天賦還是為自己的選擇感到自豪？

Founding Amazon
創辦亞馬遜

I got the idea to start Amazon 16 years ago. I came across the fact that Web usage was growing at 2,300 percent per year. I'd never seen or heard of anything that grew that fast, and the idea of building an online bookstore with millions of [5)]**titles**—something that simply couldn't exist in the physical world—was very exciting to me. I told my wife MacKenzie that I wanted to quit my job and go do this crazy thing that probably wouldn't work since most [6)]**start-ups** don't. MacKenzie told me I should **LG** go for it. I'd always wanted to be an inventor, and she wanted me to follow my passion.

我在十六年前有了創辦亞馬遜的點子。當時我偶然發現，網路的使用每年成長 2300%。我從來沒看過或聽過任何其他事物能成長如此之快，而打造一家擁有數百萬種圖書的網路書店——實體書店不可能容納這麼多本——這個點子令我興奮不已。我告訴我的妻子麥肯齊，我想辭職，好完成這件瘋狂的事，但很可能會失敗，因為大部分新創公司最後都失敗了。麥肯齊告訴我，我應該放手去做。我一直想當發明家，而她希望我能追隨自己的熱情。

VOCABULARY 🎧 28

1) **seduce** [sɪ`dus] (v.) 吸引，引誘
The audience was seduced by the singer's beautiful voice.

2) **detriment** [`dɛtrəmənt] (n.) 損害
Working too hard can be a detriment to your health.

3) **astonish** [ə`stɑnɪʃ] (v.) 使驚訝、驚嘆
The magician astonished the audience with his tricks.

4) **generate** [`dʒɛnə͵ret] (v.) 產生（光、熱、電）
Waves can be used to generate power.

5) **title** [`taɪtəl] (n.) 電影、書等作品
Our bookstore has all of the latest titles.

6) **start-up** [`stɑrt͵ʌp] (n.) 新創企業
Alvin works as an engineer at a tech start-up.

7) **light** [laɪt] (n.) 角度，觀點
After watching the interview, I saw the star in a different light.

8) **haunt** [hɔnt] (v.) （被心理陰影）糾纏
His experiences in the war haunted him for years.

I was working at a financial firm in New York City with a bunch of very smart people, and I had a brilliant boss that I much admired. I went to my boss and told him I wanted to start a company selling books on the Internet. He said, "That sounds like a really good idea, but it would be an even better idea for someone who didn't already have a good job." Seen in that [7]**light**, it really was a difficult choice, but ultimately, I decided I had to  give it a shot. I didn't think I'd regret trying and failing. And I suspected I would always be [8]**haunted** by a decision to not try at all. After much consideration, I took the less safe path to follow my passion, and I'm proud of that choice.

> " In the old world, you devoted 30% of your time to building a great service and 70% of your time to shouting about it. In the new world, that inverts.
>
> 在過去的世界裡，你要投入三成的時間建立良好的服務，和七成的時間大力宣傳。在新的世界，剛好相反。
>
> 貝佐斯談新時代商務

我當時在紐約一家金融公司上班，有一群非常聰明的同事，還有令我非常欣賞的優秀老闆。我去找我老闆，告訴他我想創業，在網路上賣書。他說：「聽起來真是個好主意，但這更適合還沒找到好工作的人來做。」從那個角度來看，的確是很難的選擇，但我最終還是決定要放手一搏。就算嘗試過後失敗，我也不認為我會後悔。而且我認為，假如我連試都不去試，這件事反而會一直縈繞在我心頭。思考再三後，我還是選擇了比較不安全的路，追隨我的熱情，而且我為這個選擇感到自豪。

What Choices Will You Make?
你會做什麼選擇？

Tomorrow, in a very real sense, your life—the life you author from scratch on your own—begins.

明天，說真的，你的人生——一個從頭開始，由你自己作主的人生——就此展開。

How will you use your gifts? What choices will you make?

Will you ¹⁾**inertia** be your guide, or will you follow your passions?

Will you follow dogma, or will you be original?

Will you choose a life of ease, or a life of service and adventure?

Will you ²⁾**wilt** under criticism, or will you follow your ³⁾**convictions**?

Will you guard your heart against rejection, or will you act when you fall in love?

When it's tough, will you give up, or will you be relentless?

Will you be a ⁴⁾**cynic**, or will you be a builder?

Will you be clever at the expense of others, or will you be kind?

© ali asaria

你要如何運用你的天賦，你會做什麼選擇？

你要因循怠惰，還是要追隨你的熱情？

你要墨守成規，還是要創新？

你要選擇安逸的人生，還是要奉獻和冒險的人生？

你會因為受到批評而退縮，還是要堅守自己的信念？

你會因為怕被拒絕而不表白，還是不顧一切墜入愛河？

當處境艱難時，你會放棄，還是堅持不懈？

你要當一個憤世嫉俗的人，或是一個有作為的人？

你要將自己的精明建立在他人的痛苦上，或是對人體貼？

I will ⁵⁾**hazard** a ⁶⁾**prediction**. When you are 80 years old, and in a quiet moment of reflection ⁷⁾**narrating** for only yourself the most personal ⁸⁾**version** of your life story, the telling that will be most ⁹⁾**compact** and meaningful will be the series of choices you have made. In the end, we are our choices. Build yourself a great story. Thank you and good luck!

我要大膽做個預測。當你們八十歲的時候，在某個靜下來反思的時刻，想對自己訴說一個最貼近自己的人生故事，而且是最精簡、也最有意義的版本，那就是你所做的一連串選擇。最終，我們的選擇，將決定我們成為什麼樣的人。為你自己打造一個精彩的人生故事。謝謝各位，祝各位好運！

VOCABULARY 30

1) **inertia** [ɪˋnɝʃə] (n.) 慣性
Martha finally overcame her inertia and went back to school.

2) **wilt** [wɪlt] (v.) 退縮，失去信心
We need somebody who won't wilt under pressure.

3) **conviction** [kənˋvɪkʃən] (n.) 信念
What are your religious convictions?

4) **cynic** [ˋsɪnɪk] (n.) 憤世嫉俗的人
Jeffrey is too much of a cynic to believe in love.

5) **hazard** [ˋhæzəd] (v.) 大膽提出
If I had to hazard a guess, I'd say she's around 40.

6) **prediction** [prɪˋdɪktʃən] (n.) 預測，預言
Scientists hope to make more accurate earthquake predictions in the future.

7) **narrate** [ˋnæret] (v.) 敘述，作旁白
The series is narrated by a famous actor.

8) **version** [ˋvɝʒən] (n.) 版本
Which version of Windows do you have on your computer?

9) **compact** [ˋkɑmpækt] (a.) 簡潔的，精簡的，小型的
The book provides a compact introduction to Hawaiian history.

look forward to 期待，盼望

這個句型後面加上名詞使用，表示對某個人事物非常喜悅而殷切的期待，一般可以在信件結尾加上這個句型，例如 I'm looking forward to your e-mail / reply. 表示「我很期待收到你的電子郵件／回覆／消息」。

A: I'll be arriving in San Francisco on the 25th.
　我會在二十五號抵達舊金山。
B: Great! I'm really looking forward to your visit.
　太好了，我很期待你的到訪。

at any rate 無論如何，不管怎樣

這個片語從字面上就很好理解：「在任何狀況下」，後方常接既定的狀況、結果或決定。類似的表達也可以用 in any case。

A: Isn't it about time that we got a new car?
　我們不是應該買台新車了嗎？
B: But our old car still runs great. And at any rate, we can't afford a new one.
　但我們的舊車性能還很好。而且不管怎樣，我們買不起新車。

burst into tears 突然哭起來

burst 有「爆裂，衝出」的意思，burst into 表示「開始（做某事）」，經常與 tears/laughter/applause 連用，表示「突然飆淚」、「笑起來」、「爆出如雷掌聲」。

A: What did Karen do when you broke up with her?
　你跟凱倫分手時，她作何反應？
B: She burst into tears.
　她哭了起來。

過去完成進行式 vs. 過去進行式

到底何時該用過去完成進行式（had been + Ving）、何時該用過去進行式（was/were + Ving）？兩者之間的微妙差異時常讓人一個頭兩個大。其實很簡單，只要記得過去完成進行式是強調過去某個動作的「持續」就好。也就是說，這個動作在過去的某段時間持續進行著（過去完成進行式），直到在過去的某個時間點有另一件事發生（過去簡單式）。

● 以本篇演講中這句話為例：

 My grandfather, who had been driving（過去完成進行式）**in silence, pulled**（過去簡單式）**over onto the shoulder of the highway.**
　一直默默開車的爺爺，將車子停在高速公路的路肩上。

解 如果用 had been driving（過去完成進行式），強調的是爺爺「一直」在開車，直到他將車子停下來的時間點。

● 現在來看看如果單純用過去進行式，在語意上會有什麼差別：

例 **My grandfather, who was driving**（過去進行式）**in silence, pulled**（過去簡單式）**over onto the shoulder of the highway.**
　正默默開著車的爺爺，將車子停在高速公路的路肩上。

解 看出來了嗎？如果用過去進行式，純粹是說爺爺當時正在開車，沒有強調他一直在開車這件事。

come in handy 派上用場

handy 的意思是「手邊（立即可用）的」，It'll come in handy. 則是指某樣東西先準備起來，未雨綢繆，未來說不定可以派上用場。

A: How come you're buying a down jacket in June?
　你為什麼要在六月買羽絨外套啊？
B: It'll come in handy in the winter.
　冬天的時候就會用到了。

go for it 儘管去做

go 有「追尋某個目標」的意思，it 是代名詞，代表前面所說想做的事情。下次再有人猶豫不決，你就可以說 Go for it! 鼓勵他囉。

A: I'm thinking of trying out for cheerleading, but I hear it's really hard to get in.
　我正在考慮去參加啦啦隊徵選，但聽說非常難考進去。
B: I think you should go for it!
　我認為你應該放手一試！

give sth. a shot 試試看

shot 這個字有許多意思，在此指做某事的「機會」，平常如果要說「放手一試」會用 give it a shot/go 或 have a shot at sth.。

A: Hey, how about trying some stinky tofu?
　嘿，要不要吃吃看臭豆腐？
B: OK, let's give it a shot.
　好啊，我們來試試。

from scratch 從頭做起

scratch 當名詞有「起跑線」的意思，from scratch 就表示「從頭開始」，用來描述一樣東西從最基本的食材、原料做起。經常搭配的動詞有 bake/do/make/start sth. from scratch。

A: This cake is delicious! What's your secret?
　這個蛋糕好好吃！你的祕訣是什麼？
B: I baked it from scratch.
　我用食材從頭烤起。

at the expense of 以……為代價

expense 有「犧牲，代價」的意思，除了 at the expense of sb./sth.，也經常會說 at sb.'s/sth.'s expense，表示犧牲了某人或某事物。

A: Robert seemed a little insulted by my joke.
　羅伯特似乎被我的玩笑冒犯了。
B: Yeah. It's not nice to laugh at the expense of others.
　的確。把快樂建築在別人身上並不厚道。

傑夫貝佐斯這篇演說發表於二〇一〇年五月普林斯頓大學部畢業典禮（Baccalaureate），距離創立 Amazon 已有十六年，他的傳奇創業故事已廣為人知，在這次演講中難免要舊事重提；但貝佐斯先講了一段故事，回顧對他影響深遠的外公說過的一句話，讓這篇以「勇於選擇自己的路」為主的簡單演說，成為一篇引人深思的佳作。

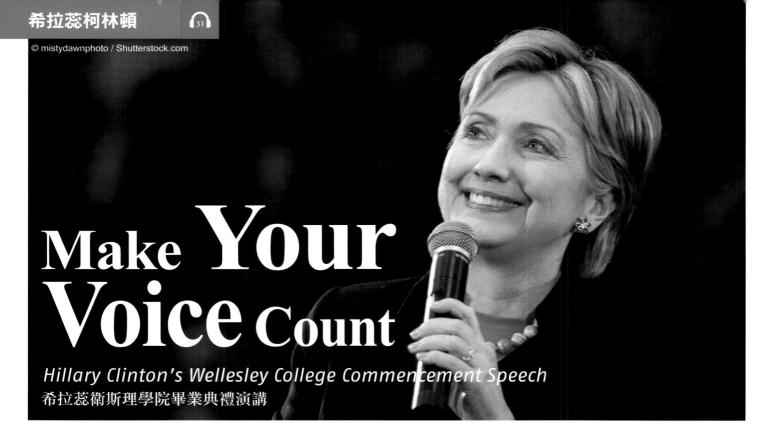

© mistydawnphoto / Shutterstock.com

Make Your Voice Count

Hillary Clinton's Wellesley College Commencement Speech
希拉蕊衛斯理學院畢業典禮演講

A Second Chance
第二次機會

This is my second chance to speak from this [1)]**podium**. The first was 23 years ago, when I was a graduating senior. My classmates selected me to address them as the first Wellesley student ever to speak at a commencement.

這是我第二次有這個機會在這個講台上演講。第一次是在二十三年前，當時我是應屆畢業生。我是衛斯理學院有史以來首位被同學選為代表畢業生致詞的學生。

I can't claim that 1969 speech as my own; it reflected the hopes, values, and [2)]**aspirations** of the women in my graduating class. We passionately rejected the notion of limitations on our abilities to make the world a better place. We saw a gap between our expectations and realities, and we were inspired, in large part by our Wellesley education, to bridge that gap. Wellesley [3)]**nurtured**, challenged, and guided me; it [4)]**instilled** in me not just knowledge, but a reserve of [5)]**sustaining** values.

一九六九年那場演講，我不能說是屬於我自己一個人的，那場演講代表著我們畢業班全體女同學的希望、價值和志向。女性在改善世界這一方面的能力有限，關於這樣的觀點我們是強烈反對的。在期待和現實之間，我們看到了差距，而我們之所以深受啟發而決心彌補這道差距，主要是因為我們在衛斯理學院所受的教育。衛斯理培育我、鞭策我、指導我，不僅灌輸知識給我，還有深厚的人生價值。

Dreams and Disillusionments
夢想和幻滅

When I arrived as a freshman in 1965 from my
🄛 Ozzie and Harriet suburb of Chicago, both the

VOCABULARY 🎧 32

1) **podium** [ˋpodɪəm] (n.) 講台
The speaker stepped up to the podium and addressed the crowd.

2) **aspiration** [͵æspəˋreʃən] (n.) 渴望達到的目的
Heather's aspiration is to become a doctor and save lives.

3) **nurture** [ˋnɝtʃə] (v.) 栽培，養育
Parents have a duty to nurture and protect their children.

4) **instill** [ɪnˋstɪl] (v.) 栽培，灌輸，徐徐地教導
We hope to instill good values in our children.

5) **sustain** [səˋsten] (v.) 維持，支撐，支援
Very few planets are capable of sustaining life.

6) **tumultuous** [tuˋmʌltʃʊəs] (a.) 混亂的，激烈的，狂暴的
The small country has a tumultuous history.

7) **disillusionment** [͵dɪsɪˋluʒənmənt] (n.) 幻滅，理想破滅，醒悟
There is increasing disillusionment with the president.

College and the country were going through a period of rapid, sometimes [6]**tumultuous** changes. We grew up in a decade dominated by dreams and [7]**disillusionments**: dreams of the civil rights movement, of the Peace Corps, of the space program; disillusionments starting with President Kennedy's [8]**assassination**, accelerated by the [9]**divisive** war in Vietnam, and the deadly mixture of poverty, racism, and despair that burst into flames in the hearts of some cities and which is still burning today.

一九六五年我離開芝加哥純樸的郊區，踏進校園，成為大一新生時，當時的大學和國家都正在經歷一段迅速、偶有動盪的變化。我們生長的年代，是一個充滿夢想的年代，但也是夢想幻滅的年代：有民權運動、和平工作團和太空計畫的夢想；但自從甘迺迪總統遇刺後夢想就開始幻滅了，接著引起社會分裂的越戰更加速夢想破裂，加上致命的貧困、種族歧視、灰心喪志等問題，在某些城市的心臟地帶燃起熊熊烈火，至今仍在延燒。

Much has changed—and much of it for the better—but much has also stayed the same. Each new generation takes us into new territory. But while change is certain, progress is not. Change is a law of nature; progress is the challenge for both a life and society. Describing an [10]**integrated** life is easier than achieving one. Yet, what better place to speak on integrating the [11]**strands** of women's lives than Wellesley, a college that not only [12]**vindicates** the [13]**proposition** that there is still an essential place for an all-women's college, but which defines its mission as seeking "to educate women who will make a difference in the world."

許多事情已經變了，雖然大多是正面的改變，不過還是有很多事情沒變。每一個新生代都會帶領我們前往新的境界。改變雖然是一定會發生的，但進步卻不一定。改變是自然的法則，進步則是人生和社會的挑戰。描述一個完整的人生要比實現它簡單多了。不過，要談論婦女

要如何創造出完整的人生，還有什麼地方比衛斯理學院更適合？衛斯理不僅證明了女子學院仍佔有重要地位這一論點，也追求著明確的宗旨：「為將來影響世界的女性提供教育」。

" We're always going to argue about abortion. It's a hard choice and it's controversial, and that's why I'm pro-choice, because I want people to make their own choices.

我們永遠都會吵墮胎問題。這是一個困難的選擇，而且極具爭議性，那就是我支持選擇權的原因，因為我希望人們為自己做決定。

希拉蕊談墮胎

Hillary Clinton
希拉蕊柯林頓

© Everett Collection /
Shutterstock.com

生於一九四七年，為美國第四十二屆總統比爾柯林頓（Bill Clinton）的夫人。希拉蕊出身伊利諾州富商家庭，早年曾是共和黨支持者，但到一九六八年因不滿尼克森政府，並出於對非裔人權運動的支持，轉投民主黨。

一般認為希拉蕊是美國史上最具實權的第一夫人。她於柯林頓總統任期內參選紐約州參議員成功，二〇〇八年參加民主黨總統候選人初選，雖然敗給歐巴馬，但後來出任歐巴馬的國務卿。希拉蕊已正式宣佈參選二〇一六年美國總統大選。

Hillary Rodham Clinton

---

8) **assassination** [ə͵sæsə`neʃən] (n.) 刺殺
The president's assassination led to violent demonstrations.

9) **divisive** [dɪ`vaɪsɪv] (a.) 引起不合、分裂的
Gay marriage is a very divisive issue.

10) **integrated** [`ɪntə͵gretɪd] (a.) 完整的，整合的
Our school takes an integrated approach to learning.

11) **strand** [strænd] (n.) （構成整體的）一方面、組成部分
There are many different stands within the Christian religion.

12) **vindicate** [`vɪndə͵ket] (v.) 證明為正確，證實，辯明
The latest research vindicates the scientist's theory.

13) **proposition** [͵prɑpə`zɪʃən] (n.) 主張，論點，提議
The U.S. was founded on the proposition that all men are created equal.

Women Are Struggling
婦女都在努力

And what better time to speak than in the spring of 1992, when women's concerns are so much in the news. I've traveled all over America, talking and listening to women who are struggling to raise their children and somehow **LG** make ends meet; bumping up against the **LG** glass ceiling; watching their insurance [1]**premiums** increase; coping with inadequate or [2]**nonexistent** child support payments; [3]**anguishing** over the [4]**prospect** that [5]**abortions** will be criminalized again.

還有比一九九二年的春季（現在）更適合談論的時間點嗎？現在正是新聞上常看到女性議題的時候。我造訪過美國各地，與婦女們談話，傾聽她們的聲音。她們有的要努力撫養孩子、僅靠微薄收入維生；有的要在職場中對抗無形的晉升障礙；有的要面對保險費不斷上升；有的必須面對不足夠的贍養費，甚至完全拿不到；有的則要再度為墮胎可能再度非法化而苦惱不已。

Women who pack lunch for their kids, or take the early bus to work, or stay out late at the [6]**PTA**,

> Oftentimes when you face such an overwhelming challenge as global climate change, it can be somewhat daunting—it's kind of like trying to lose weight, which I know something about.
>
> 當全球氣候變遷等重大問題迎面而來，經常讓人感到氣餒——這有點像嘗試減肥，關於這點我略知一二。

希拉蕊談減肥

or spend every spare minute taking care of aging parents don't need lectures from Washington about values. We need understanding and a helping hand to solve our own problems. We're doing the best we can to find the right balance in our lives.

忙著幫孩子準備便當、搭早班公車上班、參加家長教師聯誼會到很晚才回家，或一有空就得照顧年邁雙親的婦女們，不需要聽白宮關於各種價值的訓誡。為了解決我們自己的問題，我們需要的是體會和協助。為了尋找人生中良好的平衡，我們一直是全力以赴。

Family, Work and Service
家庭、工作、服務

For me, the elements of that balance are family, work and service.

對我來說，平衡的元素是家庭、工作和服務。

First, your personal relationships. **LG** When all is said and done, **GM** it is the people in your life, the friendships you form and the [7]**commitments** you maintain, that give shape to your life—your friends and your neighbors, the people at work or church, all those who touch your daily lives. And if you choose, a marriage filled with love and respect.

首先，是妳個人的人際關係。畢竟妳生活周遭的人、妳所建立的友情和維持的承諾，都在塑造妳的人生——妳的朋友、鄰居、同事、教友，所有妳每天生活中要接觸的人。還有，如果妳這麼選擇的話，一個充滿愛和尊重的婚姻。

Second, your work. For some of you, the future might not include work outside the home (and I don't mean involuntary [8]**unemployment**); but most of you will at some point in your life work for pay, maybe in jobs that used to be [9]**off-limits** for women.

VOCABULARY 🎧34

1) **premium** [ˈprimiəm] (n.) 保險費
Which insurance plan has the lowest premium?

2) **nonexistent** [ˌnɑnɪɡˈzɪstənt] (a.) 不存在的
The team's chances of winning the competition are nonexistent.

3) **anguish** [ˈæŋgwɪʃ] (v./n.)（感到）極度的痛苦
The widow anguished over the death of her husband.

4) **prospect** [prəˈspɛkt] (n.) 可能性，可能發生的事
The doctor says the patient has little prospect of improving.

5) **abortion** [əˈbɔrʃən] (n.) 墮胎
Do you support a woman's right to have an abortion?

6) **PTA**（美國）家長教師聯誼會，即 Parent Teacher Association 的縮寫
Will your parents be coming to the PTA meeting?

第二，是妳們的工作。對妳們當中一些人來說，未來可能不包括家庭以外的工作（我指的不是非自願失業）；但妳們大部分人在一生當中或多或少都會去上班賺錢，也許從事的工作在過去還是限制女性的禁區。

Third, your service. As students, we debated passionately what responsibility each individual has for the larger society. The most [10]**eloquent** explanation I have found of what I believe now and what I argued then is from 🄻🄶 Vaclav Havel, the [11]**playwright** and first freely-elected president of Czechoslovakia. In a letter from prison to his wife, Olga, he wrote:

第三，是妳們的服務。身為學生時，我們曾熱烈討論每一個人對廣大社會的責任。我發現最有說服力的說法，也是我現在所相信和當時所主張的，是劇作家、也是捷克斯洛伐克第一任民選總統哈維爾說的一段話。是他在監獄中寫給妻子奧爾加的信中提到的一段話：

Only by looking outward, by caring for things that, in terms of pure survival, you needn't bother with at all, and by throwing yourself over and

❝ I'm one of those people who thinks that changing one's hair is the only part of the body that you can change at will.

我屬於那種人，認為髮型是人身上唯一能隨意改變的部分。

希拉蕊談自我形象

over again into the tumult of the world, with the intention of making your voice count—only thus will you really become a person.

唯有向外探索、去關心那些就純粹生存而言，一點都不需要勞妳費心的事，設法讓世界聽到妳的聲音，一再投身這動盪的世界——唯有如此，妳才能真正成為一個人。

I first recognized what I cared most about while I was in law school where I worked with children at the Yale New Haven Hospital and Child Study Center and represented children through legal services. My experiences [12]**gave voice** to deep feelings about what children deserved from their families and government. I discovered that I wanted my voice to count for children.

就讀法學院時，我在耶魯紐哈文醫院和兒童研究中心與孩童一起工作，並代表兒童處理法律事務，那是我第一次意識到我最關心的事情是什麼。這段經歷讓我深深感覺到，兒童理應從家庭或政府獲得些什麼。我發現自己原來想要為兒童發聲。

---

7) **commitment** [kə`mɪtmənt] (n.) 承諾，承擔的義務
Stacy wants to get married, but her boyfriend is afraid of commitment.

8) **unemployment** [ˌʌnɪm`plɔɪmənt] (n.) 失業
The government has promised to reduce unemployment.

9) **off-limits** [`ɔf`lɪmɪts] (a.) 禁止（進入、使用等）的
This area is off-limits to hotel guests.

10) **eloquent** [`ɛləkwənt] (a.) 有說服力的，口才好的
I was moved by the speaker's eloquent words.

11) **playwright** [`pleˌraɪt] (n.) 劇作家
Shakespeare is England's most famous playwright.

12) **give voice to** [gɪv vɔɪs tu] (phr.) 發聲，表達（情緒、意見）
The protesters gave voice to their anger.

Some of you may have already had such a life-shaping experience; for many, it lies ahead. Recognize it and nurture it when it occurs. Some of you may be saying to yourselves, "I've got to [1)]**pay off** my student loans. I can't even find a good job, [2)]**let alone** someone to love. How am I going to worry about the world? Our generation has fewer dreams, fewer [3)]**illusions** than yours."

妳們之中可能已有些人有過這樣塑造人生的經驗；對許多人來說，這樣的經驗正在前方等著妳去體驗。當它發生時，要認清它、滋養它。妳們之中可能有些人會對自己說：「我還要還學貸，我連好工作都找不到，更別說找個人去愛了，我哪有精力去擔心這世界？比起你們，我們世代的夢想更少、幻想更少。」

And I hear you. As women today, you face tough choices. You know the rules are basically as follows: If you don't get married, you're [4)]**abnormal**; If you get married but don't have children, you're a selfish 🄛 yuppie. If you get married and have children, but work outside the home, you're a bad mother. If you get married and have children, but stay home, you've wasted your education.

我聽到妳們的心聲了。現今身為女人，妳們面臨著艱難的抉擇。妳們都很清楚人生規則基本上就是這樣：假如妳不結婚，妳就不正常；假如妳結婚，但不生小孩，妳就是自私的雅痞；假如妳結了婚，也生小孩，但要外出工作，妳就不是個好媽媽；假如妳結了婚、生了小孩、在家當主婦，妳就浪費了妳所受的教育。

Hold onto Your Dreams
守住妳的夢想

So you see, if you listen to all the people who make these rules, you might just conclude that the safest course of action is just to take your diploma and crawl under your bed. But let me propose an [5)]**alternative**. Hold onto your dreams. Take up the challenge of [6)]**forging** an identity that [7)]**transcends** yourself. Transcend yourself and you will find yourself. Care about something you needn't bother with at all. Throw yourself into the world and make your voice count!

所以，妳看，假如妳聽從那些人制訂的規則，妳可能會得出一個結論：最好的做法就是拿著畢業證書躲到床底下。不過，先讓我提出一項替代方案。緊緊抓住妳的夢想。接受挑戰，打造一個超越自己的身份。超越自己，才能找到自己。關懷那些一點都不需要勞妳費心的事，投身這個世界，讓世界聽到妳的聲音！

VOCABULARY 🎧 36

1) **pay off** [pe ɔf] (phr.) 清償
Steven is working two jobs to pay off his debts.

2) **let alone** [lɛt əˋlon] (phr.) 更不必說，遑論
She never reads magazines, let alone books.

3) **illusion** [ɪˋluʒən] (n.) 幻想，幻覺，錯覺
Some people believe that love is just an illusion.

4) **abnormal** [æbˋnɔrməl] (a.) 不正常的
The abnormal weather is damaging crops.

5) **alternative** [ɔlˋtɜnətɪv] (n.) 選擇，替代方案
What are the alternatives to this treatment?

6) **forge** [fɔrdʒ] (v.) 鍛造，創造，打造
The actor is forging a new career as a director.

7) **transcend** [trænˋsɛnd] (v.) 超越，超出，超過
The band makes music that transcends cultural barriers.

Ozzie and Harriet 歐茲與哈莉愛特

© catwalker / Shutterstock.com

The Adventures of Ozzie and Harriet《歐茲與哈莉愛特的冒險》是橫跨美國五〇、六〇年代的電視家庭劇,劇中的夫妻 Ozzie 和 Harriet 及兩個兒子 Rick 和 David 在現實生活中就是一家人。在搬上電視之前,這個節目已從一九四〇年代中期起,以廣播劇形式放送八年,是美國電視史上播放時間最長的即時播出情境喜劇(live-action sitcom),劇中的情境也成為美國五、六〇年代理想家庭生活的代表。

Peace Corps 和平工作團

於一九六〇年由正在競選總統的甘迺迪(John F. Kennedy)所發起的志工團,主要宗旨是促進世界的和平和友誼。和平工作團的志工至今在一百三十九個國家都有活動。從事的內容包括將受訓過的志願人士送到發展中國家提供教育、醫療、農業等方面的幫助、促進各國人民對美國人的瞭解,同時也促進美國對別國人士的瞭解。參加和平工作團的志工必須融入當地生活,和當地人做一樣的工作,吃一樣的食物,説一樣的語言,努力為世界和平作出貢獻。

make ends meet 維持生計

此片語照字面上解釋是「使兩端相接」,大家可以想成記帳時「收入」與「支出」兩欄的數字至少要「入能敷出」,才不會還沒月底就月光光、心慌慌,所以 make ends meet 可解釋為「收支平衡、勉強餬口」等。

A: How's the pay at your company?
你公司的薪資待遇如何?
B: Pretty bad. I'm barely making enough to make ends meet.
很差,我幾乎賺不夠錢來維持生計。

glass ceiling 玻璃天花板效應

指企業對女性職員晉升的障礙,以透明的 glass(玻璃)來形容一種外面看似男女平等,但就是橫在女性上面的障礙,像 ceiling(天花板)一樣讓女性無法突破。

學希拉蕊如何振振有辭的表達:以 it 為首的強調句型

當我們想強調句子裡某事件、某時、某人等等的時候,可把欲強調事物前面加上虛主詞 it,並將整段話置於句首,之後再用 that 引導出真正的句子。

希拉蕊用這種虛主詞 it 代替 that 子句(名詞子句)的句型來強調,你的人生跟你周遭的「人」有密不可分之關係。這樣的用法也常見於英文文章中。

● It is/was + 欲強調事物 + that 主詞 + 動詞
例 **His words made me angry.**(直述句)
例 **It was his words that made me angry.**(強調句)

● 虛主詞後也可接形容詞,形容 that 子句
例 **It was obvious that Roger was lying.**

when all is said and done 塵埃落定,整體來說

這句俗語用在表示等一切紛擾底定、綜觀全局之後,你覺得整個來説最重要的事。

A: Prices in California are so expensive!
加州的物價好高喔!
B: Yeah. But when all is said and done, it's a great place to live.
對啊。但整體來説,這裡是很好的居住環境。

Vaclav Havel 瓦茲拉夫哈維爾

哈維爾(一九三六至二〇一一年)是捷克劇作家,著名反(共產黨)政府異議人士,長期受到監控與迫害。一九八九年,哈維爾當選捷克斯洛伐克總統,一九九二年捷克共產政權瓦解,隔年哈維爾當選捷克共和國總統,並於一九九八年連任。

© haak78 / Shutterstock.com

yuppie 雅痞

雅痞是八〇年代興起的名詞,yuppie 的前三個字母是 young urban professional 的縮寫,代表「年輕、都會、專業」,亦即靠著自身的專業能力,在競爭激烈的大都會占有一席之地,掙得錦衣玉食的年輕人。但經常用於負面評論,指涉膚淺、過度著重物質生活、自私自利的都會男女。

© fran west

衛斯理學院畢業傳統 hooprolling(滾輪圈),傳説跑第一名的人能最快獲得成功。© www.wellesley.edu

這篇演説是希拉蕊成為第一夫人之前一年,回到母校 Wellesley College(衛斯理學院)的畢業典禮演講。衛斯理學院這所女子文理學院位於麻州,創立於一八七五年,名列美國七姊妹學院(Seven Sisters)之一,與麻省理工學院及哈佛大學交流密切,是美國最頂尖的女子學院,在全美文理學院中排名第六(二〇一三年)。除希拉蕊之外,著名校友還有前國務卿歐布萊特(Madeleine Albright)。蔣中正的夫人宋美齡也畢業於此。

I, Too, Battled Self-Doubt

Natalie Portman's Harvard Class Day Speech

娜塔莉波曼哈佛畢業聯歡日演講

© magicinfoto / Shutterstock.com

You Are Here for a Reason
你存在的理由

Hello, class of 2015. I am so honored to be here today. I have to admit that today, even 12 years after graduation, I'm still [1)]**insecure** about my own [2)]**worthiness**. I have to 🅖🅜 remind myself today, "You are here for a reason." Today, I feel much like I did when I came to Harvard Yard as a freshman in 1999. I felt like there must have been some mistake—that I wasn't smart enough to be in this company and that every time I open my mouth, I have to prove that I'm not just a dumb actress.

哈囉，二〇一五年畢業班，今天很榮幸能來到這裡。我必須承認，就算已經畢業十二年了，我到現在對自己的價值還是缺乏信心。我現在還是要提醒自己：「妳存在是有理由的。」今天，我覺得自己跟一九九九年剛進哈佛時的我沒什麼兩樣。當年剛進哈佛時，我覺得一定是哪裡搞錯了——因為我不夠聰明，沒有資格加入這個大家族，而且每次開口說話時，我都要證明自己不是愚笨的女演員。

I went to a public high school on Long Island. Since I'm ancient and the Internet was just starting when I was in high school, people didn't really pay that much attention to the fact that I was an actress. I was known mainly at school for having a backpack bigger than I was. I was voted for my senior yearbook "most likely to be a [3)]**contestant** on 🅛🅖 *Jeopardy*," or code for [4)]**nerdiest**.

我在長島就讀一所公立高中。我的年代有點久遠了，網路是在我念高中時才剛剛開始，所以當時校園裡沒有多少人注意到我是女演員。我在學校裡之所以出名，主要是因為我背的書包比我個子還大。在畢業

VOCABULARY 🎧38

1) **insecure** [ˌɪnsəˋkjʊr] (a.) 缺乏安全感的，沒有自信的
(n.) **insecurity** [ˌɪnsəˋkjʊrəti]
Michelle is very insecure about her looks.

2) **worthiness** [ˋwɜðinəs] (n.) 值得尊重，有價值
New employees must work hard to prove their worthiness.

3) **contestant** [kənˋtɛstənt] (n.) 參賽者
The contestants on the show are all so talented.

4) **nerdy** [ˋnɜdi] (a.) 書呆子的，宅的
How can you go out with such a nerdy guy?

5) **overwhelmed** [ˌovɚˋwɛlmd] (a.) 無力的，無法承受的，不知所措的
Sarah's busy schedule left her feeling overwhelmed.

6) **unimaginable** [ˌʌnɪˋmæɡɪnəbəl] (a.) 無法想像的，想不到的
Losing a child can cause unimaginable grief.

紀念冊裡，我被票選為「最有可能成為《危險邊緣》節目的參賽者」，說白一點就是頭號書呆子。

I Was Completely Overwhelmed
我完全不堪負荷

When I got to Harvard, just after the release of *Star Wars: Episode I*, I knew I'd be starting over in terms of how people viewed me. I feared people would assume I'd gotten in just for being famous, and it wouldn't have been far from the truth. When I came here, I'd never written a 10-page paper before. I was completely 5)**overwhelmed**, and thought that reading 1,000 pages a week was 6)**unimaginable**, that writing a 50-page 7)**thesis** was something I could never do.

我剛進入哈佛時，是《星際大戰首部曲》剛上映的時候，我知道自己要重新建立別人對我的看法。我擔心大家會認為我之所以能進哈佛，靠的只是名氣，而事實上也差不多是如此。我剛進來時，還沒寫過十頁以上的報告。我完全不堪負荷，每星期要念一千頁的書更是令我難以想像，覺得寫五十頁的論文也是我做不到的事。

Driven by these 1)**insecurities**, I decided that I was going to find something to do at Harvard that was serious and meaningful, that would change the world and make it a better place. So, freshman fall, I decided to take 8)**Neurobiology** and Advanced Modern Hebrew Literature. But I saw friends around me writing papers on sailing and pop culture magazines, and professors teaching classes on fairy tales and *The Matrix*. I realized that seriousness for seriousness' sake was its own kind of 9)**trophy**, and a 10)**dubious** one.

受到這些不安全感的驅使，我決定要在哈佛做些嚴肅且有意義的研究，而且是可以改變世界的研究，讓世界變得更好。於是，在大一上學期時，我決定修讀神經生物學和進階現代希伯來文學。但我發現身邊朋友寫的報告內容都是關於帆船和流行文化雜誌，教授講課的內容也是關於童話和電影《駭客任務》。我這才意識到，為了嚴肅而嚴肅本身就是件虛榮的事，而且也不是件真正光彩的事。

> 66 I don't love studying. I hate studying. I like learning. Learning is beautiful.
>
> 我不愛讀書。我討厭讀書。我喜歡學習。學習是很美的事。
>
> 娜塔莉波曼談學習

Natalie Portman
娜塔莉波曼

一九八一年出生於以色列耶路薩冷的美國演員，一九九四年以盧貝松執導的《終極追殺令》*Léon*（美國上映片名 *The Professional*）步入影壇。於喬治魯卡斯的《星際大戰》系列飾演納卜星球年輕女王 Padmé Amidala 成名。二〇一〇年以《黑天鵝》奪下奧斯卡最佳女主角獎。近期的作品是在《雷神索爾》系列飾演索爾女友 Jane Foster。

© DFree / Shutterstock.com

Natalie Portman

《終極追殺令》海報及劇照

7) **thesis** ［ˈθisɪs] (n.) 論文，畢業論文，製作
How long did it take to write your master's thesis?

8) **neurobiology** ［ˌnʊrobaɪˈɑlədʒi] (n.) 神經生物學
Neurobiology is the study of nerve and brain function.

9) **trophy** ［ˈtrofi] (n.) 獎盃，獎品，戰利品
The tennis player's living room is filled with trophies.

10) **dubious** ［ˈdubiəs] (a.) 可疑的，半信半疑的
His story seemed a little dubious to me.

I Wanted to Tell Stories
我想說故事

When I got to my graduation, sitting where you sit today, after four years of trying to get excited about something else, I admitted to myself that I couldn't wait to go back and make more films. I wanted to tell stories, to imagine the lives of others, and help others do the same. I'd found, or perhaps [1)]**reclaimed**, my reason.

我畢業時，就坐在你們現在坐的位子，那時已經花了四年時間試著尋找其他能讓我提得起勁的事，但我承認自己是迫不及待想回去拍更多電影。我想說故事，想詮釋別人的人生，也幫助其他人完成同樣的事。我找到了，或者應該說我又找回了我存在的理由。

In my professional life, it also took me time to find my own reasons for doing my work. The first film I was in came out in 1994. I was 13 years old upon the film's release, and I can still quote what the *New York Times* said about me, "Miss Portman poses better than she acts." The film went on to [2)]**bomb** commercially. That film was called *The Professional*. And today, 20 years and 35 films

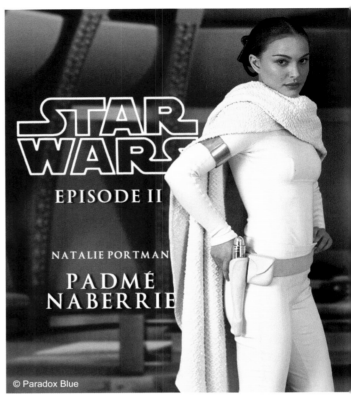

© Paradox Blue

later, it's still the film people approach me about the most, to tell me how much they loved it. I feel lucky that my first experience releasing a film was initially such a disaster by all standard measures. I learned early that my meaning had to be from the experience of making the film and the possibility of connecting with individuals rather than the [3)]**foremost** trophies in my industry: financial and critical success.

在我的職業生涯中，找到自己做這份工作的理由也花了我不少時間。我第一次拍電影是在一九九四年，電影上映時我十三歲，我還記得當時《紐約時報》這樣形容我：「波曼小姐擺姿勢的功力比她的演技好得多。」這部電影結果成了票房毒藥，片名是《終極追殺令》。不過，二十年過去了，我已經拍了三十五部電影，直到現在，這部仍是最多人來告訴我他們有多喜歡的電影。從任何標準來說，我拍第一部電影的經歷基本上是個災難，但這點對我來說算是幸運的。因為這樣讓我很早就學到，我存在的意義必須來自拍電影的經歷，以及與人接觸的可能性，而不是這一行的最高榮耀：票房和影評方面的成功。

" I am not someone who sacrifice all for the cinema. My life will be always more important.

我不是那種為電影犧牲一切的人，我的生活永遠比較重要。

娜塔莉波曼談生活

VOCABULARY 🎧 40

1) **reclaim** [rɪˋklem] (v.) 取回，奪回
The golfer hopes to reclaim the title of world champion.

2) **bomb** [bɑm] (v.) 不賣座，大敗
The play bombed on Broadway.

3) **foremost** [ˋforˏmost] (a.) 最重要的，最先的
Albert Einstein was the foremost scientist of the 20th century.

4) **passionate** [ˋpæʃənɪt] (a.) 有熱忱的，熱情的
Brazilians are passionate about soccer.

5) **Inquisition** [ˏɪnkwəˋzɪʃən] (n.) （中世紀天主教審判異端的）宗教法庭
Thousands of people were killed during the Inquisition.

6) **terrorist** [ˋtɛrəɪst] (n.) 恐怖份子，恐怖主義者
The terrorists responsible for the bombing were never caught.

7) **immune** [ɪˋmjun] (a.) 不受影響的，免疫的
Few people are immune to criticism.

> ❝ My dad's a doctor, and when I was 8, I went to one of his medical conferences where they were demonstrating laser surgery on a chicken. I was so mad that a chicken had to die, I never ate meat again.

我爸是個醫生，當我八歲時跟他去參加一場醫學會議，他們用一隻雞示範雷射手術。我好生氣那隻雞必須被殺，從此我就不再吃肉了。

娜塔莉波曼談吃素的原因

Owning My Meaning
自己決定存在的意義

I started choosing only jobs I was 4)**passionate** about. I made *Goya's Ghosts*, a foreign independent film, and studied art history, visiting the 🔲 Prado every day for four months as I read about 🔲 Goya and the Spanish 5)**Inquisition**. I made *V for Vendetta*, a studio action movie for which I learned everything I could about freedom fighters, who otherwise might be called 6)**terrorists**. I was able to own my meaning and not have it be determined by box office receipts.

從此我只選擇自己熱愛的電影去拍。我主演了一部外國獨立電影《哥雅畫作下的女孩》，還要學習藝術史，四個月來每天都去參觀普拉多博物館，並閱讀關於哥雅和西班牙宗教裁判的資料。我還拍了大片廠動作片《V 怪客》，從這部片中我學到一切關於自由鬥士的事，換一個角度，這些人可能被稱為恐怖份子。我得以自己決定存在的意義，而不是讓票房收入來決定。

By the time I got to making *Black Swan*, the experience was entirely my own. I felt 7)**immune** to the worst things anyone could say or write about me, and to whether an audience felt like going to see my movie or not. Authoring your own experience was very much what *Black Swan* itself was about. Because my character, Nina, is only artistically successful when she finds perfection and pleasure for herself, not when she's trying to be perfect in the eyes of others.

等到拍《黑天鵝》的時候，我打造了完全屬於自己的經歷。不管是誰說到或寫到關於我最糟糕的評論、是否有觀眾願意看我的電影，我都不會受到影響。打造自己的經歷，也就是《黑天鵝》這部電影的主旨。我的角色妮娜之所以能在藝術事業上功成名就，就是因為找到了自己的理想和喜悅，而不是成為別人眼中的完美形象。

《哥雅畫作下的女孩》

本片透過哥雅的畫家之眼和他的作品，紀錄歐洲最黑暗動盪的拿破崙攻進西班牙、宗教法庭時代。娜塔莉波曼在《哥雅畫作下的女孩》片中分飾母女，故事前段娜塔莉飾演哥雅的繆斯，也就是《裸體的馬哈》當中的美麗女子。她被構陷入獄，受到宗教審判酷刑，哥雅受女子父親之託，找宗教法庭的羅倫佐修士斡旋，女子卻因而與修士生下女兒。

© Kanzaman S.A.I

《V 怪客》

V for Vendetta 改編自英國漫畫家艾倫摩爾（Alan Moore）的同名作品，他是以蓋伊福克斯（Guy Fawkes）為藍本創造 V 怪客這個角色。蓋伊福克斯參與了 1605 年 11 月 5 日的火藥陰謀（Gunpowder Plot），企圖炸掉國會並暗殺英格蘭國王詹姆士一世，抗議其對天主教徒的迫害。Guy Fawkes 因消息走漏被逮捕並處死，此後英國在每年的 11 月 5 日舉辦煙火節（Guy Fawkes Day 或 Bonfire's Day）以慶祝 Guy Fawkes 被捕。

A Scary Challenge
一場可怕的挑戰

People told me that *Black Swan* was an artistic risk, a scary challenge to try to portray a professional ballet dancer. When it quickly became clear, in preparing for the film, that I was maybe fifteen years away from being a 1)**ballerina**, it made me work a million times harder. If I'd known my own limitations, I never would have taken the risk. And the risk led to one of my greatest personal and professional experiences.

© Balletstar011

曾經有人告訴我,在《黑天鵝》中詮釋專業的芭蕾舞者,是一場藝術風險,也是一場可怕的挑戰。在準備拍片時,我很快就發現,如果要成為真正的芭蕾舞者,我大概還得下十五年的苦工,因此讓我多付出一百萬倍的努力。假如我早知道自己的極限在哪裡,我不會去冒這個風險。但這場風險把我帶向我個人和事業中最重要的歷程之一。

People always talk about diving into things you're afraid of. What has served me is diving into my own 2)**obliviousness**—being more confident than I should be. It can be a good thing if it makes you try things you never might have tried. Your inexperience is an 3)**asset**, and will allow you to think in original and 4)**unconventional** ways.

大家總是說要放手去做那些讓自己感到害怕的事。但對我來說受用的是,放任自己的漫不經意——讓自己變得過於自信。假如這樣能讓你嘗試從未嘗試過的事,這對你來說可能是好事。缺乏經驗也是一種優勢,因為這樣能讓你用原創和另類的方式思考。

Forge Your Own Path
打造自己的路

You here will all go on to achieve great things. There's no doubt about that. Each time you set out to do something new, your inexperience can either lead you down a path where you will 5)**conform** to someone else's values, or you can forge your own path. If your reasons are your own, your path, even if it is a strange and clumsy path, will be wholly yours. And you will control the reward of what you do by making your internal life fulfilling. To quote one of my favorite thinkers, **LG** Abraham Joshua Heschel, "To be or not to be is not the question. The 6)**vital** question is how to be and how not to be."

在座的各位將來都會功成名就,這是毫無疑問的。每當你們準備展開新的旅程時,你們的經驗不足不是帶領你們遵循其他人的價值觀,就是打造自己的路。假如你們能自己決定存在的理由,就算那是條怪異又崎嶇的路,也完全都是屬於你自己的路。而你們可以藉由充實自己的內心生活,控制自己所做的事和回報。我要引述我最喜歡的思想家之一,亞伯拉罕約書亞赫施爾的名言:「生與死並不是問題,至關重要的問題是,如何生、如何死。」

Thank you. I can't wait to see how you do all the beautiful things you will do.

謝謝各位。我迫不及待看到你們的成就。

© Alexander Kenney / Kungliga Operan

VOCABULARY 🎧 42

1) **ballerina** [ˌbæləˋrinə] (n.) 女芭蕾舞者
The ballet teacher used to be a ballerina.

2) **obliviousness** [əˋblɪvɪəsnɪs] (n.) 不注意,不經意,健忘
His obliviousness to other people's feelings is really annoying.

3) **asset** [ˋæsɛt] (n.) 才能,資產,有價值的條件
Richard's leadership skills are his greatest asset.

4) **unconventional** [ˌʌnkənˋvɛnʃənəl] (a.) 不符合習俗的,非傳統的,非常規的
Stella has unconventional taste in clothes.

5) **conform** [kənˋfɔrm] (v.) 遵從,遵守(習俗、規定等)
Most teenagers feel pressure to conform.

6) **vital** [ˋvaɪtəl] (a.) 不可缺少的,極為重要的
Foreign trade is vital to Taiwan's economy.

Jeopardy 《危險邊緣》

美國電視益智搶答節目，一九六四年開播至今，除在美國大受歡迎，也授權許多國家製作改編版本。節目進行是由三位參賽者（一名衛冕者及兩位挑戰者）按鈴搶答問題，問題包羅萬象。

搶答分為三輪，第一輪 Jeopardy! 及第二輪 Double Jeopardy! 參賽者要在六類各五題中選題回答，依題目難度賺取分數／獎金，答錯倒扣。完成 Double Jeopardy! 分數為正數者，可進入第三輪 Final Jeopardy! 爭取冠軍，及下次比賽的衛冕資格，累積更高的獎金。

Museo del Prado 普拉多博物館

位於西班牙馬德里，這所世界級博物館成立於一八一九年，收藏西班牙王室於十二世紀至十九世紀初的歐洲藝術典藏，如魯本斯（Rubens）及提香（Titian），並收有西班牙藝術家最精華、最完整的作品，

© Rodrigo Garrido / Shutterstock.com

包括哥雅、維拉斯奎茲（Velázquez）、艾爾葛雷柯（El Greco），是全球最多遊客造訪的景點之一。

remind 的常見用法

演講時，講者最常以分享自己經驗的方式，與聽眾拉近距離、感同身受；英文裡「憶起……」、「作為提醒……」就是用 remind 一字表達。常見句型如下：

● **remind sb. that + 子句**

例 **You should remind Bobby that school starts next week.**
你應該提醒巴比下星期開學。

● **remind sb. of sth.**：提醒某人過去發生的某事；因相似而使某人想起某事

例 **That love song always reminds Laura of her first date.**
那首情歌總是讓羅拉想起她第一次約會。

例 **The landscape reminds Tracy of Ireland.**
這裡的風景讓崔西想到愛爾蘭。

● **remind sb. about sth.**：提醒某人必須做某事 (= remind sb. to v.)

例 **Paul was glad that his wife reminded him about the meeting. He had completely forgotten about it.**
保羅很高興他太太提醒他開會的事，他壓根兒忘了這件事。

Francisco Goya 哥雅

西班牙畫家 Francisco Goya（1746-1828）原本為宮廷作畫，一八〇八年拿破崙入侵，半島戰爭爆發，哥雅留在馬德里以畫作記錄戰爭的殘酷，其後他畫了許多描繪戰爭、死亡和疾病的畫作，晚年留下十四幅壁畫《黑色繪畫》（Black Paintings）系列。他一生畫風多變，對後來的現實主義、浪漫主義及印象畫派影響深遠，啟發了馬奈、畢卡索、培根等畫家。

哥雅擔任宮廷畫師時的畫作《查理四世一家》，收藏於普拉多博物館

哥雅描寫早期半島戰爭的名畫《1808年5月3日》，收藏於普拉多博物館

哥雅晚年黑色繪畫系列中最有名的一幅《農神吞噬其子》，描繪農神為避免兒子們奪權，將他們全部吃掉。收藏於普拉多博物館

普拉多博物館哥雅門外的哥雅雕像，下方石柱四面刻有其名畫的浮雕，正面為《裸體的馬哈》
© Elias H. Debbas II / Shutterstock.com

Abraham Joshua Heschel 亞伯拉罕約書亞赫施爾

Abraham Joshua Heschel（1907-1972）為波蘭裔猶太拉比（rabbi，猶太祭司），咸認為是二十世紀最重要的猶太神學家之一。相較於大多猶太學者著重於鑽研古籍，赫施爾拉比更注重精神層面的探討，也更積極入世，是反越戰與推動美國人權運動的重要角色。

亞伯拉罕約書亞赫施爾和金恩博士
© huc.edu

年輕美貌加上少年得志的公眾人物，無論如何都躲不過受放大鏡檢視的命運，這就是成名的代價，娜塔莉波曼就是其中之一。既然無論如何都不可能躲過，又為何要隨別人的眼光起舞呢？娜塔莉波曼在演講中把過往所有對她的負評都攤開來講，不迴避不閃躲，成就了一篇動人的演說。

Get on a Rocket Ship

雪柔桑伯格哈佛大學畢業典禮演講
Sheryl Sandberg's Harvard Commencement Speech

© Stuart Isett/Fortune Most Powerful Women

🚀 **Social Marketing**
社會行銷

When I was a student here 17 years ago, I studied 🄻🄶 social marketing with professor Kash Rangan, and one of the many examples Kash used to explain the concept of social marketing was the lack of organ [1]**donors** in this country, which kills 18 people every single day. Earlier this month, Facebook launched a tool to support organ donations, something that stems directly from Kash's work.

十七年前我在哈佛大學就讀時，選修了卡席蘭根教授的社會行銷課程，卡席教授用了許多例子解說社會行銷的概念，其中一個例子是這個國家缺乏器官捐贈者，而且每天有十八人因為等不到器官捐贈而死亡。這個月稍早，臉書推出一項支持器官捐贈的功能，想法源自卡席教授的研究成果。

It used to be that in order to reach more people than you could talk to in a day, you had to be rich and famous and powerful, but that's not true today. Now ordinary people have a voice, not just those of us lucky to go to HBS, but anyone with access to Facebook, Twitter, a mobile phone. This is [2]**disrupting** traditional power structures and

VOCABULARY 🎧 44

1) **donor** [ˈdonɚ] (n.) 捐贈者，**donation** [doˈneʃən] 即「捐獻，捐款」
The country urgently needs more blood donors.

2) **disrupt** [disˈrʌpt] (v.) 使瓦解，使混亂，使中斷
A group of protesters tried to disrupt the conference.

3) **hierarchy** [ˈhaɪɚˌrɑrki] (n.) 等級制度，統治集團
(a.) **hierarchical** [ˌhaɪɚˈrɑrkɪkəl]
He swiftly rose to the top of the company hierarchy.

4) **institution** [ˌɪnstɪˈtuʃən] (n.) 機構
This university is the largest educational institution in the country.

5) **MBA** (n.) 企業管理碩士，即 master of business administration
How many MBA programs are you applying to?

6) **spreadsheet** [ˈsprɛdˌʃit] (n.) 試算表
Do you know how to use Excel spreadsheets?

leveling traditional [3]**hierarchy**. Voice and power are shifting from [4]**institutions** to individuals.

在過去，為了能觸及一天中所能面對的人以外的群眾，你必須有錢、有名、有權，但現在不需要這樣了。現在一般人也可以發聲，不一定只有像我們這群有幸能就讀哈佛商學院的人，而是只要你能使用臉書、推特或手機就好。這種現象打破了傳統的權力結構和階層等級制度。原本掌握在組織機構裡的聲音和力量已轉移到個人手上。

 ## Career Paths Are Shifting
職涯發展正在改變

As the world becomes more connected and less [3]**hierarchical**, traditional career paths are shifting as well. In 2001, I moved out to Silicon Valley to try finding a job. My timing wasn't really that good. The bubble had crashed. After a while I had a few offers and I had to make a decision. I'm [5]**MBA** trained, so I made a [6]**spreadsheet**. One of the jobs on that sheet was to become Google's first business unit general manager, which sounds good now, but at the time no one thought consumer Internet companies could ever make money. So I sat down with Eric Schmidt, who had just become the CEO, and I showed him the spreadsheet and I said, "This

job meets none of my criteria." He looked at me and said, "Don't be an idiot." And then he said, "Get on a rocket ship." When companies are growing quickly and they are having a lot of impact, careers take care of themselves.

隨著全球網路普及率越高、等級制度消退，傳統的職涯發展也跟著改變。二〇〇一年，我搬到矽谷找工作。但時間點不太好，遇到了網路泡沫破滅。找了一段時間，有幾家提出工作機會，所以我必須做出決定了。我受過企業管理訓練，因此我列出了一份試算表。表格上的其中一項工作是擔任 Google 公司的第一位業務部經理，那份工作現在聽起來很棒，但在當時，沒有人認為消費者網路公司會賺錢。於是我和艾立克史密特坐下來談，他那時剛剛擔任執行長，我給他看我的試算表，我說：「這份工作似乎不符合我的標準。」他看了看我說：「別傻了。」然後他說：「有火箭就坐上去。」當公司迅速成長，並帶來大量效應時，事業自然會水到渠成。

> 66 The No. 1 impediment to women succeeding in the workforce is now in the home.
>
> 目前女人在職場上成功的最大絆腳石，來自家庭。
>
> 雪柔桑伯格談職業女性

© Stuart Isett/Fortune Most Powerful Women

Sheryl Sandberg 雪柔桑伯格

一九六九年生於美國華盛頓特區，現任 Facebook 營運長，同時為首位女性董事會成員。她畢業於哈佛商學院，曾任職於麥肯錫公司、美國財政部及 Google，二〇〇八年進入 Facebook，讓該公司「從一個很酷的網站，變成一個獲利的公司」。

雪柔桑伯格長期關注女性職場問題，二〇一〇年，她在 TED 以「為什麼太少女性成為領導者」Why we have too few women leaders 發表演說；二〇一一年被《富比世》雜誌選入百大最具影響力女性（100 Most Powerful Women）第五名；二〇一二年進入 Facebook 董事會；二〇一三年出版女權主義商管書籍 Lean In。

LEAN IN

WOMEN, WORK, AND THE WILL TO LEAD

SHERYL SANDBERG

本書中文版為《挺身而進》

Why Work for a 23-year-old?
為何幫二十三歲小夥子工作？

About 6 and half years later, when I was leaving Google, I 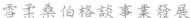 took that advice to heart. I was offered CEO jobs at a bunch of companies, but I went to Facebook as [1)]**COO**. At the time people said, "Why are you going to work for a 23-year-old?" The traditional [2)]**metaphor** for careers is a ladder, but I no longer think that metaphor holds. It doesn't make sense in a less hierarchical world.

大約六年半後，我要離開 Google 時，我將他的建議放在心上。有一堆公司請我當執行長，但我選擇到 Facebook 公司擔任營運長。當時大家都問我：「妳為什麼要去幫一個二十三歲的年輕人工作？」晉升階梯是職涯發展的傳統比喻，但我不再認為這種比喻現在還適用。在一個階級制度日漸消弭的世界中，這種比喻不再有意義。

> 66 Careers are a jungle gym, not a ladder.
>
> 事業發展是在爬遊戲場上的攀爬架，不是爬梯子。

雪柔桑伯格談事業發展

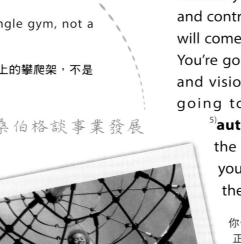

Jungle gym

Build Your Skills, Not Your Résumé
累積技能，而非履歷

As you start your post-HBS career, look for opportunities, look for growth, look for impact. Build your skills, not your résumé. Evaluate what you can do, not the title they're going to give you. Don't plan too much, and don't expect a direct climb. If I had [3)]**mapped out** my career when I was sitting where you are, I would have missed my career.

當你們離開哈佛商學院展開職涯時，要尋求機會、發展和效應。要累積技能，而不是累積履歷。衡量自己能做什麼，而不是別人能給你什麼頭銜。不需要做太多的規劃，也不要期待平步青雲。假如我當年畢業時就按既定標準規劃我的職涯，我可能就沒有今天的事業成就。

You are entering a different business world than I entered. As traditional structures are breaking down, leadership has to [4)]**evolve** as well—from hierarchy to shared responsibility, from command and control to listening and guiding. Your strength will come from building trust and earning respect. You're going to need talent, skill, and imagination and vision, but more than anything else, you're going to need the ability to communicate [5)]**authentically**, to speak so that you inspire the people around you and to listen so that you continue to learn each and every day on the job.

你們現在進入的商界已經和我當年不一樣了。傳統的結構正在瓦解，領導方式也必須改變——要從階級制度演變成分擔責任，從指揮和管控演變成聆聽和指導。你們的力量將來自建立信任和贏得尊敬。你們將需要才華、技能、想像力和願景，但更重要的是，你們需要真正溝通的能力。發言，可以鼓舞周遭的人；聆聽，可以讓你持續從每天的工作中學習。

VOCABULARY 🎧46

1) **COO** (n.) 營運長，即 chief operating officer
The company is thinking of bringing in a new COO.

2) **metaphor** [ˋmɛtə͵fɔr] (n.) 隱喻，象徵
Chess is often used as a metaphor for war.

3) **map out** [mæp aʊt] (phr.) 安排，策劃
His future was mapped out for him by his parents.

4) **evolve** [ɪˋvɑlv] (v.) 演變，演化
Is it true that humans evolved from apes?

5) **authentically** [ɔˋθɛntɪklɪ] (adv.) 真實地，真正地
The novel authentically portrays wartime London.

6) **setup** [ˋsɛt͵ʌp] (n.) （事物的）安排，組織，結構，體制
How do you like my home office setup?

7) **burst out** [bɝst aʊt] (phr.) 突然開始（說、笑、哭）
I burst out laughing when I saw his new haircut.

Speak and Hear the Truth
說真話，聽真相

臉書創辦人馬克祖克柏（Mark Zuckerberg）和本篇主講者 © Dan Farber

If you watch young children, you'll immediately notice how honest they are. As adults, we are never this honest, and that's not a bad thing. But it's not always a good thing either—because all of us, and especially leaders, need to speak and hear the truth. The workplace is an especially difficult place for anyone to tell the truth, because no matter how flat we want our organizations to be, all organizations have some form of hierarchy. This is not a [6]**setup** for honesty.

觀察一下小朋友，你立刻就能發現他們有多真誠。反觀成年人，我們從來沒這麼真誠，而這並不是壞事。但也不總是件好事，因為我們所有人，尤其是領導者，必須說真話和聆聽真話。職場尤其是難以讓人說真話的地方，因為不管我們希望組織有多平等，所有組織總是會有某種程度的階級制度存在。這不是一個能培養真誠的體制。

Last year Mark decided to learn Chinese, and as part of studying, he would spend an hour or so each week with some of our employees who were native Chinese speakers. One day, one of them was trying to tell him something about her manager, so she said this long sentence and he said "Simpler please." And then she said it again and he said, "No, I still don't understand, simpler please." Finally, she [7]**burst out**, "My manager is bad." Simple and clear and very important for him to know. People rarely speak this clearly in the [8]**workforce** or in life.

去年祖克柏決定學中文，為了學中文，他每週會花一兩個小時跟公司裡母語是中文的員工相處。有一天，其中一人想告訴他關於她主管的事，她用冗長的句子述說這件事，於是他說：「請簡單一點。」然後她又說了一次，他說：「不行，我還是聽不懂，請簡單一點。」終於她激動地說：「我的經理很壞。」簡單明瞭，而且對他來說是重要訊息。人們鮮少在職場上或人生中把話說得這麼清楚。

❝ I'm not telling women to be like men. I'm telling us to evaluate what men and women do in the workforce and at home without the gender bias.

我不是叫女人要變得跟男人一樣。我是要我們評價男人和女人在職場及家庭的貢獻時，不要有男女之別。

雪柔桑伯格談性別待遇

8) **workforce** [ˋwɝk͵fɔrs] (n.) 勞動力，勞動人口
Millions left the workforce during the recession.

They Applauded
他們竟然鼓掌

When I first started at Google, I had a team of four people and it was really important to me that I interview everyone—being part of my team meant I had to know you. When the team had gotten to 100 people, I realized it was taking longer to schedule my interviews, so one day at my meeting of just my [1]**direct reports**, I said maybe I should stop interviewing, fully expecting them to jump in and say, "No, your interviews are a critical part of the process." They applauded.

我開始在 Google 工作時，我的團隊有四人，對我來說，與每一個人面談是非常重要的——因為我覺得，既然是我團隊的一份子，我就必須了解你。當團隊增加到一百人時，我發現安排面談行程就要花不少時間。所以，某天跟直屬員工開會時，我說，也許我該停止面談，我以為他們會立刻回答：「不行，和妳面談是非常重要的程序。」結果他們全體鼓掌。

I was embarrassed, then I was angry. Why didn't they tell me I was a [2]**bottleneck**? Then I realized that if they hadn't told me, that was my fault. I hadn't been open enough to tell them I wanted that [3]**feedback**, and I would have to change that going forward.

我先是感到丟臉，然後生氣，為什麼他們不早告訴我，我讓他們為難了？然後我發現，他們沒告訴我，那也是我的錯。因為我還不夠坦率到告訴他們，我想多聽聽他們的意見，而我之後必須要改變。

How Will You Lead?
你將如何領導？

As you graduate today, ask yourself, "How will you lead?" Will you use simple and clear language? Will you seek out honesty?

When you get honesty back, will you react with anger or with gratitude? As we strive to be more authentic in our communication, we should also strive to be more authentic in a broader sense.

在你們畢業這天，問問自己：「你要怎麼領導？」你們會用簡單明瞭的表達方式嗎？你們會追求真誠嗎？你們得到真誠的回應時，你們的反應會是憤怒，還是感激？當我們在溝通上努力做到真誠時，我們也應該努力讓自己在各方面都做到真誠。

Motivation comes from working on things we care about, but it also comes from working with people we care about. And in order to care about someone, you have to know them. You have to know what they love and hate, what they feel, not just what they think. If you want to win  hearts and minds, you have to lead with your heart as well as your mind.

動力來自於我們為自己所關心的事物工作，也來自於和我們所關心的人一起工作。為了關心他人，你必須了解他們。你必須知道他們喜歡什麼、討厭什麼，還有他們的感受，而不只是他們的想法。假如你想贏得人心，領導上除了用頭腦，還要用心。

VOCABULARY 48

1) **direct report** [dɪˋrɛkt rɪˋport] (n.) 直屬員工
   How many direct reports does the marketing manager have?

2) **bottleneck** [ˋbatl͵nɛk] (n.) 瓶頸，障礙
   A lack of parts has caused a production bottleneck.

3) **feedback** [ˋfid͵bæk] (n.) 意見，反應
   Jim asked for feedback from the audience after his presentation.

social marketing 社會行銷

「社會行銷」一詞始於七○年代，在此之前，各項社會政策都是執政者規劃制定後直接推行，但社會行銷將商業的「行銷」觀念引進公共政策領域，強調追求商業的 consumer（消費者／社會大眾）的利益，以 target audience（目標族群／想向其宣導某種觀念或作法的對象）能接受的手法，推廣 product（產品／想宣導的觀念或作法）。社會行銷較常被運用在疾病防治、反毒宣導等公共衛生領域。

bubble 網際網路泡沫化

bubble 即經濟泡沫（economic bubble），是指股票、債券、不動產抵押等虛擬資本交易過度增長，證券、地產等投機交易極度活躍，造成社會經濟虛假繁榮，終至經濟崩潰。

文中所說的 bubble，是指一九九五年到二○○一年間與資訊科技、網路產業相關的投機泡沫。由於許多網路公司名稱都以 .com 結尾，加上許多既有公司為了賺網路財，也跟風在原公司名稱後面加上 .com，因此這波經濟泡沫，被稱作 dotcom bubble。

take sth. to heart 銘記在心，放在心上

把某件事好好放進心裡，很慎重的記下來，當然不會輕易忘記。不論是好的想法或壞的印象，都可以用這種說法表示。

A: I'm really upset about what Jack said about me.
　傑克關於我的評論讓我很難過。
B: Don't take it to heart. He was just joking.
　別放在心上。他只是在開玩笑。

英文裡的連體嬰「對詞」

英文修辭中常用 and 或 or 連接兩個意思相近或相反的詞，此二字結構通常有押韻，所以念起來非常順口，而且兩個詞的順序是固定的，不能隨意改變，譬如 rock and roll（搖滾）、hide and seek（捉迷藏），還有文中的 hearts and minds（人心）。因此英文稱這種詞組為 Siamese twins（連體嬰）或 freezes（凍結字）。

● 以下舉例一些常見對詞：

例 **back and forth** 來來回回
deaf and dumb 聾啞
now and then 偶爾
dos and don'ts 可與不可（小眉角）
more or less 差不多
fight or flight 打或跑
room and board 食宿
lost and found 遺失物招領（處）
24/7 全年無休

這篇演說於二○一二年發表於哈佛商學院（Harvard Business School），曾獲媒體評選，與賈伯斯二○○五年史丹佛大學畢業演講、J.K. 羅琳二○○八年哈佛大學畢業演講並列「一百年內最佳畢業演說 Top 7」。

本書因篇幅所限，無法囊括所有優秀演講，以下列出上述「一百年內最佳畢業演說 Top 7」名單，希望各位讀者找時間上網搜尋：

© ari/flickr.com

David Foster Wallace, Kenyon College, 2005
美國前作家大衛佛斯特華萊士，肯揚學院
講題："This Is Water: Some Thoughts, Delivered on a Significant Occasion, about Living a Compassionate Life"
「這是水，生活中平淡無奇，又十分重要之事」

Sheryl Sandberg, Harvard Business School, 2012
雪柔桑伯格，哈佛大學（本書收錄）

John F. Kennedy, American University, 1963
美國前總統約翰甘迺迪，美國大學（見本書 p.125）

Steve Jobs, Stanford University, 2005
史蒂夫賈伯斯，史丹佛大學（本書收錄）

J.K. Rowling, Harvard University, 2008
J.K. 羅琳，哈佛大學（本書收錄）

Winston Churchill, Harrow School, 1941
英國前總理溫斯頓邱吉爾，哈羅公學
名句："Never give in. Never give in. Never, never, never, never—In nothing, great or small, large or petty—never give in, except to convictions of honour and good sense."
「決不屈服，決不屈服，決不、決不、決不、決不——事無分大小鉅細，除非為了榮譽和良知，絕不向任何事物屈服。」

© Olga Popova /Shutterstock.com

Barbara Kingsolver, Duke, 2008
美國作家芭芭拉金索弗，杜克大學
她以一首詩 Hope; An Owner's Manual（希望，人生的使用手冊）為演說作結。

© Annie Griffiths

Taking on the World's Inequities

比爾蓋茲哈佛畢業典禮演講
Bill Gates' Harvard Commencement Speech

I've been waiting more than 30 years to say this: "Dad, I always told you I'd come back and get my degree." I want to thank Harvard for this timely honor. I'll be changing my job next year, and it will be nice to finally have a college degree on my résumé.

這句話我等了三十多年了：「爸，我說過，我會回來領我的學位的。」我要謝謝哈佛，這份榮耀來得真是時候。我明年要換工作了，有個大學學歷放在我的履歷表上真是不錯。

The Founding of Microsoft
微軟的創立

One of my biggest memories of Harvard came in January 1975, when I made a call to a company in Albuquerque that had begun making the world's first personal computers. I offered to sell them software. I worried that they would realize I was just a student in a dorm and [1)]**hang up** on me. Instead, they said: "We're not quite ready, come see us in a month," which was a good thing, because we hadn't written the software yet. From that moment, I worked day and night on this little extra credit project that marked the end of my college education and the beginning of a remarkable journey with 💿 Microsoft.

我在哈佛最難忘的回憶之一，是在一九七五年的一月，當時我打電話到阿布里基的一家公司，那家公司正在製造全世界第一款個人電腦。我向他們推銷軟體。我擔心他們會發現我只是從宿舍打過去的學生而

VOCABULARY 🎧 50

1) **hang up (on)** [hæŋ ʌp] (phr.) 掛斷電話
Don't forget to hang up the phone when you're finished talking.

2) **midst** [mɪdst] (n.) 當中，中間，in the midst of 即「在…之中」
The country is in the midst of a severe recession.

3) **inequity** [ɪn`ɛkwɪti] (n.) 不公平
There is still a great deal of inequity in the education system.

4) **appalling** [ə`pɑlɪŋ] (a.) 可怕的，駭人的
Conditions inside the prison were appalling.

5) **disparity** [dɪs`pærəti] (n.) 不平等，差異
There is growing disparity between the rich and poor.

6) **condemn** [kən`dɛm] (v.) 迫使…於不幸的狀況
Tom's lack of education condemned him to a life of poverty.

掛我電話。出乎意料，他們說：「我們還沒準備好，一個月後再來見我們吧。」這是好事，因為我們當時也還沒把軟體寫好。從那一刻起，我日夜趕工，好完成這項額外加分的研究專案，也是這份專案讓我提早結束大學教育，帶我展開非凡的微軟旅程。

One Big Regret
一大遺憾

 What I remember above all about Harvard was being in the [2)]**midst** of so much energy and intelligence. It was an amazing privilege. But taking a serious look back, I do have one big regret. I left Harvard with no real awareness of the awful [3)]**inequities** in the world—the [4)]**appalling** [5)]**disparities** of health, and wealth and opportunity that [6)]**condemn** millions of people to lives of [7)]**despair**.

置身在智慧的殿堂中，周遭圍繞著滿滿的能量，是我對哈佛最重要的記憶。我很幸運能有這樣的機會。但認真回顧，我確實有一大遺憾。我離開哈佛時，沒有真正意識到這世界有著可怕的不平等現象——財富、健康和機會的懸殊差異極其嚴重，迫使千萬人的生活陷入絕望。

You graduates came to Harvard at a different time. You know more about the world's inequities than the classes that came before. In your years here, I hope you've had a chance to think about how, in this age of [8)]**accelerating** technology, we can finally [9)]**take on** these inequities, and we can solve them.

你們這群畢業生是在不同時間點進哈佛的。相較於比你們早進哈佛的學生，你們更瞭解這世界的不公。我希望你們在哈佛的日子裡，已經有機會思考，在科技日新月異的時代，我們該如何承擔這些不公平的現象，並解決這些問題。

Imagine, just for the sake of discussion, that you had a few hours a week and a few dollars a month to [10)]**donate** to a cause—and you wanted to spend that time and money where it would have the greatest impact in saving and improving lives.

Where would you spend it? For [LG] Melinda and for me, the challenge is the same.

為了方便我們討論，試想一下，你一個星期可以奉獻出幾個小時、一個月幾塊美元來捐助一項公益事業——而且你希望這些時間和金錢可以在拯救生命和改善生活方面發揮最大功效。那麼你要捐到哪裡？對梅琳達（比爾蓋茲的妻子）和我來說，要面臨的挑戰也是一樣的。

> 66 I choose a lazy person to do a hard job. Because a lazy person will find an easy way to do it.
>
> 我會選懶惰的人做困難的工作。因為懶惰的人會找出輕鬆的方法完成。

比爾蓋茲談懶惰

© Paolo Bona / Shutterstock.com

Bill Gates
比爾蓋茲

William Henry "Bill" Gates III 生於一九五五年，以創立微軟公司聞名於世。他對電腦工業的貢獻，正如當年 亨利福特（Henry Ford）對汽車工業的決定性影響，讓原本只有少數人能接觸的物品普及化，成為家家戶戶都用得到的商品，因此經常有人將 Bill Gates 比做電腦業的 Henry Ford。

他於二〇〇〇年卸下微軟 CEO 職位，並於二〇〇六年宣布全職投入 Bill & Melinda Gates Foundation 的慈善工作。

William H. Gates III

7) **despair** [dɪˋspɛr] (n.) 絕望
The destruction of the earthquake left the villagers in despair.

8) **accelerate** [ækˋsɛləˏret] (v.) 增速，促進
The government has promised to accelerate economic growth.

9) **take on** [tek ɑn] (phr.) 承擔
We're looking for employees who are willing to take on new challenges.

10) **donate** [ˋdonet] (v.) 捐助
Michael donated some of his old clothes to charity.

Bill Gates 的妻子 Melinda Gates 二〇一五年三月於聯合國發表演講。她畢業於杜克大學，因任職於 Microsoft 時與 Bill Gates 相識，兩人於一九九四年結婚

© JStone / Shutterstock.com

We Were Shocked
我們很震驚

During our discussions on this question, Melinda and I read an article about the millions of children who were dying every year in poor countries from diseases that we had long ago made harmless in this country. We were shocked. We had just assumed that if millions of children were dying and they could be saved, the world would make it a [1)]**priority** to discover and deliver the medicines to save them.

我和梅琳達在討論這個問題時，看到了一篇文章，其中提到貧窮國家每年有千百萬名兒童死於疾病，而這些疾病在美國已經銷聲匿跡很久了。我們很震驚。我們原本以為，如果有千百萬名兒童面臨死亡，而且有辦法拯救他們，那麼世界一定會把研發並提供藥物拯救他們擺在優先位置。

How could the world let these children die? The answer is simple, and harsh. The market did not reward saving the lives of these children, and governments did not [2)]**subsidize** it. So the children died because their mothers and their fathers

had no power in the market and no voice in the system. But you and I have both. If we can find approaches that meet the needs of the poor in ways that generate profits for business and votes for politicians, we will have found a [3)]**sustainable** way to reduce inequity in the world.

這個世界怎麼能讓這些孩子死去？答案很簡單，而且苛刻。在市場經濟中，拯救這些兒童是一項沒有利潤的工作，政府也不會提供補助。這些孩子之所以死亡，是因為他們的父母在市場中沒有力量，在體制中也沒有聲音。但這兩者你們和我皆有。假如我們能找出辦法滿足窮人所需，還能為企業產生利潤，並為政治人物帶來選票，那麼我們就等於找到了一種永續方式，可以減少世界上的不平等現象。

Cutting Through Complexity
化繁為簡

All of us here in this 🄻🄶 Yard, at one time or another, have seen human tragedies that broke our hearts, and yet we did nothing—not because we didn't care, but because we didn't know what to do. If we had known how to help, we would have acted. The barrier to change is not too little caring; it is too much [4)]**complexity**.

在哈佛園的我們，都曾經看過令人心痛的人間悲劇，但我們卻袖手旁觀——不是因為我們不關心，而是因為我們不知道該怎麼做。假如我們知道該怎麼幫忙，我們一定會行動。改變世界的阻礙不是因為關懷太少，而是情況過於複雜。

[5)]**Cutting through** complexity to find a solution runs through four predictable stages: determine a goal, find the highest [6)]**leverage** approach, discover the ideal technology for that approach, and in the meantime, make the smartest application of the technology that you already have—whether it's something [7)]**sophisticated**, like a drug, or something simpler, like a bed net.

> " Flipping burgers is not beneath your dignity. Your Grandparents had a different word for burger flipping — they called it opportunity.
>
> 在速食店煎漢堡不會降低你的尊嚴。你的祖父母對相同的工作有不同的稱呼——他們說那是機會。

比爾蓋茲談工作

VOCABULARY 🄻🄶

1) **priority** [praɪˋɔrəti] (n.) 優先（事項），重點，目標
Providing good service to customers is our top priority.

2) **subsidize** [ˋsʌbsəˌdaɪz] (v.) 補助
Primary education is subsidized by the government.

3) **sustainable** [səˋstenəbəl] (a.) 永續的，能維持的
The UN is working to promote sustainable agriculture.

4) **complexity** [kəmˋplɛksəti] (n.) 複雜
Many complain about the complexity of modern life.

5) **cut through** [kʌt θru] (phr.) 穿過，克服
We need to cut through the red tape and find a solution.

6) **leverage** [ˋlɛvərɪdʒ] (n.) 槓桿作用，力量，影響力
Ron's value to the company gave him leverage to ask for a raise.

© Thomas Hawk

want to inspire people to participate, you have to show more than numbers; you have to convey the human impact of the work—so people can feel what saving a life means to the families affected.

最後一個步驟——在看到問題並找出辦法後——就是衡量你的成果所帶來的影響，並分享你的成功和失敗之處，讓其他人從你的努力成果中學習。不過，假如你想激勵其他人參與，你要展現出的就不只是數字；你必須傳遞這份工作對人的影響——這樣大家才能感受到，原來拯救一條生命，是可以影響到整個家庭。

And how you do that is a complex question. Still, I'm optimistic. Yes, inequity has been with us forever, but the new tools we have to cut through complexity have not been with us forever. The defining and [8]**ongoing** [9]**innovations** of this age—[10]**biotechnology**, the computer, the Internet—give us a chance we've never had before to end extreme poverty and end death from preventable disease.

要怎麼做到這點也是一個複雜的問題。不過，我還是很樂觀的。是的，不平等現象永遠都存在，但是我們用來化繁為簡的新辦法卻是近年才有的。這個時代持續不斷的重大創新發展——比如生物科技、電腦、網路——賦予我們前所未有的機會，讓我們可以終止貧困和防止可預防疾病帶來的死亡。

化繁為簡以找出解決辦法，要經過四個既定步驟：確定目標，尋找槓桿效應最高的辦法，並為此辦法找出理想的技術，同時也以你手邊現成的技術做最聰明的應用——不論是高階的東西，像是藥物；或是更簡單的東西，比如蚊帳。

The final step—after seeing the problem and finding an approach—is to measure the impact of your work and share your successes and failures so that others learn from your efforts. But if you

---

7) **sophisticated** [sə`fɪstɪˌ ketɪd] (a.) 精密的，高度發展的
The company manufactures sophisticated scientific instruments.

8) **ongoing** [`ɑnˌɡoɪŋ] (a.) 持續不斷的
Many have lost their jobs in the ongoing financial crisis.

9) **innovation** [ˌɪnəˋveʃən] (n.) 創新
Innovation is the key to success in the global economy.

10) **biotechnology** [ˌbaɪotɛkˋnɑlədʒi] (n.) 生物科技
The investor made millions in biotechnology stocks.

© John Wollwerth / Shutterstock.com
以科技解決缺水地區的問題，是蓋茲基金會的志業之一

The [1]**emergence** of low-cost personal computers [2]**gave rise** to a powerful network that has transformed opportunities for learning and communicating. It also dramatically increases the number of brilliant minds we can have working together on the same problem—and that [3]**scales up** the rate of innovation to a [4]**staggering** degree.

低價的個人電腦出現後，威力強大的網路隨之興起，學習和溝通的機會也跟著轉變。優秀人才也隨之大幅增加，因此能夠一起合作，解決共同的問題——這能將創新發展的速度提高到驚人的程度。

Members of the Harvard family, here in the Yard is one of the great collections of intellectual talent in the world. When you consider what those of us here in this Yard have been given—in talent, privilege, and opportunity—there is almost no limit to what the world has a right to expect from us.

哈佛園的哈佛家族成員們，是全世界最傑出的一群菁英。只要你們想一下，身在哈佛園的我們都獲得了什麼——才華、特權和機會——那麼這世界也就有權利對我們抱有最大的期待。

Take on the Big Inequities
挑戰不平等現象的大問題

In line with the promise of this age, I want to [5]**exhort** each of the graduates here to take on an [6]**issue**—a complex problem, a deep inequity, and become a [7]**specialist** on it. If you make it the focus of your career, that would be [8]**phenomenal**. But you don't have to do that to make an impact. For a few hours every week, you can use the growing power of the Internet to get informed, find others with the same interests, see the barriers, and find ways to cut through them. Don't let complexity stop you. Be [9]**activists**. Take on the big inequities. It will be one of the great experiences of your lives!

在這個前景光明的年代，我想敦促在座每一位畢業生，找一個議題來努力——一個複雜的問題，一個嚴重的不平等問題，然後成為解決這個問題的專家。假如你能把這個問題當成你職業生涯的重點，那就太棒了。但你不必這麼做才能有貢獻。你可以每星期花幾個小時，利用日益強大的網路取得訊息，尋找志同道合的人，找出並設法克服阻礙。不要因為問題複雜而卻步。積極行動，挑戰不平等現象的大問題。這將成為你人生中最重要的經歷之一。

VOCABULARY 🎧54

1) **emergence** [ɪˋmɝdʒəns] (n.) 出現，浮現
The professor gave a lecture on the emergence of the middle class.

2) **give rise (to)** [gɪv raɪs] (phr.) 引起，產生，導致
Some believe that human activity gave rise to global warming.

3) **scale up** [skel ʌp] (phr.) 擴大，相應增加
The company scaled up production to meet growing demand.

4) **staggering** [ˋstægərɪŋ] (a.) 驚人的，難以置信的
The army suffered a staggering defeat.

5) **exhort** [ɪgˋzɔrt] (v.) 力勸，激勵，敦促
The teacher exhorted his students to study hard for the exam.

6) **issue** [ˋɪʃju] (n.) 問題，爭議
What are the biggest issues facing our country today?

7) **specialist** [ˋspɛʃəlɪst] (n.) 專家
The company hired a network specialist to set up its computer network.

8) **phenomenal** [fəˋnɑmənəl] (a.) 傑出的，極好的，驚人的
The movie was a phenomenal success.

9) **activist** [ˋæktəvɪst] (n.) 行動主義者，社運人士
Dozens of human rights activists were arrested at the demonstration.

Microsoft 微軟公司

微軟公司是由 Bill Gates 及 Paul Allen 在一九七五年成立於美國新墨西哥州的阿布奎基市（Albuquerque, New Mexico）。Bill 和 Paul 早在大學頂校 Lakeside School（一所位於西雅圖 Haller Lake 附近的私校，據估計每年有四分之一畢業生進入長春藤盟校，百分之九十九的畢業生都能進入大學）就是同學，兩人當年就已開始用校內分時共享的電腦（time-shared computer）設計井字遊戲軟體。

© enzodebernardo / Shutterstock.com

Microsoft 成立之初，在一九七九年設計推出 MS-DOS 作業系統，是一系列 DOS 作業系統中最常被運用的一支，是八〇及九〇年代個人家用電腦（personal computer）最主要使用的作業系統。其後又推出 Windows 作業系統、商務套裝軟體 Office 以及網路瀏覽器 Internet Explorer，並買下 Skype。硬體方面，Microsoft 擁有 XBOX 遊戲機及 Surface 平板電腦，買下 Nokia 之後，也開始進軍行動電話市場。據估計，Microsoft 是目前全球總收入最高的軟體公司。

© tanuha2001 / Shutterstock.com

© manaemedia / Shutterstock.com

© rvlsoft / Shutterstock.com

© julie deshaies / Shutterstock.com

© charnsitr / Shutterstock.com

© charnsitr / Shutterstock.com

認識 Bill & Melinda Gates Foundation 蓋茲基金會

簡稱 B&MGF 或 Gates Foundation，是全球最大的財務公開私人基金，由科技富豪比爾蓋茲及妻子梅琳達蓋茲於兩千年創立。蓋茲基金會旨在全球普及醫療照顧（healthcare）、減少赤貧（extreme poverty），也在美國廣泛提供教育機會、幫助更多人有能力使用資訊科技。

巴菲特（Warren Buffett）於二〇〇六年捐出一千萬股波克夏 B 股（Berkshire Hathaway Class B stock）給蓋茲基金會時，設下三個條件：第一，比爾蓋茲或梅琳達蓋茲至少一人還在世，並實際參與會務；第二，這個基金會必須持續符合慈善機構的資格；第三，基金會每年必須將前一年波克夏 B 股持股獲利加上 5% 的淨資產捐出。

Harvard Yard 哈佛園

哈佛校園中最古老的區域，為大約二十二英畝的寬廣綠地，四周環繞圍籬，開有二十七道門，畢業典禮以及許多學生活動皆在此舉行。哈佛園中有許多該校代表建築，包括大部份的新生宿舍、總圖懷德納圖書館（Widener Library）、紀念教堂（Memorial Church），以及哈佛校園中最古老的建築 —— 麻薩諸塞樓（Massachusetts Hall）。

Harvard Yard 大門

就算是比爾蓋茲也要謙虛：避免每句話都用 I 當主詞開頭 ——用句子當主詞

用句子當主詞的意思是，以 wh-、if、whether、that 引導句子，使其變為名詞子句，讓這句話能在一個敘述長句裡當主詞用，讓敘述聽起來富有情境，又不至於太囉唆。名詞子句的常見用法如下：

● 名詞子句當主詞

例 **That Ben skipped class shocked his parents.**（主詞是子句，shocked 才是這句真正的動詞）

● 名詞子句當主詞補語

例 **Judy's mistake was that she skipped class.**（子句放在 was 之後，說明 mistake）

● 名詞子句當動詞的受詞

例 **I don't know how Jason was able to go to work when he was so sick.**（子句接在動詞 know 之後當受詞）

● 名詞子句當介系詞的受詞

例 **Rick didn't listen to what Mary said.**（子句也可以當介系詞 to 的受詞）

● 名詞子句當同位語

例 **George's problem, what career path he should follow, was hard to solve.**

Widener Library
© Will Hart

Memorial Church

微軟創辦人 Bill Gates 於二〇〇七年接受哈佛大學頒發榮譽法學博士，並發表畢業演說。這位「哈佛史上最成功中輟生」早年以強悍的經營風格聞名於世，隨著微軟公司的成功，他多年蟬聯世界首富，也讓跟他畫上等號的微軟飽受批評，更在一九九八年面臨反托拉斯訴訟。

Bill Gates 全心投身公益之後，不只是捐大錢，還積極投入各項濟貧計劃，扭轉了他在世人心中的評價。無論他「君子愛財」是否「取之有道」，但他「用之有道」已無庸置疑。

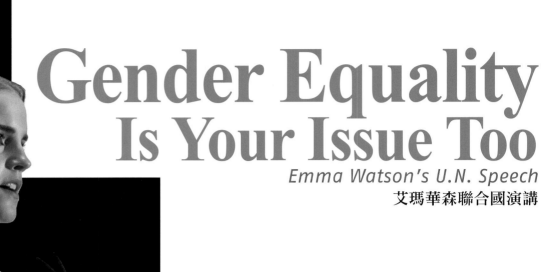

Gender Equality Is Your Issue Too

Emma Watson's U.N. Speech

艾瑪華森聯合國演講

© UN Women/Simon Luethi

We Need Your Help
我們需要你們的幫忙

Today we are launching a campaign called **LG** HeForShe. I am reaching out to you because we need your help. We want to end [1]**gender** [2]**inequality**, and to do this, we need everyone involved. This is the first campaign of its kind at the U.N. We want to try and [3]**galvanize** as many men and boys as possible to be [4]**advocates** for change. And we don't just want to talk about it. We want to try and make sure that it's [5]**tangible**.

我們正在推出一項「HeForShe」活動。我之所以向各位介紹這個活動，是因為我需要你們的幫忙。我們想終止兩性不平等的現象，為了做到這點，我們需要每一個人參與。這是聯合國有史以來第一次推行這樣的活動。我們希望能盡量激發更多男性加入，包括男人和男孩，一起宣導改變這個現象。我們不只是說說而已，我們要試著去做，並務必落實這項活動。

I was appointed as **LG** Goodwill Ambassador for U.N. Women six months ago. And the more I've spoken about [6]**feminism**, the more I have realized that fighting for women's rights has too often become [7]**synonymous** with man-hating. If there is one thing I know for certain, it is that this has to stop.

我半年前獲命擔任聯合國婦女署親善大使。我談論女性主義越多次，就越發現女權運動往往就變成憎恨男性的代名詞，但這種誤解必須停止，這一點我是非常肯定的。

Equal Rights and Opportunities
平等的權利和機會

For the record, feminism, by definition, is the belief that men and women should have equal rights and opportunities. It is the theory of the political, economic and social equality of the sexes.

VOCABULARY 56

1) **gender** [ˋdʒɛndɚ] (n.) 性別
I'm thinking of taking a gender studies class.

2) **inequality** [ˌɪnɪˋkwɑlətɪ] (n.) 不平等，不均等
There is still great inequality between men and women in many countries.

3) **galvanize** [ˋgælvəˌnaɪz] (v.) 激勵，刺激，激起
The group hopes to galvanize public opinion agaist the law.

4) **advocate** [ˋædvəkɪt] (n.) 提倡者，擁護者
The new media law has been criticized by free speech advocates.

5) **tangible** [ˋtændʒəbəl] (a.) 明確的，實際的，具體的
The construction project brought tangible economic benefits to the town.

6) **feminism** [ˋfɛməˌnɪzəm] (n.) 女性主義，女權運動
The second wave of feminism began in the 1960s.

我在此聲明，女性主義，根據定義，就是認為男性和女性應享有平等的權利和機會。這是兩性在政治、經濟和社會上平等的理論。

I started questioning gender-based [8]**assumptions** a long time ago. When I was 8, I was confused at being called [9]**bossy** because I wanted to direct the plays that we would put on for our parents, but the boys were not. When at 14, I started to be [10]**sexualized** by certain elements of the media. When at 15, my girlfriends started dropping out of sports teams because they didn't want to appear [11]**muscly**. When at 18, my male friends were unable to express their feelings.

我很久以前就已經開始質疑建立在性別上的成見。我八歲時，因為想要主導一齣在家長面前表演的舞台劇而被大家形容為「跋扈」，但假如換做是男孩子就不會被說成跋扈，這點令我感到困惑。我十四歲時，開始被某些媒體情色化。十五歲時，我的女性朋友們因為不想看起來太男性化而退出球隊。十八歲時，我的男性朋友們無法表達自己的情緒。

I decided that I was a feminist, and this seemed uncomplicated to me. But my recent research has shown me that feminism has become an unpopular word. Women are choosing not to identify as feminists. Apparently, I'm among the ranks of women whose expressions are seen as too strong, too aggressive, isolating, and anti-men—unattractive, even.

於是我決定成為一名女性主義者，這對我來說並不難理解。但我最近研究發現，女性主義這個詞越來越不受歡迎。女性開始避免標榜自己是女性主義者。看來，我已經被列為表現太強勢、太激進、孤傲、反男人，甚至沒有魅力的女性族群。

> ❝ I threw my 20th birthday party at Brown, and I didn't even have to say to anyone not to put pictures on Facebook. Not a single picture went up. That was when I knew I'd found a solid group of friends, and I felt like I belonged.

我的二十歲派對是在布朗大學舉辦，而我甚至不必跟任何人說請勿把照片放上臉書。連一張照片都沒上傳。我那時候就知道我已經找到一群真正的朋友，讓我很有歸屬感。

艾瑪華森談朋友

Emma Watson
艾瑪華森

© UN Women/Celeste Sloman

一九九〇年生於巴黎，五歲回到英國。艾瑪華森因《哈利波特》系列電影成名，由童星演到成年，在各部片中的演技都頗受肯定。

儘管十歲起就成為世界級明星，艾瑪仍非常重視自己的課業，二〇一四年自名校布朗大學畢業，取得英國文學學士學位。大學畢業後，艾瑪華森隨即獲任命為聯合國婦女權能署（UN Women）親善大使。

Emma Watson

---

7) **synonymous** [sɪˋnɑnəməs] (a.) 同義詞的
Picasso's name is synonymous with modern art.

8) **assumption** [əˋsʌmpʃən] (n.) 假設，假定
Your argument is based on false assumptions.

9) **bossy** [ˋbɑsɪ] (a.) 霸道的，跋扈的
Karen is so bossy—she's always telling people what to do.

10) **sexualize** [ˋsɛʃʊəˏlaɪz] (v.) 情色化，性感化
It's wrong to sexualize children.

11) **muscly** [ˋmʌslɪ] (a.) 有肌肉的
Kathy likes muscly guys.

Why has the word become such an uncomfortable one? I am from Britain, and I think it is right that I am paid the same as my male [1]**counterparts**. I think it is right that I should be able to make decisions about my own body. I think it is right that women be involved on my behalf in the policies and the decisions that will affect my life.

為什麼這個詞變得這麼令人感到不舒服？我來自英國，我認為女人的薪資與男性同事要同工同酬才是對的。我認為女人擁有自己身體的自主權才是對的。我認為女人有權參與會影響到自己人生的政策和決策才是對的。

But sadly, I can say that there is no one country in the world where all women can expect to receive these rights. GM No country in the world can yet say that they have achieved gender equality. These rights, I consider to be human rights, but I am one of the lucky ones.

> 66 I remember reading this thing that Elizabeth Taylor wrote. She had her first kiss in character, on a movie set. It really struck me. I don't know how or why, but I had this sense that if I wasn't really careful, that could be me: that my first kiss could be in somebody else's clothes, and my experiences could all belong to someone else.
>
> 我記得曾經讀到伊麗莎白泰勒寫的東西。她在演戲時獻出初吻，是電影的一景。這讓我很震撼。我不知道為什麼，但我感覺到如果不好好注意，我也會那樣：我會穿著扮演某人的戲服獻出初吻，我的經驗會全都屬於別人。
>
> 艾瑪華森談初吻

但悲哀的是，我可以說這世上沒有一個國家可以讓所有女性指望得到這些權利。這世上沒有一個國家敢說他們已經實現了兩性平等。我認為這些權利等同於人權。不過，我算是幸運的。

My life is a [2]**sheer** privilege because my parents didn't love me less because I was born a daughter. My school did not limit me because I was a girl. My [3]**mentors** didn't assume that I would go less far because I might give birth to a child one day. They may not know it, but they are the [4]**inadvertent** feminists who are changing the world today. We need more of those.

我的人生完全就像是享有特權，因為我的父母並不會因為我是女兒而少愛我一點。我的學校不會因為我是女孩而限制我的發展。我的導師們不會因為我可能有一天會生兒育女而對我少有期待。他們自己可能不知道，但已經無意中成為女性主義者，而且正在改變現在的世界。我們需要更多像這樣的人。

In 1997, LG Hillary Clinton made a famous speech in Beijing about women's rights. Sadly, many of the things that she wanted to change are still true today. But what [5]**stood out** for me the most was that less than thirty percent of the audience were male. How can we effect change in the world when only half of it is invited or feel welcome to participate in the conversation?

一九九七年，希拉蕊在北京發表一場關於女性權益的知名演說。可悲的是，她當時想改變的事情，現在有許多依然存在。但其中最引起我注意的，是觀眾當中的男性比例不到三成。當這個世界只有一半的人受邀或欣然參與這場對話，我們要怎麼去實現這個改變？

A Formal Invitation
正式邀請

Men, I would like to take this opportunity to extend your formal

VOCABULARY 58

1) **counterpart** [ˈkaʊntɚ‚pɑrt] (n.) 極相似的人（物），相配對之人事物
The U.S. president is the counterpart of the U.K prime minister.

2) **sheer** [ʃɪr] (a.) 全然的，純粹的
Listening to Katie sing karaoke was sheer torture.

3) **mentor** [ˈmɛntɚ] (n.) 精神導師，良師益友
You should find a mentor to advise you on your career.

4) **inadvertent** [‚ɪnədˈvɝtənt] (a.) 無意的，偶然的，碰巧的
We had an inadvertent encounter with a bear while hiking.

consequence. If men don't have to be aggressive in order to be accepted, women won't feel [9]**compelled** to be [10]**submissive**. If men don't have to control, women won't have to be controlled.

我們往往不會談論關於男性也受到性別刻板印象的禁錮，但我認為，只要他們能擺脫這樣的束縛，關於女性的一切自然而然也會隨之改變。假如男人不一定要大男人才能獲得認同，女人也就不用逆來順受。假如男人不一定要掌控全局，女人也就不用受到控制。

invitation. Gender equality is your issue too. Because to date, I've seen my father's role as a parent being valued less by society, despite my need of his presence as a child, as much as my mother's. I've seen young men suffering from mental illness, unable to ask for help for fear it would make them less of a man. I've seen men made [6]**fragile** and insecure by a [7]**distorted** sense of what constitutes male success. Men don't have the benefits of equality either.

男性們，我想藉這個機會正式邀請你們。兩性平等也是屬於你們的議題。因為至今為止，我發現父親的親職角色，在這個社會已經越來越不受重視，儘管我在孩提時代對父親的需要並不亞於母親。我看到年輕男性因為精神疾病而受苦，卻無法求助，因為害怕求助會讓自己看起來沒有男子氣概。我也看到男性因為曲解了成功男人的定義而變得脆弱、沒有安全感。男人也同樣沒有獲得兩性平等。

We don't often talk about men being imprisoned by gender [8]**stereotypes**, but I can see that they are, and that when they are free, things will change for women as a natural

5) **stand out** [stænd aut] (phr.) 突出，顯著
Wearing green makes your eyes stand out.

6) **fragile** [ˋfrædʒəl] (a.) 脆弱的，虛弱的
Be careful with that glass bowl—it's very fragile.

7) **distorted** [dɪˋstɔrtɪd] (a.) 曲解的，扭曲的
The textbook presents a distorted view of the nation's history.

8) **stereotype** [ˋstɛrɪəˌtaɪp] (n.) 刻板印象
Matthew doesn't fit the stereotype of a typical American.

9) **compel** [kəmˋpɛl] (v.) 強迫，使不得不
The court compelled the man to appear as a witness.

10) **submissive** [sʌbˋmɪsɪv] (a.) 服從的，柔順的
It's hard for men to find submissive wives these days.

It's about Freedom
與自由息息相關

If we stop defining each other by what we are not, and start defining ourselves by who we are, we can all be freer, and this is what HeForShe is about. It's about freedom.

假如我們停止互相貼標籤，開始認同真實的自己，我們就可以活得更加自由，這就是「HeForShe」的目的，自由。

I want men to 🔵take up this mantle so that their daughters, sisters and mothers can be free from [1)]**prejudice**, but also so that their sons have permission to be [2)]**vulnerable** and human too, reclaim those parts of themselves they abandoned, and in doing so, be a more true and complete version of themselves.

我希望男性可以接下這個衣缽，這樣不但能讓他們的女兒、姊妹和母親都能免受歧視，也能讓他們的兒子表現脆弱的一面，做一個真正的人，找回被自己拋棄的部分，如此一來，他們也能活得更真實，做個更完整的自己。

You might be thinking, "Who is this Harry Potter girl, and what is she doing speaking at the U.N.?" And it's a really good question. I've been asking myself the same thing.

你可能會想：「這個曾經演過《哈利波特》的女孩是誰？她怎麼會在聯合國大會上演講？」這真是個好問題，我也一直在問自己同樣的問題。

All I know is that I care about this problem, and I want to make it better. And having seen what I've seen, and given the chance, I feel it is my responsibility to say something.

我只知道我很關心這個問題，而我希望能有所改善。當我看盡世間百態後，又有機會來到這裡，我覺得我有責任說點什麼。

Statesman 🔵Edmund Burke said, "All that is needed for the forces of evil to triumph is for good men and women to do nothing."

政治家埃德蒙伯克曾說：「想要讓邪惡的力量戰勝一切，只要讓善良的男女什麼都不做就行了。」

If you believe in equality, you might be one of those inadvertent feminists that I spoke of earlier, and for this, I applaud you. We are struggling for a uniting world, but the good news is, that we have a uniting movement. It is called HeForShe. I am inviting you to step forward, to be seen and to ask yourself, "If not me, who? If not now, when?"

假如你相信平權，你可能就是我剛剛說的，已經在無意中成為了女權主義者，對此我為你感到驕傲。為了讓世界團結起來，我們一直辛苦奮戰著，不過有個好消息是，我們發起了一個團結運動，名稱是「HeForShe」。我現在邀請你們向前一步，挺身而出並自問：「我不做，誰會來做？不現在開始，還要等到什麼時候？」

© FOKUS_kvinner

VOCABULARY 🎧 60

1) **prejudice** [ˈprɛdʒədɪs] (n.) 偏見，損害
   We must continue to fight against racial prejudice.

2) **vulnerable** [ˈvʌlnərəbəl] (a.) 易受傷害的
   Your eyes are one of the most vulnerable parts of your body.

HeForShe 兩性平權運動

HeForShe 是 U.N. Women 為提倡性別平權所發起的社會運動，在過去，「性別平權運動」被視作女人為女人爭權，HeForShe 主張性別平權不是半數人口的問題，而是全體人類的問題，希望透過引導男性加入思考性別問題，達成共同保障婦女權益、追求性別自由的目標。

© www.hillaryclinton.com

U.N. Goodwill Ambassador 聯合國親善大使

親善大使是對等機構間（如國對國、城市對城市）派出的代表，以交換贈禮或是提供人道救援為目的出訪，經常由知名人士擔任，如莎莉賽隆（Charlize Theron）擔任聯合國和平大使（U.N. Messenger of Peace）、維多利亞貝克漢（Victoria Beckham）擔任聯合國愛滋防治大使（UNAIDS Goodwill Ambassador）等。

© Everett Collection / Shutterstock.com

© United Nations Photo

Hillary's Speech at Fourth U.N. Conference on Women 希拉蕊於第四次聯合國婦女大會演講

一九九五年（艾瑪華森演講口誤為一九九七年），希拉蕊以美國第一夫人身份出席第四次聯合國婦女大會（Fourth U.N. Conference on Women），在北京發表了一篇重要演講，其中最令人印象深刻的一句話為：Human rights are women's rights and women's rights are human rights once and for all.（人權終究就是婦權，婦權終究就是人權。）

take up the mantle 繼承某人的衣缽

mantle 有「披風，斗篷」的意思，引申為象徵權力的「衣缽」，take up / assume / accept / take on the mantle 都是「繼承衣缽」，若要強調是「什麼的衣缽」，可以在後面加上 of sth.。

A: Why aren't you voting for that candidate?
你為什麼不投票給那個候選人？
B: I don't think he's ready to take up the mantle of leadership.
我不覺得他已經準備好要接掌領導大任。

Edmund Burke 艾德蒙伯克

艾德蒙伯克是十八世紀的愛爾蘭政治家、作家和政治理論家，於一七六五年進入英國國會。他最主要的主張包括反對英王無限制擴權、同情並支持美國殖民地，影響了英國退出美洲，轉向印度等其他地區發展，走上大國之路。

對於法國大革命，伯克則採取批判的態度，反對破除所有制度與文明的激烈革命，主張社會安定大於一切，改革就算有必要，也須漸進推行，被視為「保守主義」健將。

Grammar Master

No country in the world can yet say...
用雙重否定句，加強語氣

雙重否定句通常是為了要加強語氣與美化句子，讓句子看起來較有變化、靈活。

● 雙重否定句中一定同時有兩個「否定詞」

解 最常見的否定詞有 no、not、never 等，也可以是帶有否定意味的單字 seldom（難得）、yet（還沒）、little（少許）、hardly（幾乎不）等。

例 They **don't** call economics "the dismal science" for **nothing.**

例 Henry **never** leaves home **without** his cell phone.

例 There **isn't** a day that goes by that I **don't** think of you.

例 I **can't hardly** read your handwriting.

這篇演說是艾瑪華森於二○一四年接任 U.N. Women 親善大使兩個月後，在聯合國紐約總部發表的演說，為新發起的 HeForShe 運動揭開序幕。

儘管艾瑪華森已經是世界巨星，也有無數公開受訪經驗，但可以看出她在發表公開演說時，還是非常緊張。儘管聲音顫抖，肢體僵硬，但她以自身成長經驗撰寫出一篇真摯動人的講稿，仍讓她獲得全場起立鼓掌。

Ellen Comes Out

Ellen Page's Time to THRIVE Speech
艾倫佩姬「發光發熱」座談會演講

© s_bukley / Shutterstock.com

Thank you, Chad, for those kind words and for the even kinder work that you and the **LG** Human Rights Campaign foundation do every day—especially on behalf of the **LG** lesbian, gay, bisexual and transgender young people here and across America.

謝謝查德主席，感謝您的美言，更感謝您和人權戰線組織每日的善舉，尤其是為了在座和全美各地的女同性戀、男同性戀、雙性戀和跨性別者的年輕人。

Deep Admiration
深感佩服

It's such an honor to be here at the [1]**inaugural** **LG** Time to THRIVE conference. But it's a little [2]**weird**, too. Here I am, in this room because of an organization whose work I deeply admire. And I'm surrounded by people who make it their life's work to make other people's lives better—[3]**profoundly** better. Some of you teach young people—people like me. Some of you **GM** help young people heal and to find their voice. Some of you listen. Some of you take action. Some of you are young people yourselves—in which case, it's even weirder for a person like me to be speaking to you.

很榮幸參加「發光發熱」座談會的開幕致詞。不過也是有點奇怪。我之所以來到這裡，是因為我對組織所做的工作深感佩服。在座的各位將這份工作視為終生志業，讓其他人過更好的生活——而且是大幅度的改善。在座之中有些人擔任教導年輕人的工作——就像我一樣的年輕人。有些則幫助年輕人療癒，尋找自己的聲音。有些人傾聽，有些人採取實際行動。還有些人自己本身就是年輕人，所以在這樣的情況下，由像我這樣的人來發表演說更是奇怪了。

VOCABULARY 62

1) **inaugural** [ɪnˋɔgjərəl] (a.) 首屆的，開幕的，就任的
The president will give his inaugural address tomorrow.

2) **weird** [wɪrd] (a.) 奇怪的，怪異的
Michael has weird taste in music.

3) **profoundly** [prəˋfaʊndli] (adv.) 極度地，深切地
We're profoundly grateful for all your help.

4) **crushing** [ˋkrʌʃɪŋ] (a.) 嚴厲的，壓倒的
The death of their son was a crushing blow.

5) **push back** [pʊʃ bæk] (phr.) 抵抗，反擊
Home owners are pushing back against plans to raise property taxes.

6) **authentic** [ɔˋθɛntɪk] (a.) 真實的，真正的，道地的
That restaurant serves authentic Cantonese food.

Crushing Standards
嚴苛的標準

It's weird because here I am, an actress, representing—at least in some sense—an industry that places [4]**crushing** standards on all of us. Not just young people, but everyone: standards of beauty, of a good life, of success. Standards that, I hate to admit, have affected me. You have ideas planted in your head, thoughts you never had before, that tell you how you have to act, how you have to dress and who you have to be. I have been trying to [5]**push back**, to be [6]**authentic**, to follow my heart, but it can be hard.

之所以奇怪，是因為身為演員的我來到這裡，代表著某個行業——至少在某種程度上——而這個行業卻在我們所有人身上建立嚴苛的標準。不只是年輕人，而是在每一個人身上：美麗的標準、美好生活的標準、成功的標準。我真不想承認，但這些標準已經影響到我。你的腦海中已植入了既定的觀念，是自己從未有過的想法，都在告訴你該怎麼行為處事、該怎麼穿著、該成為什麼樣的人。我試著把這些想法都擋回去，試著真心追隨自己的心，但很難。

But that's why I'm here. In this room, all of you, all of us, can do so much more together than any one person can do alone. And I hope that thought [7]**bolsters** you as much as it does me. I hope the [8]**workshops** you'll go to over the next few days give you strength. Because I can only imagine that there are days when you've worked longer hours than your boss realizes or cares about, just to help a kid you know can make it; days where you feel completely alone, [9]**undermined** or hopeless.

不過這也是我出現在這裡的原因。在這場座談會上，你們所有人，我們所有人，只要團結一致，絕對比孤軍奮戰能有更大的作為。希望這樣的想法能支撐你們走下去，就像它一直支撐著我一樣。我希望接下來幾天的研討會也都能帶給你們力量，因為我可以想像，有些時候你們願意長時間加班，時間長到超乎你們老闆所能理解或關心的，只為了幫助那些你們相信有能力走出陰影的年輕人；也有些時候你們會感到徹底孤獨、受到打擊或絕望。

Ellen Page
艾倫佩姬

© s_bukley / Shutterstock.com

一九八七年出生於加拿大，二〇〇七年以喜劇《鴻孕當頭》 Juno 成名，並獲奧斯卡最佳女主角提名。她在劇中飾演意外懷孕後獨排眾議，決定生下孩子交給他人撫養的少女，引發廣大迴響，Ellen 因此成為女性對人生有自由選擇權的象徵，二〇〇八年獲《時代雜誌》提名百大最具影響力人物。

Ellen Page 所主演《鴻孕當頭》海報
© 2007, Fox Searchlight Pictures

---

7) **bolster** [ˋbolstɚ] (v.) 支持，提高，加強
The player's win bolstered his confidence.

8) **workshop** [ˋwɝkˏʃɑp] (n.) 研討會，工作室
I'm going to a drama workshop on Saturday.

9) **undermine** [ˏʌndɚˋmaɪn] (v.) （暗中）打擊
All the criticism undermined his confidence.

Worrying about the Future
擔心未來

I know there are people in this room who go to school every day and get 🅻🅶 treated like shit for no reason. Or you go home and you feel like you can't tell your parents the whole truth about yourself. Beyond putting yourself in one box or another, you worry about the future—about college or work or even your physical safety. Trying to create that mental picture of your life—of what on earth is going to happen to you—can crush you a little bit every day. It is [1]**toxic** and painful and deeply unfair.

我知道在座有人每天在學校無緣無故遭到唾棄，或是回到家也不敢向父母坦言自己的一切。除了把自己塞進各種不同的框框裡，還要擔心未來——關於升大學、就職，或甚至人身安全。試著描繪一下你們的人生——未來到底會怎樣——每天光是這樣想就能讓你一點一滴崩潰。不但有害，而且痛苦，也十分不公平。

Sometimes it's the little, [2]**insignificant** stuff that can 🅻🅶 tear you down. I try not to read gossip as a rule, but the other day a website ran an article with a picture of me wearing sweatpants on the way to the gym. The writer asked, "Why does this

> 66
> I don't care if people like my character. I just want them to think about the movie's message.
>
> 我不在乎大家喜不喜歡我的角色。我只希望他們能思考電影要傳達的訊息。
>
> 艾倫佩姬談電影

[3]**petite** beauty insist upon dressing like a [4]**massive** man?" Because I like to be comfortable. There are [5]**pervasive** stereotypes about [6]**masculinity** and femininity that define how we are all supposed to act, dress and speak. They serve no one. Anyone who [7]**defies** these [8]**so-called** [9]**norms** becomes [10]**worthy** of comment and [11]**scrutiny**. The LGBT community knows this [12]**all too** well.

有時候會把你擊垮的都是些微不足道的小事。我基本上不看八卦新聞，但有天我看到網站上有一篇文章，上面附有我的照片，照片中的我穿著運動褲，正在往健身房的路上。文章作者問道：「為什麼這位嬌小的美女偏要穿得像個彪形大漢？」因為我只是想穿得舒服一點。用來界定男人和女人該怎麼行事、怎麼穿和怎麼說話的刻板印象是無所不在的。但這些對任何人都沒有好處。只要有人違反這些規範，就會有人理所當然地拿來批評和檢視。LGBT 族群都太瞭解這點了。

Courage All around Us
勇氣可嘉

Yet there is courage all around us: the football hero Michael Sam; the actress Laverne Cox; the musicians Tegan and Sara Quinn; the family that supports their daughter or son who has come out. And there is courage in this room—all of you. I'm inspired to be in this room because every single one of you is here for the same reason.

不過，勇氣可嘉的例子依然隨處可見：美式足球英雄麥可山姆、女演員拉佛恩考克斯、樂手泰根和莎拉奎恩，以及那些支持自己兒女出櫃的家庭，還有在座的你們也都是勇氣可嘉。我之所以在這裡受到鼓舞，是因為你們每一個人也都出於同樣理由來到這裡。

You're here because you've adopted as a [13]**core** motivation the simple fact that this world would be a whole lot better if we just made an effort to be less horrible to one another. If we took just five minutes to recognize each other's beauty, instead of attacking each other for our differences. That's

VOCABULARY 🎧64

1) **toxic** [ˈtɑksɪk] (a.) 有毒的，有害的
The company was fined for dumping toxic chemicals in the river.

2) **insignificant** [ˌɪnsɪɡˈnɪfɪkənt] (a.) 無足輕重的，無意義的
You shouldn't worry about insignificant details.

3) **petite** [pəˈtit] (a.) 嬌小的
Greg is attracted to petite women.

4) **massive** [ˈmæsɪv] (a.) 巨大的，龐大的
The bus was crushed by a massive boulder.

5) **pervasive** [pɚˈvesɪv] (a.) 普遍的，彌漫的
Sex and violence are pervasive in the media.

6) **masculinity** [ˌmæskjəˈlɪnəti] (n.) 男子氣概，男性特質，femininity 即「女子氣質，女性特質」
Some men see powerful women as a threat to their masculinity.

7) **defy** [dɪˈfaɪ] (v.) 違反，反抗
The court's decision seems to defy logic.

8) **so-called** [ˈsoˌkɔld] (a.) 所謂的，號稱的
His so-called friends all abandoned him.

9) **norm** [nɔrm] (n.) 常態，常規
These days, smaller families have become the norm.

Michael Sam 是 NFL（國家美式足球聯盟）首位出櫃球星。他與男友 Vito Cammisano 於二〇一五年一月訂婚
© Helga Esteb / Shutterstock.com

Laverne Cox 為變性女星，以影集《女子監獄》 Orange Is the New Black 走紅，是第一位登上《時代雜誌》封面的變性人
© FashionStock com / Shutterstock.com

Tegan and Sara 樂團的雙胞胎樂手 Tegan Quin 及 Sara Quin
© JStone / Shutterstock.com

not hard. It's really an easier and better way to live. And ultimately, it saves lives.

你們之所以來到這裡，是因為你們抱持著一個核心動機，而且道理簡單，那就是只要我們努力減少對彼此的惡意，只要我們願意花五分鐘，互相肯定對方的美好之處，而不是互相攻擊彼此的不同之處，這個世界就會變得更美好。這並不難。這樣做真的會讓人生更輕鬆、更美好。而最終，還能挽救生命。

Then again, it's not easy at all. It can be the hardest thing, because loving other people starts with loving ourselves and accepting ourselves. I know many of you have struggled with this. I [14)]**draw upon** your strength and your support, and have, in ways you will never know.

不過，這樣做也可能一點都不簡單，也可能會是最困難的一件事，因為要愛他人之前，首先要懂得愛自己、接受自己。我知道你們當中有許多人經歷過這樣的掙扎，所以我借用了你們的力量和支持，而且是許多你們意想不到的地方。

I'm here today because I am gay. And because maybe I can make a difference. To help others have an easier and more hopeful time. [15)]**Regardless**,

> " Yeah, people following me down the street and at the airport and all that. I can't imagine what it must be like for people who are, you know, actually famous.

的確，有人會沿路跟著我，在機場和其他地方也是。我真不能想像那些真的很出名的人，會碰到什麼局面。

艾倫佩姬談成名

for me, I feel a personal [16)]**obligation** and a social responsibility.

我今天之所以在這裡，是因為我是同性戀，也因為我或許可以發揮我的影響力，或許可以幫助別人過上更自在、更有希望的生活。不論如何，對我來說，我覺得我有個人義務和社會責任。

---

10) **worthy** [ˋwɚðɪ] (a.) 值得的，配得上的
Few politicians are worthy of people's trust.

11) **scrutiny** [ˋskrutənɪ] (n.) 仔細的觀察，詳細的檢查
Political funding should be open to public scrutiny.

12) **all too** [ɔl tu] (adv.) （負面）很
Our vacation ended all too quickly.

13) **core** [kor] (a./n.) 核心（的），基本（的）
Beijing has stated that the South China Sea is a core national interest.

14) **draw upon** [drɔ əˋpɑn] (phr.) 利用（自己的特質），亦作 draw on
Actors often draw upon their own life experiences.

15) **regardless** [rɪˋgɑrdlɪs] (adv.) 不管，不顧
Gary knew the milk was past its expiration date, but he drank it regardless.

16) **obligation** [ˌɑbləˋgeʃən] (n.) （道義或法律上的）義務，責任
You can try our product with no obligation to buy.

Tired of Hiding
厭倦躲躲藏藏

I also do it selfishly, because I am tired of hiding and I am tired of lying by 1)**omission**. I suffered for years because I was scared to be out. My spirit suffered, my mental health suffered and my relationships suffered. And I'm standing here today, with all of you, on the other side of all that pain. I am young, yes, but what I have learned is that love, the beauty of it, the joy of it and yes, even the pain of it, is the most incredible gift to give and to receive as a human being. And we deserve to experience love fully, equally, without shame and without 2)**compromise**.

我這麼做也是出於私心,因為我厭倦了躲躲藏藏,厭倦了迴避事實而隱瞞真相。多年來因為害怕出櫃而承受著痛苦,包括我的心靈、精神健康和人際關係也都飽受折磨。於是我今天站在這裡,與你們一起,拋開所有痛苦。是的,我還年輕,但我已經學到,是愛本身,以及伴隨著愛而來的美好、歡樂,甚至痛苦,才是人類應該互相給予和接受的最美妙禮物。我們都應該有權全心地、平等地談戀愛,無須羞愧,也不需妥協。

There are too many kids out there suffering from 3)**bullying**, rejection, or simply being 4)**mistreated** because of who they are—too many 5)**dropouts**, too much 6)**abuse**, too many homeless, too many suicides. You can change that, and you are changing it.

有太多青少年因為遭到霸凌和排擠而承受著痛苦,或只是因為他們本身的與眾不同而受到不公平對待。有太多人因此輟學、飽受凌虐、無家可歸和自殺。你們可以改變這些情況,而且你們已經開始這麼做了。

But you never needed me to tell you that. That's why this was a little bit weird. The only thing I can really say is what I've been LG building up to for the past five minutes. Thank you. Thank for inspiring me. Thank you for giving me hope, and please keep changing the world for people like me. Happy Valentine's Day. I love you.

不過,你們從來不需要我告訴你們這些,所以我一開始才說這有點奇怪。我真正能說的其實只有一句話,我過去五分鐘一直在做準備。謝謝你們。感謝你們激勵了我。謝謝你們給我希望,也請繼續為像我這樣的族群改變這個世界。情人節快樂。我愛你們。

VOCABULARY 🎧66

1) **omission** [ə`mɪʃən] (n.) 省略,遺漏
We're sorry for the omission of your name from the list.

2) **compromise** [`kɑmprə,maɪz] (n./v.) 妥協,折衷
After a long discussion, we finally reached a compromise.

3) **bullying** [`bulɪɪŋ] (n.) 霸凌
Students should report bullying to school officials.

4) **mistreat** [mɪs`trit] (v.) 虐待
The suspect claims that he was mistreated by the police.

5) **dropout** [`drɑp,aʊt] (n.) 中輟生
Bill Gates is a college dropout.

6) **abuse** [ə`bjus] (n./v.) 虐待,濫用
The parents were accused of child abuse.

© a katz / Shutterstock.com

Human Rights Campaign 人權戰線

人權組織「人權戰線」（Human Rights Campaign，HRC）成立於一九八〇年，倡導 LGBT（女同性戀、男同性戀、雙性戀、跨性別）平權（其標誌就是一個等號），是美國最大的多元性別人權團體。

LGBT 多元性別

LGBT（或 GLBT）是由女同性戀者（lesbian）、男同性戀者（gay）、雙性戀者（bisexual）、跨性別者（transgender）這四個字的第一個字母組成。其他常見的相關縮寫為 LGBTQ，當中的 Q，代表酷兒（queer，反對界定何謂正常、區分性別、追求家庭契約的自由性別者）或是性別認同障礙者。LGBTI 的 I 代表同時具備兩種生理特徵的陰陽人（intersex）。

但一般來說，目前 LGBT 這個縮寫的含意已超過字面上的四種族群，已涵蓋所有非異性戀者（non-heterosexual）。

關於 help，你必須知道的正確用法

不論是在書面或是口語，help 都是高頻率用字，運用範圍也很廣，但卻是大家常常容易用錯的字，記住這兩種 help 句型的意思，你就不會再用錯了。

● 表達「幫助某人某事」的句型：

help + 人 + (to) V = help + 人 + with + 事

例 **I helped him fill out the application form.**

= **I helped him with the application form.**
　　我幫他填寫申請表。

例 **Can you help me wash the dishes?**

= **Can you help me with the dishes?**
　　你能不能幫我洗碗？

● **help 另一種常見用法為 can't/couldn't help + Ving**

意指「忍不住做某事、不能停止做某事」，與原先的「幫助」相去甚遠。使用時，請注意要使用 V-ing 的型式。

can't/couldn't help + Ving

例 **She can't help crying whenever she hears that song.**
　　她每次聽到那首歌都會忍不住哭泣。

例 **I couldn't help laughing when the man slipped and fell.**
　　那個人滑倒的時候，我忍不住笑了出來。

Time to THRIVE 「發光發熱」座談會

為 HRC 為年輕 LGBTQ 族群舉辦的年度座談會，邀集社會工作者、中小學教師、宗教領袖、運動教練，以及青少年團體職員進行研討，藉由認識 LGBTQ、了解這個族群所受到的壓迫，進而交流改善方法，以增進這群社會弱勢者在家庭、學校，乃至社會生活的安全與福祉。

treat sb. like shit 視……如敝屣

treat 是「對待」，shit 是「屎」，被人當作屎來對待，當然是毫無尊嚴了。

A: Why did you break up with your boyfriend?
　　你為什麼和你男友分手？
B: Because he treated me like shit.
　　因為他對我很差。

tear sb. down 貶低，毀謗

tear 當動詞是「撕破、扯掉」的意思，tear down 表示「拆毀」。tear 用在「人」身上代表「讓人精神受折磨」，tear down 就是「詆毀」了。

A: Why don't you like Melissa?
　　你為什麼不喜歡梅麗莎？
B: It seems like she's always tearing people down.
　　她似乎總喜歡貶低別人。

build up to 慢慢準備（說或做），醞釀

build 有一步一步、按部就班構築的意思，當你慢慢醞釀，讓一件事成形，就可以說 build up to。

A: You didn't tell the boss you were quitting till Friday?
　　你禮拜五才告訴老闆你要辭職？
B: It took me all week to build up to it.
　　我花了一個星期的時間準備告訴他。

這次演說發表於二〇一四年二月十四日情人節，為 Time to THRIVE 的開幕演說。儘管 Ellen Page 在十九歲時，就已向父母坦承同志身份，但在演藝圈內一直用絕口不提和假緋聞來掩蓋。

八分半鐘的演說中，Ellen Page 一路鋪陳同志的處境，語氣漸趨激昂，甚至顫抖哽咽，正在令人起疑之際，她於第六分鐘公開出櫃，全場為之震撼。

Let This End with Us
Malala's Nobel Speech
馬拉拉諾貝爾和平獎獲獎演講

© European Parliament

 The Youngest Nobel Recipient
年紀最輕的諾貝爾和平獎得主

Dear sisters and brothers, today is a day of great happiness for me. I am humbled that the Nobel Committee has selected me for this precious award. I am very proud to be the first 🔲 Pashtun, the first Pakistani, and the youngest person to receive this award. Along with that, I am pretty certain that I am also the first [1]**recipient** of the Nobel Peace Prize who still fights with her younger brothers. I want there to be peace everywhere, but my brothers and I are still working on that.

親愛的兄弟姊妹們，今天是我非常快樂的日子。能獲得諾貝爾委員會頒發這項殊榮，我實在是受寵若驚。我很榮幸能成為第一位獲得諾貝爾獎的普什圖族人和巴基斯坦人，以及最年輕的得主。此外，我相信我也是還在和我的弟弟們吵架的第一位諾貝爾和平獎得主。我希望世界和平，但我和我的弟弟們還在努力當中。

This award is not just for me. It is for those forgotten children who want education. It is for those frightened children who want peace. It is for those voiceless children who want change. I am here to 🔲 stand up for their rights, to raise their voice. It is not time to pity them. It is time to take action so it becomes the last time that we see a child [2]**deprived** of education.

VOCABULARY 🎧68

1) **recipient** [rɪˋsɪpɪənt] (n.) 獲得者
Scholarship recipients will be informed by mail.

2) **deprive** [dɪˋpraɪv] (v.) 剝奪
Nobody should be deprived of quality health care.

3) **laureate** [ˋlɔrɪət] (n.) 獲獎者，享有殊榮者
Our professor is a Nobel laureate in chemistry.

4) **blessing** [ˋblɛsɪŋ] (n.)（神的）賜福，值得慶幸的事
The good weather has been a blessing for farmers.

這個獎項不只屬於我，也屬於那些渴望受教育，卻被遺忘的孩子們；屬於那些希望和平，卻要擔驚受怕的孩子們；屬於那些希望改變，但聲音被淹沒的孩子們。為了他們的權益，我挺身而出，為他們發聲。現在不是可憐他們的時候，而是要採取行動，讓他們成為最後一批失學的孩子。

教育是人生的幸事之一，也是必要之一。這是我人生十七年來的經驗談。過去在我如同天堂的家鄉斯瓦特時，我一直樂於學習和發現新事物。我們渴望接受教育，因為我們的未來就在教室裡。我們樂於穿著整潔的校服，坐在教室裡時，眼睛都綻放出遠大夢想的光芒。

Shot by the Taliban
遭塔利班槍擊的女孩

I have found that people describe me in many different ways. Some people call me the girl who was shot by the **LG** Taliban; and some, the girl who fought for her rights; some people call me a Nobel [3]**Laureate** now. As far as I know, I am just a committed and even stubborn person who wants to see every child getting quality education, who wants to see women having equal rights and who wants peace in every corner of the world.

我發現人們用各種不同的方式形容我。有些人形容我是「遭塔利班槍擊的女孩」；有些人形容我是「爭取自身權益的女孩」；現在有些人稱我為「諾貝爾獎得主」。就我所知，我只是一個心志堅定、甚至執著的人，我想要看到每一個孩子都能接受優質教育，想要看到女性們擁有平等權利，想要看到世界每一個角落都充滿和平。

Education is one of the [4]**blessings** of life—and one of its necessities. That has been my experience during the 17 years of my life. In my paradise home, **LG** Swat, I always loved learning and discovering new things. We had a thirst for education, because our future was right there in that classroom. We loved to wear neat and tidy school uniforms and we would sit there with big dreams in our eyes.

Malala Yousafzai
馬拉拉約薩輔栽

© Marta B. Haga/MFA, Oslo

生於一九九七年，巴基斯坦人，自幼受父親影響，對政治極感興趣，尤其關注教育權問題。她十二歲冒險為 BBC 撰寫部落格，記錄塔利班禁止女孩上學、破壞學校的情況，受到國際媒體注意，開始投入人權運動。

具國際知名度的馬拉拉，在巴基斯坦公開主張女性受教權，越來越多的死亡威脅隨之而來。二〇一二年開始籌組馬拉拉教育基金會，援助貧困女童上學；十月，馬拉拉於放學途中遭塔利班份子襲擊遇刺，轉送英國救治，大難不死，現居英國繼續受教。二〇一四年獲諾貝爾和平獎，年僅十七歲。

Dreams Turned into Nightmares
夢想變成惡夢

But things did not remain the same. Swat, which was a place of tourism and beauty, suddenly changed into a place of 1)**terrorism**. I was just ten when more than 400 schools were destroyed. Women were 2)**flogged**. People were killed. And our beautiful dreams turned into nightmares. Education went from being a right to being a crime. Girls were stopped from going to school.

但好景不常。斯瓦特原本是一處美麗的旅遊勝地，突然之間變成恐怖主義蔓延的地方。當四百多所學校遭到摧毀時，我只有十歲。婦女們遭到鞭打，人民遭到殺害。我們懷抱的美夢變成了惡夢。教育從應得的權益變成了罪行。女孩們被禁止上學。

When my world suddenly changed, my priorities changed too. I had two 3)**options**. One was to remain silent and wait to be killed. And the second was to speak up and then be killed. I chose the second one. We decided to raise our voice and tell them, "Have you not learnt that in the Holy 4)**Koran** 5)**Allah** says: if you kill one person it is as if you kill the whole humanity?"

❝ There are so many figures in our history that did not believe they could make a change, and they did.

我們的歷史上有許多人物，原本都不相信自己能造成改變，但他們都做到了。

馬拉拉談改變

我的世界瞬間改變，我的生活重心也變了。我只剩兩個選擇。一是保持沉默，等著被殺害。二是勇於發聲，然後被殺害。我選擇第二個。我們決定大聲對他們說：「你們難道不知道，《古蘭經》中真主阿拉說，『你殺害一個人，就等於殺害全人類』？」

The terrorists tried to stop us and attacked me and my friends—who are here today—on our school bus in 2012, but neither their ideas nor their bullets could win. We survived. And since that day, our voices have grown louder and louder.

I tell my story, not because it is unique, but because it is not. It is the story of many girls.

恐怖份子想阻止我們，所以攻擊我和我的朋友們 —— 他們今天都在場 —— 恐怖份子在二〇一二年襲擊我們搭乘的校車，但不論是他們的信條或槍彈攻擊都沒有得逞。我們逃過一劫。從那一天起，我們發出的聲音只會越來越大聲。我說出我的故事，不是因為它有多獨特，而是因為它一點也不獨特。有許多女孩都遭遇到同樣的事。

I Am Not a Lone Voice
我不是孤軍奮戰

Today, I tell their stories too. I have brought with me some of my sisters from Pakistan, from Nigeria and from Syria, who share this story. Though I appear as one girl, I am not a lone voice, I am many. I am those 66 million girls who are deprived of education. And today I am not raising my voice, it is the voice of those 66 million girls.

今天，我也要說出她們的故事。我帶了幾位來自巴基斯坦、奈及利亞和敘利亞的姊妹來，她們的遭遇和我一樣。雖然只有我一人出現在大家面前，但我並不是孤軍奮戰，我背後站著許多人，我代表著六千六百萬名失學的女孩。今天我發出的不只有我一人的聲音，而是六千六百萬名女孩的聲音。

Dear sisters and brothers, today, in half of the world, we see rapid progress and development. However, there are many countries where millions still suffer from the very old problems of war,

VOCABULARY 70

1) **terrorism** [ˋtɛrə͵rɪzəm] (n.) 恐怖行動，恐怖主義
Governments must work together to fight terrorism.

2) **flog** [flɑg] (v.) 鞭打
The prisoner was flogged for trying to escape.

3) **option** [ˋɑpʃən] (n.) 選項，可選擇的東西
What payment options do you offer?

4) **Koran** [koˋræn] (n.) 古蘭經
The Koran dates back to the 7th century.

5) **Allah** [ˋælə] (n.) 阿拉，真主
Muslims pray to Allah five times a day.

6) **taboo** [təˋbu] (n.) 戒律，禁忌
Marrying a relative is a taboo in many cultures.

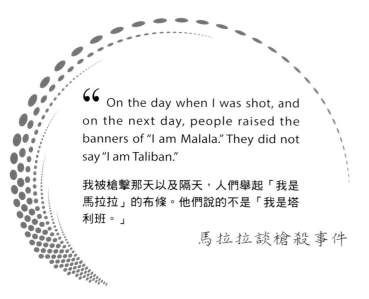

> **❝** On the day when I was shot, and on the next day, people raised the banners of "I am Malala." They did not say "I am Taliban."
>
> 我被槍擊那天以及隔天，人們舉起「我是馬拉拉」的布條。他們說的不是「我是塔利班。」
>
> 馬拉拉談槍殺事件

親愛的兄弟姊妹們，今天我們看到有一半的世界正快速進步和發展。不過，也有許多國家的數以百萬計人口長久以來因為戰爭、貧困和不公等問題而受苦。非洲有許多孩子因為貧困而無法受教育。還有許多孩子，尤其是在印度和巴基斯坦，因為社會禁忌，他們接受教育的權利遭到剝奪，或是被迫童婚，或成為童工。

One of my very good school friends dreamed of becoming a doctor. But at the age of 12, she was forced to get married. And then soon she had a child when she herself was still a child—only 14. I know that she could have been a very good doctor. But she couldn't, because she was a girl. Her story is why I dedicate the Nobel Peace Prize money to the **LG** Malala Fund, to help give girls quality education, everywhere, anywhere in the world.

我在學校裡有一位非常要好的同學夢想成為醫生。但在十二歲時，她被迫結婚。過不久她生了孩子，但自己還只是個孩子，當時才十四歲。我知道她本來可以當個好醫生的，卻因為身為女生而不能圓夢。因為她的故事，我將諾貝爾和平獎獎金捐獻給馬拉拉基金會，幫助世界各地的女孩接受優質教育。

poverty, and injustice. Many children in Africa do not have access to education because of poverty. Many children, especially in India and Pakistan, are deprived of their right to education because of social [6)]**taboos**, or they have been forced into child marriage or into child labor.

#EduSummitOslo 6-7 JULY 2015
EDUCATION FOR DEVELOPMENT

In my own village, there is still no **LG** secondary school for girls. And it is my wish and my commitment, and now my challenge, to build one so that my friends and my sisters can go there to school and get quality education and get this opportunity to fulfill their dreams. This is where I will begin, but it is not where I will stop. I will continue this fight until I see every child in school.

在我自己的村莊，沒有中學讓女孩就讀。建造一所學校，讓我的朋友和姊妹們可以上學，接受優質教育，並有機會實現夢想，這是我的願望，也是我的承諾，現在已成為我的挑戰。這是我的出發點，但不是我的終點，我要繼續抗爭，直到我看到每一個孩子都能接受教育。

A 1)**Plea to World Leaders**
對世界領導人的請願

It is not time to tell the world leaders to realize how important education is. They already know it—their own children are in good schools. Now it is time to 2)**call** on them to **LG** take action for the rest of the world's children. We ask the world leaders to unite and make education their top priority.

Leaders must seize this opportunity to guarantee a free, quality, primary and secondary education for every child.

現在不是告訴世界領導人認識到教育有多重要的時候，他們早已經知道這點，因為他們的孩子都就讀好學校。現在是呼籲他們為世界上其他孩子採取行動的時候。我們請求世界領導人團結起來，將教育列為優先考量的任務。請所有領導人務必抓住這個機會，保證為每一個孩子提供免費和優質的中小學教育。

Let us become the first generation that decides to be the last that sees empty classrooms, lost childhoods and wasted 3)**potentials**. Let this be the last time that a girl or a boy spends their childhood in a factory. Let this be the last time that a girl is forced into early child marriage. Let this be the last time that a child loses life in war. Let this be the last time that we see a child out of school. Let this end with us.

讓我們成為最後一次看到教室空置、孩子失去童年與浪費潛力的第一代人。讓我們最後一次看到女孩或男孩的童年在工廠中度過，讓我們最後一次看到女孩被迫童婚，讓我們最後一次看到孩子在戰爭中喪生，讓我們最後一次看到孩子失學。就讓這一切在我們這一代結束。

© Nicholas Frisardi

VOCABULARY 72

1) **plea** [pli] (n./v.) 請求
The police ignored the crime victim's plea for help.

2) **call on** [kɔl ɑn] (v.) 呼籲，請求
Human rights groups called on the government to end the death penalty.

3) **potential** [pəˋtɛnʃəl] (n.) 潛力，可能性
Going to university will help you reach your full potential.

Pashtun 普什圖人

普什圖族是阿富汗第一大民族，在馬拉拉的祖國巴基斯坦則為第二大民族。這兩個國家聚居了全球絕大多數的普什圖人，約有五千萬人，信奉伊斯蘭教，大多屬遜尼派（正統派，相對於什葉派）。

stand up for 支持

字面上的意思是「為了……站起來」，也就是起而聲援、表示支持的意思。

A: Thanks for standing up for me at the meeting.
多謝你在會議上為我挺身而出。
B: Sure. I can't believe Eddie tried to steal your idea.
這是當然。真不敢相信艾迪竟想剽竊你的點子。

Taliban 塔利班

波斯語「學生」的意思，也被譯為「神學士」，屬於伊斯蘭教遜尼派，是發源於阿富汗的原教旨主義運動組織。這支興起於阿富汗難民營的學生軍以鏟除軍閥、重建國家、反對腐敗、恢復商業為號召，以激進的觀點詮釋伊斯蘭教，成立宗教警察，以暴力手段執行伊斯蘭律法，禁止女性就學、就業，將電視、電影、音樂、舞蹈視為淫穢腐敗的事物。塔利班政權因協助隱匿賓拉登（911恐怖攻擊首謀），一直被視為恐怖份子同路人。

Swat 斯瓦特縣

位於巴基斯坦西北，座落於斯瓦特河（Swat River，在普什圖語代表如水晶般清澈的天藍色河水）上游，當地環山攬翠風景秀麗，伊麗莎白二世造訪時，稱這裡為「東方的瑞士（Switzerland of the East）」。

By Aisha Nadim

By Green Giant

> Let us remember: One book, one pen, one child, and one teacher can change the world.

我們要記住：一本書、一支筆、一個孩子、加上一個老師，就能改變世界。

馬拉拉談教育

Malala Fund 馬拉拉基金會

提倡女性受教權的非營利組織，幫助貧困女童能在安全無虞的環境中接受優質教育，成為社會的中堅。馬拉拉及其父親 Ziauddin Yousafzai 為共同創辦人之一。

secondary school 中學

世界各國家地區的學制不盡相同，但大約都可區分為三級：
初：primary education 初等教育（小學）
中：secondary education 中等教育（中學）
高：tertiary education 高等教育（大學）

take action 採取行動

take action 的意思從字面上不難了解，它還有一個常見的用法，是表示「提出訴訟」。

A: The crime rate here is getting worse and worse.
這一帶的犯罪率真的是每況愈下。
B: Yeah. The government should really take action to fight crime.
對啊。政府該好好採取行動打擊犯罪了。

© JStone / Shutterstock.com

since 的兩種用法

● 用 since 表示時間點

解 since 可以用來表示「自從……起」，常用句型是 since + 時間點，接在現在完成式（have + p.p.）或現在完成進行式（have been + Ving）後面。

例 **Michael has lived in Taiwan since 2002.**
麥可從二〇〇二年起就住在台灣了。

例 **Pam has been studying French since last October.**
潘從去年十月開始學法文。

● 用 since 表示原因

解 since 的另外一個意思是「因為，由於」，用法近似 because 和 as，後面會接表示原因的名詞子句，例如 Since/As + 子句 ..., S. + V....

例 **Since she loves music so much, Carrie decided to become a musician.**
因為凱莉熱愛音樂，所以她決定要當個音樂家。

這篇演講發表於二〇一四年十二月的諾貝爾和平獎頒獎典禮。儘管用字簡單（看單字數量即知），依然是一篇激勵世人的演講。馬拉拉流利的英語，受教於她的父親，他是一位詩人、教育改革家，也經營多家連鎖的私立學校，原本想成為醫生的馬拉拉，也是受到父親鼓勵，決定投入政治，因為「醫生只能救病人，但政治家能讓人免於苦難。政治家能採取行動，讓明日不再有人恐懼。」

Woody Hayes' Ohio State Commencement Speech

Paying Forward

伍迪海耶斯俄亥俄州立大學畢業典禮演講

© Steve Grant

A Great Education
優質的教育

Today is the greatest day of my life. I appreciate it so much being able to come here and talk to our graduating class at Ohio State University, the great University that you and I love.

今天是我一生中最棒的一天，很感謝能來到這所我和在座各位都熱愛的俄亥俄州立大學，為畢業班演講。

I'd like to start out with something that I use in almost every speech, and that is the idea of [LG] paying forward. That is the thing that you folks with your great education from here can do for the rest of your lives. I was so happy the other day when I saw in the paper about Jim Lachey, who played here one year ago and comes back after one year of professional football to give a six-figure gift to the University. And what he said was, "I received a great education here and I got to play great football under a great football system here. I want to help some other youngsters do the same thing."

© mcdermottography

VOCABULARY [74]

1) **accumulate** [ə`kjumjə͵let] (v.) 累積，積聚
Mark's debts began accumulating after he lost his job.

2) **corrupt** [kə`rʌpt] (a.) 貪污的，腐敗的
The corrupt official was sentenced to life in prison.

3) **marine** [mə`rin] (n.) （常大寫）海軍陸戰隊隊員
Justin wanted to be a Marine ever since he was a little boy.

4) **corps** [kor] (n.) （常大寫）部隊，兵團
My father served in the Army Corps of Engineers.

5) **outfit** [`aut͵fɪt] (n.) 部隊，團體，組織
All the other soldiers in his outfit were killed.

一開始，我想先談談我幾乎在每一場演講都會提到的概念，也就是回饋。這是在此接受優質教育的各位在接下來的人生當中可以做的事。我最近在報紙上看到關於吉姆拉奇的消息，令我非常開心。一年前他在俄亥俄州大踢球，在當了一年的職業美式足球員後，捐款六位數字給俄亥俄州大。他說：「我在這裡接受了優質教育，也曾在這所學校的優秀球隊裡踢足球。我也想幫助其他年輕學子加入足球隊。」

You Can Always Pay Forward
你可以隨時回饋

Take that attitude toward life, because GM so seldom can we pay back. Those whom you owe—your parents and other people—will be gone. Emerson had something to say about that. He said

> " Any time you give a man something he doesn't earn, you cheapen him. Our kids earn what they get, and that includes respect.
>
> 讓一個人不勞而獲，就是貶低他。我們隊上的孩子什麼都得靠自己爭取，包括尊重。

伍迪海耶斯談尊重

you can pay back only seldom, but you can always pay forward. He said beware of too much good [1]**accumulating** in your palm or it will fast [2]**corrupt**. No one put it better than he did.

請以這種態度面對人生，因為能報答他人的機會並不多。你的恩人——你的父母等其他人——都會離開。愛默生說過類似的話。他說，你報答別人的機會不多，但你總是能隨時回饋。他說，手中積累太多利益就要注意了，否則很快就會墮落。沒有誰能比他形容得更好了。

Two weeks ago in Michigan, a former football player of ours passed away. He had been in the [3]**Marine** [4]**Corps** during World War II, on Okinawa. There were only 30 from his [5]**outfit** that survived. That made a difference in him. He came back to coaching and he was a great coach. His name was Jack Castignola. Jack Castignola won nine championships, but he did something bigger—he coached 126 players who went on to college. That was his way of paying forward.

兩星期前，我們有位前足球員在密西根州過世。第二次世界大戰時，他在參與沖繩島戰役的海軍陸戰隊服役，他的部隊只有三十人存活下來。這對他的人生帶來了影響。他回來後當了教練，而且還是非常優秀的教練。他就是傑克卡斯蒂諾拉。傑克卡斯蒂諾拉贏過九次冠軍，但他更大的成就是——他指導的一百二十六位球員都升上了大學，這就是他回饋的方式。

© Robert Patton

Woody Hayes 伍迪海耶斯

生於一九一三年，卒於一九八七年。他擔任大學足球校隊教練生涯締造 238 勝、72 負、10 平的輝煌戰績，絕大多數都是在他任教俄亥俄州立大學的二十八年（一九五一年至一九七八年）間締造。

俄亥俄七葉樹隊（Ohio State Buckeyes）在海耶斯的帶領下，拿下五座全國冠軍、十三次 Big Ten（十大聯盟，美國中西部十所大學聯盟）冠軍，備受該校師生尊敬。一九八三年，海耶斯以教練身份進入美式足球大學名人堂，他也被稱為 NCAA（國家大學體育學會，National Collegiate Athletic Association）歷史上的五大名帥之一。

The Ohio State vs. Michigan University（密西根大學）是美國大學足球世仇，兩軍對壘為美國體壇年度盛事，就算駐紮伊拉克的部隊也很關心
© The National Guard

We had a great [1)]**dean** of agriculture here 🄻🄶 by the name of Roy Kottman. And on his retirement, I said, "Roy, how did you [2)]**happen to** go to Iowa State?" He said, "I was working back during the Depression for $1.50 a day pumping gas and I couldn't save any money. But an old man in that community in Iowa came to me and said, 'Roy, if you'll go to Iowa State, I'll pay your [3)]**tuition**.' So I went to Iowa State, graduated, went into the [4)]**service**, came back, got my master's, my doctorate, and then I came to Ohio State." He was here 23 years, and in those 23 years, he [5)]**virtually** doubled food production in Ohio. On top of that, he graduated thousands of youngsters. All because of that old man back in Iowa. That's paying forward.

俄亥俄州立大學體育場向伍迪海耶斯致敬的橫幅
© Sam Howzit

我們以前有位優秀的農學院院長，名叫羅伊考特曼。他退休時，我問他：「羅伊，你是怎麼進入愛荷華州大的？」他說：「經濟大蕭條時，我在加油站打工，一天工資一塊五毛，我存不了錢。有天，

我住的愛荷華州社區裡一位老人來找我，告訴我：『羅伊，假如你能去念愛荷華州大，我就幫你付學費。』所以我就去念愛荷華州大了，畢業後去服了兵役，再回學校修碩士和博士學位，然後就來到俄亥俄州大服務了。」他在這裡待了二十三年，這二十三年裡，他幫助俄亥俄州的糧食生產量增加了幾乎兩倍。最重要的是，他為成千上萬名年輕人授予畢業證書。這全都是因為愛荷華州的那位老人。這就是回饋。

In football, we always say, "That other team can't beat us. We have to make sure that we don't beat ourselves." And that is what a person has to do, too— make sure that they don't beat themselves. So many times I've found people smarter than I was. I found them in football— bigger, they could run faster, could block harder, they were smarter people than I.

66 Perfect preparation prevents piss-poor performance.

好好練習就不怕上場失利。

伍迪海耶斯談練習
編註：請注意，全部都是 P 開頭喔！

伍迪海耶斯帶領俄亥俄州立大學的戰術手冊
© Steve Grant

VOCABULARY 🄷76

1) **dean** [din] (n.) （大學）學院院長，教務長
The dean of the law school is retiring next year.

2) **happen (to)** [ˋhæpən] (v.) （偶然）發生，碰巧
I happened to meet an old friend at the post office.

3) **tuition** [tuˋɪʃən] (n.) 學費
Students held a protest against the tuition increase.

4) **service** [ˋsɜvɪs] (n.) 軍隊，軍方，兵役
Tony joined the service after graduating from high school.

5) **virtually** [ˋvɜtʃʊəlɪ] (adv.) 幾乎
The city was virtually destroyed during the war.

6) **fatheaded** [ˋfætˌhɛdɪd] (a.) 愚笨的
Why do you have to be so fatheaded all the time?

在足球場上，我們總是說：「對手無法擊敗我們。我們只要確保不敗在自己手上。」這也是身為一個人要做的事——千萬不要敗在自己手上。我常常碰到比我聰明的人，在足球場上，他們塊頭比我大，跑得比我快，比我更會用力防守，他們都是比我聰明的人。

But you know what they couldn't do? They couldn't outwork me. And I ran into coaches that I coached against who knew a lot more football than I did, but they couldn't work as long as I could. And I had a wonderful wife who put up with that—she'd allow me to stay and work. And I had great associations with my coaches. There was no one who had better people than I did, or better football players. And we outworked the other teams. The only way we'd get beaten was if we got a little [6]**fatheaded**, if we didn't train right, if we had [7]**dissension** on the [8]**squad**.

但你們知道他們有什麼是做不到的？他們沒有我努力。我遇到對手的教練有的比我懂足球，但他們工作的時間還是沒有我長。我有個很棒的妻子，她能體諒我這點——她讓我在外面長時間工作。我也跟隊上其他教練們合作愉快。沒有其他球隊的團員或球員比我的還棒了。而且我們比其他球隊都更努力。我們若是被擊敗，原因就只有我們稍微懈怠了、訓練的方式不對，或球隊中意見分歧。

Family is so enormously important. I'm going to tell you about a student in your University right now—a 🔲 Rhodes Scholar, Mike Lanese. I talked to his dad. I said, "When did you know he was going to be a great athlete?" He said, "By the time he was in the seventh grade,

> "
> Nobody despises to lose more than I do. That's got me into trouble over the years, but it also made a man of mediocre ability into a pretty good coach.
>
> 沒人比我更討厭輸。多年來我為此吃了不少苦頭，但這能讓一個能力平平的教練，變成相當好的教練。
>
> *伍迪海耶斯談得失心*

he was [9]**coming along** physically. But I found out something else—he was listening to his coaching instruction and the instruction we gave him." There's your good family.

家庭是極其重要的。我要告訴你們關於貴校一位在校學生的事——羅德獎學金得主麥可藍尼西。我曾和他的父親談過話。我問他：「你什麼時候知道他會成為優秀的運動員？」他說：「他在七年級的時候，身體已變得相當強壯。但我還發現另一件事——他有在聽教練的指導，還有我們給他的指導。」這就是家庭的影響力。

俄亥俄州立大學體育吉祥物 Brutus Buckeye 被打扮成伍迪海耶斯的招牌造型 © atalou

© www.petful.com

---

7) **dissension** [dɪˋsɛnʃən] (n.) 意見不合，不和
There are signs of dissension within the ruling party.

8) **squad** [skwɑd] (n.) 球隊，小組
Which squad are you cheering for?

9) **come along** [kʌm əˋlɔŋ] (phr.) 進展，進行
How is your project coming along?

For me, this goes all the way back to my grandmother and then right on LG down the line. She didn't tell my dad, "Go to the study table." She said, "I'll meet you at the study table." And that's where your good parents and good teachers are. They're talking now about all of this tutoring you need for athletes. We were doing that 35 years ago. I didn't send those football players to the study table—I met them at the study table. When you deal with youngsters, when you get into jobs of any kind, don't send people to do it, meet them there and help them do it, and you'll be amazed how it works.

俄亥俄州立大學七葉樹隊戰術磋商（huddle）
© Sam Howzit

以我的例子來說，這要從我的奶奶開始說起，然後一路影響到後來的我。她從沒這樣要求我爸爸：「到你的書桌去。」她說的是：「我在書桌那裡等你。」這就是好父母和好老師會做的事。現在許多人在談運動員所需的教導。三十五年前我們已經在提供這樣的教導。我不會要求那些足球員到書桌去——而是到書桌那裡等他們。當你跟年輕人共事時，或從事任何工作時，不要指使別人去做事，要跟他們相約一起做事，並幫助他們，你會發現成效非常驚人。

In football, we do learn some wonderful things, and one of them is this—when you get knocked down, which is plenty often, you get right up in a hurry. Then do you know what you do? You probably need more strength. You know where you get it? You get it in a 1)**huddle**. You get it by going back and getting a new play and running that play together. And in your lifetime, how well you can work with people will depend on how quickly you get back to them and get together.

在足球場上，我們確實會學到一些美妙的事，其中一件是——當你被撞倒時（這是經常會發生的事）你要趕快站起來。然後你知道要做什麼嗎？你大概需要更多力量。你知道要從哪裡獲得力量嗎？從球隊的戰術聚商中。你要回到聚商中，討論出新戰術，然後一起執行新戰術。在你這一生中，你能否跟別人合作無間，就看你要多快才能回到團隊中，一起商討戰術。

In football, you learn there's nothing that comes easy that's LG worth a dime. LG As a matter of fact, I never saw a football player make a 2)**tackle** with a smile on his face. And I have no idea, but you may have the attitude and the capacity and the ability to go on from here and help to make this a greater world. 3)**Godspeed** to all of you!

在足球場上，你會學到，得來容易的東西是一文不值的。說實在的，我從來沒看過一個撲倒對手的足球員是面帶微笑的。我無法預言，但也許你們從這裡離開後，心態已調整好，並有資格和能力幫助這個世界變得更美好。祝你們一帆風順。

VOCABULARY 🎧78

1) **huddle** [ˋhʌdəl] (n./v.)（美式足球）隊員靠攏磋商戰術，聚在一起，擠成一團
The players formed a huddle to discuss the next play.

2) **tackle** [ˋtækəl] (v./n.)（美式足球等球類）擒抱，撲倒
The player was tackled before he could catch the ball.

3) **Godspeed** [ˋɡɑd͵spid] (int.) 祝成功，祝一路平安
Godspeed on your journey!

pay...forward
把這份心意或行動傳下去

這個說法的使用情境，通常與金錢無關。當你釋出善意，對方想要回報（pay back），你可以請他不必放在心上，只要把這份善意傳下去（pay forward），讓更多人受益就夠了。也可以說 pay sth./it forward。

A: I can never pay you back for all your help.
　我永遠都無法報答你對我的幫助。
B: You don't have to. Just make sure to pay it forward.
　你不需要這樣。只要把這份心傳出去就好了。

by the name of 名為

也可以說 go by the name of，意思就是「名字叫做……」。

A: Who worked on your car at the garage?
　在修車廠幫你修車的人是誰？
B: A mechanic by the name of Gary.
　一個名叫蓋瑞的師傅。

伍迪海耶斯送給美國福特總統（Gerald Ford）的簽名球，上面是福特總統在密西根大學足球隊打球那三年，該隊與俄亥俄州立大學對戰的得分紀錄

表否定意味的倒裝句法

英文句子的語序有兩種：自然語序與倒裝語序，後者所形成的句子就是倒裝句（inverted sentence）。本文中 seldom 是具有否定意義的副詞，而當否定副詞（片語）置於句首表示強調意義時，其後的主詞、動詞須用倒裝形式。

● 表否定意味的倒裝句型：否定副詞 + 助動詞 + 主詞 + 動詞
解 比較以下意思完全相同的兩句話，用直敘表達與倒裝句，語意上便能產生不同的效果：

例 **Angie had never been so confused.**（直述句）
= **_Never_ had Angie been so confused.**（倒裝句）

例 **Jason was rarely home before nine.**
= **_Rarely_ was Jason home before nine.**

例 **We had no sooner left home than it started to rain.**
= **_No sooner_ had we left home than it started to rain.**

Rhodes Scholar 羅德學者

羅德獎學金，又稱羅氏獎學金（Rhodes Scholarship），是由英國殖民時期的南非礦業大亨 Cecil John Rhodes 於一九〇二年創設，目的在於以全額獎學金（含來回機票及生活費）獎助德智體群兼備的菁英本科生前往牛津大學研習。羅德獎學金評審每年十一月在十八個國家地區，選取八十位應屆畢業生成為羅德學者（Rhodes Scholar），前往牛津攻讀碩士或博士，全球錄取率為萬分之一，是最難申請的獎學金，而成為羅德學者，也被視為學術界最高榮譽之一。

Rhodes House Oxford

down the line 往後，未來

也可以說 down the road，一條線拉到最後，一條路走到最後，總會看到止盡，所以 down the road / line 就表示「到最後，未來」的意思。

A: Are you planning on having kids?
　你有計畫要生小孩嗎？
B: Not now, but we probably will sometime down the line.
　目前沒有，但是我們以後或許會想要生。

(not) worth a dime 一文不值

dime 是美國的一毛硬幣，與 not/never/nothing 等否定詞連用：(not) worth a dime 就表示連一毛錢都不值，也就是全無價值了。意思類似的說法還有 a dime a dozen，一毛錢就能買到一打，當然是普通到不行，一文不值了。

A: That painting you bought is a fake?
　你買的那幅畫是仿造的嗎？
B: Yeah. It isn't worth a dime.
　是呀。這幅畫一文不值。

as a matter of fact 其實

要表示「事實上」、「實際上」、「老實說」的片語很多，如 as a matter of fact、in fact、actually 等，常用於句首，後面接著敘述真正想說的話，建議大家可以交替使用，增加自己說英文的豐富性。

A: Have you been to that new Thai restaurant?
　你去過那間新開的泰國餐廳了嗎？
B: As a matter of fact, I ate there last night.
　事實上，我昨晚去那兒吃吃飯。

這篇演說發表於一九八六年，距離伍迪海耶斯去世不到一年。儘管演講主題 Paying Forward（把善意傳下去）現在聽來像是老生常談，但在伍迪海耶斯演講的當時並不陳腐。這篇演講曾被美國記者選為「歷史上最佳畢業演說 Top 12」的第八名，連甘迺迪總統、歐普拉及 J.K. 羅琳都得乖乖排在他後頭，其地位可見一斑。

Tear Down This Wall

Ronald Reagan's Berlin Wall Speech
隆納雷根柏林圍牆演講

Speaking of Freedom
論自由

Twenty-four years ago, President John F. Kennedy visited Berlin, speaking to the people of this city and the world at the City Hall. Well, since then two other presidents have come, each in his turn, to Berlin. And today 🔵 I, myself, make my second visit to your city.

二十四年前，甘迺迪總統造訪柏林，在柏林市政廳向柏林和世界的人民說話。那麼，自那時候起，還有另外兩位總統在任內造訪柏林。而今天，是我本人第二次造訪柏林。

We come to Berlin, we American presidents, because it's our duty to speak, in this place, of freedom. But I must confess, we're drawn here by other things as well: by the feeling of history in this city, more than 500 years older than our own nation; by the beauty of the 🔵 Grunewald and the Tiergarten; most of all, by your courage and determination.

我們以美國總統的身分來到柏林，是因為我們有責任來到這個地方談論自由。但我必須承認，吸引我們來到這裡還有其他原因：對這座城市的歷史感，柏林比我們國家多了五百多年的歷史；以及古納森林和蒂爾加滕的美；最重要的，是你們的勇氣和決心。

There Is Only One Berlin
柏林只有一個

Our [1]**gathering** today is being broadcast throughout Western Europe and North America. I understand that it is being seen and heard as well in the East. To those listening throughout Eastern Europe, a special word: Although I cannot be with you, I address my remarks to you just as surely as to those standing here before me. For I join you, as I join your fellow countrymen in the West, in this firm, this 2)**unalterable** belief: Es gibt nur ein Berlin.

我們今天齊聚一堂的盛會，在西歐和北美實況轉播。據我了解，東方也正在收看和收聽這場盛會。對於那些在東歐收聽的人，我要特地說一句話：雖然我無法與你們同在，但我現在對你們發表的言論，與在場的人所聽到的是一樣的。因為我要加入你們，如同我加入西方的同胞，堅守這個永恆不變的信念：柏林只有一個。

Behind me stands a wall that 3)**encircles** the free 4)**sectors** of this city, part of a vast system of barriers that divides the entire continent of Europe. From the Baltic, south, those barriers cut across Germany in a 5)**gash** of 6)**barbed wire**, concrete, dog runs and guard towers. Farther south, there may be no visible, no obvious wall. But there remain armed guards and 7)**checkpoints** all the same—still a restriction on the right to travel, still an instrument to 8)**impose** upon ordinary men and women the will of a 9)**totalitarian** state. Yet it is here in Berlin where the wall emerges most clearly. Standing before the Brandenburg Gate, every man is a German, separated from his fellow men. Every man is a Berliner, forced to look upon a 10)**scar**.

在我背後有一道圍牆，包圍著這座城市的自由區，是龐大屏障的一部分，分裂著整個歐洲大陸。北從波羅的海到南部，那些屏障以帶刺的鐵絲網、水泥牆、巡邏犬和哨塔的形式，在德國刻畫出一道深長的傷口。在更遠的南方，也許沒有看得見或明顯的牆，但還是一樣，仍有武裝警衛和檢查站——依然有對旅行權的限制，也依然是極權主義國家用來控制一般人民的工具。不過，在柏林這裡，這道牆最顯而易見。站在布蘭登堡門前，每個人都是德國人，被迫與同胞分離；每個人都是柏林人，被迫面對這個傷疤。

66 The Wall was brought down, not by Washington or Moscow, but by courageous people from the east.

這座牆被打倒，不是被華府或莫斯科，而是被牆東的英勇人民打倒。

前德國總理格哈特施羅德
（Gerhard Schröder）

Ronald Reagan
隆納雷根

生於一九一一年，美國第四十任總統。被視為打垮蘇聯英雄的雷根，原本是民主黨員，由於相信共和黨更能對抗共產主義，他於一九六二年轉投共和黨。從此仕途大開。一九六七年至一九七五年擔任加州州長，一九七六年雖然爭取共和黨提名失敗，但他對核子戰爭危機與蘇聯威脅的演說，令許多人印象深刻，終於在一九八〇年成功問鼎白宮。

雷根於內政上大幅減稅、降低利率、擴大軍費開支、高舉國債，並撤銷對商業的管制，使美國經濟於一九八二年開始起飛。對外，他貫徹反共主義，在蘇聯經濟疲軟之際與其直接對抗。他大幅擴張軍備，提出在外太空建立飛彈防禦網的「星戰計畫」，並秘密支援全球反蘇聯勢力；更於電腦快速發展之際，禁止美國和盟國對蘇聯輸出高科技技術。一九九一年，蘇聯各國紛紛宣布獨立正式瓦解。柴契爾夫人對此評論：「雷根不開一槍便贏得了冷戰。」

Ronald Reagan

© Courtesy of Ronald Reagan Library

雷根在柏林圍牆上親筆寫下「戈巴契夫先生，拆掉這座牆！」（Mr. Gorbachev - Tear Down This Wall!）」© 360b / Shutterstock.com

7) **checkpoint** [ˋtʃɛk͵pɔɪnt] (n.) 檢查站，關卡
The guards at the checkpoint asked to see my passport.

8) **impose (on)** [ɪmˋpoz] (v.) 加（負擔）於，徵（稅）
The government was criticized for imposing restrictions on trade.

9) **totalitarian** [to͵tæləˋtɛrɪən] (a.) 極權主義的
Many people still live under totalitarian governments.

10) **scar** [skɑr] (n.) 疤，傷痕，創傷
The war left deeps scars on the country.

A Message of Hope
希望的訊息

President von Weizsacker has said, "The German question is open as long as the Brandenburg Gate is closed." Today I say: As long as the gate is closed, as long as this scar of a wall is permitted to stand, it is not the German question alone that remains open, but the question of freedom for all mankind. Yet I do not come here to [1]**lament**. For I find in Berlin a message of hope, even in the shadow of this wall, a message of triumph.

魏茨澤克總統曾說：「只要布蘭登堡門還是關著，德國的問題就一直存在。」今天我要說：只要布蘭登堡門還是關著，只要圍牆的傷疤依舊存在，就不只是德國的問題還沒解決，而是所有人類的自由問題都還沒解決。但我不是來這裡唉聲嘆氣的。我在柏林所看到的是希望的訊息，勝利的訊息，就算是站在這道圍牆的陰影下。

In this season of spring in 1945, the people of Berlin emerged from their [2]**air raid** shelters to find [3]**devastation**. Thousands of miles away, the people of the United States reached out to help.

And in 1947 Secretary of State George Marshall announced the creation of what would become known as the LG Marshall Plan. Speaking precisely 40 years ago this month, he said: "Our policy is directed not against any country or [4]**doctrine**, but against hunger, poverty, [5]**desperation** and [6]**chaos**."

一九四五年春季，柏林人走出防空洞時，滿目瘡痍，百廢待興。遠在千里的美國人伸出了援手。一九四七年，美國國務卿馬歇爾宣布制訂歐洲復興計劃，也就是所謂的「馬歇爾計畫」。正好就是四十年前這個月，他說：「我們的政策不是針對任何國家或主義，而是針對飢餓、貧困、絕望和混亂。」

 ## Political and Economic Rebirth
政治和經濟的重生

A strong, free world in the West, that dream became real. Japan rose from ruin to become an economic giant. Italy, France, Belgium—virtually every nation in Western Europe saw political and economic rebirth. In West Germany and here in Berlin, there [7]**took place** an economic miracle. Adenauer, Erhard, Reuter, and other

> Since it represents a resounding confession of failure and of political weakness, this brutal border closing evidently represents a basic Soviet decision which only war could reverse.
>
> 因為這等同徹底承認失敗和政治無能，這次粗暴的邊界關閉足證只有開戰才能讓蘇維埃政權收回成命。
>
> JFK 致前德國總理威利布蘭特（Willy Brandt）

一九六一年，柏林圍牆沿著伯諾爾大街（Bernauer Strasse）築起。貼臨圍牆的房屋一邊窗戶對著西柏林，另一邊窗戶對著東柏林，是有名的投奔自由地點。

VOCABULARY 82

1) **lament** [ləˋmɛnt] (v./n.) 悲嘆，痛惜
   The couple lamented the death of their child.

2) **air raid** [ɛr red] (phr.) 空襲
   Many buildings were destroyed in the air raid.

3) **devastation** [ˌdɛvəˋsteʃən] (n.) 毀滅，蹂躪
   The earthquake that hit Nepal caused widespread devastation.

4) **doctrine** [ˋdɑktrɪn] (n.) 教條，信條
   Do you believe in Church doctrine?

5) **desperation** [ˌdɛspəˋreʃən] (n.) 絕望，極度渴望
   The eyes of the starving villagers were filled with desperation.

6) **chaos** [ˋke͵ɑs] (n.) 混亂，雜亂
   The country was in chaos after the war.

7) **take place** [tek ples] (phr.) 進行，舉行，發生
   The royal wedding took place at Buckingham Palace.

8) **flourish** [ˋflɝɪʃ] (v.) 繁榮，繁盛
   Art and music flourished in Europe during the Renaissance.

> **"** The same rightists who decades ago were shouting, 'Better dead than red!' are now often heard mumbling, 'Better red than eating hamburgers.'"
>
> 數十年前高喊「進棺材比共黨統治好」的同一批右翼份子，現在經常聽到他們抱怨「共黨統治比吃漢堡好」。
>
> 斯拉沃熱齊澤克
> （Slavoj Žižek 斯洛維尼亞社會學家）

從英國托管區遠望布蘭登堡門

蒂爾加滕區的柏林圍牆。柏林圍牆於一九九〇年拆除

leaders understood the practical importance of liberty—that just as truth can [8)]**flourish** only when the journalist is given freedom of speech, so prosperity can come about only when the farmer and businessman enjoy economic freedom. The German leaders reduced [9)]**tariffs**, expanded free trade, lowered taxes. From 1950 to 1960 alone, the standard of living in West Germany and Berlin doubled.

在西方建立強大的自由世界，這樣的夢想實現了。日本從戰敗的廢墟中崛起，成為經濟強國。義大利、法國、比利時——西歐幾乎每一個國家都歷經了政治和經濟的重生。在西德和柏林這裡，出現了經濟奇蹟。艾德諾、艾哈德、羅伊特等政治領袖都知道自由的實際意義——就像是只有新聞記者擁有言論自由，真相才能散播；農民和商人享有經濟自由，社會才能繁榮。德國領導人已降低了關稅、拓展自由貿易、降低課稅。單單在一九五〇年到一九六〇年，西德和柏林的生活水準就已上升了一倍。

Where four decades ago there was [10)]**rubble**, today in West Berlin there is the greatest industrial [11)]**output** of any city in Germany—busy office blocks, fine homes and apartments, proud avenues. Where a city's culture seemed to have been destroyed, today there are two great universities, orchestras and an opera, [12)]**countless** theaters, and museums. Where there was want, today there's [13)]**abundance**—food, clothing, automobiles—the wonderful goods of the LG Ku'damm. From devastation, from [14)]**utter** ruin, you Berliners have, in freedom, rebuilt a city that once again ranks as one of the greatest on earth.

四十年前這裡是一片斷垣殘壁，今天西柏林已成為德國工業產量最高的城市——繁忙的商業區、舒適的住宅和公寓、氣派的林蔭大道。一座文化一度摧毀殆盡的城市，如今已有兩所優秀的大學、管弦樂團和一間歌劇院、無數戲院，以及博物館。曾經渴求的必需品，現在已是不虞匱乏——食物、衣服、汽車——以及庫杜姆街賣的各種精品。你們柏林人已從滿目瘡痍的廢墟中，在自由之下重建了這座城市，使其再次榮登全世界最棒的地方之一。

---

9) **tariff** [ˈtærɪf] (n.) 關稅
Steel tariffs were introduced to protect local steel producers.

10) **rubble** [ˈrʌbəl] (n.) 瓦礫堆，碎石
The earthquake reduced the building to rubble.

11) **output** [ˈaʊtˌpʊt] (n.) 產量，出產
Manufacturing output fell 15% in the third quarter.

12) **countless** [ˈkaʊntlɪs] (a.) 無數的，數不清的，大量的
I've heard that song on the radio countless times.

13) **abundance** [əˈbʌndəns] (n.) 豐富，豐饒，大量
There was an abundance of food at the wedding.

14) **utter** [ˈʌtɚ] (a.) 完全的，徹底的，十足的
That meeting was an utter waste of time.

Freedom Leads to Prosperity
自由才能帶動繁榮

In the 1950s, **LG** Khrushchev predicted: "We will bury you." But in the West today, we see a free world that has achieved a level of prosperity and well-being [1)]**unprecedented** in all human history. In the [2)]**Communist** world, we see failure, technological [3)]**backwardness**, [4)]**declining** standards of health, even want of the most basic kind—too little food. Even today, the **LG** Soviet Union still cannot feed itself. After these four decades, then, there stands before the entire world one great and [5)]**inescapable** conclusion: Freedom leads to prosperity. Freedom is the victor.

一九五〇年代，赫魯雪夫預言：「我們會消滅你們。」但是在今天的西方，我們看到一個自由世界實現了人類史上前所未有的繁榮和福祉。在共產世界，我們看到了失敗、科技落後、衛生水準下降，甚至最基本的生活所需都沒有──糧食不足。就算是在今天，蘇聯仍無法過上溫飽的日子。這四十年來，全世界只得出一個重大的必然結論：自由才能帶動繁榮；自由才是勝利者。

And now the Soviets themselves may, in a limited way, be coming to understand the importance of freedom. We hear much from Moscow about a new policy of reform and openness. Some political prisoners have been released. Certain foreign news broadcasts are no longer being [6)]**jammed**. Some economic [7)]**enterprises** have been permitted to operate with greater freedom from state control.

現在蘇聯可能已開始逐漸瞭解自由的重要性，雖然程度有限。我們聽說了不少關於莫斯科開始實行新改革開放政策的消息，一些政治犯已經獲得釋放，也不再阻擋某些國外新聞的播放，部分企業已獲得比以往多一點自由，在有限的範圍內免受國家掌控。

 ## An Unmistakable Sign
一個明確無誤的徵兆

Are these the beginnings of [8)]**profound** changes in the Soviet state? Or are they [9)]**token** gestures, intended to raise false hopes in the West, or to strengthen the Soviet system without changing it? We welcome change and openness; for we believe that freedom and security go together, that the advance of human liberty can only strengthen the cause of world peace. There is one sign the Soviets can make that would be [10)]**unmistakable**, that would advance dramatically the cause of freedom and peace.

這些是否代表蘇聯正在開始進行徹底改變？或者他們只是在擺出象徵性的姿態，有意讓西方燃起不實的希望，或只是為了加強蘇聯體制，其實無意進行改革？我們歡迎他們改革和開放；因為我們相信，自由和國安是息息相關的，唯有促進人類自由，才能鞏固世界和平的事業。有一種明確無誤的表現是蘇聯可以做出的，會極力促進自由和平的事業。

General Secretary Gorbachev, if you seek peace, if you seek prosperity for the Soviet Union and Eastern Europe, if you seek [11)]**liberalization**: Come here to this gate! Mr. Gorbachev, open this gate! Mr. Gorbachev, tear down this wall!

戈巴契夫總書記，假如你在追求和平，假如你在追求蘇聯和東歐的繁榮，假如你在追求自由化：到布蘭登堡門這裡來！戈巴契夫先生，打開這扇門！戈巴契夫先生，拆掉這道圍牆吧！

VOCABULARY 84

1) **unprecedented** [ʌnˋprɛsə͵dɛntɪd] (a.) 前所未有的，空前的
The economy entered a period of unprecedented growth.

2) **communist** [ˋkɑmjə͵nɪst] (a./n.) （常為大寫）共產的，共產黨的；共產主義者，共產黨員
There are very few Communist countries left in the world.

3) **backwardness** [ˋbækwədnɪs] (n.) 落後，進步遲緩
Many in the rural area are living in backwardness and poverty.

4) **decline** [dɪˋklaɪn] (v./n.) 下跌，衰退
Wages have declined over the past several years.

5) **inescapable** [͵ɪnəˋskepəbəl] (a.) 不可避免的，逃不掉的
Death is an inescapable fact of life.

6) **jam** [dʒæm] (v.) 干擾（廣播等），堵住
The airplane has equipment to jam enemy radio signals.

7) **enterprise** [ˋɛntə͵praɪz] (n.) 事業，企業，公司
The Taiwan Power Company is a government enterprise.

8) **profound** [prəˋfaʊnd] (a.) 深刻的，深遠的
Pollution has profound effects on human health.

9) **token** [ˋtokən] (a.) 象徵性的，意思意思的，充場面的
Only a few token women have been promoted to management positions.

10) **unmistakable** [͵ʌnmɪˋstekəbəl] (a.) 不會認錯的，明顯的
The smell of stinky tofu is unmistakable.

11) **liberalization** [͵lɪbərələˋzeʃən] (n.) 自由化，開放
The government is considering a new trade liberalization plan.

馬歇爾計畫的宣傳海報，表示此計畫是要拉西歐諸國一把

Grunewald and the Tiergarten
古納森林和蒂爾加滕

Grunewald 是德文 green wood（綠色樹林），是柏林地區最大的綠地。Tiergarten 是德文 animal garden（動物公園），是德國境內第二大都會公園，僅次於慕尼黑的英國公園（Englischer Garten）。這兩個處處湖光瀲豔的綠林區，都位於柏林西半部，是當年被柏林圍牆圍住的西柏林人難得的休憩去處。

Brandenburg Gate 布蘭登堡門

位於柏林市正中心的布蘭登堡門，建於十八世紀末年，是為了紀念普魯士（Prussia）在七年戰爭中獲勝而興建，頂上的「勝利女神四馬戰車（Quadriga）」雕像面向當時的柏林城內，象徵凱旋歸來。這座雅典衛城風格的建築，見證了歐洲乃至世界許多歷史事件，其中最著名的，就是柏林圍牆的興建與倒塌。

德國於第二次世界大戰後分裂，位於東德境內的柏林，則被分為東、西柏林，在東柏林的布蘭登堡門位於柏林圍牆隔離區內，無論東西柏林人都不能進出，是德國分裂、歐洲分裂和冷戰的象徵。

一九九〇年，德國統一，布蘭登堡門又成為歐洲重新統一的象徵。

Marshall Plan 馬歇爾計畫

以當時美國國務卿喬治馬歇爾（George Marshall）為名，也稱為歐洲復興計畫（European Recovery Program），是美國對飽受納粹摧殘的西歐進行各項經濟援助、協助重建的計劃，也藉此鞏固美國在歐洲的勢力，以與蘇聯抗衡。

馬歇爾計畫從一九四七年七月開始執行，共持續四年。計畫結束時，西歐除德國之外，大多國家經濟都已恢復戰前水準。這項計畫並未讓西歐成為美國的附庸國，反因打破了各國間的關稅及貿易壁壘，最終走向一體化，成為能與美國平起平坐的勢力。

Ku'damm 選帝侯大街

Ku'damm 是當地人對 Kurfürstendamm 的簡稱，也常音譯為庫達姆大街，是柏林最高級的時尚購物街，堪稱德國的香榭麗舍大道。在柏林分割時期，這裡是西柏林的商業中心。

Khrushchev 赫魯雪夫

史達林死後，赫魯雪夫於一九五六年成為蘇聯最高領導人，他在內政上，推行文藝自由化、進行農業改革。外交上，他與美國和西歐針鋒相對，成為冷戰代表人物。

一九六一年六月，赫魯雪夫與甘迺迪會議，討論柏林問題，他再度要求英美法撤出西柏林（第一次提出是在一九五八年），遭甘迺迪斷然拒絕，同年八月，蘇聯與東德築起柏林圍牆。一九六二年，他策劃的古巴飛彈危機使美俄幾近發動核子戰爭。一九六四年因政變下台，赫魯雪夫從此淡出政壇。

圖片提供 manhhai

Soviet Union 蘇聯

蘇維埃社會主義共和國聯邦（CCCP）的簡稱，存在於一九二二年至一九九一年，是當時世界上面積最大的國家。蘇維埃是俄語「代表會議」的意思。儘管蘇聯憲法規定這是一個聯邦國家，由十五個平等的蘇維埃社會主義共和國自願聯合組成，但其實權力高度集中，由蘇聯共產黨一黨執政。

一九八〇年代，長期與美國及西歐冷戰的蘇聯國力衰弱，蘇聯領導人戈巴契夫開始進行改革（Perestroika），但自由民主化及放寬對衛星國箝制的結果，是一九九一年的蘇聯解體。其後由俄羅斯聯邦繼承蘇聯大部分的軍事、經濟力量，及國際地位。

GM

Grammar Master

用反身代名詞「鄭重強調」

英文的反身代名詞，就是中文「……自己」，概念對台灣人來說不困難，但如何巧妙使用在文章之中表達，便要了解這個詞在英文文法上的作用有哪些。

● **主詞與受詞為同一人**

解 表達做動作的人跟接受動作反應的人是同一個，也就是句子裡主詞與受詞為同一人。

例 **We treated ourselves to dinner at an expensive restaurant.**
我們到一家昂貴的餐廳犒賞自己一頓晚餐。

例 **Pam blamed herself for the mistakes.**
潘將錯誤歸咎於自己。

● **跟在主詞或受詞後作語氣上的強調**

解 此用法中就算拿掉句中的反身代名詞，仍不影響句意。

例 **The house itself was cheap compared to the land.**
房子本身的價值要比土地便宜。（強調主詞）

例 **I want her to finish the work herself.**
我要她自己完成工作。（強調受詞）

這篇演說發表於一九八七年的六月十二日。Tear down this wall!（推倒高牆！）這句話被視為與柏林圍牆有關的最經典名言，但當初差點就因被認為太過極端而被幕僚刪除。但派駐西德的美國官員和總統文稿寫手衡酌西柏林輿論，認為這句話並無不妥，雷根也很喜歡，最後決定保留。

儘管演講稿不是自己寫的，但雷根的演說風格與迷人風采，讓他被媒體譽為「偉大的溝通者」（The Great Communicator），也一直是美國人心目中最偉大的總統之一。

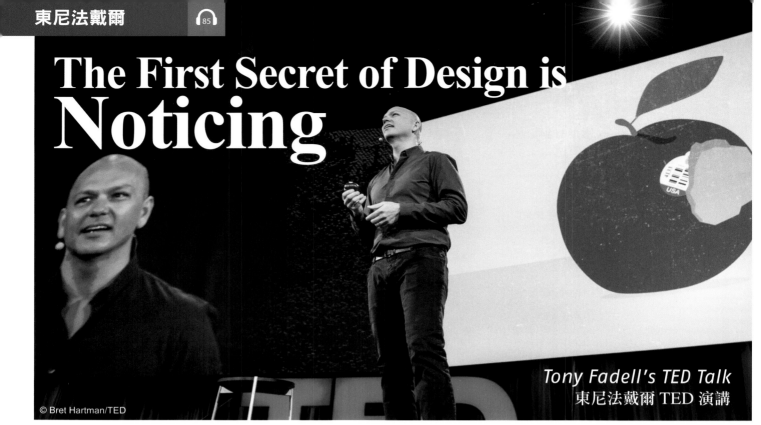

The First Secret of Design is Noticing

Tony Fadell's TED Talk
東尼法戴爾 TED 演講

© Bret Hartman/TED

 You Won't Even Notice It
你會習以為常

In the great 1980s movie 🔲 *The Blues Brothers*, there's a scene where John Belushi goes to visit Dan Aykroyd in his apartment in Chicago for the very first time. As John sits on Dan's bed, a train goes rushing by, [1]**rattling** everything in the room. John asks, "How often does that train go by?" Dan replies, "So often, you won't even notice it."

一九八〇年代有一部經典電影《福祿雙霸天》，裡面有一個場景，是約翰貝魯西第一次到丹艾克洛德在芝加哥的公寓。約翰坐在丹的床上時，一列火車呼嘯而過，房間裡所有東西都跟著嘎嘎作響。約翰問：「火車多久來一次？」丹回答：「很頻繁，頻繁到你會習以為常。」

We all know what he's talking about. As human beings, we get used to everyday things really fast. As a product designer, it's my job to see those everyday things, to feel them, and try to improve upon them. Why do we get used to everyday things? As human beings, we have limited brain power. And so our brains [2]**encode** the everyday things we do into habits so we can 🔲 free up space to learn new things. It's a process called [3]**habituation**.

我們都懂他的意思。身為人類，我們很快就能習慣日常生活的一切事物。但身為產品設計師，我的工作就是觀察這些日常事物，感受它們，並試著改善它們。我們為何會習慣日常事物？身為人類，我們的腦力有限。所以我們的大腦會將每天做的事情編碼成為習慣，好讓大腦空出更多容量學習新事物。這樣的過程稱為習慣性。

Now, habituation isn't always bad. Remember learning to drive? I sure do. It's a [4]**nerve-wracking** experience. But as the weeks went by, driving became easier and easier. You habituated it. So there's a good reason why our brains habituate

VOCABULARY 86

1) **rattle** [ˈrætəl] (v.) 發出咯咯聲
The windows rattled all night in the storm.

2) **encode** [ɪnˈcod] (v.) 編碼
Lasers are used to encode music on CDs.

3) **habituation** [hə͵bɪtʃuˈeʃən] (n.) 成為習慣，適應
(v.) **habituate** [həˈbɪtʃu͵et]
Feeding wild animals can lead to habituation to humans.

4) **nerve-wracking** [ˈnɜv͵rækɪŋ] (a.) 令人非常不安的，極為惱人的
The sound of that car alarm is really nerve-racking.

5) **exhausting** [ɪgˈzɔstɪŋ] (a.) 令人精疲力盡的
I had an exhausting day at work today.

things. **GM** If we didn't, we'd notice every little detail, all the time. It would be [5]**exhausting**, and we'd have no time to learn about new things.

習慣性並非全都是不好的。還記得學開車的時候嗎？我還記得很清楚。那是一個令人膽戰心驚的體驗。但幾個星期過後，開車變得越來越輕鬆，因為你習慣了。所以，這就是為什麼我們的大腦會習慣事物。假如不習慣的話，我們無時無刻都會注意到每一個小細節。這會讓人筋疲力盡，也不會有時間去學習新事物。

Habituation Isn't Always Good
習慣性並非全都是好事

But sometimes, habituation isn't good. **GM** If it stops us from noticing the problems that are around us, that's bad. But designers, [6]**innovators** and [7]**entrepreneurs**, it's our job to not just notice those things, but to go one step further and try to fix them. Why? Because it's easy to solve a problem that almost everyone sees. But it's hard to solve a problem that almost no one sees.

不過，有時候習慣性並不是好事。假如我們因為習慣而沒注意到周遭發生的問題，這就不是好事了。但身為設計師、發明家和創業家，我們的工作不只是要去注意這些事物，還要進一步修正這些事物。為什麼呢？因為解決一個幾乎每個人都會發現的問題是很簡單的，但要解決一個幾乎沒有人發現的問題是很難的。

During my years at Apple, Steve Jobs challenged us to come into work every day, to see our products through the eyes of the customer, the new customer, the one that has fears and possible frustrations and hopeful [8]**exhilaration** that their new technology product could work [9]**straightaway** for them. He called it staying beginners, and wanted to make sure that we focused on those tiny little details to make them faster, easier and [10]**seamless** for the new customers.

我在蘋果公司時，賈伯斯要求我們每天來上班，都要從顧客的角度看待我們的產品，尤其是新顧客，對於新買的科技產品是否能馬上發揮功效，是帶著擔憂和些許挫敗、卻又滿懷希望的興奮心情。他說，這就是保持初心，並要我們專注於這類小細節，好讓新顧客更加快速上手、更不費力、更順手。

> 66 With most tech guys, it's the same outfit every day—they wear their company logo.
>
> 對大多科技業者而言，他們每天打扮都一樣——都把公司的商標穿在身上。
>
> *東尼法戴爾談科技業者*

Tony Fadell
東尼法戴爾

© OFFICIAL LEWEB PHOTOS

生於一九六三年，二○○六至二○○八年間任職蘋果公司，主導 iPod 研發設計，因此被稱為 iPod 之父。後因工作時間過長離職，以便有更多時間與家人相處。

打造自家住宅時，東尼法戴爾開始研究家用空調系統，得到許多靈感，二○一○年與友人創建 Nest Lab 公司，專攻智慧家用設備。該公司於二○一四年以三十二億美元售予 Google，東尼法戴爾仍繼續執掌公司業務。

© Vdovichenko Denis / Shutterstock.com

---

6) **innovator** [ˈɪnəˌvetə] (n.) 創新者，先驅
Steve Jobs was a true innovator.

7) **entrepreneur** [ˌɑntrəprəˈnɜ] (n.) 創業者，企業家
Silicon Valley has the highest concentration of entrepreneurs in the world.

8) **exhilaration** [ɪɡˌzɪləˈreʃən] (n.) 愉快的心情，歡喜，興奮
All the players on the team felt the exhilaration of victory.

9) **straightaway** [ˌstretəˈwe] (adv.) 立刻，馬上
If we don't leave straightaway, we'll be late.

10) **seamless** [ˈsemlɪs] (a.) 天衣無縫的，順利的
The new owners have promised a seamless change in management.

Charge Before Use
使用前先充電

So I remember this clearly in the very earliest days of the  iPod. I'd take all the time to get to the store, I'd [1)]**check out**, I'd come back home, I'd start to [2)]**unbox** it. And then, there was a little [3)]**sticker**: "Charge before use." What? I can't believe it! I just spent all this time buying this product and now I have to charge before use. It was crazy.

我還清楚記得，iPod 剛推出的時候，我特地花時間親自走進商店裡，結了帳，把東西帶回家後，開始打開包裝。然後看到裡面有張小貼紙寫著：「使用前先充電。」什麼？我真不敢相信！我花了那麼多時間買了這個產品，現在還必須在使用前先充電。真是太誇張了。

Well, Steve noticed that and he said, "We're not going to let that happen to our product." So that customer, with all that exhilaration, could just start using the product. It was great, and it worked. People liked it. Today, almost every product that you get that's battery powered comes out of the box fully charged. But back then, we noticed that detail and we fixed it, and now everyone else does that as well.

嗯，賈伯斯注意到了，他說：「我們不能讓這件事發生在我們的產品上。」所以我們要讓顧客帶著愉快的心情，直接開始使用產品。這個想法很棒，而且有用，大家都喜歡這樣的設計。如今，幾乎所有產品在打開包裝時，電池都是已經充好電了。但在以前，是我們注意到這個細節，然後修正它，現在其他公司也都如法炮製。

> 66 Studies have shown that children are less likely to wake up to a horn than the sound of a mother's voice.
>
> 研究顯示，兒童聽到媽媽的聲音，比聽到喇叭聲還容易醒來。

東尼法戴爾談兒童

So why am I telling you this? Well, it's seeing the invisible problem, not just the obvious problem, that's important, not just for product design, but for everything we do. So, I'm [4)]**hesitant** to give you any tips about [5)]**neuroscience** or psychology. But let me leave you with a few tips that I do, that we all can do, to fight habituation.

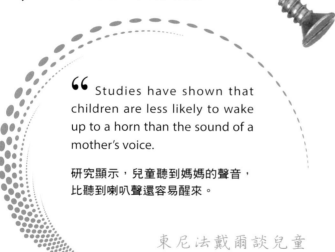

VOCABULARY 🎧 88

1) **check out** [tʃɛk aʊt] (phr.) 結帳
   I can check you out over here, sir.

2) **unbox** [ʌnˋbɑks] (v.) 從箱子、包裝拿出來
   Have you unboxed your new video game yet?

3) **sticker** [ˋstɪkɚ] (n.) 貼紙，標籤
   Take the price sticker off her present before you wrap it.

4) **hesitant** [ˋhɛzɪtənt] (a.) 猶豫的，遲疑的，不願意的
   Many consumers are hesitant to purchase products online.

5) **neuroscience** [ˋnʊroˌsaɪəns] (n.) 神經科學
   Neuroscience is the scientific study of the nervous system.

6) **tackle** [ˋtækəl] (v.) 著手處理，對付
   The government has promised to tackle unemployment.

For my second tip, it's to look closer. One of my greatest teachers was my grandfather. I remember one story he told me about screws, and about how you need to have the right screw for the right job. Our job is to make products that are easy to install for all of our customers themselves without professionals. So what did we do? We thought, "How many different screws can we put in the box? Because there are so many different wall types." So we came up with three different screws to put in the box.

我的第二個秘訣，就是注意細節。我人生中最偉大的老師之一，就是我爺爺。我記得他告訴過我關於螺絲的故事，對的螺絲要用在對的工作上。我們的工作是要讓所有顧客都能毫不費力地安裝我們的產品，而不必另外請人來裝。那麼，我們怎麼做？我們是這樣思考的：「我們要在包裝盒裡放多少螺絲？因為牆壁的種類有這麼多。」於是我們決定把三種螺絲放進包裝盒裡。

那麼，為什麼我要告訴你們這些？因為我們要注意的是看不見的問題，而不只是顯而易見的問題，這才是重點，不只是在產品設計上，而是我們所做的每一件事。嗯，我不太想跟你們提關於神經學或心理學的事。不過，還是讓我告訴你們幾個對抗習慣性的秘訣，這幾個秘訣我都在用，大家也都能做到。

So we shipped the product, and people weren't having a great experience. So what did we do? We designed a special screw, a [7] **custom** screw. There was just one screw in the box that was easy to [8] **mount** and put on the wall.

我們就這樣將產品包裝發貨，結果顧客的體驗並不愉快。我們該怎麼辦？我們又設計出了一種特別的螺絲，就是特製螺絲。只在包裝盒裡放一種螺絲，而且可以輕易就固定在牆壁上。

Look Broader, Look Closer
眼界放大，注意細節

My first tip is to look broader. You see, when you're [6] **tackling** a problem, sometimes there are a lot of steps that lead up to that problem, and sometimes a lot of steps after it. If you can take a step back and look broader, maybe you can change some of those steps before the problem. Maybe you can combine them. Maybe you can remove them altogether to make that better.

我的第一個秘訣是眼界要放大。是這樣，當你在處理一個問題時，有時問題是因為許多步驟所導致的，有時是因為問題而衍生出許多步驟。假如能退一步，放大眼界，也許能在問題產生前改變一些步驟，也許是結合一些步驟，也許是移除所有步驟，好讓一切更順利。

7) **custom** [ˋkʌstəm] (a.) 訂做的，特製的
The CEO wears only custom suits.

8) **mount** [maʊnt] (v.) 固定在…上，鑲嵌，裱貼
Can you help me mount this painting on the wall?

 ### Think Younger
讓想法更年輕

My last piece of advice is to think younger. Every day, I'm [1)]**confronted** with interesting questions from my three young kids. My son came to me the other day and I told him, "Go run out to the mailbox and check it." He looked at me, [2)]**puzzled**, and said, "Why doesn't the mailbox just check itself and tell us when it has mail?"

我最後一個建議是讓想法更年輕。我的三個小孩每天都會問我很有趣的問題。我兒子最近跑來找我，我告訴他：「去信箱那裡，看看有沒有信。」他看著我，滿臉疑惑，問道：「為什麼信箱不會自己看看，有信時再來通知我們？」

The more we're [3)]**exposed** to something, the more we get used to it. But kids haven't been around long enough to get used to those things. So when they run into problems, they immediately try to solve them, and sometimes they find a better way. We all saw the world more clearly when we saw it for the first time, before a lifetime of habits got in the way. Our challenge is to get back there, to feel that [4)]**frustration**, to see those little details, to look broader, look closer, and to think younger so we can stay beginners.

我們接觸的事物越多，對事物就越是習慣。但小孩對事物的接觸時間並不長，還沒習慣這些事物。所以，當他們遇到問題時，會立刻想辦法解決，而且有時能找到更好的辦法。我們第一次看到這個世界時，是看得最清楚的時候，之後就是讓一生養成的習慣阻礙我們看這個世界。我們要挑戰的，就是回到最初的心態，感受那些挫敗，看到那些小細節，看得更廣、更仔細，讓想法更年輕，好讓我們永遠保持初心。

It's not easy. It requires us pushing back against one of the most basic ways we 🔵 make sense of the world. But if we do, we could do some pretty amazing things. For me, hopefully, that's better product design. For you, that could mean something else, something powerful.

這並不容易。因為我們要抵抗的，卻是用來理解這個世界的最基本方式之一。但假如我們能這麼做，就可以完成一些非常美妙的事。對我來說，就是希望能完成更好的產品設計。對你們來說，可能會是其他事情，一些有影響力的事。

VOCABULARY 🎧 90

1) **confront** [kən`frʌnt] (v.) 面對，面臨
It takes courage to confront our fears.

2) **puzzled** [`pʌzəld] (a.) 困惑的，搞糊塗的，茫然的
I'm puzzled that he didn't return my call.

3) **expose (to)** [ɪk`spoz] (v.) 使接觸到，使暴露於
The goal of the program is to expose students to art.

4) **frustration** [frʌ`streʃən] (n.) 挫折（感），挫敗
This software is causing me nothing but frustration.

The Blues Brothers
《福祿雙霸天》

這部一九八〇年的電影，敘述一對玩藍調音樂的混混兄弟，為了幫助當初收養他們的孤兒院，決定完成上帝指派的任務，重組他們的 The Blues Brothers 樂團，到處巡迴籌錢，卻搞得雞飛狗跳。這部非主流喜劇電影受到特定族群喜愛，已成為一部「邪典」cult classic。

© Pedro Rebelo

片中有許多藍調、爵士樂大咖客串甚至獻唱，像是 James Brown 飾演牧師、Ray Charles 飾演樂器當鋪老闆、Aretha Franklin 飾演餐廳女侍，片中還能看到 Cab Calloway、Chaka Khan、John Lee Hooker、Pinetop Perkins 及 Joe Walsh，甚至連大導演史匹柏也有軋一角。

free up 挪出（時間，空間，錢等）

free 在這邊當動詞「使……有空的」，free up 指設法挪出餘裕。

A: Will you have time to help me move this weekend?
　這周末你可以挪出一些時間幫我搬家嗎？
B: Well, I have plans, but I can free up some time to help you.
　我有安排事情了，但是我還是可以挪出一些時間幫你的。

設計，從「假設」開始：善用表達「如果……就……」的 if 子句

假設語氣是使用頻率相當高的語氣，句型也只有三種，但台灣人常被「與現在事實相反要用……，與未來相反要……」的口訣搞不清楚要用哪一種。其實只要回到你要說的話本身該用的時態，就可以清楚判斷了，不用管是跟什麼事實「相反」。

● 未來的事：「如果明天下雪，學校應該就會關閉。」
例 *If it snows tomorrow, schools will probably close.*
解 不論是講未來或常態性的事情，if 子句都用現在簡單式，另一句則用未來式。（因為是在講未來可能發生的事情）

● 不可能的事：「如果我是小鳥，就可以在天空自在飛翔。」
例 *If I were a bird, I could fly freely in the sky.*
解 敘述目前幾乎不可能的事，if 子句跟另一句都用過去簡單式。（因為若用現在式時態不就等於有發生的事實了嗎？）

● 過去的事：「如果當時沒有你相助，我就完蛋了。」
例 *If you hadn't helped me, I would have gotten into big trouble.*
解 這是在講「當時、過去」沒有發生的事，if 子句跟另一句都用過去完成式。（跟上一個原理一樣，若正常使用過去式，那就是講過去真正有發生的事了！）

iPod

二〇〇一年十月，蘋果公司推出 iPod 這款可攜式影音播放器，透過 iTunes 軟體向 iPod 傳輸音樂，使用者可以輕鬆在自用電腦及 iPod 上管理音樂庫，不必再像之前其他播放器那樣燒來燒去，成功在三年內搶下超過九成的音樂播放器市場，完全改變音樂使用習慣及音樂消費市場，對文化產生極大衝擊。

© Pedro Rebelo

make sense of 搞懂，理解

sense 是「意義，道理」，想從一樣事物當中找出道理，就是「搞懂，理解」的意思。

A: Did you understand the teacher's explanation?
　你聽懂老師的說明了嗎？
B: No. I couldn't make sense of it.
　沒有。我還是沒搞懂。

The First Secret of Design is Noticing（設計的首要秘訣就是注意力）是東尼法戴爾二〇一五年於 TED 發表的演講。（TED 是 technology、entertainment、design 的縮寫，美國非營利機構，組織 TED 大會邀集各領域傑出人士演講，分享科技、設計、娛樂等領域的心得。）

東尼法戴爾設計 iPod 一戰成名之後，又因他創立的 Nest Labs 公司被 Google 相中買下造成轟動。他究竟為何能順利從「影音播放器」領域跳進「智慧家用品」，相當令人好奇。但東尼告訴大家，原來設計哪有什麼領域之別？「拒絕習以為常」而已。

Why It's Time to Forget the Pecking Order at Work

Margaret Heffernan's TED Talk

瑪格麗特赫弗南 TED 演講

© Ryan Lash / TED Conference

Superchickens
超級雞群

An [1]**evolutionary** biologist at Purdue University named William Muir studied chickens. He was interested in [2]**productivity**—I think it's something that concerns all of us—but it's easy to measure in chickens because you just count the eggs. He wanted to know what could make his chickens more productive, so he devised a beautiful experiment. Chickens live in groups, so first of all, he selected just an average flock, and he let it alone for six generations. But then he created a second group of the individually most productive chickens—you could call them superchickens—and he put them together in a superflock, and each generation, he selected only the most productive for breeding.

普度大學有一位研究雞的進化生物學家，名叫威廉繆爾。他對生產力的研究感興趣——我想這也是我們都關心的事——不過，評估雞的生產力是比較簡單的，因為你只要數雞蛋就行了。他想知道如何增加雞的生產力，於是他設計了一套美妙的實驗。雞是群居動物，所以，首先他挑選了一群普通的雞群，讓牠們自行繁衍六代。然後他挑選第二群雞，而且每一隻雞的生產力都是最高的——你可以稱牠們為超級雞——這群雞就是超級雞群，接下來的每一代都只挑出生產力最高的雞來繁殖。

After six generations had passed, what did he find? Well, the first group, the average group, was doing just fine. They were all [3]**plump** and fully feathered and egg production had increased dramatically. What about the second group? Well, all but three were dead. They'd [4]**pecked** the rest to death. The individually productive chickens had only achieved their success by [5]**suppressing** the productivity of the rest.

繁殖六代過後，他發現了什麼？嗯，第一群雞，也就是普通雞群，表現得還不錯。牠們都長得很肥碩、羽翼豐滿，生產的雞蛋量也急遽增加。那第二群雞呢？嗯，除了三隻，其他都死了。是牠們把其他雞啄死的，牠們壓制其他雞的生產量，好讓自己成功繁殖。

VOCABULARY

1) **evolutionary** [ˌɛvəˈluʃəˌnɛri] (a.) 進化的，發展的
The researcher is an expert in evolutionary biology.

2) **productivity** [ˌprodʌkˈtɪvəti] (n.) 生產力，生產率
The company is looking for ways to improve productivity.

3) **plump** [plʌmp] (a.)（肉類食物）多肉的
We bought a plump turkey to serve on Thanksgiving.

4) **peck** [pɛk] (v.) 啄，啄食，啄穿
The chickens pecked at their feed.

5) **suppress** [səˈprɛs] (v.) 抑制，阻止
The virus suppresses the body's immune system.

That's My Company
那跟我的公司一樣

Now, as I've gone around the world talking about this and telling this story in all sorts of organizations and companies, people have seen the [6]**relevance** almost instantly. And they come up and they say things to me like, "That superflock, that's my company." Or, "That's my country." Or, "That's my life."

現在，我在世界各地為各種不同的組織和公司演講時，都會說這個故事，大家幾乎可以立刻聯想到其中的關連性。然後他們會過來跟我說類似這樣的話：「那個超級雞群，就跟我的公司一樣」，或是「那跟我的國家一樣」，或是「那跟我的人生一樣」。

All my life I've been told that the way we have to get ahead is to compete: get into the right school, get into the right job, get to the top, and I've really never found it very inspiring. I've started and run businesses because invention is a joy, and because working alongside brilliant, creative people is its own reward. And I've never really felt very motivated by **LG** pecking orders or by superchickens or by superstars.

我這一生一直有人告訴我，我們想成功的話，就要有競爭力，例如：要進好學校、要找到好工作、要晉升到最高職位，但我從不覺得這有多激勵。我創業經商，是因為我覺得創造力本身就是一種快樂，也因為跟聰明、有創意的人一起工作很有收穫。而且我從不覺得打造競爭制度，或打造超級雞群、超級巨星有多激勵人心。

But for the past 50 years, we've run most organizations and some societies along the superchicken model. And the result has been just the same as in William Muir's experiment: [7]**aggression**, [8]**dysfunction** and waste.

不過，在過去五十年，我們都是以打造超級雞群的模式在經營大部分組織和部分社會。而且結果一直都跟繆爾的實驗一樣：侵略好鬥、機能失調和耗費資源。

> 66 There is a strange pecking order among actors. Theater actors look down on film actors, who look down on TV actors. Thank God for reality shows, or we wouldn't have anybody to look down on.

在演員當中有一種很奇怪的階級觀念。舞台劇演員瞧不起電影演員，電影演員不屑電視演員。感謝老天爺，還好有真人實境秀，不然我們就沒有人可以鄙視了。

喬治克隆尼談啄序

Margaret Heffernan
瑪格麗特赫弗南

© James Duncan Davidson / TED Conference

一九五五年出生於美國德州，在荷蘭長大，劍橋大學畢業，曾任職於 BBC 廣播公司，製作橫跨多種領域的廣播和電視節目。定居美國期間，曾經營管理多家科技、資訊公司。回到英國後，負責創辦英國貝斯大學（University of Bath）。

瑪格麗特赫弗南是一位優秀的公司執行長、作家、劇作家及網路專欄作家。她善於書寫自身經驗，並從心理學、腦神經科學及管理學的角度，點出人性的盲點，剖析現代公司組織的弊病，並提出建議。

本書中文版為《大雞時代》

'Entertaining and compellingly argued'
SUNDAY TIMES

WILFUL BLINDNESS
Why we ignore the obvious at our peril

MARGARET HEFFERNAN
Shortlisted for the FT/Goldman Sachs
Business Book of the Year Award

---

6) **relevance** [ˈrɛləvəns] (n.) 關聯，切題
I don't see the relevance of your question.

7) **aggression** [əˈgrɛʃən] (n.) 侵略（行動），侵犯（行為）
Dogs that show aggression toward people should be kept inside.

8) **dysfunction** [dɪsˈfʌŋkʃən] (n.) 機能不良，機能障礙
Poor management can lead to organizational dysfunction.

What Determines Success?
成功的決定因素

So what is it that makes some groups obviously more successful and more productive than others? Well, that's the question a team at MIT took to research. They brought in hundreds of volunteers, they put them into groups, and they gave them very hard problems to solve. And what happened was exactly what you'd expect—that some groups were very much more successful than others. But what was really interesting was that the high-achieving groups were not those where they had one or two people with [1)]**spectacularly** high [2)]**IQ**.

那麼，有些群體為何明顯比其他群體更成功、更有成效？嗯，這就是麻省理工學院一個團隊拿來研究的問題。他們徵集了幾百位自願受試者，將他們分組後，分配非常困難的問題讓他們解決。結果就跟你猜的一樣——有些小組的表現就是遠比其他小組成功。但非常有趣的是，表現優異的小組並不是那些有一、兩個人智商特別高的小組。

Instead, they had three characteristics. First of all, they showed high degrees of social [3)]**sensitivity** to each other. Secondly, the successful groups gave roughly equal time to each other, so that no one voice dominated. And thirdly, the more successful groups had more women in them. [applause]

成功的小組反而有三項特質。首先，他們的成員對彼此都有高度的社會敏感性。第二，成功小組的成員互相給予的時間都差不多一樣，所以沒有一個人的意見是佔主導地位的。第三，比較成功的小組，女性成員也較多。[掌聲]

So how does this [4)]**play out** in the real world? Well, it means that what happens between people really counts, because in groups that are highly

[5)]**attuned** and sensitive to each other, ideas can flow and grow. People don't get stuck. They don't waste energy down dead ends.

那麼，如何把這樣的道理放到現實生活中呢？嗯，這表示人與人之間的互動也非常重要，因為在群體中，對彼此有高度的理解和感受，創意才能源源不絕地湧出和成長。大家才不會停滯不前，也不會卡在死胡同裡浪費精力。

Getting to Know Each Other
互相瞭解

When I was running my first software company, I realized that we were getting [6)]**stuck**. There was a lot of [7)]**friction**, but not much else, and I gradually realized the brilliant, creative people that I'd hired didn't know each other. They were so focused on their own individual work, they didn't even know who they were sitting next to, and it was only when I insisted that we stop working and invest time in getting to know each other that we achieved real [8)]**momentum**.

我在經營第一家軟體公司時，發現我們開始停滯不前，發生了許多摩擦，也沒有什麼進展，而且我逐漸意識到，我聘請的聰明、有創意的員工都彼此不熟。他們太專注於自己的工作，根本不知道隔壁坐的是誰，只有在我堅持要他們放下工作，花時間認識彼此後，我們才終於獲得真正的動力。

Now, that was 20 years ago, and now I visit companies that have [9)]**banned** coffee cups at desks because they want people to ᴸᴳ hang out around the coffee machines and talk to each other. The [10)]**Swedes** even have a special term for this. They call it ᴸᴳ *fika,* which means more than a coffee break; it means collective [11)]**restoration**. Companies don't have ideas; only people do. And

---

VOCABULARY 🎧 94

1) **spectacularly** [spɛkˋtækjələli] (adv.) 極其，非常，壯觀地
The founder of the company is spectacularly wealthy.

2) **IQ** [ˋaɪˋkju] (abbr.) 智商，intelligence quotient 的縮寫
Have you ever taken an IQ test?

3) **sensitivity** [ˌsɛnsɪˋtɪvɪti] (n.) 敏感性
People vary greatly in their sensitivity to pain.

4) **play out** [ple aʊt] (phr.) 發展，結果
Nobody knew how the situation would play out.

5) **attuned** [əˋtund] (a.) 非常熟悉、了解的
Nurses must be attuned to the needs of their patients.

6) **stuck** [stʌk] (a.) 卡住的，困住的
Marge is stuck in a dead-end career.

7) **friction** [ˋfrɪkʃən] (n.) 摩擦（力），不和
The incident has caused friction between the two countries.

8) **momentum** [məˋmɛntəm] (n.) 氣勢，動力
The politician's campaign is gaining momentum.

9) **ban** [bæn] (v./n.) 禁止，取締
The city is considering banning smoking in restaurants.

million dollars, and employee satisfaction went up 10 percent. Not a bad return on social capital, which compounds even as you spend it.

那麼，如果把這些全部整理一下，你會發現這是一種稱為「社會資本」的東西。社會資本就是依存和互相依賴，而信任是從這點建立起來的。這實際上是什麼意思？意思是時間就是一切，因為社會資本是隨著時間增長的。所以在團隊中，成員共同合作的時間越長，效果越好，因為想得到真正的坦誠和敞開胸懷，你需要花時間建立所需的信任。艾利克斯佩特蘭曾建議一家公司，統一喝咖啡的休息時間，讓員工有時間互相聊天，後來公司的盈利增加了一千五百萬美元，員工滿意度也上升百分之十。從社會資本來看，回報率還不錯，而且隨著你的付出，回報率還是加倍增長。

what motivates people are the bonds and loyalty and trust they develop between each other.

那是二十年前的事了，現在我拜訪的公司有些已經禁止在辦公桌上放咖啡杯，因為他們要讓員工到咖啡機旁相聚、聊天。瑞典人甚至發明了一個特別的專有名詞來形容這件事：fika，這表示休息時不再獨自一個人喝咖啡，而是大家一起充電的時刻。公司本身沒有想法，有想法的是員工。而員工的動力是來自於互相建立的凝聚力、忠誠和信任。

Now, when you put all of this together, what you get is something called social capital. Social capital is the 12)**reliance** and 13)**interdependency** that builds trust. What does this mean in practical terms? It means that time is everything, because social capital 14)**compounds** with time. So teams that work together longer get better, because it takes time to develop the trust you need for real 15)**candor** and openness. When Alex Pentland suggested to one company that they 16)**synchronize** coffee breaks so that people would have time to talk to each other, profits went up 15

---

10) **Swede** [swed] (n.) 瑞典人
Most Swedes are fluent in English.

11) **restoration** [ˌrɛstəˋreʃən] (n.) 恢復，修復
Both sides are hoping for the restoration of peace.

12) **reliance** [rɪˋlaɪəns] (n.) 依賴，信賴
The government is working to decrease the country's reliance on oil.

13) **interdependency** [ˌɪntədɪˋpɛndənsi] (n.) 互相依靠
There is increasing economic interdependency between the U.S. and China.

14) **compound** [kəmˋpaʊnd] (v.) （以複利）增加，加重
You need time to let your savings compound.

15) **candor** [ˋkændə] (n.) 坦率，真誠
Thank you for your candor.

16) **synchronize** [ˋsɪŋkrəˌnaɪz] (v.) （使）協調、同步
It takes a lot of practice for the dancers to synchronize their movements.

Things Have to Change
事情必須改變

Once you appreciate truly how social work is, a lot of things have to change. Management by talent contest has routinely **LG** pitted employees against each other. Now, **1)rivalry** has to be replaced by social capital. For decades, we've tried to motivate people with money, even though we've got a vast amount of research that shows that money **2)erodes** social connectedness. Now, we need to let people motivate each other. And for years, we've thought that leaders were **3)heroic** **4)soloists** who were expected, all by themselves, to solve complex problems. Now, we need to redefine leadership as an activity in which conditions are created in which everyone can do their most courageous thinking together.

一旦真正體會到工作的社交層面有多麼重要，許多事情也就必須改變。人才競爭的管理方式通常會讓員工互相對立。現在，對立必須要用社會資本取代。數十年來，我們試著用金錢激勵員工，儘管我們有大量研究顯示，金錢會削弱社會聯結。現在，我們要讓人們互相激勵。多年來，我們以為領導者是唱獨腳戲的英雄，眾人期待他們能全靠自己解決複雜問題。現在，我們需要重新將領導力界定為一種行動，在這個行動中創造出一種環境，讓每個人都可以一起集思廣益，分享最大膽的想法。

> " For good ideas and true innovation, you need human interaction, conflict, argument, debate.
>
> 好的創意和真正的創新，需要有人際互動、衝突、爭執和辯論。
>
> 瑪格麗特赫弗南談創新

There was a lot **LG** at stake then, and there's a lot at stake now, and we won't solve our problems if we expect them to be solved by a few supermen or superwomen. Now we need everybody, because it is only when we accept that everybody has value that we will **5)liberate** the energy and imagination and momentum we need to create the best beyond measure.

過去有許多嚴重問題要解決，現在還是有許多嚴重問題尚待解決，假如我們期待少數的超人或超女解決問題，問題將無法解決。現在我們需要每一個人，因為唯有認可每一個人的價值，我們才能釋放出所需的能量、想像力、動力，創造不可估量的最佳成果。

VOCABULARY 96

1) **rivalry** [ˈraɪvəlrɪ] (n.) 競爭（行為），對抗（行為）
There's a bitter rivalry between the Red Sox and the Yankees.

2) **erode** [ɪˈrod] (v.) 削弱，侵蝕
Support for the candidate is slowly eroding.

3) **heroic** [hɪˈroɪk] (a.) 英勇的，英雄的
The soldiers received medals for their heroic actions.

4) **soloist** [ˈsoloɪst] (n.) 獨奏者，獨唱者
The orchestra hired a new violin soloist.

5) **liberate** [ˈlɪbəˌret] (v.) 解放，使獲自由
The town was liberated near the end of the war.

pecking order
啄序,階級尊卑制度

「啄食順序理論」說法源自一九二〇年代挪威動物學家 Thorleif Schjelderup-Ebbe 對母雞群的觀察,他發現母雞是以啄啄較弱的個體來確認彼此的地位高下,後續許多禽類研究也都觀察到類似的行為。pecking order 後來用來泛指動物界(包含人類)的階級尊卑制度,即較具資歷/實力者欺壓弱小的行為。

© William

hang out 一起混(玩)

hang out 是指朋友聚一聚,感情才不會散。也可以用 get together 表示「一起混(玩)」。

A: What do you like to do on weekends?
你週末喜歡幹嘛?
B: I usually hang out at the mall with my friends.
我經常找朋友一起逛賣場。

© Ruvi Leider, www.ruvileider.com/

© ruminatrix

fika 喝咖啡,聊是非

有人說:學瑞典文第一個要會的字是 tack(thank you),第二個字是 hej(hello),第三個字就是 fika 了。形式上,fika 是在日常生活中休息一下,喝杯咖啡;但對瑞典人來說,最重要的是與人相聚的社交意涵。

在瑞典,隨時隨地都能 fika,對象可以是親朋好友、同事乃至你有興趣認識的陌生人。除了喝咖啡,瑞典人還喜歡配個餅乾、蛋糕,其中楓糖肉桂捲(cinnamon rolls)就是最具代表性的 fika 點心。

pit (sb./sth.) against 使……與……對抗

pit 當名詞時表「鬥雞場」,當動詞時有「使……與……相鬥」之意。

A: I can't wait to see the Pacquiao-Mayweather fight!
我等不及要看帕奎奧對上梅威瑟的大戰!
B: Yeah. It's gonna pit the world's top two boxers against each other.
對啊!這將是全球最頂尖兩位拳擊手的對決。

at stake 處於危急關頭,吉凶未卜

stake 有「危險,風險」的意思,某樣人事物處於 at stake 的狀況,就代表前途不明,有遭逢厄運的危險。

A: The town should be evacuated before the hurricane hits.
這個鎮應該在颱風侵襲前撤離居民。
B: I know. Thousands of lives are at stake.
對啊。成千上萬的生命遭受威脅。

使文筆更通暢:運用形容詞或副詞表示「……得多」

當想要在兩者中互相比較時,會用形容詞的比較級來修飾,譬如:America is bigger than Singapore. 若想強調不只是比較大,而是「大很多」,便要用另一個有「更……」含義的形容詞或副詞放在 bigger 前。常見用來修飾形容詞的字有 much、far、way、a lot 等。

● much、far、way、a lot + bigger / taller / more…

例 **Gina is much taller than her older sister.**
吉娜比她姐姐高得多。

例 **Kenny drives far more carefully than Hank.**
肯尼開車比漢克小心多了。

例 **Nathan is a lot smarter than he looks.**
奈森比外表看起來聰明多了。

這場演說發表於二〇一五年五月的 TEDWomen,在這個以 Revealing the ideas of women and girls(展現女性與女孩的想法)為號召的場合中,長期關注女性上班族議題的 Margaret Heffernan 在第二跨頁第二段提出:「比較成功的小組,女性成員也較多」,難怪會獲得滿堂喝彩。

© JoffreyM / Shutterstock.com

MICHAEL JACKSON
1958 - FOREVER + EVER

Madonna's *Tribute* to Michael Jackson

Long Live the King

瑪丹娜向麥可傑克森致敬

© JStone / Shutterstock.com

⭐ The World's Most Beloved Child
世上最受寵愛的孩子

Michael Jackson. *[cheers]* I have a little bit more to say than that. OK, here we go again. Michael Jackson was born in August 1958. **GM** So was I. Michael Jackson grew up in the suburbs of the Midwest. **GM** So did I. Michael Jackson had eight brothers and sisters. **GM** So do I. When Michael Jackson was six, he became a ²⁾**superstar**, and was perhaps the world's most ³⁾**beloved** child. When I was six, my mother died. I think he **LG** got the shorter end of the stick. I never had a mother, but he never had a childhood. And when you never get to have something, you become ⁴⁾**obsessed** by it.

麥可傑克森（歡呼聲）。我要說的不只這個。好了，我再從頭開始。麥可傑克森生於一九五八年八月，我也是。麥可傑克森生長在中西部的郊區，我也是。麥可傑克森有八個兄弟姊妹，我也是。麥可傑克森八歲時就成了巨星，可能是世上最受寵愛的孩子。我六歲時，我的母親過世。但我覺得他比我更不幸。我雖然從小失去母親，但他是失去了童年。當你從沒擁有過某樣東西時，你就會對這樣東西念念不忘。

I spent my childhood searching for my mother figures. Sometimes I was successful, but how do

VOCABULARY 🎧 98

1) **tribute** [ˈtrɪbjut] (n.) 稱頌，致敬
The painting is a tribute to the artist's genius.

2) **superstar** [ˈsupɚˌstɑr] (n.) 巨星
Beyoncé is one of pop's biggest superstars.

3) **beloved** [bɪˈlʌvd] (a.) 深受喜愛的
Terry's beloved aunt passed away recently.

4) **obsessed** [əbˈsɛst] (a.) 著迷的
Debbie is obsessed with boy bands.

5) **magnifying glass** [ˈmægnəˌfaɪɪŋ ˌglæs] (n.) 放大鏡
The teacher had us look at leaves with a magnifying glass.

6) **elegance** [ˈɛləgəns] (n.) 優雅，典雅
The designer's dresses have a timeless elegance.

you recreate your childhood when you are under the [5] **magnifying glass** of the world?

我在童年時不斷尋找可以代替母親的角色。有時候雖然成功了，但在這個世界的放大鏡下，你又要如何重建童年？

Inexplicable Magic
難以言喻的魅力

There is no question that Michael Jackson is one of the greatest talents the world has ever known. That when he sang a song at the LG ripe old age of eight he could make you feel like an experienced adult was squeezing your heart with his words. That when he moved he had the [6] **elegance** of Fred Astaire and LG packed the punch of Muhammad Ali. That his music had an extra layer of [7] **inexplicable** magic that didn't just make you want to dance but actually made you believe you could fly, dare to dream, be anything that you wanted to be. Because that is what heroes do, and Michael Jackson was a hero.

毫無疑問，麥可傑克森是全世界最有才華的藝人之一。他以八歲的「高齡之姿」，唱起歌來就像是歷盡滄桑的老大人，歌詞扣人心弦。跳起舞來不但有佛雷亞斯坦的優雅，也有拳王阿里的震撼力。他的音樂有一種莫名的魅力，不只會讓你想跳舞，也讓你相信自己能飛起來、勇於夢想、成為你想成為的一切。這是英雄才能做到的事，所以麥可傑克森就是英雄。

> ❝ One thing I've learned is that I'm not the owner of my talent; I'm the manager of it.
>
> 我學到一件事，我不是自己天賦的擁有者，而是管理者。
>
> 瑪丹娜談天賦

He performed in soccer stadiums around the world, and sold hundreds of millions of records and dined with prime ministers and presidents. Girls fell in love with him, boys fell in love with him, everyone wanted to dance like him. He seemed [8] **otherworldly**, but he was a human being.

他在世界各地的大巨蛋表演，賣出了好幾億張專輯，還與各國首相和總統一起進餐。不只女孩們愛上他，男孩們也愛他，每個人都想和他跳得一樣棒。他看似不食人間煙火，但其實是個平凡人。

© Everett Collection / Shutterstock.com

Madonna 瑪丹娜

一九五八年出生於密西根州，二十歲到紐約追求舞者夢。她於一九八三年獲得唱片合約，推出暢銷專輯《瑪丹娜》，開始以挑戰主流尺度的歌詞、MV 影帶及大膽言行闖蕩演藝界。

根據《金氏世界紀錄》統計，瑪丹娜的唱片銷售紀錄僅次於披頭四、貓王，以及麥可傑克森，同時擁有最多告示牌排行榜冠軍單曲（12 首）及最多冠軍專輯（8 張），並被告示牌排行榜評為流行音樂最成功藝人第二名（僅次於披頭四）。

7) **inexplicable** [ˌɪnɪkˈsplɪkəbəl] (a.) 莫名其妙的，難以解釋的
For some inexplicable reason, all the dogs began barking.

8) **otherworldly** [ˌʌðəˈwɜldlɪ] (a.) 超脫世俗的
The star was known for her otherworldly beauty.

Like most [1]**performers**, he was shy and [2]**plagued** with [3]**insecurities**. I can't say we were great friends, but in 1991 I decided I wanted to try to get to know him better. I asked him out to dinner, I said "My treat, I'll drive—just you and me."

就像大部分藝人，他其實很害羞，深受缺乏安全感之苦。我不敢說我們是多好的朋友，但在一九九一年時，我決定要多認識他一點。我約他出來吃晚餐，我跟他說：「我請客，我來開車，只有我們兩個人。」

Sunglasses at Night
晚上戴墨鏡

He agreed and showed up to my house without any [4]**bodyguards**. We drove to the restaurant in my car. It was dark out, but he was still wearing sunglasses.

I said, "Michael, I feel like I'm talking to a [5]**limousine**. Do you think you can take off your glasses so I can see your eyes?" Then he tossed the glasses out the window, looked at me with a wink

> I think the biggest reason I was able to express myself and not be intimidated was by not having a mother. For example, mothers teach you manners. And I absolutely did not learn any of those rules and regulations.
>
> 我覺得我能無畏的表達自己，原因就在我沒有媽媽。比如說，媽媽會教小孩禮貌。而我絕對沒有學過那些規矩。
>
> 瑪丹娜談表現自我

and a smile and said, "Can you see me now? Is that better?"

他答應了，來到我住處時沒有帶任何保鑣。我開車帶他到餐廳，當時天已經黑了，但他還戴著墨鏡。我說：「麥可，我覺得我好像在跟一輛豪華轎車說話。你是不是可以摘下墨鏡，讓我能看著你的眼睛說話？」於是他把墨鏡扔出窗外，看著我眨了眨眼，微笑說道：「你現在看得到我嗎？有沒有好一點？」

In that moment, I could see both his [6]**vulnerability** and his charm. The rest of the dinner, I was [7]**hell-bent** on getting him to eat French fries, drink wine, have dessert and say bad words—things he never seemed to allow himself to do.

那一刻，我在他眼中同時看到了脆弱和魅力。接下來的晚餐，我拼命說服他吃薯條、喝紅酒、吃甜點、罵髒話，這些都是他似乎從來不允許自己做的事。

Later, we went back to my house to watch a movie and sat on the couch like two kids, and somewhere in the middle of the movie, his hand [8]**snuck** over and held mine. It felt like he was looking for more of a friend than a romance, and I was happy to [9]**oblige**. In that moment, he didn't feel like a superstar. He felt like a human being.

然後，我們回到我住處，像兩個小孩一樣坐在沙發上看電影。電影看到一半時，他的手悄悄伸過來握住我的手，感覺像是在尋找友情的溫暖，而不是愛情，而我也很樂意幫他。那一刻，他給我的感覺不是巨星，而是一個普通人。

I Felt His Pain
我感受到他的痛苦

We went out a few more times together, and then for one reason or another we [LG] fell out of touch. Then the [LG] witch hunt began, and it seemed like one negative story after another was coming out about Michael. I felt his pain, I

VOCABULARY 100

1) **performer** [pɚˋfɔrmɚ] (n.) 表演者，演奏者
The audience clapped when the performers walked onto the stage.

2) **plague** [pleg] (v.) 困擾，為…所苦
The neighborhood has been plagued by crime for years.

3) **insecurity** [ˏɪnsɪˋkjʊreti] (n.) 不安全感
Many new graduates have a sense of insecurity about their future.

4) **bodyguard** [ˋbadɪˏgard] (n.) 保鑣
The star never goes anywhere without his bodyguards.

5) **limousine** [ˋlɪməˏzin] (n.) 豪華轎車
The couple rented a limousine for their wedding.

6) **vulnerability** [ˏvʌlnərəˋbɪləti] (n.) 柔弱，容易受傷害
Engineers are testing the operating system's vulnerability to viruses.

© gigi_nyc

know what it's like to walk down the street and feel like the whole world is turned against you. I know what it's like to feel helpless and unable to defend yourself because the roar of the [10]**lynch mob** is so loud you feel like your voice can never be heard. But I had a childhood, and I was allowed to make mistakes and find my own way in the world without the [11]**glare** of the [12]**spotlight**.

我們後來又一起出去了幾次，然後出於各種原因漸漸失去聯絡。接著捕風捉影開始了，關於麥可的負面新聞一個接著一個冒出來。我能感受到他的痛苦，我知道這種感覺就像是走在街上時，整個世界都把你當箭靶。我知道這種無助、無法為自己辯護的感覺，因為憤怒群眾的怒吼是如此喧囂，已經淹沒了自己的聲音。但是我有童年，身為孩童是可以有犯錯空間的，在沒有刺眼的鎂光燈下的世界裡，我還可以自己找到出口。

When I first heard that Michael had died, I was in London, days away from the start of my tour. Michael was going to perform in the same venue as me a week later. All I could think about in this moment was, "I had abandoned him." That we had abandoned him; that we had allowed this

> ❝ I didn't have many friends; I might not have had any friends. But it all turned out good in the end, because when you aren't popular and you don't have a social life, it gives you more time to focus on your future.
>
> 我那時沒幾個朋友，可能沒人算得上是朋友。但到頭來卻還不錯，因為當你不受歡迎，缺乏社交生活，就比較有時間專注於自己的未來。
>
> 瑪丹娜談交友

magnificent creature who had once 🔲 set the world on fire to somehow 🔲 slip through the cracks.

當我剛聽到麥可過世的消息時，我人在倫敦，距離巡迴演唱開始只有幾天，一星期後麥可要在同一場地演出。那一刻我腦海中只有一個想法：「是我棄他不顧。」是我們棄他不顧的，是我們讓這位曾經轟動全世界的偉大人物在不經意間從指縫中溜走了。

7) **hell-bent** [ˋhɛlˋbɛnt] (a.) 不顧一切的，拚命的
Our team is hell-bent on winning the championship.

8) **sneak** [snik] (v.) 偷偷地做、溜、走
The boys snuck into the movie theater without paying.

9) **oblige** [əˋblaɪdʒ] (v.) 答應…的請求，幫忙
If a friend needs a favor, I'm always ready to oblige.

10) **lynch mob** [lɪntʃ mɑb] (n.) （行私刑的）烏合之眾，憤怒群眾
Be careful what you post, or you may be attacked by an Internet lynch mob.

11) **glare** [glɛr] (n.) 刺眼的光
I shielded my eyes from the glare of the sun.

12) **spotlight** [ˋspɑtˏlaɪt] (n.) 聚光燈，公眾注意的目光
The famous singer is tired of living in the spotlight.

He Was a King
他是一代歌王

While he was trying to build a family and rebuild his career, we were all **LG** passing judgment. Most of us had **LG** turned our backs on him. In a desperate attempt to hold onto his memory, I went on the Internet to watch old [1]**clips** of him dancing and singing on TV and on stage and I thought, "My God, he was so unique, so original, so rare, and there will never be anyone like him again. He was a king."

他在試著建立家庭和重建事業生涯時，我們都在批判他。我們大部分人已背棄了他。我上網去看他以前在電視節目和舞台上又唱又跳的影片，在絕望中極力想抓住關於他的回憶，心想：「我的天，他是那麼獨特、那麼有創意、那麼傑出，不會再有人像他一樣了。他是一代歌王。」

© travelfoto / Shutterstock.com

But he was also a human being, and [2]**alas** we are all human beings, and sometimes we have to lose things before we can appreciate them. I want to end this on a positive note and say that my sons, age nine and four, are obsessed with Michael Jackson. There's a whole lot of **LG** crotch grabbing and moon walking going on in my house. And, it seems like a whole new generation of kids have discovered his genius and are bringing him to life again. I hope that wherever Michael is right now he is smiling about this.

但他也是個凡人，唉，我們都是凡人，我們必須失去某些東西之後才懂得珍惜。我想要用正面的訊息結束這段演講，我九歲和四歲的兒子都很迷麥可傑克森，他們常在家裡模仿麥可的抓褲襠和月球漫步。新一代的年輕人似乎已經發現他的天賦，再次賦予他生命。不論麥可現在在哪裡，我希望他能因此感到欣慰。

Yes, Michael Jackson was a human being, but he was a king. Long live the king!

是的，麥可傑克森是凡人，但他也是一代歌王，歌王萬歲！

© jejim / Shutterstock.com

crotch grab 抓胯下與
moonwalk 月球漫步

crotch 是指胯下「該邊」部位，crotch grab 以右手扣住胯下扭動臀部，是 Michael Jackson 的招牌舞蹈動作，而 moonwalk 看似向前走的姿態實為後退的舞蹈技巧，在 MJ 採用之後紅遍全球，成為 MJ 的招牌舞步。他的其他招牌舞步還有 anti-gravity lean（反重力前傾）及 toe stand（腳尖撐地）等。

VOCABULARY 102

1) **clip** [klɪp] (n.) 一段影片，剪輯片段
Have you seen the clip of the cat playing the piano?

2) **alas** [əˋlæs] (int.)（表示悲痛、憐憫、遺憾、關切等）唉呀
I asked her to marry me, but alas, she said no.

get the short end of the stick 吃虧，倒霉

short end of the stick 是切一半之後比較小的一邊、等級比較差的東西、挑到最後沒人要的工作……總之就是比較差的部分。所以當一個人 get the short / shorter end of the stick，就是得到比較差的待遇。也可以說 end up with the short end of the stick。

A: The boss told me to finish the report and let everyone else go home.
老闆叫我完成報告，讓其他人回家。
B: Wow, you really got the short end of the stick!
哇，你也太衰了吧！

ripe (old) age 熟齡

ripe 是「成熟」的意思，ripe age 字面上的意思就是「足夠成熟的年齡」，口語中也可用於反諷，表示「年紀輕輕就已經……」。

A: What kind of work does your brother do?
你的哥哥在哪高就？
B: He doesn't. He retired at the ripe old age of 35.
他沒工作。他三十五歲就退休了。

pack a punch 極具威力

punch 是指「（拳擊手的）一記重拳」，當我們說某樣東西 pack a punch，或是 pack the punch of... 的時候，表示它擁有讓人招架不住的力量。

A: How many of those martinis did you have?
你到底喝了幾杯馬丁尼？
B: Just two—but they really pack a punch!
才兩杯——但那酒的後勁真強！

fall out of touch 斷了音訊

touch 有「聯繫」的意思，因此 (be) in touch、get in touch 表示「保持聯絡」，(be) out of touch、fall out of touch、lose touch 就是「失去聯絡」。

A: Are you still in touch with Eric?
你還有跟艾瑞克聯絡嗎？
B: No. We fell out of touch after he moved away.
沒。他搬家之後我們就失聯了。

冷戰時期漫畫封面，描繪美國遭共產黨赤化的景象

witch hunt 獵巫行動

大約在一四五〇年到一七五〇年這三百年間，歐洲及北美洲盛行獵巫行動，數以萬計所謂的的巫師（絕大多數為女性）被以施行巫術，或是不敬上帝為名處決。到了一九三〇年代，witch hunt 一詞被媒體引用，代表政府或大企業利用起底的方式，引導大眾相信某人背德無恥、不愛國……，造成集體唾棄以整肅對手，美國冷戰時期對共產黨員的迫害就是一例。

演講稿中提到針對 Michael Jackson 的 witch huut，是指大眾對他狂整形、老戴墨鏡、口罩拒人於千里之外的負面輿論；媒體對他收藏象人屍骨、發狂把小嬰兒懸空放在陽台外的醜化報導，以及 Michael 遭控告性侵猥褻男童，以致他必須在鑑識人員面前脫光，拍攝生殖器特寫照等司法審判折磨。

set the world on fire 席捲全球

所有藝人都夢想能夠揚名國際、帶動風潮，在全世界各地發燒，set the world on fire 字面上的意思「讓全世界著火」，就是這個意思。

A: Do you want to become a famous actor?
你想要成為大明星嗎？
B: I don't want to set the world on fire. I just want to be able to make a living.
我不想要紅遍全球。我只求能夠糊口。

slip through the cracks 被（制度）忽略、犧牲

也可以說 fall though the cracks。crack 是「裂縫」，使用有裂縫的容器，裡面裝的東西自然會無聲無息的漏掉。slip through the cracks 就是在沒被注意的情況下遺漏、犧牲掉的部分，經常用在表示制度的缺失。

A: Lots of kids with learning problems seem to slip through the cracks.
許多有學習障礙的孩子似乎都被忽略了。
B: Yeah. The education system really needs to be reformed.
對啊。教育制度真的需要好好重整。

pass judgment 批評，無的放矢

這個說法除了用於法律相關場合，也用於日常會話，表示批評有欠公允。

A: The movie is supposed to be really boring.
這部電影應該會相當無聊。
B: You shouldn't pass judgment until you've seen it.
你都還沒看過不要亂批評。

turn one's back on 放棄，拋棄

turn one's back on sb./sth. 可以表示字面上的意思「轉身背對」，也可如同課文中引申為「背棄」

A: Did you hear? Robert ran off with his secretary.
你聽說了嗎？羅伯特跟他的祕書私奔了。
B: How could he turn his back on his wife and kids like that?
他怎麼可以就這樣拋妻棄子？

　精簡句子，**so** 的用法

so 可以用來代替前面說過的話，避免句子太過重複、冗長。瑪丹娜說出自己許多與麥可傑克遜一樣的背景時，就用了很多 so 來代替，例如文中 Michael Jackson had eight brothers and sisters. So do I. so 便代替 eight brothers and sisters。

例 **I think so.** 我同意。（用來贊同對方說過的話）
例 **I'm afraid so.** 恐怕是如此。（用來回應對方說的事）
例 **I hate to say it, but I told you so.**
雖然我很不願意這麼說，但我早就跟你講過了。

Madonna 於二〇〇九年的 MTV 音樂錄影帶獎（MTV Video Music Awards，簡稱 VMA）發表這段演說。不同於一般悼念致詞的歌功頌德、矯情裝熟，Madonna 一秉直言不諱的風格，坦承自己跟 MJ 算不上朋友，MJ 落難時，她跟所有人一樣棄他不顧，卻也因此讓她這篇對 MJ 的致敬更具說服力。

Man's Best Friends
Dogs and...
Whiskey?

人類的最好朋友是狗……還有威士忌？

A Tribute to Dogs
狗的禮讚

Gentlemen of the [1]**Jury**, the best friend a man has in the world may turn against him and become his enemy. His son or daughter that he has [2]**reared** with loving care may prove ungrateful. 🆖 Those who are nearest and dearest to us, 🆖 those whom we trust with our happiness and our good name may become [3]**traitors** to their faith. The money that a man has, he may lose. It flies away from him, perhaps when he needs it most. A man's reputation may be sacrificed in a moment of [4]**ill-considered** action. The people who are [5]**prone** to fall on their knees to do us honor when success is with us, may be the first to throw the stone of [6]**malice** when failure settles its cloud upon our heads.

陪審團的各位先生們，一個人在世上最好的朋友，有一天可能會背叛他，成為他的敵人。他一直悉心照顧的兒子或女兒，到頭來也有可能忘恩負義。那些跟我們關係最親近、最心愛的人，那些讓我們將幸福和名譽寄託在他們身上的人，也有可能成為叛徒，失信於我們。一個人擁有的金錢，有一天可能都會失去，而且可能會是在最需要的時候就不翼而飛。一個人的聲譽可能會因為一時考慮不周的行為而犧牲。當我們飛黃騰達時，人們容易對我們卑躬屈膝；但是當失敗降臨，烏雲罩頂時，他們可能會是最先對我們落井下石的人。

The one absolutely unselfish friend that man can have in this selfish world, the one that never deserts him, the one that never proves ungrateful or [7]**treacherous** is his dog. A man's dog stands by him in prosperity and in poverty, in health and in

VOCABULARY 🎧 104

1) **jury** [ˈdʒʊri] (n.) 陪審團
The jury found the suspect guilty of murder.

2) **rear** [rɪr] (v.) 撫養，飼養
The author has written several books on rearing children.

3) **traitor** [ˈtretɚ] (n.) 叛徒，叛國者
During the war, all traitors were executed.

4) **ill-considered** [ˈɪlkənˈsɪdɚd] (a.) 未深思的，考慮欠佳的，不明智的
The ill-considered plan was destined to fail.

5) **prone (to)** [pron] (a.) 易於，有…傾向的
Taiwan is prone to earthquakes.

6) **malice** [ˈmælɪs] (n.) 惡意，敵意，怨恨
John claimed that his criticism was without malice.

sickness. He will sleep on the cold ground, where the [8]**wintry** winds blow and the snow drives fiercely, if only he may be near his master's side. He will kiss the hand that has no food to offer. He will lick the wounds and sores that come in encounters with the roughness of the world. He guards the sleep of his [9]**pauper** master as if he were a prince. When all other friends desert, he remains. When riches take wings, and reputation  falls to pieces, he is as constant in his love as the sun in its journey through the heavens.

在這個自私的世界裡，有一種絕對無私的朋友，這個朋友絕不會拋棄我們，不會忘恩負義，不會不忠不信，那就是狗。不論富貴還是貧賤，不論健康還是生病，狗都會一直陪伴在主人身邊。不論是寒風來襲或大雪紛飛，牠都可以睡在冰冷的地上，只為了緊緊跟在主人身邊。就算不是給牠食物，牠也願意親吻主人的手。當你在這坎坷的世界遭遇挫折，牠會舔舐你所受到的創傷和痛處。主人睡覺時，牠守在一旁，就算主人窮如乞丐，牠也像對待王子一般守護他。當所有朋友棄你而去，只有牠會留在你身邊。當財富不翼而飛，名聲掃地，牠對你的愛還是像太陽一樣，永恆不變，誓死追隨。

George Graham Vest
喬治格拉漢衛斯特

喬治格拉漢衛斯特（George Graham Vest，一八三〇至一九〇四）曾在一八七九年至一九〇三年擔任美國密蘇里州聯邦參議員，並成為當代首屈一指的演説家和辯論家。他早期在密蘇里州一座小鎮擔任律師，一八五五年，他在法庭上代表一位男子控告另一名男子殺害他的狗時，發表了這篇有趣的演講。在審訊時，衛斯特不顧對方的證詞，輪到他向陪審團提出總結時，他發表了以下演講，贏得這場官司。

If fortune drives the master forth, an [10]**outcast** in the world, friendless and homeless, the faithful dog asks no higher privilege than that of accompanying him, to guard him against danger, to fight against his enemies. And when the last scene of all comes, and death takes his master in its [11]**embrace** and his body is laid away in the cold ground, no matter if all other friends pursue their way, there by the graveside will the noble dog be found, his head between his paws, his eyes sad, but open in alert [12]**watchfulness**, faithful and true even in death.

若是不敵命運作弄，主人成了世界的棄兒，眾叛親離，流離失所，忠心耿耿的狗除了陪伴主人、保護主人免於危難和對抗敵人之外，不會再要求其他特權。當人生來到最後一幕，死神將主人擁入懷中，遺體

---

7) **treacherous** [ˈtrɛtʃərəs] (a.) 背叛的，奸詐的，危險的
The king was murdered by his treacherous brother.

8) **wintry** [ˈwɪntrɪ] (a.) 寒冷的，冬天的，冬天似的
The wintry weather is unusual for this time of year.

9) **pauper** [ˈpɔpə] (n.) 窮人，貧民，乞丐
If you spend like a millionaire, you'll end up a pauper.

10) **outcast** [ˈaʊtˌkæst] (n.) 被拋棄的人，被逐出的人
In some countries, people with AIDS are treated like outcasts.

11) **embrace** [ɪmˈbres] (n./v.) 擁抱，接納
The two friends embraced and said goodbye.

12) **watchfulness** [ˈwɑtʃfəlnɪs] (n.) 警覺（性）
Driving on icy roads requires watchfulness.

The Whiskey Speech
威士忌演說

My friends, I had not intended to discuss this [1)]**controversial** subject at this particular time. However, I want you to know that I do not [2)]**shun** controversy. LG On the contrary, I will LG take a stand on any issue at any time, regardless of how [3)]**fraught** with controversy it might be. You have asked me how I feel about whiskey. All right, this is how I feel about whiskey:

朋友們，我原本無意要在這個時刻討論這項具有爭議的議題。不過，我希望讓你們知道，我不會迴避爭議。相反地，我可以在任何時刻，對任何議題表達立場，不管這個議題是否充滿爭議。你們曾經問過我對威士忌的看法。好吧，以下就是我對威士忌的看法：

If when you say whiskey you mean the devil's [4)]**brew**, the poison [5)]**scourge**, the bloody monster, that [6)]**defiles** innocence, [7)]**dethrones** reason, destroys the home, creates misery and poverty, [8)]**literally** takes the bread from the mouths of little children; if you mean the evil drink that [9)]**topples** the Christian man and woman from the [10)]**pinnacle** of [11)]**righteous**, gracious living into the bottomless pit of [12)]**degradation**, and despair, and shame and helplessness, and hopelessness, then certainly I am against it.

當大家提到威士忌時，就會聯想到這是惡魔釀的酒，是毒害的禍根，是血腥的怪物，會玷污清白，消滅理智，破壞家庭，製造苦難和貧困，簡直就是將小孩嘴邊的麵包搶走；假如你認為這種邪惡的飲料會讓信奉基督教的男男女女從過著正當、優裕生活的頂峰，跌到墮落、灰心喪志、羞恥、無助、絕望的無底洞，那麼，我肯定是反對的。

Noah S. Sweat
諾亞史威特

諾亞史威特（Noah S. Sweat，一九二二年至一九九六年）曾擔任法官、法學教授、美國密西西比州眾議員，一九五二年在密西西比州議會的議員席上發表一篇關於威士忌的知名演講。據說這篇演講花了史威特兩個半月寫成。

這篇演講有名的地方在於運用華麗的修辭，對議題的正反兩面皆表達了堅決和明確的論述。史威特是在一九四七年二十四歲時當選為州眾議員。他只做了一任，並在任期結束時發表這篇演講。他後來從事法律相關的工作。

VOCABULARY 106

1) **controversial** [ˌkɑntrəˈvɝʃəl] (a.) 有爭議的
Gun control is a very controversial issue.

2) **shun** [ʃʌn] (v.) 躲開，避開，迴避
After the divorce, Carl was shunned by many of his friends.

3) **fraught (with)** [frɔt] (a.) 充滿（問題危險）
Investing in the stock market is fraught with risk.

4) **brew** [bru] (n.) 啤酒，釀製／沖泡出來的飲料
Let's have a few brews after work.

5) **scourge** [skɝdʒ] (n.) 禍根，亂源
Gangs are a scourge on society.

6) **defile** [dɪˈfaɪl] (v.) 弄髒，敗壞，褻瀆
The man was arrested for defiling a church.

7) **dethrone** [diˈθron] (v.) 罷黜，罷免，使下臺
The tennis champion was finally dethroned.

8) **literally** [ˈlɪtərəli] (adv.) 確實地，簡直
We saw literally thousands of animals on the safari.

9) **topple** [ˈtɑpəl] (v.) 推翻，顛覆
The government was toppled by rebel forces.

10) **pinnacle** [ˈpɪnəkəl] (n.) 頂峰，極點
Winning an Oscar was the pinnacle of the actor's career.

11) **righteous** [ˈraɪtʃəs] (a.) 正義的，正當的
The crowd was filled with righteous anger.

12) **degradation** [ˌdɛɡrəˈdeʃən] (n.) 墮落，羞辱
Millions of Africans suffer the degradation of poverty.

不是藝術家，
也可以翻轉玩藝術！

0~80 歲都該認識的 37 幅藝術大師名畫
欣賞臨摹、塗塗畫畫
剪它貼它、改造惡搞
經典名畫×個人 style
誰說你沒有藝術細胞？畫上去就好！

／藝術涵養、創意體驗、靈感刺激、培養想像力
／不只是著色！三十七幅經典畫作的名畫小檔案，鑑賞、創作一次滿足
／特別邀請創意人及讀者示範畫作，讓你發現「原來名畫還可以這樣玩？！」
／內頁採用適於上色的厚磅道林紙；畫完了，就是屬於你自己的名畫冊！

「好想畫畫喔！可是我是手殘的美術白痴…。」
「覺得好煩喔！想要找件能讓頭腦放空的事來做。」

不管是「星光燦爛的星夜」、「橋上吶喊著的扭曲人形」，
或是「戴著珍珠耳環回眸的少女」…選一張喜歡的名畫，
跟著原畫上色。拿起身邊任何可以用來創作的物品發揮
創意。完成屬於自己獨一無二的作品。

○ Yes24 網路書店藝術類熱銷超過二十週
○ SBS 節目特別介紹創意書籍

書名|動手玩名畫：
　　　跟著梵谷和他的朋友們，徹底解放你的創意！
定價|$320

各界名人推薦

專文推薦	創意畫作示範
邱建一	**王建民** - 藝術家 ／ **徐德寰** - 拾參樂團主唱小寶
藝術史學者 / 台北市立大學視覺藝術系助理教授	**Belle 莊蕙如** - 旅行繪畫家　（依姓氏筆畫排列）

But, if when you say whiskey you mean the oil of conversation, the philosophic wine, the [1]**ale** that is consumed when good fellows get together, that puts a song in their hearts and laughter on their lips, and the warm glow of contentment in their eyes; if you mean 🄻🄶 Christmas cheer; if you mean the [2]**stimulating** drink that puts the spring in the old gentleman's step on a frosty, crisp morning; if you mean the drink which enables a man to [3]**magnify** his joy, and his happiness, and to forget, if only for a little while, life's great tragedies, and heartaches, and sorrows; if you mean that drink, the sale of which pours into our [4]**treasuries** [5]**untold** millions of dollars, which are used to provide tender care for our little crippled children, our blind, our deaf, our dumb, our pitiful aged and [6]**infirm**; to build highways and hospitals and schools, then certainly I am for it.

不過，假如你認為威士忌是聊天的潤滑劑，是富有哲理的酒，好人聚在一起時喝的麥芽酒，能讓他們由衷歡唱、歡笑、雙眼流露出滿足的溫暖光芒；假如你認為威士忌能為耶誕節帶來歡樂；假如你認為這種提神的酒可以讓老人家的步伐在清冷的早晨中增添活力；假如你認為這種飲料可以讓人更幸福、更快樂，還能忘卻人生巨大的悲痛和憂傷，就算只有一下子也好；假如你認為這種酒的販售可以幫助我們的國庫增加難以估量的億萬稅收，並用來為殘疾兒童、視障人士、聾啞人士、年邁體弱者提供體貼的照顧，以及興建公路、醫院和學校，那麼，我當然是支持的。

This is my stand. I will not retreat from it. I will not compromise.

這就是我的立場，我不會退縮，也不會妥協。

❝ My God, so much I like to drink Scotch that sometimes I think my name is Igor Stra-whiskey.

老天，我好愛喝威士忌，有時候我會以為自己名叫伊格史特拉威士忌。

史特拉文斯基
Igor Stravinsky，俄國作曲家

VOCABULARY 🎧108

1) **ale** [el] (n.) 黑啤酒，烈啤酒，麥芽酒
I'd like a pint of brown ale.

2) **stimulating** [ˈstɪmjəˌletɪŋ] (a.) 令人精神充沛的，激勵人心的
We had a stimulating conversation over lunch.

3) **magnify** [ˈmægnəˌfaɪ] (v.) 放大，擴大
The microscope can magnify objects up to 1,000 times.

4) **treasury** [ˈtrɛʒəri] (n.) 國庫，金庫，寶庫
The official was accused of stealing from the treasury.

5) **untold** [ˌʌnˈtold] (a.) 數不清的，無限的，無法形容的
The prisoners of war endured untold misery.

6) **infirm** [ɪnˈfɜm] (a.) 體弱的，衰弱的
The virus mostly attacks the old and infirm.

fall to pieces 瓦解，失敗，崩潰

fall to pieces 字面上的意思就是「摔成碎片」，自然會衍生出「失敗，瓦解」之意。go to pieces 和 fall apart 也是相同的意思。

A: Are Paul and Shelly still together?
　保羅與雪麗還有在一起嗎？
B: No. Their marriage fell to pieces.
　沒有了。他們的婚姻破裂了。

on the contrary 正好相反

contrary 是指「對立的一方，反面」，on the contrary「在相反那一方」，就是正好相反的意思了。

A: Was the professor's lecture boring?
　教授的演講無聊嗎？
B: No. On the contrary, it was quite interesting.
　沒有，而且正好相反，他講得相當有趣。

take a stand 採取某立場

stand 當名詞有「立場，態度」的意思，要求人 take a stand 就表示「選邊站」，表明自己的立場。

A: Why are you voting for Hillary?
　你為什麼要投給希拉蕊？
B: Because she's taken a stand on women's rights.
　因為她採取女性權益的立場。

eggnog

以熱牛奶、蛋黃、糖、鮮奶油、威士忌、蘭姆酒，加入香草及肉豆蔻（nutmeg）調味而成。

spiced cider

以蘋果汁（apple cider）、威士忌、檸檬汁、糖漿及肉桂等香料調成。

耶誕節傳統 whiskey 雞尾酒

說到耶誕節宴會上喝的調酒飲料，第一個想到的就是摻了威士忌的奶蛋酒（eggnog）。以下是耶誕節常見的威士忌雞尾酒。

hot toddy

以威士忌、檸檬汁、蜂蜜、檸檬片，沖熱水用肉桂棒調成。常被當成冬夜暖身、舒緩感冒症狀的飲品。

Manhattan

以威士忌、甜苦艾酒（sweet vermouth）加冰塊調成。

whiskey sour

以柳橙汁、威士忌、檸檬汁、橙皮酒（triple sec）加冰塊調成。

大有學問的關係代名詞 who & whom

雖然 whom 跟 who 兩者的區分現在已經不那麼明顯，但非常正式的文章中幾乎還是會看到 whom，寫作上還是得知道兩者的正確用法。

要了解 who 跟 whom 使用的差別，只要能分辨關係代名詞為句子的主詞或受詞即可：

● 關係代名詞後面若是動詞，使用主格 who。
例 **Anyone who trespasses will be punished severely.**

● 關係代名詞後面若是代名詞，使用受格 whom。
例 **My grandfather, whom I greatly respected, passed away last year.**

因此演講中 Those who are nearest and dearest to us, those whom we trust with our happiness...，第一句 those 的關係代名詞後面接的是 be 動詞 are，所以用 who。第二句 those 後接的是代名詞 we，則用 whom 比較正式。

《狗的禮讚》是 George Graham Vest 為一隻被牧羊人殺死的獵犬老鼓（Old Drum）打官司的結辯，現存的僅是其中部分文字，其他已經散失。接下官司委託時，Vest 誓言要「打贏官司，否則就向全密蘇里州的狗謝罪」。Vest 勝訴之後一戰成名，他通篇未提審理過程證詞，僅以華美辭藻讚頌「狗德」的奇文，也不斷流傳下來。

立於這場審判所在法院前的 Old Drum 雕像

另一篇「威士忌演說」的作者 Noah S. Sweat, Jr. 也是法界出身，他針對密西西比是否應廢止直至當時（一九五二年）還在執行的禁酒令（Prohibition，美國全國禁酒時期為一九二〇年至一九三三年）發表這篇演說，但他滔滔不絕採用了正反雙方的語彙，讓雙方陣營聽完都能感到滿意，也使得 if-by-whiskey 一詞成為「兩邊不得罪，兩面討好」的代名詞。

Yes we can

Obama's 2008 Victory Speech
歐巴馬二〇〇八年勝選演講

© Everett Collection / Shutterstock.com

 All Things Are Possible
一切皆有可能

Hello, Chicago. If there is anyone out there who still doubts that America is a place where all things are possible, who still wonders if the dream of our founders is alive in our time, who still questions the power of our democracy, tonight is your answer.

哈囉,芝加哥!假如還有人在懷疑,美國是否真的是一切皆有可能實現的地方,還有人在懷疑我們開國元勳的夢想今天是否依然存在,還有人在懷疑我們民主的力量;今夜,就是你們的答案。

It's the answer told by lines that stretched around schools and churches in numbers this nation has never seen, by people who waited three hours and four hours, many for the first time in their lives, because they believed that this time must be different, that their voices could be that difference.

全國各地的學校和教堂的投票所外面,出現了前所未有的大排長龍,這就是答案。有人等了三、四個小時,其中有許多人還是第一次投票。他們之所以願意這麼做,是因為他們相信這次一定會不一樣,他們的聲音會帶來不一樣的結果。

🔊 It's the answer spoken by young and old, rich and poor, 1)**Democrat** and Republican, black, white, 2)**Hispanic**, Asian, Native American, 3)**gay**, straight, 4)**disabled** and not disabled—Americans who sent a message to the world that we have never been just a collection of individuals or a collection of

VOCABULARY 🎧 110

1) **Democrat** [ˈdɛmə͵kræt] (n.) 美國民主黨人;
Republican [rɪˈpʌblɪkən] (n.) 共和黨人
Democrats and Republicans disagree on many issues.

2) **Hispanic** [hɪˈspænɪk] (a./n.) (美國)拉丁裔(的),以西班牙文為母語的(人)
The candidate is very popular with Hispanic voters.

3) **gay** [ge] (a./n.) 同性戀的,同性戀;
straight [stret] (a./n.) 異性戀的,異性戀
I'm not sure whether Allen is gay or straight.

4) **disabled** [dɪˈsebəld] (a.) 殘障的,有生理缺陷的
The accident left Frank severely disabled.

5) **cynical** [ˈsɪnɪkəl] (a.) 憤世嫉俗的,悲觀的
Voters are becoming more and more cynical about politics.

6) **arc** [ɑrk] (n.) 弧形,(持續的)發展
I was impressed by the story's dramatic arc.

red states and blue states. We are, and always will be, the United States of America.

這個答案是所有美國人共同訴說的，不分老少、貧富、民主黨、共和黨、黑人、白人、西班牙裔、亞裔、美洲原住民、同性戀、異性戀、身障和非身障，大家都在向全世界傳送一個訊息，那就是，我們從來不只是由個體組成的群體，也不只是由紅州和藍州拼湊而成的國家。我們現在是，未來也永遠是，美利堅合眾國。

It's the answer that led those who've been told for so long by so many to be ⁵⁾**cynical** and fearful and doubtful about what we can achieve to put their hands on the ⁶⁾**arc** of history and bend it once more toward the hope of a better day. It's been a long time coming, but tonight, because of what we did on this date in this election at this defining moment change has come to America.

長久以來，我們明明可以做到的事，卻一直被許多人告誡要抱著悲觀、戒慎恐懼和懷疑的態度。這個答案引導我們掌握歷史的舵盤，再次朝向充滿希望的美好明天駛去。這個答案讓我們等了很久，但就在今夜，就因為我們在這個投票日、在這個關鍵性的一刻做出了抉擇，我們終將為美國帶來改變。

A Brave and Selfless Leader
勇敢、無私的領袖

A little bit earlier this evening, I received an ⁷⁾**extraordinarily** gracious call from ⁸⁾**Senator** McCain. Senator McCain fought long and hard in this campaign. And he's fought even longer and harder for the country that he loves. He has endured sacrifices for America that most of us cannot begin to imagine. We are better off for the service ⁹⁾**rendered** by this brave and selfless leader.

今晚稍早，我接到馬侃參議員打來的電話，他的態度格外親切。馬侃參議員也打了一場漫長又艱苦的選戰。他也曾為他所愛的國家打了一場更漫長、更艱困的戰役。他為美國所承受的犧牲，是我們大部分人無法想像的。因為這位領袖勇敢且無私的奉獻，我們現在才能過著比較寬裕的生活。

Barack Obama
巴拉克歐巴馬

© Joseph Sohm / Shutterstock.com

一九六一年八月四日生。是美國民主黨籍政治家，也是第四十四任美國總統，為第一位非裔美國總統，於二〇〇八年初次當選，並於二〇一二年成功連任。

他就任總統後，對內全面實施恢復美國經濟的計劃，對移民、公民醫療保健、教育等領域進行變革；對外主張從阿富汗和伊拉克撤軍，並向伊斯蘭世界表示友善，還和核武大國俄羅斯簽署削減核武器的《布拉格條約》。二〇〇九年十月九日，獲頒諾貝爾和平獎。

John McCain 約翰馬侃

美國共和黨重量級人物，祖父及父親都是美國海軍上將，他自己也因參加越戰期間被俘五年半成為越戰英雄。二〇〇八年代表共和黨與歐巴馬角逐總統大位，他的競選搭擋莎拉裴林（Sarah Palin）不但是共和黨第一位參加美國總統大選的女性、阿拉斯加州最年輕的州長，也是第一位女性州長，因此獲得極高媒體曬目，但兩人最後落敗。

© Perspectives - Jeff Smith / Shutterstock.com

---

7) **extraordinarily** [ɪkˋstrɔrdə͵nɛrɪli] (adv.) 異常地，格外地
Dogs have an extraordinarily keen sense of smell.

8) **senator** [ˋsɛnətə] (n.) 參議員
The scandal destroyed the senator's reputation.

9) **render** [ˋrɛndə] (v.) 給予，提供
The charity was established to render assistance to the poor.

I was never the likeliest candidate for this office. We didn't start with much money or many [1])**endorsements**. Our campaign was not hatched in the halls of Washington. It began in the backyards of Des Moines and the living rooms of Concord and the front porches of Charleston. It was built by working men and women who dug into what little savings they had to give $5 and $10 and $20 to the cause.

我從來就不是最被看好的總統候選人。我們一開始的競選資金並不多，為我背書的人也不多。我們這場選戰不是從華府的大廳開始的，而是從狄蒙市的後院、康科的客廳、查爾斯頓市的門廊出發的。是來自勞工階層的男男女女，從他們僅有的存款中擠出五元、十元、二十美元來共襄盛舉的。

It drew strength from the young people who rejected the [2])**myth** of their generation's [3])**apathy** who left their homes and their families for jobs that offered little pay and less sleep. It drew strength from the not-so-young people who braved the bitter cold and [4])**scorching** heat to knock on doors of perfect strangers, and from the millions of Americans who volunteered and organized

> 66 If the people cannot trust their government to do the job for which it exists—to protect them and to promote their common welfare—all else is lost.
>
> 如果人民不信任政府執行它的任務——保護人民、為人民謀福利——一切都失去意義了。
>
> 歐巴馬談政府

and proved that more than two centuries later a government of the people, by the people, and for the people has not [5])**perished** from the Earth. This is your victory.

這場選戰有年輕世代出力，他們為此離開家人，投入收入微薄、犧牲睡眠時間的競選工作，並以此證明他們不是傳說中冷漠的世代。這場選戰也有非年輕族群共同出力，他們鼓起勇氣，冒著寒冬酷暑，挨家挨戶敲著陌生人的門，還有好幾百萬人自發性組織志工，證明在經過兩百多年後，由人民自治、由人民選出、為人民服務的政治體制並未在地球上消失。這是屬於你們的勝利。

Many Firsts and Many Stories
許多第一次和許多故事

This election had many firsts and many stories that will be told for generations. But one that's on my mind tonight's about a woman who cast her [6])**ballot** in Atlanta. She's a lot like the millions of others who stood in line to make their voice heard in this election except for one thing: Ann Nixon Cooper is 106 years old.

這次選舉有許多第一次，也有許多故事可以傳承給後代。但在今夜，令我難忘的是一位女士，她在亞特蘭大投下她的一票。她跟其他千百萬名選民一樣排隊投票，在這次選舉中表達自己的意見，唯一與他人不同的是，安尼克森庫帕今年 106 歲了。

She was born just a generation past [7])**slavery**; a time when there were no cars on the road or planes in the sky; when someone like her couldn't vote for two reasons—because she was a woman and because of the color of her skin.

她出生的年代，是廢除奴隸制度後的下一代，一個路上沒有汽車、天上沒有飛機的年代。在當時，像她那樣的人出於兩個原因而沒有投票權，一是身為女性，二是膚色。

And tonight, I think about all that she's seen throughout her century in America—the heartache and the hope; the struggle and the progress; the

VOCABULARY 🎧112

1) **endorsement** [ɪnˋdɔrsmənt] (n.) 背書，支持，批准
The candidate received the endorsement of the former president.

2) **myth** [mɪθ] (n.) 迷思，神話
Some people think global warming is just a myth.

3) **apathy** [ˋæpəθi] (n.) 冷漠，漠不關心
Young people's apathy toward politics isn't very surprising.

4) **scorching** [ˋskɔrtʃɪŋ] (a.) 炎熱的，極熱的
Most people stay indoors during the scorching summer months.

5) **perish** [ˋpɛrɪʃ] (v.) 死去，消滅
Dozens of people perished in the fire.

6) **ballot** [ˋbælət] (n.) 選票
It will take several days for all the ballots to be counted.

7) **slavery** [ˋslevəri] (n.) 奴隸制度，奴役；**slave** [slev] (n.) 奴隸
Slavery in the U.S. ended in 1865.

> The thing about hip-hop today is it's smart, it's insightful. The way they can communicate a complex message in a very short space is remarkable.
>
> 今日嘻哈動人之處，在於其機智、具有洞見。在有限空間溝通複雜訊息的方式令人激賞。
>
> 歐巴馬談嘻哈

times we were told that we can't, and the people who pressed on with that American [8)**creed**: Yes we can.

而在今夜，我想到了她這一生看盡美國這一世紀以來歷經的一切，有悲痛、有希望；有掙扎、有進步；那些別人告訴我們做不到的年代，還有那些人堅守著美國信條：是的，我們做得到。

Yes We Can
是的，我們做得到

At a time when women's voices were silenced and their hopes dismissed, she lived to see them stand up and speak out and reach for the ballot. Yes we can. When there was despair in the Dust Bowl and depression across the land, she saw a nation conquer fear itself with a **LG** New Deal, new jobs, a new sense of common purpose. Yes we can. When the bombs fell on our harbor and [9)**tyranny** threatened the world, she was there to witness a generation rise to greatness and a democracy was saved. Yes we can.

這位女士一生中歷經了女性聲音受到壓制和希望渺茫的年代，也見證到女性站起來、大聲表達自己的意見、爭取到投票權。是的，我們

做得到。當全國發生令人絕望的大沙塵暴和經濟大蕭條時，她親眼見證了一個國家如何運用新政、新的工作機會、新的共同目標來戰勝恐懼。是的，我們做得到。當珍珠港遭到轟炸，獨裁專制威脅著全世界時，她也親眼見證了一個世代崛起成為強者，拯救民主。是的，我們做得到。

She was there for the buses in **LG** Montgomery, the hoses in **LG** Birmingham, a bridge in **LG** Selma, and a [10)**preacher** from Atlanta who told a people that "We Shall Overcome." Yes we can. A man touched down on the moon, a wall came down in Berlin, a world was connected by our own science and imagination.

在反對種族隔離的蒙哥馬利公車運動中、在伯明罕運動中遭到水柱鎮壓時、在塞爾瑪城外的橋上示威遊行爭取非裔投票權時，還有在亞特蘭大的一位傳教士告訴大家「我們終將勝利」時，她也都在。是的，我們做得到。人類登上了月球，柏林圍牆已倒塌，世界已經因為科學和創造力而連結在一起。

8) **creed** [krid] (n.) 信條，信念，主義
The U.S. is home to people of every race and creed.

9) **tyranny** [ˈtɪrəni] (n.) 暴政，專制，專橫
The people struggled bravely to free themselves from tyranny.

10) **preacher** [ˈpritʃə] (n.) 講道者，牧師
The religious leader started out as a street preacher.

America Can Change
美國可以改變

And this year, in this election, she touched her finger to a screen, and cast her vote, because after 106 years in America, through the best of times and the darkest of hours, she knows how America can change. Yes we can.

在今年，在這次選舉，她用手指輕觸電子投票機的螢幕，投下她的一票。因為她知道，美國經過了一百零六年，歷經了輝煌的年代，也歷經過最黑暗的年代，她知道美國可以改變。是的，我們做得到。

America, we have come so far. We have seen so much. But there is so much more to do. So tonight, let us ask ourselves—if our children should live to see the next century; if my daughters should be so lucky to live as long as Ann Nixon Cooper, what change will they see? What progress will we have made? This is our chance to answer that call. This is our moment.

美國，我們已經走了這麼遠的路，見證了這麼多的事，但還是有許多事情要做。所以，就在今夜，讓我們捫心自問：假如我們的孩子能跨越到下個世紀 ，我的女兒有幸跟庫帕一樣長壽，他們會看到什麼樣的改變？我們會取得什麼樣的進展？這是我們回應這種號召的機會。這是屬於我們的時刻。

This is our time, to put our people back to work and open doors of opportunity for our kids; to $^{1)}$**restore** $^{2)}$**prosperity** and promote the cause of peace; to reclaim the  American Dream and $^{3)}$**reaffirm** that fundamental truth, that, out of many, we are one; that while we breathe, we hope. And where we are met with cynicism and doubts and those who tell us that we can't, we will respond with that timeless creed that $^{4)}$**sums up** the spirit of a people: Yes, we can.

這是我們的時代，讓我們的人民重返就業市場，為我們的下一代開啟機會之門，恢復繁榮發展，推動和平事業；重拾美國夢，再次肯定美國夢的基本真理，那就是，我們是合眾為一，團結一致的；只要我們活著，就不會放棄希望。當有人嘲諷我們、懷疑我們，還說我們做不到時，我們就用那千古不變、可用來概括我們民族精神的信條回應他們：是的，我們做得到。

Thank you. God bless you. And may God bless the United States of America.

謝謝你們。願上帝保佑你們。也願上帝保佑美國。

VOCABULARY 114

1) **restore** [rɪˋstor] (v.) 復原，修復
The operation to restore the patient's sight was a success.

2) **prosperity** [prɑˋspɛrəti] (n.) 繁榮
The railroads brought prosperity to the American West.

3) **reaffirm** [ˌriəˋfɝm] (v.) 再次確認，重申
Voters reaffirmed their support for the ruling party.

4) **sum up** [sʌm ʌp] (phr.) 總結
At the end of the lecture, the professor summed up his main points.

American Dream 美國夢

指每個美國人只要肯努力，都有相同機會的理想狀態，其精神主要奠基於《獨立宣言》（Declaration of Independence）的這段話：

We hold these truths to be self-evident, that all men are created equal, that they are endowed by their Creator with certain unalienable Rights, that among these are Life, Liberty and the pursuit of Happiness.

我們認為下述真理是不言而喻的：人人生而平等，造物主賦予他們若干不可讓與的權利，其中包括生存權、自由權和追求幸福的權利。

Language Guide

© Angr / Wikipedia

red state 紅州與 blue state 藍州

紅色和藍色是美國國旗的兩個主要顏色，分別指美國總統選舉中支持共和黨（Republican Party）各州（紅），與支持民主黨（Democratic Party）各州（藍）。這個說法起源於二〇〇〇年美國政論節目 The Today Show。

這個分類法很籠統，各州屬紅或藍並非絕對，也不是非紅即藍。在過去四次（二〇〇〇年到二〇一二年）美國大選當中，都被共和黨取下的州大致分佈在中西部及南部，都被民主黨取下的州分佈在北部及西部沿岸（如圖所示），紫色代表兩黨各贏兩次，天藍色則表示民主黨獲勝三次的地區，而粉紅色表示共和黨獲勝三次的地區。

New Deal 新政

新政主要是指美國總統小羅斯福（Franklin Delano Roosevelt）於一九三三年到一九三八年間，以增加政府干預的方式，對美國經濟大蕭條（Great Depression）所做出一系列失業救濟及振興經濟的措施。

同一時期，美國南方農業區（主要位於奧克拉荷馬州）因土地長期過度使用，表土嚴重破壞，造成長達十年的沙塵暴乾旱，整個大平原地區（Great Plains）變成黃沙滾滾的沙漠，被稱為 Dust Bowl。馬修麥康納（Matthew MaConaughey）主演電影《星際效應》（Interstellar），就在模擬未來發生第二次 Dust Bowl 的故事，大家從片中幾段老人的獨白（取自真實的一九三〇年代紀錄片 The Dust Bowl）可以一窺當時的慘狀。

Grammar Master

It's the answer spoken by...
歐巴馬教你「被動語態」的奧義

此原句為 It's the answer that is spoken by...；「be+p.p. by...」為被動語態句型，常用在新聞報導、演說及小說文章中，有別於口語常用、較為直白的主動語態，同樣一句話用被動語態敘述時，會讓句子聽起來比較簡潔、正式，也能用來強調事件。以下是兩種非常適合選擇使用被動語態的狀況：

● 說話者認為事件中執行動作的人不重要、未知或是不願提及此人時。

例 **A new cancer drug has been discovered.**
　發現了一種癌症新藥。（誰發明的不是重點）

例 **Three banks were robbed last night.**
　三家銀行昨晚被搶了。（不知道搶匪是誰）

● 說話者想刻意強調施動者（agent，被動語態 by 之後的原主詞），因此用被動語態將想強調的 agent 放在句子最後面。

例 **The patient was murdered by his own doctor!**
　該病患被他自己的醫生殺死了。（強調語意，「竟然」是被自己的醫生所害）

例 **My mother was hit by a drunk driver.**
　我的母親被酒醉的駕駛撞了。（重點是 driver，my mother 是句子的主題）

歐巴馬演說中的這個句子就是要強調出這些述說答案的美國人，並一一列名，語意中顯示自己對各階層、人種、性向等全美人民之重視與平等對待。

Civil Rights Movement 民權運動

一直到第二次世界大戰結束，美國南方都還是個實行種族隔離（racial segregation）的地區。戰後十年間，美國黑人爭取平等自由的民權運動團體受到政府鎮壓，只能在法院進行鬥爭。由於美國法院偏袒種族主義，黑人轉向呼籲國際重視此問題。為改變美國在國際上的形象，美國最高法院於一九五四年做出「公立學校實行種族隔離教育是不平等的」之判決。

由於訴諸法律的進度太過緩慢，黑人不再寄望於修法，轉而靠自身的力量。一九五五年，黑人女性帕克斯（Rosa Parks）在阿拉巴馬州蒙哥馬利市（Montgomery）的公車上拒絕讓座給白人，因而被捕入獄。當時還很年輕的馬丁路德金恩博士（Martin Luther King, Jr. 即 MLK）領導全城五萬黑人拒搭公車長達一年，迫使公車的種族隔離規定取消，開啟了美國黑人摧毀種族隔離制度的希望。

一九五七年，馬丁路德金恩博士帶頭組成南方基督教領袖會議（Southern Christian Leadership Conference, SCLC），將民權運動推廣到美國南部的各個生活角落。一九六〇年，北卡羅萊納州格林斯伯勒市（Greensboro）有四位黑人大學生進入一間餐廳，遭到白人服務員斥離，四個大學生靜坐不動，此舉獲得美國南部廣大黑人學生響應，進而發展成大規模靜坐，最後有將近兩百個城市取消餐廳隔離制。美國民權運動持續發燒，一九六一年迫使南部各州取消州際公車上的種族隔離制。

一九六三年，金恩博士在南部種族隔離極嚴重的伯明罕組織示威遊行（Birmingham Campaign），要求取消全市隔離制，示威群眾受到殘酷鎮壓。最後該市的種族隔離制全部取消。民權運動勢力從此迅速擴大，八月二十八日更集結二十五萬人向華府進軍（March on Washington），同時部分黑人展開以暴制暴的鬥爭，終於在一九六四年迫使詹森總統（Lyndon Johnson）簽署《民權法案》（Civil Rights Act）。

但上有政策，下有對策，南部各州仍用各種手段阻撓黑人選民登記。金恩博士於是前往極端種族主義的阿拉巴馬州塞爾馬市（Selma, Alabama）推動黑人選民登記運動，並於一九六五年三月七日冒著被恐嚇暗殺的風險發起另一次行動，向阿拉巴馬州首府蒙哥馬利市進軍，抗議群眾遭到州警及地方警力毆打，甚至催淚瓦斯攻擊，史上將這天稱為「血腥星期日」（Bloody Sunday）。終於，美國政府在全球輿論壓力下，於八月要求國會通過《選民登記法》，後來發展成《一九六五年選舉權法》（Voting Rights Act of 1965），保證所有美國人都享有投票選舉的權利。

《民權法案》及《選民登記法》實際上未能完全消弭美國南部的種族隔離制度與歧視，長期的紛擾反而挑起美國北部的種族歧視情緒。一九六八年三月，金恩博士發起另一次「貧民進軍」（亦稱「窮人運動」），途經田納西州孟菲斯市（Memphis）時，不幸被種族主義分子槍殺。而演講中所述 We Shall Overcome 即金恩博士遇刺前最後一次佈道中引用的歌曲《我們必勝》，為六〇年代人權運動代表歌曲。

這篇演講是歐巴馬二〇〇八年十一月四日勝選後，在伊利諾州芝加哥市的格蘭特公園發表的歷史性演說。歐巴馬雄辯滔滔的演講魅力，是許多人認為他能獲勝的一大關鍵。而他能從代表伊利諾州的資淺參議員一躍成為民主黨總統候選人，就是靠他在二〇〇四年民主黨全國代表大會上的演講一夕爆紅。

他在那場演講當中談到國家團結問題，就有提到 red state、blue state，但不論紅藍，他（和他的團隊）都效忠星條旗（美國）。他在勝選演說中再次提到作為呼應，別具意義。歷時四十三年，美國黑人終於從爭取投票權，到出現第一位總統，歐巴馬這一晚的演說，不但深具意義，也格外激勵人心。

Ask Not
What Your Country
Can Do for You
John F. Kennedy's [1]***Inaugural*** *Address*
甘迺迪總統就職演講

A Celebration of Freedom
自由的慶典

GM We observe today not a victory of party but a celebration of freedom, **GM** [2]**symbolizing** an end as well as a beginning, [3]**signifying** renewal as well as change. For I have sworn before you and [4]**Almighty** God the same [5]**solemn** [6]**oath** our [7]**forebears** [8]**prescribed** nearly a century and three quarters ago.

我們不會將今天視為政黨的勝利，而是自由的慶典。今天象徵著一種結束，也象徵著一種開始，代表著復興，也代表著改變。因為我在你們和全能的上帝面前鄭重宣誓的誓言，是我們的先人在將近一又四分之三世紀前制訂的。

The world is very different now. For man holds in his [9]**mortal** hands the power to [10]**abolish** all forms of human poverty and all forms of human life. And yet the same revolutionary beliefs for which our forebears fought are still **LG** at issue around the globe—the belief that the rights of man come not from the generosity of the state but from the hand of God.

現在的世界已經變得很不一樣了，因為凡人手中握有的權力，足以消除一切形式的人類貧困，又足以毀滅一切形式的人類生命。然而我們先人所奮鬥的革命理念，現在依然是全世界爭論的議題——那理念就是，人類的權利不是國家所慷慨贈予的，而是上天所賦予的。

We dare not forget today that we are the [11]**heirs** of that first revolution. Let the word go forth from this time and place, to friend and [12]**foe** alike, that the [13]**torch** has been passed to a new generation of Americans—born in this century, [14]**tempered** by war, disciplined by a hard and bitter peace, proud of our ancient [15]**heritage**.

VOCABULARY 🎧116

1) **inaugural** [ɪnˋɔɡjərəl] (a.) 就任的，開幕的
Many important people attended the inagural ball.

2) **symbolize** [ˋsɪmbəˌlaɪz] (v.) 象徵，代表
The stars on the American flag symbolize the 50 states.

3) **signify** [ˋsɪɡnəˌfaɪ] (v.) 表示，意味著
What does the man's strange behavior signify?

4) **almighty** [ɔlˋmaɪtɪ] (a./n.)（常用大寫）全能的（神）
Let us pray to Almighty God.

5) **solemn** [ˋsɑləm] (a.) 嚴肅的，鄭重的，正式的
The man made a solemn promise to stop drinking.

6) **oath** [oθ] (n.) 誓言
The soldier took an oath to defend his country.

7) **forebear** [ˋforˌbɛr] (n.)（常複數）祖先
We strive to honor the traditions of our forebears.

8) **prescribe** [prɪˋskraɪb] (v.) 規定，指定
The rules prescribe that all employees must wear a uniform.

9) **mortal** [ˋmɔrtəl] (a.) 會死的，凡人的
Steve's heart attack made him realize that he's mortal.

我們至今仍不敢忘記，我們是第一代革命的繼承人。就在此時此地，我們要告訴我們的朋友和敵人，薪火已經傳到了新一代的美國人——在這一世紀出生的美國人，已歷經過戰爭的磨練，為了得來不易的和平歷經了嚴苛的考驗，也為我們的古老傳統感到自豪。

We Shall Pay Any Price
我們將付出任何代價

Let every nation know, whether it wishes us well or ill, that we shall pay any price, bear any burden, meet any hardship, support any friend, oppose any foe to assure the survival and the success of liberty.

我們要讓每一個國家都知道，不管他們是希望我們興盛或衰落，為了確保自由的延續和實現，我們將付出任何代價、承擔一切重任、應付一切困難、支援所有朋友、對抗所有敵人。

To those old [16]**allies** whose cultural and spiritual origins we share, we [17]**pledge** the loyalty of faithful friends. United, there is little we cannot do in a host of cooperative ventures. Divided, there is little we can do.

對於那些我們源自共同文化和信仰的老盟友，我們保證會像摯友一樣忠誠相待。只要我們團結一致，在眾多的合作事業中，沒有什麼做不到的。我們若是分裂，便什麼都做不了。

To those new states whom we welcome to the ranks of the free, we pledge our word that one form of [18]**colonial** control shall not have passed away merely to be replaced by a far more iron tyranny. We shall not always expect to find them supporting our view. But we shall always hope to find them strongly supporting their own freedom.

對於那些新建立的國家，我們歡迎他們加入自由國度的行列，我們保證，讓殖民統治的形式消失，絕對不是為了讓另一種更為殘酷的暴政取代。我們不會一直要求他們支持我們的觀點，但會希望他們能大力支持他們自己的自由。

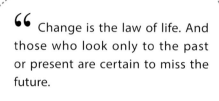

> Change is the law of life. And those who look only to the past or present are certain to miss the future.
>
> 改變是生命的法則。那些只看過去和眼前的人，一定會錯失未來。
>
> *JFK 談改變*

John F. Kennedy
約翰甘迺迪

© U.S. Embassy New Delhi

甘迺迪生於一九一七年五月，於一九六一年就任美國第三十五任總統，年僅四十三歲，不但是美國歷史上當選總統最年輕的一位（希奧多羅斯福 Theodore Roosevelt 一九〇一年因威廉麥金利 William McKinley 遇刺繼任時四十二歲，競選連任時四十六歲），也是唯一的羅馬天主教徒。

被美國人暱稱為 JFK 的甘迺迪，一直被許多美國人視為史上最偉大的總統之一。他任內歷經古巴飛彈危機、柏林圍牆建立、黑人民權運動，並繼續支持越戰，以及與蘇聯的太空競賽，並成立和平工作團（Peace Corps）。一九六三年十一月二十二日，甘迺迪於德州達拉斯市遭到暗殺身亡，得年四十六歲。

---

10) **abolish** [əˋbɑlɪʃ] (v.) 廢除，取消
The citizens fought to abolish the unfair law.

11) **heir** [ɛr] (n.) 繼承人，（傳統、才能、性格等的）繼承者
The young man was the heir to a large fortune.

12) **foe** [fo] (n.) 敵人，敵軍，反對者
The two countries fought against their common foe.

13) **torch** [tɔrtʃ] (n.) 火把
The fishermen used torches to attract fish at night.

14) **temper** [ˋtɛmpər] (v.) 鍛鍊，使變堅韌
The troops were tempered by battle.

15) **heritage** [ˋhɛrətɪdʒ] (n.) 遺產，留給後人的事物
The Greeks are proud of their cultural heritage.

16) **ally** [ˋælaɪ] (n.) 同盟者，同盟國
Germany and Japan were allies in World War II.

17) **pledge** [plɛdʒ] (v.) 許諾，承諾給予
The candidate has pledged to improve the economy if elected.

18) **colonial** [kəˋloniəl] (a.) 殖民地的，殖民的
The city is known for its colonial architecture.

Because It Is Right
因為這是正確的事

To those peoples in the huts and villages of half the globe struggling to break the bonds of mass misery, we pledge our best efforts to help them help themselves, for whatever period is required—not because the communists may be doing it, not because we seek their votes, but because it is right. If a free society cannot help the many who are poor, it cannot save the few who are rich.

對於那些生活在地球另一半的茅舍和村落中，正奮力破除眾生苦難枷鎖的人，我們保證，我們會盡最大努力幫助他們自救，不管需要多久時間——這不是因為共產主義者會這麼做，也不是為了爭取選票，而是因為這是正確的事。如果一個自由的社會不能幫助眾多的窮人，那麼也就無法保全少數的富人。

To that world assembly of [1]**sovereign** states, the United Nations, our last best hope in an age where the instruments of war have far [2]**outpaced** the instruments of peace, we renew our pledge of support—to prevent it from becoming merely a [3]**forum** for [4]**invective**, to strengthen its [5]**shield** of the new and the weak, and to enlarge the area in which its [6]**writ** may run.

對於主權國家的世界大會，也就是聯合國，因為它是我們在這個戰爭手段遠勝於和平手段的時代中，最後一個、也最大的希望，所以我們要重申我們對它的支持承諾——避免讓它淪為互相謾罵的論壇，並加強對新國家和弱小國家的保護，以及擴大推行聯合國規範的區域。

Finally, to those nations who would make themselves our [7]**adversary**, we offer not a pledge but a request: that both sides begin anew the [8]**quest** for peace, before the dark powers of destruction [9]**unleashed** by science [10]**engulf** all humanity in planned or accidental self-destruction.

最後，對於那些與我們為敵的國家，我們不做出承諾，而是提出請求：雙方應重新開始尋求和平，不要等到科技引發毀滅性的黑暗力量，吞噬了所有人類，不論那是有預謀或是意外的自我毀滅。

We dare not [11]**tempt** them with weakness. For only when our arms are sufficient beyond doubt can we be certain beyond doubt that they will never be employed. But neither can two great and powerful groups of nations take comfort from our present course—both sides [12]**overburdened** by the cost of modern weapons, both rightly alarmed by the steady spread of the deadly atom, yet both racing to [13]**alter** that uncertain balance of terror that stays the hand of mankind's final war.

我們不能示弱，以免引誘他們來犯。因為，唯有我們的武力是無庸置疑的，才能無庸置疑地確保武力永遠不會加以使用。不過，兩方強盛的國家集團都不會對目前的方針感到滿意——現代武器所花費的成本已讓雙方不堪負荷，雙方也確實都對致命原子武器的威脅不斷擴散感到驚恐，不過雙方仍在競相改變這種不穩定、阻止人類發動終極戰爭的恐怖平衡。

A New Beginning
新的開始

So let us begin anew, remembering on both sides that [14]**civility** is not a sign of weakness, and sincerity is always  subject to proof. Let us

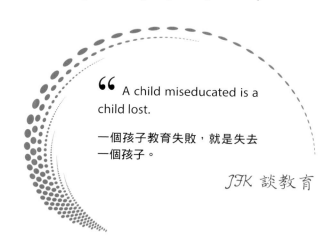

66 A child miseducated is a child lost.

一個孩子教育失敗，就是失去一個孩子。

JFK 談教育

1) **sovereign** [ˈsɑvrɪn] (a.) 主權獨立的
China denies that Taiwan is a sovereign state.

2) **outpace** [aʊtˈpes] (v.) 趕過，勝過
The company has successfully outpaced its competition.

3) **forum** [ˈforəm] (n.) 論壇，討論會
The town held a public forum to discuss traffic safety.

4) **invective** [ɪnˈvɛktɪv] (n.) 惡言謾罵
The speech was filled with invective against the government.

5) **shield** [ʃild] (n.) 盾，防護物，護罩
The missile system provides a shield against enemy attack.

6) **writ** [rɪt] (n.) 令狀
The judge issued a writ ordering the man to appear in court.

7) **adversary** [ˈædvɚˌsɛri] (n.) 敵人，對手
The candidate was attacked by his political adversaries.

8) **quest** [kwɛst] (n.) 探索，追尋
Iran refuses to give up its quest for nuclear energy.

9) **unleash** [ʌnˈliʃ] (v.) 引發，使爆發，突然釋出
The president's assassination unleashed violent protests.

never negotiate out of fear. But let us never fear to negotiate.

所以，讓我們重新開始，雙方都應記住，謙恭不是軟弱的表現，而真誠一直有待驗證。我們永遠都不要因為恐懼而協商，但絕不要懼怕協商。

Let both sides, for the first time, ¹⁵⁾**formulate** serious and precise proposals for the inspection and control of arms—and bring the absolute power to destroy other nations under the absolute control of all nations.

讓我們雙方開創先河，為審查和管制武器制訂認真且明確的提議——讓那種能夠徹底毀滅其他國家的武力都能受到所有國家的完全控制。

Let both sides seek to ¹⁶⁾**invoke** the wonders of science instead of its terrors. Together let us explore the stars, conquer the deserts, ¹⁷⁾**eradicate** disease, tap the ocean depths and encourage the arts and commerce.

讓雙方設法藉助科學的神奇力量，而不是它的恐怖威力。讓我們一起探索星際、征服沙漠、消滅疾病、開發海洋深處、鼓勵藝術和貿易。

66 Written in Chinese, the word crisis is composed of two characters. One represents danger and the other represents opportunity.

用中文寫危機這個詞，包含兩個字。一個代表危險，另一個代表機會。

JFK 談機會

All this will not be finished in the first one hundred days. Nor will it be finished in the first one thousand days, nor in the life of this ¹⁸⁾**Administration**, nor even perhaps in our lifetime on this planet. But let us begin.

這些都不可能在短短一百天內完成，不會在一千天內完成，也不會在我的任期內完成，甚至可能無法在我們有生之年完成，但就讓我們開始吧。

---

10) **engulf** [ɪn`gʌlf] (v.) 吞沒，捲入
Within minutes, the building was engulfed in flames.

11) **tempt** [tɛmpt] (v.) 吸引，引誘
I'm on a diet, so don't tempt me with candy.

12) **overburden** [ˌovɚ`bɝdən] (v.) 使負擔過重，使過於勞累
I've been overburdened with work lately.

13) **alter** [`ɔltɚ] (v.) 改變，修改
We may have to alter our plans.

14) **civility** [sɪ`vɪləti] (n.) 禮貌，客氣
All people should be treated with civility.

15) **formulate** [`fɔrmjəˌlet] (v.) 規劃（制度等），想出（計劃等）
The government formulated a new strategy to fight crime.

16) **invoke** [ɪn`vok] (v.) 召喚，喚起，訴諸
The traditional dance is performed to invoke the gods.

17) **eradicate** [ɪ`rædɪˌket] (v.) 根絕，消滅
Polio has been eradicated in most of the world.

18) **administration** [ədˌmɪnə`streʃən] (n.)（某位總統的）政府、任期
Millions of jobs were created during the Reagan administration.

It's in Your Hands
這一切都掌握在你們手中

In your hands, my fellow citizens, more than mine, will rest the final success or failure of our course. Since this country was founded, each generation of Americans has been [1)]**summoned** to give [2)]**testimony** to its national loyalty. The graves of young Americans who answered the call to service surround the globe.

同胞們，我們的方針最後成功或失敗，不僅僅在我身上，更操在你們手中。自從美國建國以來，每一代美國人都會受到徵召以證明自己對國家的忠誠。而那些響應徵召而服役的美國青年，他們的墳墓遍及了全球。

Now the trumpet summons us again, not as a call to bear arms, though arms we need, but a call to bear the burden of a long [3)]**twilight** struggle, **LG** year in and year out, a struggle against the common enemies of man: tyranny, poverty, disease and war itself.

現在，徵召的號角又響起了，但這次的徵召不是要我們扛槍荷彈，雖然我們需要軍備，而是要我們扛起年復一年的長期重任，對抗人類共同的敵人：暴政、貧困、疾病和戰爭本身。

紐約聯合國總部前的雕塑，以打結的槍管象徵追求和平
© Marco Rubino / Shutterstock.com

Can we forge against these enemies a grand and global [4)]**alliance**, North and South, East and West, that can assure a more [5)]**fruitful** life for all mankind? Will you join in that historic effort?

我們是否能結成全球性的大聯盟，遍及東西南北，共同對抗這些敵人，為全人類保障更豐裕的生活？你們願意加入這場歷史性的奮鬥嗎？

Defending Freedom
捍衛自由

In the long history of the world, only a few generations have been granted the role of defending freedom in its hour of maximum danger. I do not shrink from this responsibility—I welcome it. The energy, the faith, the [6)]**devotion** which we bring to this [7)]**endeavor** will light our country and all who serve it—and the glow from that fire can truly light the world.

在世界悠久的歷史中，只有少數幾代人在遭遇最大危機的時刻，能獲得扮演捍衛自由的角色。我不會迴避這個責任，而是欣然接受。我們為這場努力付出的精力、信念和奉獻精神，將照亮我們國家和所有為國家效勞的人，而這道光芒肯定也能照亮全世界。

And so, my fellow Americans: ask not what your country can do for you—ask what you can do for your country.

因此，我的美國同胞們：不要問國家能為你做什麼，要問你能為國家做什麼。

My fellow citizens of the world: ask not what America will do for you, but what together we can do for the freedom of man.

我的世界公民同胞們：不要問美國會為你做什麼，要問我們能一起為人類的自由做什麼。

VOCABULARY 120

1) **summon** [ˋsʌmən] (v.) 召喚，召集
The manager summoned the employee to his office.

2) **testimony** [ˋtɛstəˌmonɪ] (n.) 證明，證言，公開表白
The state of the economy is testimony to the failure of the government's policies.

3) **twilight** [ˋtwaɪˌlaɪt] (n.) 黃昏，晚期
The singer is in the twilight of her musical career.

4) **alliance** [əˋlaɪəns] (n.) 聯盟，同盟，結盟
The two countries have formed a military alliance.

5) **fruitful** [ˋfrutfəl] (a.) 收益好的，富有成效的
Christopher had a long and fruitful career as a writer.

6) **devotion** [dɪˋvoʃən] (n.) 投入，忠誠，熱愛
The man was admired for his devotion to charity.

7) **endeavor** [ɪnˋdɛvəˋ] (n.) 努力，力圖，事業
I hope you succeed in all your endeavors.

at issue 爭議中，討論中

issue 是「待解決的問題，受到爭論的議題」，當我們說某樣東西 at issue，就表示還處於被討論、未解決的階段。

A: What's keeping them from signing the contract?
是什麼讓他們還不簽合約？
B: The point at issue is how the profits should be divided.
因為還在爭議利潤應該怎麼分。

subject to 以……為條件的

subject 在這裡是形容詞，有「取決於……的，受……管制的，容易遭受……的」等含義，需視上下文了解。演講稿中 sincerity is always subject to proof 表示「誠意必須拿出實際證明」。

A: Have the new traffic rules been implemented?
新的交通規則實施了嗎？
B: Not yet. They're still subject to approval by the city council.
還沒。還在等市議會通過。

year in and year out 一年又一年地

表示一年接著一年、過了好幾年，用來形容恆久不變的事物。也可以說 year in, year out。

A: Is that the only suit that Roger owns?
那是羅傑唯一的西裝嗎？
B: Yeah. He wears the same suit year in and year out.
是呀。他年復一年都穿同一套西裝。

© NASA/MSFC

We observe today..., symbolizing..., signifying... 在一句話中使用多個動詞的方法

若想把兩、三句話變成一句時，最簡單的方式就是用連接詞（and, so, because……等）把話連接起來。另一種更簡潔的處理方式則是將話中相同的主詞省略，並將動詞改為 Ving（現在分詞）或 Ved 的形式，這就稱為「分詞構句」，簡單吧？

● 原句的動詞是「主動語態」，用 Ving 來做分詞構句
原句
Patrick didn't want to work such long hours, so he decided to quit his job.
分詞構句
Not wanting to work such long hours, Patrick decided to quit his job.
派屈克不想這麼長時間工作，就離職了

● 原句的動詞是「被動語態」，用 Ved 來做分詞構句
原句
The country is blessed with abundant natural resources and the country has attracted traders and explorers for centuries.
分詞構句
Blessed with abundant natural resources, the country has attracted traders and explorers for centuries.
這國家幸運地擁有豐沛的自然資源，幾世紀以來吸引商人和探險家絡繹不絕。

甘迺迪是美國口才最好的總統之一，而 Ask not what your country can do for you（不要問國家能為你做什麼），要算是他最常被人引用的一句話了。甘迺迪這篇就職演說，被認為與小羅斯福總統（Franklin D. Roosevelt）的首次就職演說並列二十世紀最動人的美國總統就職演說。

這篇講稿共計 1355 個字，是由甘迺迪親自撰寫，儘管當時越戰持續進行、與蘇聯的太空競賽也已展開，但他放棄在演說中加入激化對立的字句，而是訴求公民各盡義務，成為一篇經典之作。

除了本篇，甘迺迪於一九六三年美國大學（American University）畢業典禮上的演說（本篇刊頭照片即是這次演講現場），也是各大最佳演說榜的常客，以下是其中名句：

"…So, let us not be blind to our differences—but let us also direct attention to our common interests and to the means by which those differences can be resolved. And if we cannot end now our differences, at least we can help make the world safe for diversity. For, in the final analysis, our most basic common link is that we all inhabit this small planet. We all breathe the same air. We all cherish our children's future. And we are all mortal."

「不要被彼此的歧見蒙蔽——讓我們轉而看向共同的利益，從而解除那些歧見。畢竟到頭來，我們都一起住在這個小小的地球上，我們都呼吸相同的空氣。我們都珍惜孩子的未來。我們都難逃一死。」

For the Sake of Our Unity

Al Gore's Concession Speech 高爾敗選演講

Words of Congratulation
賀詞

Good evening. Just moments ago, I spoke with George W. Bush and congratulated him on becoming the 43rd President of the United States, and I promised him that I wouldn't call him back this time. I offered to meet with him as soon as possible so that we can start to heal the divisions of the campaign and the contest through which we just passed.

各位晚安。就在剛才，我與小布希通話，恭喜他當選第四十三任美國總統。我向他保證，這次我不會對他的當選提出質疑。我表示願意盡快與他會面，好開始彌補我們過去因選戰和爭議造成的分裂。

Almost a century and a half ago, Senator Stephen Douglas told Abraham Lincoln, who had just defeated him for the [1]**presidency**, "[2]**Partisan** feeling must [3]**yield** to [4]**patriotism**. I'm with you, Mr. President, and God bless you." Well, in that same spirit, I say to President-elect Bush that what remains of partisan [5]**rancor** must now be put aside, and may God bless his [6]**stewardship** of this country.

約一個半世紀前，參議員道格拉斯告訴在總統大選中擊敗他的林肯，「在愛國主義面前，黨派意識必須讓步。我支持你，總統先生，願上帝保佑你。」本著同樣的精神，我要對剛當選總統的布希說，我們必須將黨派的積怨放在一邊，願上帝保佑他帶領國家。

GM Neither he nor I [7]**anticipated** this long and difficult road. Certainly GM neither of us wanted it to happen. GM Yet it came, and now it has ended, resolved, as it must be resolved, through the honored institutions of our democracy.

不論是他或是我，都沒料到這條路會如此漫長和艱辛。當然我們兩人都不希望發生這樣的情況，但還是發生了。不過現在也結束了，也解決了，而且理所當然地是通過崇高的民主體制解決。

VOCABULARY 122

1) **presidency** [ˋprɛzədənsi] (n.) 總統任期、職權、職位
The author is writing a book about the Clinton presidency.

2) **partisan** [ˋpɑrtəzən] (a.) 不公平偏袒的，黨派性強的
The newspaper was accused of partisan reporting.

3) **yield** [jild] (v.) 讓於，屈服
You shouldn't yield to their demands.

4) **patriotism** [ˋpetriəˌtɪzəm] (n.) 愛國精神，愛國主義
No one can question the politician's patriotism.

5) **rancor** [ˋræŋkɚ] (n.) 仇恨，激烈的憎惡
The rancor between the two parties has only grown stronger.

6) **stewardship** [ˋstuwɚdˌʃɪp] (n.) 管理、保護的職責
Stewardship of the environment is everyone's responsibility.

7) **anticipate** [ænˋtɪsəˌpet] (v.) 預料，期待
The project took longer than we anticipated.

8) **inscribe** [ɪnˋskraɪb] (v.) 刻，雕
Edward wore a ring inscribed with his initials.

9) **motto** [ˋmɑto] (n.) 座右銘，格言
"Service with a smile" is our company's motto.

Under God and Law
遵從上帝和法律

Over the library of one of our great law schools is [8]**inscribed** the [9]**motto**, "Not under man but under God and law." That's the ruling principle of American freedom, the source of our democratic liberties. I've tried to make it my guide throughout this contest as it has guided America's [10]**deliberations** of all the complex issues of the past five weeks.

國內一所傑出法學院的圖書館內刻著一句格言：「遵從上帝和法律，而非遵從於人。」這是美國自由精神的治國原則，也是我們民主自由的根源。在這次選戰中，我試著以此為指引，如同在過去五個星期以來，美國在所有複雜的議題審議中也都以此為指引。

哈佛法學院圖書館入口上雋刻拉丁文 NON SVB HOMINE SED SVB DEO ET LEGE（Not under man, but under God and the law.）
© Herkko Hietanen

Now the U.S. [11]**Supreme** Court has spoken. Let there be no doubt, while I strongly disagree with the court's decision, I accept it. I accept the [12]**finality** of this outcome which will be [13]**ratified** next Monday in the Electoral College. And tonight, for the sake of our unity of the people and the strength of our democracy, I offer my [14]**concession**.

現在美國最高法院做出了判決，就讓我們平息所有疑慮，就算我極力反對法院的判決，我也接受判決。我接受這個已成定局的結果，而下週一選舉人團也將批准這項結果。今晚，為了我們人民的團結和民主的健全，我承認敗選。

I also accept my responsibility, which I will [15]**discharge** [16]**unconditionally**, to honor the new

president-elect and do everything possible to help him bring Americans together in fulfillment of the great vision that our Declaration of Independence defines and that our Constitution [17]**affirms** and defends.

我也要接受並無條件履行我的責任，尊重新當選的總統，盡一切可能幫助他帶領美國人完成偉大的願景，也就是我國《獨立宣言》所界定的，以及我國憲法所申明和捍衛的願景。

> 66 Airplane travel is nature's way of making you look like your passport photo.
>
> 長途飛行自然會讓你變成護照上那張照片的樣子。
>
> *高爾談長途飛行*

© stocklight / Shutterstock.com

Al Gore
艾爾高爾

一九四八年生，美國政治家及環保運動人士，於一九九三年至二○○一年 Bill Clinton 執政期間擔任美國副總統，二○○○年參選總統落敗。

高爾敗選後更加積極投入環保運動，二○○六年推出親自製作的紀錄片《不願面對的真相》*An Inconvenient Truth*，得到國際廣大迴響，還贏下奧斯卡最佳紀錄片獎。二○○七年，高爾與聯合國政府間氣候變化專門委員（Intergovernmental Panel on Climate Change，IPCC）共同獲頒諾貝爾和平獎。

10) **deliberation** [dɪ͵lɪbəˋreʃən] (n.) 審議，深思熟慮
After long deliberation, the committee came to a decision.

11) **supreme** [səˋprim] (a.) 頂級的，最高等的，Supreme Court即「最高法院」
Kim Jong-un is North Korea's supreme leader.

12) **finality** [faɪˋnælətɪ] (n.) 定局，決定性，不可挽回、改變
It's difficult to face the finality of death.

13) **ratify** [ˋrætə͵faɪ] (v.) 批准，認可
The treaty still has to be ratified by Congress.

14) **concession** [kənˋsɛʃən] (n.) 認輸，讓步
The candidate is busy writing his concession speech.

15) **discharge** [dɪsˋtʃɑrdʒ] (v.) 履行，執行
New lawyers must swear to faithfully discharge their duties.

16) **unconditionally** [͵ʌnkənˋdɪʃənəlɪ] (adv.) 無條件地，絕對地
Japan surrendered unconditionally at the end of World War II.

17) **affirm** [əˋfɜm] (v.) 確認，斷言，聲明
The expert affirmed that the painting was genuine.

Finding Common Ground
找到共同點

This has been an [1] **extraordinary** election. But in one of God's [2] **unforeseen** paths, this [3] **belatedly** broken [4] **impasse** can point us all to a new common ground, for its very closeness can serve to remind us that we are one people with a shared history and a shared [5] **destiny**.

這是場非比尋常的選舉。但正如上帝其他無法預期的安排，好不容易打破的僵局可以把我們帶往新的共識，因為雙方選票極為接近，反而提醒了我們，我們是團結一致的，有著共同的歷史和命運。

Indeed, that history gives us many examples of contests as hotly debated, as fiercely fought, with their own challenges to the popular will. Other disputes have [6] **dragged on** for weeks before reaching resolution. And each time, both the [7] **victor** and the [8] **vanquished** have accepted the result peacefully and in the spirit of [9] **reconciliation**. So let it be with us.

的確，歷史上有許多為選舉激辯和激戰的例子，為民意帶來挑戰。其他的選舉爭議也一樣拖了數週才解決。每一次爭議，不論是勝方或敗方，都抱著和解的精神，和平接受結果。讓我們這次也一樣。

I know that many of my supporters are disappointed. I am, too. But our disappointment must be overcome by our love of country. And I say to our fellow members of the world community, let no one see this contest as a sign of American weakness. The strength of American democracy is shown most clearly through the difficulties it can overcome.

我知道，我有許多支持者很失望。我也是。不過，我們必須用愛國心來克服失望。因為我們是愛國的。我想告訴全世界的其他人，不要將這件爭議看成是美國衰弱的跡象。克服困境，才最能體現美國民主的力量。

Some have expressed concern that the unusual nature of this election might [10] **hamper** the next president in the [11] **conduct** of his office. I do not believe it need be so. President-elect Bush inherits a nation whose citizens will be ready to assist him in the conduct of his large responsibilities.

有些人表示，擔心這次選舉的反常，可能會阻礙下一任總統的執政。我倒不這麼認為。剛當選總統的布希所接掌的，是一個全體公民都已準備好協助他擔起重責大任的國家。

Time to Come Together
團結的時候到了

I personally will be at his disposal, and I call on all Americans—I particularly urge all who stood with us to unite behind our next president. This is America. Just as we fight hard when the [12] **stakes** are high, we 🔲 close ranks and come together when the contest is done.

我個人會聽他差遣，所以我也呼籲所有美國人 ——尤其要敦促我的支持者，要團結起來、力挺下一任總統。這才是美國。輸贏難分時，我們會奮戰到底。同樣地，選戰結束後，我們就會團結一致。

> When you have the facts on your side, argue the facts. When you have the law on your side, argue the law. When you have neither, holler.
>
> 當真相站在你這邊，以真相來論證。當法律站在你這邊，以法律來論證。當兩者都不在你這邊，那就用喊的。
>
> 高爾談真相與法律

VOCABULARY

1) **extraordinary** [ɪkˋstrɔrdən͵ɛrɪ] (a.) 非凡的，特別的
The scientists made an extraordinary discovery.

2) **unforeseen** [͵ʌnforˋsin] (a.) 預料之外的
Insurance can protect you against unforeseen circumstances.

3) **belatedly** [bɪˋletɪdlɪ] (adv.) 太遲地，延遲地
He belatedly realized that his wife was leaving him.

4) **impasse** [ˋɪm͵pæs] (n.) 僵局，死路
The negotiations have reached an impasse.

5) **destiny** [ˋdɛstənɪ] (n.) 命運，天命
The couple believed it was their destiny to be together.

6) **drag on** [dræg ɑn] (phr.) 拖延，持續太久
The boring lecture dragged on for over an hour.

And while there will be time enough to debate our continuing differences, now is the time to recognize that that which unites us is greater than that which divides us. While we yet hold and do not yield our opposing beliefs, there is a higher duty than the one we owe to political party. This is America and we put country before party. We will stand together behind our new president.

儘管我們有時間繼續為彼此的異議爭論，但此刻我們必須承認，使我們團結的力量遠比讓我們分裂的歧見來得重要。雖然我們抱持著不同的理念，也不願讓步，但在效忠政黨之前，我們還有更崇高的責任。這是美國，我們認為國家比政黨重要，我們要團結一致，支持新任總統。

Some have asked whether I have any regrets and I do have one regret: that I didn't get the chance to stay and fight for the American people over the next four years, especially for those who need burdens lifted and barriers removed, especially for those who feel their voices have not been heard. I heard you and I will not forget.

有些人問我，我是否有遺憾，我確實有一個遺憾：未來四年我沒有機會留下來為美國人打拼，尤其是為那些需要解除重擔和排除障礙的人，以及那些被忽略的聲音。我聽到了，而且我不會忘記。

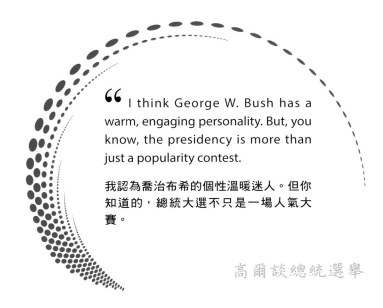

" I think George W. Bush has a warm, engaging personality. But, you know, the presidency is more than just a popularity contest.

我認為喬治布希的個性溫暖迷人。但你知道的，總統大選不只是一場人氣大賽。

高爾談總統選舉

---

7) **victor** [ˈvɪktɚ] (n.) 勝利者，戰勝者
The victor of the election was George W. Bush.

8) **vanquish** [ˈvæŋkwɪʃ] (v.) 征服，擊敗，克服
The Germans vanquished Poland in less than a month.

9) **reconciliation** [ˌrɛkənsɪliˈeʃən] (n.) 和解，和好
Peace can only be achieved through reconciliation.

10) **hamper** [ˈhæmpɚ] (v.) 阻礙
The search for the missing boat was hampered by heavy fog.

11) **conduct** [ˈkɑndʌkt] (n.) 管理，經營，處理
The court was criticized for its conduct of the trial.

12) **stake** [stek] (n.) （固定用復數）風險，代價，賭注
The bank robber raised the stakes by taking a hostage.

高爾在二〇〇八年民主黨全國代表大會最後一天，發表為歐巴馬助選的演說。

© Qqqqqq / Wikipedia

A Country Worth Fighting For
值得打拚的國家

I've seen America in this campaign and I like what I see. It's worth fighting for, and that's a fight I'll never stop. As for the battle that ends tonight, I do believe as my father once said, that no matter how hard the loss, defeat might serve as well as victory to shape the soul and let the glory out.

在這次選戰中，我看到的美國正是我所想要看到的。這是一個值得為其打拚、也值得讓我永遠為其打拚的國家。選戰在今夜結束後，我相信就如同我父親說過的，不論輸得多慘，失敗跟成功一樣，可以成就靈魂，使其綻放光芒。

So for me this campaign ends as it began: with the love of Tipper and our family; with faith in God and in the country I have been so proud to serve, from 🔲 Vietnam to the vice presidency; and with gratitude to our truly tireless campaign staff and volunteers, including all those who worked so hard in Florida for the last 36 days.

對我來說，這場選戰的結束如同開始時：有蒂波（高爾的妻子）和我家人給我的愛；帶著對上帝的信仰，以及一直讓我引以為豪的國家，從參加越戰到擔任副總統；對奮戰努力的競選團隊和義工的感激，包括過去三十六天在佛羅里達州賣力工作的人。

Now the political struggle is over and we turn again to the unending struggle for the common good of all Americans and for those [1]**multitudes** around the world who look to us for leadership in the cause of freedom.

現在政治鬥爭結束了，為了美國人的共同利益，為了全世界那些仰賴我們領導自由大業的廣大群眾，我們要再次繼續努力不懈。

In the words of our great [2]**hymn**, "America, America": "Let us crown [3]**thy** good with [4]**brotherhood**, from sea to shining sea." And now, my friends, in a phrase I once addressed to others: it's time for me to go. Thank you and good night, and God bless America.

就如同我們的愛國歌曲《美哉美國》歌詞所說：「以同胞愛之名的善行加冕，從此岸到彼岸。」現在，朋友們，就用一句我曾說過的話來總結：是我該離開的時候了，謝謝你們，晚安，天佑美國。

VOCABULARY 🎧 126

1) **multitude** [ˋmʌltəˌtud] (n.) 大批（人事物）
A multitude of protesters gathered in the square.

2) **hymn** [hɪm] (n.) 聖歌，讚美詩
Do you sing hymns at your church?

3) **thy** [ðaɪ] (a.) （古）你的，即 thou 的所有格
"Honor thy father and thy mother," says the Bible.

4) **brotherhood** [ˋbrʌðəˌhud] (n.) 手足之情，四海一家的信念
Last Sunday, our pastor talked about the importance of brotherhood.

高爾與他的競選搭檔喬李伯曼
© Joseph Sohm / Shutterstock.com

Language Guide

Electoral College 選舉人團

美國總統雖說是由人民選出，但必須透過一套「選舉人團」的機制，過程大致如下：

1. 各黨推出正、副總統候選人，在各州登記
2. 各黨在各州推出忠貞黨員作為選舉人（人數依各州人口數等條件分配，如加州最多，有五十五張，阿拉斯加州只得三張）
3. 選舉日進行全民投票，決定各州獲勝的正、副總統候選人
4. 各州獲勝正、副總統候選人所屬黨派的選舉人，成為該州選舉人
5. 各州選舉人在各州首府集會投票給參選的正、副總統候選人，決定最後當選者

由於選舉人基本上會投給所屬政黨候選人，所以只要在一州的普選中獲勝，就等於拿到該州全部選舉人票，即所謂勝者全得（winner-take-all）制度。這樣的方式讓人口較多的州成為兵家必爭之地，但也因人數稀少的州有保障票數（三票），不會被輕易犧牲。但缺點就是違反「多數決」原則，如高爾在兩千年大選中普選票數較多，最後卻落敗。

Grammar Master

善用「否定詞」，跟高爾學慎而不怒的說話術

這段連續出現好幾個否定詞：neither、nor、yet，雖充滿說話者不認同的態度，但句型上的變化與應用，便能使文句聽來流暢且不失風度。常見的否定詞句型有：

● 完全否定用法，表「既不是 A 也不是 B」、「兩者皆非」

解 neither 當形容詞，須搭配單數／不可數名詞使用

例 **Neither *statement is* true.**
兩個說法都不對。。

解 neither…nor… 須搭配複數動詞

例 **Neither Gary nor Sandy *are* good students.**
蓋瑞和姍迪都不是好學生。

解 neither of 置於代名詞或可數名詞前，動詞須為單數

例 **Neither of *my suggestions was* taken.**
我的兩個建議都沒有被採納。

解 neither + 倒裝句，表「也不」

例 **Sam doesn't work on Fridays, and neither *do I*.**
山姆週五不工作，我也是。

● yet 的用法

解 yet 作為連接詞，用以連接兩個單字、片語或子句，表示「然而」。

例 **The weather is cold, yet bright and sunny.**
天氣很冷，但天晴氣朗。

解 yet 作為副詞，表示某事到目前為止尚未發生。yet 常出現在否定或疑問句，中文意思是「還沒……」。

例 **I'm surprised that you *haven't told* him anything yet.**
我很驚訝你還沒告訴他任何事情。

Declaration of Independence 《獨立宣言》

一七七六年七月四日《美國獨立宣言》U.S Declaration of Independence 的簽署，宣告了北美洲十三個英屬殖民地自英國獨立，獨立紀念日（Independence Day）因此被視為美國的國慶，大部分的美國人稱這一天為 4th of July。

《獨立宣言》是由約翰亞當斯（John Adams）、班傑明富蘭克林（Benjamin Franklin）、湯瑪斯傑佛遜（Thomas Jefferson）、羅伯特李文斯頓（Robert Livingston）、羅傑謝爾曼（Roger Sherman）組成的五人小組（Committee of Five）起草，上呈至大陸會議（Continental Congress，美國國會的前身）獲得採用，地點為賓州獨立廳，主席為約翰漢考克（John Hancock）

宣言之原件由大陸會議出席代表共同簽署，並永久展示於華盛頓特區之國家檔案與文件局（National Archives and Records Administration）。

at sb.'s disposal 任某人差遣

disposal 是「處置，控制」，at sb.'s disposal 就表示「任由某人處置」，用在人身上，就表示「任人差遣」了。

A: Can you drive me to the airport tomorrow?
你明天可以載我去機場嗎？
B: I would, but I don't have a car at my disposal.
我願意，但我剛好沒車子可以開。

close ranks 緊密團結

rank 是指「（軍隊的）行列」，遇到敵人砲火攻擊，阿兵哥必定會靠攏共同防備，close ranks 就表示團結起來抵禦外侮。

A: What did the party do when their leader was caught accepting bribes?
這個黨的領導人受賄被抓的時候，黨內怎麼做？
B: They closed ranks and defended him.
他們團結起來，為他辯護。

Vietnam 越戰

Vietnam 是「越南」這個國家，但也代表「越戰」這場戰爭。這場為時二十年的戰爭是受到蘇聯及中國支持的北越，與受到美國支持的南越間的戰爭。高爾一九六九年哈佛大學畢業即入伍，以軍隊記者身份進入越南戰場。

高爾爭取民主黨總統提名時，挾著當時現任副總統的聲勢，受到一面倒的支持，在最初的民意調查中，更大幅領先共和黨對手小布希十一個百分點；接下來競選期間雖然頗多失誤，在二〇〇〇年十一月七日大選日開票出來，他依然大贏五十四萬票，卻因幾個關鍵州落敗輸掉選舉人票失去優勢。最後更因佛州開票作業出現爭議，使選情陷入僵局。

經過一個月重新計票，美國國內極度紛擾，高爾以五張選舉人票落敗。這篇演說，是高爾於二〇〇〇年十二月十三日發表，為這場爭議劃下句點。

We Shall Prevail
King George VI's 1939 Radio Address
英國國王喬治六世一九三九年廣播演講

喬治六世攝於一九四四年耶誕節廣播演說 © BBC Radio 4

A Grave Hour
嚴峻的時刻

In this grave hour, perhaps the most [1]**fateful** in history, I send to every household of my peoples, both at home and overseas, this message, spoken with the same depth of feeling for each one of you as if I were able to cross your threshold and speak to you myself.

在這嚴峻的時刻，或許是史上最生攸關的時刻，我要向各位國民傳達這項訊息，不論各位是在國內或海外，我都以同樣沉重的心情，猶如親自登門，向各位宣布。

We Are at War
我們正處於戰爭中

For the second time in the lives of most of us, we are at war. Over and over again, we have tried to find a peaceful way out of the differences between ourselves and those who are now our enemies, but it has been in vain.

對我們多數人來說，這是生平第二次身處戰爭之中。一次又一次，我們設法找出和平的方式解決我們與敵方之間的歧異，卻徒勞無功。

We have been forced into a conflict, for which we are called, with our allies to meet the challenge of a principle which, if it were to [2]**prevail**, would be fatal to any civilized order in the world.

我們被迫捲入這場戰爭，我們和盟友應召喚，對抗敵方實行的主義。奉行此主義的敵方若是得勝，世界上所有文明秩序都將毀於一旦。

The Selfish Pursuit of Power
自私的權力追求

It is a principle which permits a state in the selfish pursuit of power to [3]**disregard** its [4]**treaties** and its solemn pledges; which [5]**sanctions** the use of force or threat of force against the [6]**sovereignty** and independence of other states.

為了滿足追求權力的私心，在敵方奉行的主義下，政府可以無視與他國簽訂的條約和鄭重宣誓過的保證，准許以武力侵犯或恐嚇其他國家的主權和獨立。

Such a principle, stripped of all disguise, is surely the mere primitive doctrine that might is right, and if this principle were established

VOCABULARY

1) **fateful** [ˈfetfəl] (a.) 決定命運的，重大的
Hitler's decision to invade Russia was a fateful error.

2) **prevail** [prɪˈvel] (v.) 獲勝，戰勝
The Liberal Party is expected to prevail in next month's election.

3) **disregard** [ˌdɪsrɪˈgɑrd] (v./n.) 漠視，不尊重，不顧
Paul disregarded his parents' advice and dropped out of college.

4) **treaty** [ˈtriti] (n.) 條約，協定
The two nations signed a trade treaty last month.

5) **sanction** [ˈsæŋkʃən] (v.) 認可，批准，贊成
Some say the man's murder was sanctioned by the government.

6) **sovereignty** [ˈsɑvrənti] (n.) 主權，統治權
China has long claimed sovereignty over Taiwan.

throughout the world, the freedom of our own country and of the whole British Commonwealth of nations would be in danger.

這樣的主義，在扒開所有偽裝後，只不過是最原始的信條：強權即公理，但假如這樣的主義在全世界各地成立，我們國家和整個大英國協的自由都會陷入危機。

But far more than this, the peoples of the world would be kept in [7]**bondage** of fear, and all hopes of settled peace and of the security of justice and liberty among nations, would be ended.

但更重要的是，全世界人民都將因此身陷於恐懼的束縛中，各國之間所有維繫和平，以及保護正義和自由的希望都將從此終結。

The Ultimate Issue
終極議題

This is the [8]**ultimate** issue which confronts us. For the sake of all we ourselves hold dear, and of the world order and peace, it is [9]**unthinkable** that we should refuse to meet the challenge.

這是我們必須面對的終極議題。為了我們所珍惜的一切，以及世界秩序與和平，我們不可能拒絕面對這樣的挑戰。

It is to this high purpose that I now call my people at home and my people across the seas who will make our cause their own. I ask them to stand calm and firm and united in this time of trial.

為了如此崇高的目標，我現在呼籲國內外所有子民，將此目標作為己任，並請大家在這艱苦時刻保持冷靜、堅定，團結一致。

We Shall Prevail
我們必將戰勝

The task will be hard. There may be dark days ahead, and war can no longer be confined to the battlefield, but we can only do the right as we see the right, and [10]**reverently** commit our cause to God. If one and all we keep [11]**resolutely** faithful to it, ready for whatever service or sacrifice it may demand, then with God's help, we shall prevail. May He bless and keep us all.

這是項艱難的任務。我們將面臨一段黑暗的日子，戰爭也不再只侷限於戰場，但我們只有心懷正念，才能行事正當，並虔誠地將我們的目標託付給上帝。只要每個人毅然決然地信守此目標，並在必要時做出奉獻或犧牲，在上帝的幫助下，我們必將戰勝。願上帝保佑我們。

> " After I am dead, the boy will ruin himself within twelve months.
>
> 我死後，那孩子會在十二個月內毀了自己。
>
> 喬治五世談長子
> （編註：即愛德華八世，喬治六世的哥哥。後來他果真即位不到一年，就為了迎娶準備二度離婚的婦人 Wallis Simpson 退位）

George VI
喬治六世

GEORGE VI
1936-1952

© Sergey Goryachev / Shutterstock.com

生於一八九五年，身為喬治五世的次子，阿爾伯特王子殿下（His Highness Prince Albert of York）原本登基的機會不大，但一九三七年因長兄愛德華八世「不愛江山愛美人」放棄王位，他才繼任英王，為現任英國女王伊麗莎白二世的父親。

喬治六世登基未久，第二次世界大戰爆發，儘管最後獲勝，受到重創的英國已大不如前，美俄從此取代英國，成為新的世界強權。原本就抽菸的喬治六世，二戰期間的壓力讓他菸癮更重，因而罹患肺癌，一九五二年因相關併發症去世。

---

7) **bondage** [ˋbɑndɪdʒ] (n.) 束縛，奴役
Many still live under the bondage of poverty.

8) **ultimate** [ˋʌltəmɪt] (a.) 終極的，最終的，根本的
The team's ultimate goal is to win the championship.

9) **unthinkable** [ʌnˋθɪŋkəbəl] (a.) 難以想像的，不可置信的
It's unthinkable that a mother could kill her own children.

10) **reverently** [ˋrɛvərəntli] (adv.) 虔誠地，恭敬地
The monks bowed reverently before their master.

11) **resolutely** [ˋrɛzəˏlutli] (adv.) 堅決地，堅定地，不屈不撓地
The general resolutely refused to surrender to the enemy.

King George VI's 1945 VE Day Radio Address
英國國王喬治六世一九四五年二戰歐戰勝利日廣播演講

A Great Deliverance
蒙天得救

Today we give thanks to Almighty God for a great [1)]**deliverance**. Speaking from our **LG** Empire's oldest capital city, war-[2)]**battered** but never for one moment [3)]**daunted** or [4)]**dismayed**—speaking from London, I ask you to join with me in that act of thanksgiving.

今天，我們感謝萬能上帝偉大的拯救。我現在身在大英帝國歷史最悠久的首都演講，這座受到戰爭重創的城市，卻從來沒有一刻畏縮或氣餒——身在倫敦演講的我，要請你們一起與我祈禱感恩。

Germany, the enemy who drove all Europe into war, has been finally overcome. In the Far East we have yet to deal with the Japanese, a determined and cruel foe. To this we shall turn with the [5)]**utmost** resolve and with all our resources. But at this hour, when the [6)]**dreadful** shadow of war has passed far from our [7)]**hearths** and homes in these islands, we may at last make one pause for thanksgiving and then turn our thoughts to the tasks all over the world which peace in Europe brings with it.

將整個歐洲拉入戰場的敵方德國終於戰敗了。我們尚未對付在遠東的日本，他們是執著且殘忍的敵人。我們將拿出最大的決心和所有資源對抗他們。但在此時此刻，可怕的戰爭陰影才剛遠離我們島國溫暖的家園，我們終於可以先暫停一下，祈禱感恩，再將心思轉向世界各地的難題，因為這與歐洲的和平是息息相關的。

 The highest of distinctions is service to others.

為他人服務是最高的榮譽。

喬治六世談服務

Let Us Remember
先烈勿忘

Let us remember those who will not come back: their [8)]**constancy** and courage in battle, their sacrifice and [9)]**endurance** in the face of a [10)]**merciless** enemy; let us remember the men in all the services, and the women in all the services, who have **LG** laid down their lives. We have come to the end of our [11)]**tribulation** and they are not with us at the moment of our [12)]**rejoicing**.

VOCABULARY 130

1) **deliverance** [dɪˋlɪvərəns] (n.)（文）釋放，解放
Let us pray for deliverance from our sins.

2) **batter** [ˋbætɚ] (v.) 連續猛擊，搗毀
The storm battered the northeast coast of the island.

3) **daunt** [dɔnt] (v.) 使畏縮，使氣餒，嚇倒
We mustn't be daunted by the challenges that face us.

4) **dismay** [dɪsˋme] (v.) 使驚慌，使失望，使氣餒
Dana's parents were dismayed by her decision to leave school.

5) **utmost** [ˋʌt‚most] (a./n.) 最大的，極度的；極限，最大可能
These instruments should be handled with the utmost care.

6) **dreadful** [ˋdrɛdfəl] (a.)（文）可怕的，令人恐懼的
The ship was lost in a dreadful storm.

7) **hearth** [hɑrθ] (n.) 爐邊，家庭，hearth(s) and home(s) 即「家園，家庭，家」
Many were driven from hearth and home during the war.

8) **constancy** [ˋkɑnstənsɪ] (n.)（文）堅定，忠誠
He told her never to doubt the constancy of his love.

> The wildlife of today is not ours to dispose of as we please. We have it in trust and must account for it to those who come after.
>
> 目前的大自然並非供你我隨意取用。我們負有保管的責任,必須能向後世子孫交代。
>
> 喬治六世談野生自然環境

讓我們緬懷那些無法回來的人:緬懷他們在戰鬥中表現的堅定與勇氣,緬懷他們在面對殘忍的敵人時所做出的犧牲和堅忍;讓我們緬懷那些各軍種的男女,他們為國家犧牲了性命。我們的苦難結束了,但在我們歡慶的這一刻,他們卻無法與我們同慶。

Then let us ¹³⁾**salute** in proud gratitude the great host of the living who have brought us to victory. I cannot praise them to the measure of each one's service, for in a total war, the efforts of all rise to the same noble height, and all are devoted to the common purpose.

然後讓我們帶著驕傲的感激之心,向那一大群存活的戰士致敬,是他們帶領我們走向勝利。我無法一一衡量每位戰士的功勞,因為在這次全面開戰中,所有人的功勞都是同樣崇高的,而且所有人都是為了共同目標而犧牲奉獻。

Armed or unarmed, men and women, you have fought and striven and endured to your utmost. No one knows that better than I do, and as your King, I thank with a full heart those who ¹⁴⁾**bore arms** so ¹⁵⁾**valiantly** on land and sea, or in the air, and all civilians who, shouldering their many burdens,

have carried them ¹⁶⁾**unflinchingly** without complaint.

我們所有人不論是否持槍荷彈,也不論男女,都已盡全力抗戰、奮鬥和堅忍。沒有人比我更瞭解這點,身為你們的國王,我全心全意感謝那些在陸海空戰場上搏鬥的英勇戰士,以及所有肩負各種重擔仍毫不畏縮、也毫無怨言的人民。

👑 The Darkest Hours
最黑暗的時刻

In the darkest hours we knew that the ¹⁷⁾**enslaved** and isolated peoples of Europe looked to us, their hopes were our hopes, their confidence confirmed our faith. We knew that, if we failed, the last remaining barrier against a worldwide tyranny would have fallen in ruins.

在最黑暗的時刻,被奴役和孤立的歐洲人對我們有所期待,他們的希望也是我們的希望,是他們的信心加強了我們的信念。我們都知道,假如我們戰敗了,對抗世界各地暴政的最後一道防線就會崩裂瓦解。

9) **endurance** [ɪn`durəns] (n.) 耐力,忍耐
Running in a marathon takes great endurance.

10) **merciless** [`mɝsɪləs] (a.) 無情的,殘酷的
How can you support the merciless killing of innocent people?

11) **tribulation** [ˌtrɪbjə`leʃən] (n.) 苦難,磨難
Life is full of trials and tribulations.

12) **rejoice** [rɪ`dʒɔɪs] (v.) 慶祝,歡樂,欣喜
Fans rejoiced when their team won the championship.

13) **salute** [sə`lut] (v.) 向…行禮、致敬、致意
The president saluted the soldiers for their bravery.

14) **bear arms** [bɛr ɑrmz] (phr.) 帶武器,服兵役
The U.S. constitution guarantees the right to bear arms.

15) **valiantly** [`væljəntli] (adv.) 勇敢地,英勇地
The soldiers fought valiantly for their country.

16) **unflinchingly** [ʌn`flɪntʃɪŋli] (adv.) 不畏縮地
The troops marched unflinchingly onto the battlefield.

17) **enslave** [ɪn`slev] (v.) 奴役,使做奴隸,征服
The ancient Egyptians enslaved the peoples they conquered.

We Kept Faith
堅信不已

But we did not fail. We kept faith with ourselves and with one another, we kept faith and unity with our great allies. That faith, that unity have carried us to victory through dangers which at times seemed [1)]**overwhelming**.

但我們沒有戰敗。我們不但保持對自己的信任，也保持彼此的信賴，與我們偉大的盟友保持信賴與團結。這樣的信賴與團結，帶著我們歷經幾次幾乎勢不可擋的危機，最終邁向勝利。

So let us resolve to bring to the tasks which lie ahead the same high confidence in our mission. Much hard work awaits us both in the restoration of our own country after the [2)]**ravages** of war, and in helping to restore peace and sanity to a [3)]**shattered** world.

所以，讓我們下定決心，帶著這次使命中同樣高度的信心面對眼前的難題。在經過戰爭的蹂躪後，還有許多艱苦的工作等著我們，我們不但要重建自己的家園，還要幫助四分五裂的世界恢復和平和回歸正軌。

A Lasting Peace
長保和平

There is great comfort in the thought that the years of darkness and danger in which the children of our country have grown up are over and, please God, forever. We shall have failed and the blood of our dearest will have flowed in vain if the victory which they died to win does not lead to a lasting peace, founded on justice and good will.

值得安慰的是，這些年我們國家的孩子都已長大，他們這幾年所處的黑暗和危機已經結束，願上帝保佑，希望這是永遠的結束。假如我們最敬重的戰士犧牲性命後換來的勝利沒有帶來奠基於正義和良善上的持久和平，那麼我們算是失敗了，而他們的血也都白流了。

A New Task
全新挑戰

To that, then, let us turn our thoughts on this day of just triumph and proud sorrow, and then take up our work again, resolved as a people to do nothing [4)]**unworthy** of those who died for us, and to make the world such a world as they would have desired for their children and for ours.

那麼，在這正義勝利的一天，讓我們帶著既驕傲又悲痛的心情，將心思轉向這些戰士的犧牲，然後再次回到工作中，全體人民下定決心，不要愧對那些為我們犧牲生命的人，並讓這個世界成為他們渴望我們下一代能擁有的世界。

This is the task  to which now honor binds us. In the hour of danger we humbly committed our cause into the hand of God and he has been our strength and shield. Let us thank him for his mercies and in this hour of victory commit ourselves and our new task to the guidance of that same strong hand.

這是個肩負著前人使命的任務。在這危機四伏的時候，我們謙卑地將我們的目標託付給上帝之手，而祂也一直是我們的力量和守護。在這勝利的時刻，讓我們感謝上帝的憐憫，同時將自己和我們的新任務，也交給強大的上帝之手來帶領我們。

VOCABULARY 132

1) **overwhelming** [ˌovɚˋwɛlmɪŋ] (a.) 使感到無力的，使無法承受的
Sometimes the pressure at work can be overwhelming.

2) **ravage** [ˋrævɪdʒ] (v.) 蹂躪，摧毀
The country was ravaged by years of war.

3) **shatter** [ˋʃætɚ] (v.) 破滅，毀壞，粉碎
The country's economy was shattered by the war.

4) **unworthy** [ʌnˋwɝðɪ] (a.) 不值得的，不配得到的
The politician was unworthy of the people's trust.

大英國協成員國國旗，下方大面藍旗為大英國協旗幟

in vain 徒勞

vain 這個形容詞表示「沒有得到想要結果的」，in vain 也就是「徒勞無功的意思」

A: Did the search party find the missing girl?
搜救隊有找到失蹤的女孩嗎？
B: No. All their efforts were in vain.
沒有。他們的努力都白費了。

British Commonwealth
大英國協

因一次世界大戰後，英國各殖民地受民主思潮影響紛紛尋求獨立，英國遂於一九三一年成立 British Commonwealth of Nations，讓擁有共同歷史背景的成員國維持獨立平等的關係，彼此共存共榮。一九四九年進一步隱去 British 字眼，改為 Commonwealth of Nations，或以 the Commonwealth 通稱，表示「國家聯盟」。本文演講發表於一九三九年，因此仍稱 British Commonwealth。

這個國際組織由英國國王擔任元首（Head of the Commonwealth，現為英國女王伊麗莎白二世，喬治六世為首任大英國協元首），主要是由過去的英國殖民地所組成，目前包括五十三個主權國家。未曾被英國殖民的國家地區，只要通過申請審核，也可加入。

By Vadac

大英帝國於一九二一年鼎盛時期的領土分佈

British Empire 大英帝國

大英帝國是指英國自一五八八年打敗西班牙艦隊後崛起，經過三百年透過武力擴張、貿易、移民，成就了史上橫跨最多地區，涵蓋面積最大的日不落帝國（the empire on which the sun never sets）。

大英帝國於七年戰爭擊敗法國，一七六三年取得加拿大，正式成為海上霸主；一八一五年擊敗拿破崙，確立世界第一強權的地位，一九一四年德意志帝國興起之前，此一地位一直未被動搖。第一

次世界大戰後，大英帝國的領土及屬地遍及七大洲五大洋，全球四分之一土地面積及人口都受其管轄。其後隨著席捲全球的民族主義興起，大英帝國開始盛極而衰；第二次世界大戰後，英國國力大不如前，帝國逐漸瓦解。

lay down one's life 殉難，殉職

lay down 有「放棄」的意思，lay down one's life 表示為了他人或理想放棄生命。

A: There are so many tombstones at the national cemetery.
國家公墓裡有好多墓碑喔。
B: Yeah. So many soldiers laid down their lives for the country.
是啊。許多戰士為國捐軀。

喬治國王示範：
關係代名詞當受詞時的正式用法

關係代名詞代替的先行詞，可為主詞也可為受詞，若代替主詞用 who、which、that，代替受詞則用 whom、which、that。

在正式的英語寫作中，若一介系詞片語的受詞剛好是關係代名詞時，要把介系詞置於關係代名詞之前，且只能用 whom 及 which，不能用 that。

● 先行詞為受詞關代，是 listen to 的受詞

例 The music (which/that) we *listened to* last night was from Louis Armstrong's first album.
我們昨晚聽的音樂出自路易斯阿姆斯壯的第一張專輯。
解 一般寫法：關代為受詞時可被省略。

● 同句改為正式寫法

例 The music to which we *listened* last night was from Louis Armstrong's first album.
解 正式寫法：把 listened to 的介系詞放到關係代名詞受格 which 之前。

本文分別為英國宣布參加第二次世界大戰，及宣布第二次世界大戰歐戰獲勝的兩篇廣播演說。喬治六世登基時，大英帝國正逐漸步向解體，王室又因緋聞等因素名望很低。一九三九二戰爆發，嚴重口吃的喬治六世負起王室責任，努力克服說話的問題，以演說鼓舞英國人民的鬥志，重振王室在人民心中的地位，電影《王者之聲》The King's Speech 即是在記錄這段過程。

《王者之聲：宣戰時刻》海報，Colin Firth 飾演英王喬治六世，獲得奧斯卡影帝

北107.7｡ 中91.5｡ 南90.1｡ 宜蘭97.1　　www.hitoradio.com

官方APP

隨點・隨聽

獨家好禮

節目表

線上直播

即時訊息

影音專區

2015 流浪動物認養活動

毛起來愛

11/7 (六)
10:30-17:00

台北｜
四四南村中央廣場

高雄｜
夢時代幸福廣場

Do the right thing!
我要你好好的。

🐾 主辦單位

北107.7。中91.5。南90.1。宜蘭97.1

🐾 合作單位 🐾 特別支持

50位 當代名人

與 他 們 的 那 些 小 東 西

ARTISTS, WRITERS, THINKERS, DREAMERS :
Portraits of Fifty Famous Folks & All Their Weird Stuff

JAMES GULLIVER HANCOCK

WE DEFINE OURSELVES BY OUR STUFF

特色❶：輕鬆有趣的經典名人小傳

從達文西、莫札特、愛因斯坦到香奈兒、卓別林、切格瓦拉……，本書精選 50 位橫跨世紀、極具現代影響力的經典人物，並透過簡介讓讀者具體了解他們的非凡成就、輕鬆認識這些每個人都該知道的世界名人。

特色❷：圖解名人小物，另類閱讀名人的生活

愛因斯坦最不喜歡穿什麼？安迪沃荷老是戴墨鏡的原因？柴契爾夫人發明了哪種甜品？每翻一頁人名會先看到幾個引發思考的名人相關問題，作者的構圖設計，讓讀者從名人的小物中更了解、更貼近成功名人的世界。

特色❸：最夯手繪風格，創意詮釋名臉

擺脫正經八百的名人傳記式人像，透過作者別具風格的眼光與獨特的手繪筆觸，詮釋每一位名人面貌與他們的隨身小物。

作者 / 詹姆士‧格列佛‧漢考克
定價 / $350

2015
11.4
新書上市

史上最好玩的名人傳記！

最有想像力的名人錄，
探索 50 位影響當代大眾文化的名人，
充實你的文化「識力」！

有效英語學習
＝翻轉成功人生

出國留學必備
英文會話口說訓練、劍橋IELTS雅思課程

商務人士法寶
TOEIC多益證照、商務英文菁英研習營、英文寫作、英文商務秘書暨特助培訓

高階英語延伸
中英口筆議基礎養成系列、英文主題討論、外語導遊領隊証照課程

 國際語文中心

英、日、西、韓語檢定培訓課程 | 英、日、西、法、德、義、葡、越、韓語會話分級培訓課程
成人日語師資培訓班 | 中英/中日口筆譯班 | 日文祕書檢定證照班 | BJT商務日語能力試驗班
TESOL英語師資證照課程 | 劍橋TKT英語教師資格認證

文大國際語文中心 | 2356-7356#1

最激勵人心的英文演講 Words of Wisdom：EZ TALK
總編嚴選特刊 / EZ 叢書館編輯部作. -- 初版. -- 臺
北市：日月文化，2015.11
144 面；21*28 公分

ISBN 978-986-248-504-0（平裝附光碟片）

1. 英語 2. 讀本

805.18   104018467

EZ 叢書館 20

最激勵人心的英文演講
EZ TALK 總編嚴選特刊

作　　　　者：EZ TALK 編輯部
總　編　審：Judd Piggott
英　文　筆　者：Judd Piggott
專案企劃執行：陳思容
執　行　編　輯：葉瑋玲、張玉芬
特　約　編　輯：蔡佳勳、黃書英
視　覺　設　計：用視覺有限公司
內　頁　排　版：蕭彥伶、健呈電腦排版公司
錄　音　後　製：純粹錄音後製有限公司
錄　音　員：Michael Tennant、Terri Pebsworth

發　行　人：洪祺祥
副　總　經　理：洪偉傑
副　總　編　輯：曹仲堯
法　律　顧　問：建大法律事務所
財　務　顧　問：高威會計師事務所
出　　　　版：日月文化出版股份有限公司
製　　　　作：EZ 叢書館
地　　　　址：臺北市信義路三段151號8樓
電　　　　話：(02)2708-5509
傳　　　　真：(02)2708-6157
客　服　信　箱：service@heliopolis.com.tw
網　　　　址：www.heliopolis.com.tw
郵　撥　帳　號：19716071日月文化出版股份有限公司

總　經　銷：聯合發行股份有限公司
電　　　　話：(02)2917-8022
傳　　　　真：(02)2915-7212
印　　　　刷：中原造像股份有限公司
初　　　　版：2015 年 11月
初 版 十 四 刷：2020 年 6月
定　　　　價：350 元
I　S　B　N：978-986-248-504-0

日月文化集團
HELIOPOLIS
CULTURE GROUP

客服專線 02-2708-5509
客服傳真 02-2708-6157
客服信箱 service@heliopolis.com.tw

廣 告 回 函
台灣北區郵政管理局登記證
北台字第 000370 號
免 貼 郵 票

日月文化集團 讀者服務部 收

10658 台北市信義路三段151號8樓

對折黏貼後，即可直接郵寄

日月文化網址：**www.heliopolis.com.tw**

最新消息、活動，請參考 FB 粉絲團

大量訂購，另有折扣優惠，請洽客服中心（詳見本頁上方所示連絡方式）。

| 日月文化 | EZ TALK | EZ Japan | EZ Korea |

大好書屋・寶鼎出版・山岳文化・洪圖出版

日月文化集團
HELIOPOLIS
CULTURE GROUP

感謝您購買　最激勵人心的英文演講：EZ TALK 總編嚴選特刊

為提供完整服務與快速資訊，請詳細填寫以下資料，傳真至02-2708-6157或免貼郵票寄回，我們將不定期提供您最新資訊及最新優惠。

1. 姓名：＿＿＿＿＿＿＿＿＿＿＿　　性別：□男　　□女

2. 生日：＿＿＿＿年＿＿＿＿月＿＿＿＿日　　職業：＿＿＿＿

3. 電話：（請務必填寫一種聯絡方式）

　　（日）＿＿＿＿＿＿＿＿＿　（夜）＿＿＿＿＿＿＿＿＿（手機）＿＿＿＿＿＿＿

4. 地址：□□□＿＿＿＿＿＿＿＿＿＿＿＿＿＿＿＿＿＿＿＿＿

5. 電子信箱：＿＿＿＿＿＿＿＿＿＿＿＿＿＿＿＿＿＿＿＿＿＿

6. 您從何處購買此書？□＿＿＿＿＿＿＿縣/市＿＿＿＿＿＿＿書店/量販超商

　　□＿＿＿＿＿＿＿網路書店　　□書展　　□郵購　　□其他

7. 您何時購買此書？　　年　　月　　日

8. 您購買此書的原因：（可複選）

　　□對書的主題有興趣　　□作者　　□出版社　　□工作所需　　□生活所需

　　□資訊豐富　　□價格合理（若不合理，您覺得合理價格應為＿＿＿＿＿＿）

　　□封面/版面編排　　□其他＿＿＿＿＿＿＿＿＿＿＿＿＿＿＿＿＿＿

9. 您從何處得知這本書的消息：　□書店　□網路／電子報　□量販超商　□報紙
　　□雜誌　□廣播　□電視　□他人推薦　□其他

10. 您對本書的評價：（1.非常滿意 2.滿意 3.普通 4.不滿意 5.非常不滿意）

　　書名＿＿＿＿　內容＿＿＿＿　封面設計＿＿＿＿　版面編排＿＿＿＿　文/譯筆＿＿＿＿

11. 您通常以何種方式購書？□書店　　□網路　　□傳真訂購　　□郵政劃撥　　□其他

12. 您最喜歡在何處買書？

　　□＿＿＿＿＿＿＿縣/市＿＿＿＿＿＿＿書店/量販超商　　□網路書店

13. 您希望我們未來出版何種主題的書？＿＿＿＿＿＿＿＿＿＿＿＿＿＿＿＿

14. 您認為本書還須改進的地方？提供我們的建議？

　　＿＿＿＿＿＿＿＿＿＿＿＿＿＿＿＿＿＿＿＿＿＿＿＿＿＿＿＿＿＿＿

　　＿＿＿＿＿＿＿＿＿＿＿＿＿＿＿＿＿＿＿＿＿＿＿＿＿＿＿＿＿＿＿

　　＿＿＿＿＿＿＿＿＿＿＿＿＿＿＿＿＿＿＿＿＿＿＿＿＿＿＿＿＿＿＿

　　＿＿＿＿＿＿＿＿＿＿＿＿＿＿＿＿＿＿＿＿＿＿＿＿＿＿＿＿＿＿＿